REVIEWS

Margie Benedict's "prose is crisp and purposeful, charged with feeling, and always attuned to what will engage readers in each moment." -The BookLife Prize

BEFORE THE KILLING (Book One)

"Once I started I couldn't put it down!"
-Bookshelf Adventures

"Mystery fans will love this plot device, which takes a straightforward whodunit to an otherworldly level."
-The BookLife Prize

"A cleverly plotted fantasy thriller with a strong cast of characters." -The Wishing Shelf Book Awards

BEFORE SHE WAS TAKEN (Book Two)

"This was such an amazing novel to read... The characters were wonderfully written and very easy to like. I found myself unable to put it down... This novel was a fast read for me and I greatly recommend it." -Bookshelf Adventures

"The plot moves at an even pace and has a surprising ending; this supernatural mystery will be enjoyed by a diverse array of readers... the book has a strong female character who is easy to follow, smart, and displays agency."
-The BookLife Prize

BEFORE BOOKS 1-3

MARGIE BENEDICT

FIRST EDITION, MARCH 2022

This is a work of fiction. Names, characters, businesses, places, events, and incidents
are either the products of the author's imagination or used in a fictitious manner.
Any resemblance to actual persons, living or dead, or actual events is purely
coincidental.

Publisher: margiebenedict.com
Cover Design: 100covers.com

ISBN: 978-1-954584-31-0 (ebook)
ISBN: 978-1-954584-50-1 (paperback)
ISBN: 978-1-954584-46-4 (audiobook)

Printed in the United States of America

BEFORE THE KILLING

THE BEFORE SERIES BOOK ONE

For First Love

PROLOGUE
CASSIE (AGE 26)

Cassie, who lives alone, has just turned out the light in the kitchen when an unusual sight draws her gaze to the window. Countless lights fill the night sky, like bright pinpricks in a cloak of black velvet. Fascinated, she goes outside to gaze at them. The display overwhelms her with a wondrous feeling regarding the vastness of the universe. She actually finds it soothing to be reminded of the relative insignificance of her life and the mostly disastrous trajectory it's followed so far.

The lights grow brighter, or maybe just closer. One in particular increases in intensity until it seems to be heading straight for her house. Fearful, she backs inside planning to slam the door shut, but then the thing arcs downward and disappears behind the hedges. The leaves rustle.

Her cat Gio rubs against her leg. His fur is sticking straight up on his back, and his eyes bulge like yellow marbles, staring at the place where something might've landed. Cassie has goosebumps herself, but still can't resist going to check. Peering behind the bushes, she sees a small rock glowing like a piece of lit charcoal. When she moves aside branches to get a closer look, a spark flies out and pricks her bare arm. It doesn't burn but causes a tingling sensation.

The glow of the meteorite or whatever-it-is has already dimmed by the time she shifts her gaze back to it. Now it just looks like the kind of granite found everywhere in this area. Since it's sitting in the dirt not touching anything, she doesn't think it's in any danger of starting a fire even if it's still hot. She decides to leave it for now. She can collect it tomorrow when it's definitely cooled down, and possibly take it somewhere like the Museum of Science in Boston. Or maybe call them first to be sure they would be interested. It could be that meteorites land all the time and scientists already have warehouses full of them.

Under the glare of the outdoor lamp, she examines her arm. The spark left a small red mark, but it doesn't hurt when she touches it. However, a sudden sense of unease makes her quicken her steps back into the house. Gio slips between her feet before she shuts the door firmly behind them and snaps the bolt.

PART ONE: WITNESS

CASSIE (AGE 19)

1

―――――

The murder happened on June 9th or 10th, 1973, the day (or two) after Cassie came home for the summer following her first year at Syracuse. Apparently, the last breath was drawn so close to midnight, the medical examiner couldn't say with certainty whether it came before or after, though officially the death was certified as occurring on Sunday, the 10th.

Cassie woke early on the 9th, not that she had any premonition regarding what was to come, but because she couldn't wait to see Julian after so much time apart. At five a.m., diffused sunshine already filled her room, and birds were singing in a chorus outside her window.

Rising and crossing to the study that looked out toward the back of her house, she gazed at the sights she'd missed since Christmas. The still gray surface of Inner Harbor... the large grassy backyard sloping down to a border of mud where the water lapped up... the encircling branches of the gnarled oak she used to climb with her friends. From the side window, she glimpsed crows lined up on the roof of their red barn. Beyond that, past the edge of their property, the familiar gravestones poked up in a scattered formation across the hillside cemetery. She would soon pay one of them a visit.

A feeling rose inside her that was half-adrenaline, half-aching heart for this place that formed an essential part of her. She didn't know if she'd have the strength to leave it again come fall, but that was something she preferred not to think about just yet. She settled back into her father's old chair and stared out at the wakening world for an hour at least. She may have dozed off.

Eventually she returned to her bedroom to be confronted by the two suitcases and five cardboard boxes she'd carried up from the car last night. She would've rather ignored them and gone directly to Julian's, but when she spoke on the phone with him before she left Syracuse, he said he would be out with his father on the boat this morning.

Therefore, she dove into the unpacking and rather quickly had her clothes put away in her closet and dresser. But when she reached the box that held her Julian mementos, it slowed her down. She sat on the bed and flipped open the photo album, going through each picture like a preview of coming attractions. Julian and her in his father's truck, on the lobsterboat, at the beach, canoeing across Inner Harbor, on the rollercoaster at Escapade Park.

After the photos, came the contents of her special carved wooden box. The earrings he gave her for her eighteenth birthday. The roses —now dried—he bought for graduation. The letters—too few—he sent her during their separation. She raised her right hand to gaze for the millionth time at the silver ring he gave her before she left in September. It was a simple, plain band but what mattered was his pledge to be true to her forever.

Before closing up the boxes again, she removed the cassette recording of a piano recital Julian had done in high school. Debussy's *Rêverie*, one of the most exquisite songs she'd ever heard, and Julian played it masterfully. Not that she was any kind of expert, but his performance managed to silence an auditorium full of rowdy teenagers, which was saying quite a lot. She had listened to the tape often while she was away.

When nearly everything was back in its place, the phone rang, making her leap in response. She dashed down the hall and through the open door into her mother's bedroom, glad to see her mother had already risen and gone somewhere else in the house. "I'll get it!" Cassie shouted, lifting the receiver.

"Hello?" She made her voice soft and sultry, thinking it would be Julian on the other end.

Her heart sank when it wasn't. "Oh hi, Mr. Harrington." *Ew.* She felt weird having used her sexy voice on her mother's boyfriend. He was saying something to her now, but she pretended not to hear, cupping the receiver and calling out to her mother. She hung up the second the phone was picked up in the kitchen.

Cassie returned to her room to change out of her pajamas. Anticipating a hot day, she put on her bikini and topped it with a tank top and cutoffs. She braided her hair in the back, and dabbed on lipstick and eyeliner before heading downstairs to get breakfast.

Her mother was still on the phone. Cassie tried to ignore the conversation while preparing a bowl of granola with milk and sliced banana. She glanced through the newspaper headlines while she ate, though mostly she was focused on thoughts of her upcoming day.

Eventually her mother hung up and announced she was going to a party with Mr. Harrington tonight. She came up behind Cassie and played with her braid.

"That's nice," Cassie said. Since she expected to be with Julian, she wasn't sure why her mother bothered to tell her. She knew one of Mr. Harrington's daughters, making it awkward the father of this girl she hung out with a few times was now dating her mother. However, he was divorced, and Cassie's mother was a widow, and there probably weren't a lot of eligible people their age in this small town.

"Let's plan dinner together for Sunday." Her mother patted her shoulder absentmindedly. "I missed you while you were away."

"Mm, me too." She got up to rinse off her dishes. "I'm going to Julian's."

"Of course you are." Her mother smiled. "Take the car if you like."

Cassie glanced out the window at clear blue sky. "I'll ride my bike." Brumewich, Massachusetts, where she lived, was compact enough that most anywhere she might want to go lay within a thirty-minute bike ride. This, despite that homes were stretched out from one another, separated by luxurious lawns and hundreds-of-years-old trees. They were spoiled by an excess of natural beauty, here in Brumewich.

"Be careful, honey," her mother said. "Last week a car hit a bicyclist on Sand Road in Ruford. The boy broke his nose."

"Yeah, don't worry, Mom," she said, though she knew it was wasted advice. For every possible way that one might get injured or die, her mother could dig up a recent example from the news.

Fifteen minutes after setting out, Cassie approached Julian's rather rundown house, located across the street from the main commercial dock. Since it was a Saturday in June, the harbor was bustling, between the fishing boats coming back in for the day, and the pleasure boats heading out. Passing near the water, she looked out to see if Julian had arrived. She spotted the Reis boat, but only Armando, his father, was there tidying up a few things. He didn't notice her, and she didn't call out to him, figuring there would be plenty of time to greet him later.

Armando's Chevy pickup was parked in the driveway, outside their carport. She had painted an orange lobster on the back of its cargo bed last summer, and it pleased her to see the colors hadn't faded. She laid her bike down on the lawn that was more dirt and weeds than grass. The uneasy sense of someone's eyes on her made her glance back before approaching the house. A young woman, Teresa Patterson, leaned against the side of a rusty green Volkswagen Bug across the street.

Cassie remembered her from high school, though Teresa was older, a senior when she was a freshman. It really wasn't possible to forget the older girl, because of how gorgeous she was. Whenever she passed by in the corridor, every boy's eyes would be on her. Behind her back, they called her Raquel—because of the actress Raquel Welch. Seriously, she was that sexy. But despite all of them lusting after her, Cassie couldn't recall her dating anyone in particular.

Teresa looked as amazing as ever, in a little white dress that exposed cleavage on top, and long, tanned legs beneath. When she noticed Cassie looking, she shifted her gaze to the dock and waved at someone down below.

Cassie turned back to the house. Julian was likely inside taking a shower, as he always did immediately after getting off the boat, wanting to scrub off the fishy odor. Funny thing, she actually loved that smell. She was a child of the sea and always would be.

The Reis family, father and son, never locked their doors, night or day, home or not home. She assumed they kept their money in the bank, and what else would anyone want to steal? The thrift store furniture? The record player from 1943? The rickety upright piano that Julian—defying all odds and sour notes—had learned to play like a god?

An unlocked home was not unusual in Brumewich, though. Whenever a visitor encountered one, they were expected to knock first to announce their presence, then go right in before anyone inside might be forced to rise from their chair to get the door.

Cassie followed protocol, but it threw her off to find Julian frozen in the center of the family room, looking at her like she'd caught him in the middle of an embarrassing act. His hand that was balled up in a fist moved into his pocket where he may have deposited something.

Though he clearly wanted to hide the object, she would still have asked him about it if he hadn't distracted her immediately. He broke into a smile that lit up his face, sweeping away her brief suspicion. "Cass!" He crossed the room in two steps, lifted her in his arms, and swung her around in a full circle. "Cass, I missed you."

She raised her hands to his neck and kissed him, breathing in the familiar scent of warm citrus that came from his shampoo, and releasing the longing she'd felt through the snowbound winter and the drenching spring in Syracuse. Eventually they drew back just to look at each other. His expression shone with good humor, over-confidence, and carelessness in equal amounts. It made her jealous to see how brown he was already, though summer had barely begun. He'd inherited rapid-tanning skin along with glossy black hair from his Portuguese dad.

"Where were you last night?" She'd been hoping he might come to her house and surprise her.

"Me? I was home."

"I called. No one answered."

"What time?"

"I don't know. Past ten."

"Oh yeah? I was asleep."

"That's pathetic," she said.

"My father gets me up at four-thirty."

"Oh all right." She kissed him again. "Did you miss me very much?"

"Are you crazy? I couldn't think of anything else."

"Good. I hope you suffered a lot while I was gone."

"I'll suffer even more if I don't get something to eat." He went into the kitchen with Cassie following directly behind.

"You're not hungry, are you?" Julian foraged for sandwich ingredients in the fridge and cupboards. He was always famished after he came back from the boat.

"I'll take everything you have," she said to spite him. The front door opened and a moment later, Armando entered the kitchen.

"Look who's back from college." He gave her a warm smile. "You're gonna get a big hug but not before I clean up."

"Nice to see you, Armando." Mr. Reis always insisted Cassie use his first name.

"He tell you what happened?" Armando nodded in Julian's direction.

"He never tells me anything," she said.

"Papai, forget it." Julian looked annoyed.

But Armando launched into his story. "This mornin' on the boat, he's got a trap balanced on the side. I tell him to heave it. He shoves it off and stands there in a daze while rope flies out of the hot water barrel, you know, followin' the trap down." He paused for effect. "So my fool kid gets his leg in the way. Know how fast that thing goes, Cassie?"

She nodded her head, because she did know. She'd been on the boat once when Julian was setting traps.

"The line's tightening round his leg, pullin' him down, draggin' him to the edge... he's strugglin' to free himself but he can't. So who do you think saves him? I grab my knife, saw at the rope... friggin' hard to cut it. Meanwhile my son's holdin' onto the side for dear life."

"Obviously you managed it since I'm standing right here," Julian said.

"You bet I did. But thanks to you, we lost a perfectly good trap."

"How's your leg, Julian?" she said.

"Fine. My father's exaggerating."

"Gonna have a good bruise there in the morning," Armando said. "And you're welcome."

"Thanks, Papai." Julian gave him a sheepish look. Sometimes, the way they spoke to each other reminded her of brothers rather than father and son. Partly because his dad was only eighteen when Julian was born. And mostly because his mom died in childbirth and it had been just the two of them since then. Cassie had never seen a parent and child that were closer.

"Why weren't you paying attention?" she asked Julian.

"Couldn't wait to see his girl." Armando looked at Julian's developing sandwich. "You gonna share that with her?"

"Cass, you want some?" Without waiting for her reply, he added, "She's not hungry."

Just for that, she swiped a piece of cheese from on top of his bread and stuck it in her mouth.

"I taught you better manners than that," Armando told him. His gaze shifted to the table. "And after she was so nice and brought you a cookie."

She followed his eyes to a sugar cookie shaped like a heart, resting on a napkin on the table. "Oh I didn't bring that." She looked at Julian. "Where'd you get it?"

When Julian didn't answer, Armando said, "Must be from my secret admirer." He took the cookie and walked away.

"He has a secret admirer?" she whispered after he'd gone out.

Julian snorted. "Pete dropped it by earlier." She did think it was odd, though, that he hadn't said that right away.

They set out in the truck after he demolished his sandwich in several huge bites.

"Beach?" she asked him as he backed out of the driveway.

He gave her a sideways glance with half-lidded eyes that told her he had something else in mind.

"Surprise me," she said.

Before long, he drove to the end of an empty road, where a residential construction site lay deserted. "I don't think anyone works here on Saturdays." He parked the Chevy under the shade of an elm tree on the side.

It wasn't their first time doing it in the truck, and they knew how to manage the limited space. Amazing what one can accomplish when the desire is strong enough. He grabbed a condom from the glove compartment, and it did worry her a little to see what a ready supply he had despite her being out of town for months. But it could've been Armando's stash. Last summer, he'd been dating a woman ten years his junior.

The cramped quarters and months spent apart rendered their love-making frenzied and ecstatic. But the best part to Cassie was when he gathered her in his arms afterward and she listened to the rhythm of his heart. Here was home in the best possible sense.

Their repose didn't last long. At the sound of an approaching vehicle, they sprung apart and scrambled to locate discarded clothing. As soon as Julian had on his shorts, he started up the truck and headed back the way they'd come. Cassie was pulling on her T-shirt as they passed the middle-aged couple—probably the property owners—who looked amused.

When they reached the road, they exchanged a glance and burst out laughing. "Beach now?" Julian said.

"Hell yeah."

He drove them to Thorne Cove, which they liked better than Gull Beach, crowded with families this time of year. The cove had a cottage beyond the sand line, and was, strictly speaking, a private section of the coast shared among a dozen or so homeowners. But this early in the season most of the summer dwellers had not yet arrived, meaning no one was around to complain about their trespassing. The beach itself was small, with trees on one side and rocks jutting out into the water on the other.

She and Julian played like they were eight years old. They swam in the bitter-cold ocean, and when they needed to get warm, they sat near the water's edge and built a castle. Then back in to rinse off, and onto the beach where Julian buried her under the sand and threatened to leave her there.

Later while Cassie lay in the deliciously warming sun, Julian practiced diving off the rocks. She turned her head sideways to watch him. It filled her with awe that this tall man with a Grecian nose, sculpted torso, and powerful arms that must've come from all the work hauling traps... that this extraordinarily handsome man had pledged himself to her.

Three teenage girls had recently arrived and set their towels close to where he was diving. They sat there watching him while they spread baby oil all over their bodies. From the way they giggled and whispered among themselves, Cassie knew they were talking about him, maybe even daring each other to go speak to him.

When he got out of the water, he actually swaggered past the girls on his way to Cassie, showing how much he enjoyed the attention. So naturally she kicked sand on him as soon as he was close. In response he leapt on her and kissed her with the taste of salt water on his tongue.

During the drive back to his house, she asked him what they should do tonight.

"Sorry, I'm gonna be busy," he said.

"What do you mean?"

"Me and my friends are hanging out at Escapade Park."

"Can't I come?"

"It's only guys tonight. One of them just got dumped by his girlfriend."

"Which friends are these?"

"They're from Ruford. You don't know them."

"I thought you would've saved tonight for me," she said.

"Tomorrow is yours." He reached over and squeezed her hand. "Day and night. And the day and night after that. And so on for the rest of our lives, except when I need to work."

She wasn't happy, spending her first full night home without Julian. Jealousy niggled at her, and she couldn't help being afraid his plans might have something to do with Teresa Patterson, aka Raquel. She even wondered if thoughts of how he was going to choose between them might've been what distracted him on the boat this morning. But she told herself that was ridiculous.

2

A fter returning from her afternoon with Julian, she made a grilled cheese sandwich for dinner. Her mother came down while Cassie was eating. She'd really outdone herself with her makeup, a satiny silver sleeveless dress, and killer high heels.

"What'd you do with my mother?" Cassie teased. Possibly for the first time ever, she noticed the way her sky-blue eyes contrasted prettily with the rich nutty color of her hair, and how slender she still looked despite her age.

"It's still me in here," her mother said. "Are you going back to Julian's?"

She shook her head. "He's busy."

Her mother was barely listening. "Then could you bring this to Mrs. Wolcott after you finish eating?" She pointed at a large box resting on the floor. "Clothing donations. She's taking them to that non-profit where she's on the board."

"Does it have to be tonight?"

"She said she wanted to deliver everything early tomorrow." The doorbell rang. "Mr. Harrington's here." She patted down her hair and smoothed her skirt before opening the front door. "Hi Freddie."

Mr. Harrington—*Freddie*—peered into the house and across the hall at Cassie sitting at the kitchen table. "Cassie, you're home!"

She wasn't sure how to respond to such an obvious statement. "Yup, here I am."

"Ellen's back too." This was his daughter who was Cassie's age. "I know she'd love to see you."

She seriously doubted that. Ellen and her siblings had gone to private school. They had a whole different set of friends. "Sure, sounds good," she said.

"Thanks for helping me out," her mother said. "The party may go late. Don't wait up for us." She laughed at her little joke of pretending their roles were reversed, as she stepped past Mr. Harrington, heading to his Mercedes Benz parked in the driveway.

Cassie wasn't sure what her mother saw in him. She'd witnessed him bowing and scraping to Mrs. Wolcott at a Memorial Day gathering one time, and he also looked down his nose at the people who worked behind the counter at the lobster pound. Immigrants like Armando Reis, for example. If Mr. Harrington were some sort of Adonis maybe she could understand her mother's willingness to overlook his character flaws. Unfortunately, he was the opposite. Bald on top of his head, he let the thin strands of hair on the back and sides grow down to his shoulders. No doubt he believed the long hair made him cool, but actually he just looked like Benjamin Franklin. She figured her mother wanted financial stability and tried not to judge her. Cassie's father had been her soulmate, and a person couldn't expect to find more than one of those in a lifetime.

After washing her dinner dishes, Cassie hoisted the box and carried it out to the car. She approached the Wolcott place following a short drive, and couldn't help pausing to gape since she hadn't seen it in some time. The centerpiece of the estate was an enormous white Colonial house. But like a vacation resort, it also included a private dock, tennis court, putting green, swimming pool, and a matching (but considerably smaller) white Colonial guesthouse. All this spread across several acres of carpetlike lawn amid clusters of trees pruned to match each other.

Grant's mother and father, who had dementia now, occupied the entire mansion themselves. Maybe staff lived there too, she wasn't sure. Needless to say, they were the richest family in town, and probably among the top five in Massachusetts. She couldn't imagine Mrs. Wolcott needing Mom's bargain-basement hand-me-downs. The woman probably was donating silks and fur coats. But Cassie's mother had been sucking up to her lately, possibly due to Mr. Harrington's influence. He was a social climber if ever there was one.

She rounded the circular drive that led to the front door; it was like a grand hotel entrance. After parking, she ascended the marble steps flanked by pillars to ring the bell at their massive, double-sided front door. She expected a butler to answer and inform her in a British accent, "Deliveries are in the back."

But instead, Mrs. Wolcott's son Grant opened the door. It surprised Cassie to see him, though she should've expected he'd be home from school now too. He was a few years older than her; probably in his senior year. It struck her his appearance had changed significantly for the better. His hair, neatly combed and cut rather short compared to other guys his age, had a golden sheen to it. His light blue eyes were arresting, though his face might've been bland if not for the hawk nose that added character and interest. He was also taller than she remembered and had shed all of his youthful pudge.

At the moment he appeared to be annoyed about something, which she assumed was her, showing up unannounced on his doorstep. But a second later, his features formed into a pleasant mask. "Cassie?"

"Yeah, hi Grant. How are you?"

"Not bad. You're back for the summer?"

"Right, got home from Syracuse yesterday." No point in explaining she might not return there in the fall. "You too?"

"Graduated a month ago," he said. "I'm working in Boston this summer."

"Really? Doing what?"

"Interning at HarborBanks. It's kind of boring."

"I hope it gets better." She glanced around. "Are you living here?"

She tried not to sound like she was making fun of him for still being with his parents.

"In the guesthouse. Going to Wharton in the fall. You know, business school."

"Cool." *And that's how the rich get richer.* She turned back and pointed at the open trunk. "I brought a clothing donation from my mom. Can you ask someone to carry it in?" Frankly, she didn't see why she should do it, when they probably had a houseful of servants being paid for work like this.

But Grant came down the steps to lift out the box himself.

"Hey, I didn't mean you," she said.

"I don't mind. Thanks for bringing it."

It suddenly occurred to her to wonder if her mother included some of her old things in the donation. She should've checked. It mortified her imagining Grant seeing her crappy old clothing and laughing at it, or worse, feeling sorry for her.

He paused holding the box and looked at her. "Are you still seeing Julian Reis?" It was odd, but she got the impression he was trying to cover the seriousness of the question with a casual tone.

"Yeah, why?"

"Um, I just thought you would've broken up. When you went to college."

"Nope. Not at all. We're good." Her voice sounded more defensive than she felt.

"Are you sure he... never mind, it's not my business."

"What do you mean?" she said.

"Nothing. I think it's great you're still together." He stepped toward the house. "Thanks for the donation." He carried the box inside and closed the door.

She wasn't sure what to make of their conversation. Did he know something about Julian she wasn't aware of? Or was he fishing to ask her out himself? She cursed him under her breath, annoyed he reawakened the suspicions she'd been trying to suppress all day.

When she got back home it was still light out. She gathered a mixed bouquet of flowers from the garden to bring to her father, whose gravesite she hadn't visited since Christmas. The entrance to the cemetery adjoined their property and may have been what kept the price of their harborside home low enough for her parents to afford it. For a reason Cassie didn't understand, some people drew the line at having dead folks as neighbors.

The cemetery with its grassy knolls and twisted oaks was dear to her. Some of its graves were from two and a half centuries ago. There were sculptures of swans and sleeping children, and monuments to drowned sailors and soldiers that fell in battle. Their beloved Brumewich ancestors, all.

Her father's grave was on a hill overlooking Inner Harbor. She laid the flowers at his headstone and sat to watch the colors of the sunset reflected in the water while her thoughts wandered back to her memories of him. A moment of calm in an otherwise confusing day.

It was nearly dark by the time she rose again. A noise came from somewhere at the bottom of the hill. When she looked down the path, she thought she saw a shadow disappear behind a tree. Probably her imagination; hardly anyone came to the cemetery at night. Nevertheless, she quickened her pace to the gate, and from there to her house.

Afterward she went to her room and did some sketching because it was too early to go to bed. When she heard the car drive up outside, she shut off her light and peeked out her window at the front. Mr. Harrington walked her mother to the door and looked like he wanted to follow her inside. She shook her head, probably recoiling from the idea of Cassie being home and them doing it in the bedroom next to hers. At least Cassie was recoiling from that idea.

He got a little aggressive with her, but she pushed him firmly away and he finally turned back to his car. His steps wove on his way there, and he looked too drunk to get behind the wheel of any vehicle, but she just went in the house and shut the door behind her. Cassie was surprised her mother would ignore his condition, considering what happened to her father. She tried not to think about it, looking away, not wanting to see just how bad his driving might be. Not wanting to be reminded of her father's accident.

Floorboards creaked as her mother made her way upstairs. Cassie expected she would glance in and was surprised to hear her footsteps continue past the door into her own room. Within a few more minutes all was silent. Her mother might've been too plastered to remember her daughter was back from school. Most likely she fell face down on the bed and passed out immediately without even taking off her high heels.

Unlike her, Cassie was wide awake. The time was only 10:40, which made her laugh after her mother saying they were going to be out late. Apparently that was late to them.

Putting away her sketchpad, she thought of Julian, wondering if he might have gotten home from his night out with his friends. If so, it would be lovely to sneak into his house and up the stairs to his bedroom. She could think of no reason why they shouldn't sleep together tonight. And if he wasn't home yet, she could wait and surprise him when he arrived. Armando in his bedroom downstairs would never notice a thing.

She put on a light summer dress and gave her hair a quick brush. Pausing outside her mother's room, she was glad to hear her heavy breathing. Down the stairs and out the side door she went. Her first thought was to take the car, but she decided to go by bike rather than take the chance the engine would wake her mother and possibly make her worry about where Cassie had gone.

Besides, she loved riding at night when the streets were empty. She flicked on the bike light and set out along the route that skirted the shore, which was less likely to have traffic at this time. To her great surprise, however, she spotted Julian's truck parked along the side of the road just before the turnoff to Thorne Cove. She couldn't miss it with her very own lobster painted on the back.

At first she thought he and his friends must've gone to the beach with a six-pack or a nickel of grass after getting back from the amusement park. She even turned down the lane, thinking it might be fun to surprise him, though a second later she stopped. If she showed up there, it could embarrass him. His friends might mock him over his girlfriend following him wherever he went.

While she was hesitating, she noticed the rusted green VW Bug parked farther up the lane. The car Teresa had been leaning on in the morning. It had to be hers.

She breathed hard. Could it be? Had Julian lied to her? Had he been cheating with Teresa all year long?

Her initial thought was to march right onto the beach and confront them. But she realized she couldn't do it. Even imagining Teresa in his arms was too much for her. If she were to see them together with her own eyes, she might as well just tear out her own heart and stomp all over it.

She rode hard back toward home, except for pausing three times to wipe away the tears that blinded her.

3

———

"Cassie?" Her mother's shout from what sounded like two feet away woke her up.

"What?!" She was disoriented, like the space between her ears was filled with cotton instead of a brain. Failing to block out thoughts of Julian sneaking around behind her back with Teresa, she'd suffered a long, miserable, sleepless night, until finally drifting off close to sunrise.

Her mother sat on the bed beside her and rubbed her arm. "There's terrible news. Do you remember Teresa Patterson?"

Cassie blinked at her mother, thinking: *Remember her? I don't expect to ever forget her for the rest of my life.*

Her mother didn't wait for an answer. "I think she's a few years older than you. I mean, was a few years older. She's been murdered. Someone found her body early this morning at Thorne Cove." She squeezed Cassie's arm. "Thank god you didn't go out last night."

"Murdered?" Cassie couldn't wrap her head around the word. "Murdered?" she repeated, pulling herself up in the bed.

"That's what they're saying. The police haven't let out how, though. And they haven't caught anyone. If it's someone with a gun, the police ought to warn us. What if there's a shooter loose in town?"

"At Thorne Cove? Is that what you said?" Cassie's brain was struggling to keep up.

"Yes, honey. Thorne Cove. Are you all right? I know it's shocking news."

"What about Julian?" She had a horrific vision of their bullet-ridden, blood-soaked bodies side-by-side on the sand.

"Julian? What does he have to do with it?"

Her mother didn't know he'd been there with Teresa. Maybe no one knew. Except her. "Oh, I... I'm confused. I was just having a dream about him." Teresa must've died later, after Julian left. "What time was she killed?"

"How should I know? That's for the police examiner to figure out. Sometime during the night."

"Are you sure it was her?"

"Of course. Franny Thatcher lives right across from there and she's been out talking to the police."

"But are they sure it's murder? Maybe it was an accident. Or suicide."

"I don't think so. Franny sounded sure."

Her head was throbbing. Julian had been there. But it couldn't have anything to do with him. Whatever happened must have taken place after he went home. There couldn't be any doubt about that.

"Maybe it was a serial killer," her mother said. "He could've been stalking her. She was very pretty, wasn't she? That's what Franny told me."

"A serial killer? In Brumewich?" It was just like her mother to hit on a theory like that.

"Why not? Boston had the Boston Strangler. Someone like that could be anywhere. We'll have to lock all our doors and windows from now on."

"Whoever it is, they better catch him soon." Cassie lowered the sheet to get up.

"Did I ever meet Teresa? Was she a friend of yours?" her mother said.

"She was older. We weren't friends. What senior hangs out with a freshman?" She reached for her clothes.

"Where are you going?" Her mother's voice held an edge of panic.

"Julian's." It was the first thing that crossed Cassie's mind. She would go to his house and confirm for herself he had nothing to do with this.

"No. There's a killer out there. It might be some crazy person with a gun." Her mother was back on the shooter theory.

"I doubt it's anything like that. I bet whoever did this is long gone. I'll be careful though. I'm sure if there's any danger, the cops will set up a roadblock. Let me take the car." At least that would keep her mother from worrying about bike accidents.

Before they could continue their argument, the phone rang. Cassie's mother jumped up, unable to resist answering it. "Fine, but don't stay out long," she told her daughter as she hurried to her own room to pick up the call. Another one of her friends, no doubt. This would likely continue all day.

Cassie felt numb as she got dressed. She grabbed an apple on the way out the door and ate it in the car, taking the alternate route to Julian's, avoiding the turnoff to the cove. Likely that way would be blocked anyhow, to keep gawkers away while police continued to gather evidence at the cove. Town residents would be curious. An unexpected death was rare in Brumewich.

When she reached the Reis house, she found Armando outside, vacuuming the inside of the Chevy. It struck her odd that he would pick a time like this to clean it. She couldn't help wondering if it was related to the truck having been at Thorne Cove last night.

Noticing her approach, Armando shut off the vacuum. His eyes were red like he'd been weeping. "You heard the news?" he said.

She nodded.

"What kind a monster would do a thing like that?" He turned back to his truck. "Julian's inside," he said hoarsely.

He was taking it so hard, he made her fear Julian might somehow be involved. On the other hand, it made sense Armando would be anxious about the appearance of guilt that came from his son being at the wrong place at the wrong time. The Reis family was not of the privileged class. Armando had arrived in America with nothing, and since then he and his son had worked with their hands and sweat to make a passable living. Their kind of people never dared admit anything because they knew it would be used against them. They understood if anyone were going to take the fall for a crime, it was going to be them.

Entering the house, she called out to Julian. Right away he emerged from his dad's room, for some reason, and hugged her hard. His throat was thick when he spoke. "Hey. You must've heard. I can't believe it."

"I feel so bad for her." Tears stung her eyes. She longed to open up to him and tell him what she'd seen last night. She wanted to beg him for an explanation. She wanted him to swear he had nothing to do with it. But she kept quiet because—more than anything—she needed to hang onto her belief in his innocence for as long as possible.

"Is there any more news? You know, like, how she died?" he said.

She shook her head.

He echoed his father. "Who would do a thing like that?"

"A serial killer." That was her mother's theory and she was sticking to it. "When did you hear?"

"My father was up early like usual. He overheard somebody talking about it at the market."

"I guess you were out late with your friends." It was the closest she dared get to asking him what he was doing last night.

He hesitated. "Not that late. I, um…"

It seemed like he was about to speak openly. But with the worst timing possible, two police cars turned onto the harbor road and squealed to a halt right outside the house. She and Julian watched through the open door as four officers, one in plainclothes, got out of the vehicles and stalked up the driveway looking grim. Armando, now spraying the outside of the truck with hose water, looked like the proverbial cat caught with a mouthful of mouse. Julian's face paled.

The one who wasn't wearing a uniform approached Armando.

"Detective Heath." He shook Armando's hand. "Mind if we talk to your son?"

"What for?" Sweat glistened from Armando's brow.

"We have some questions for him, related to Teresa Patterson's murder."

"Got nothin' to do with Julian."

"Probably not. But it will help us if we can clear up a couple things," the detective said.

"You got a warrant?" Armando said.

The detective raised an eyebrow. "Like I said, it's just a few questions. We're trying not to escalate things. We'll get a warrant if you insist. If you're worried he's involved."

Cassie wondered if that was even legal, suggesting that insisting on getting a warrant made a person look guilty.

Julian came down the steps from the house. "Papai, it's okay, I'll talk to them."

She wanted to scream, *don't do it, make them get a warrant, give yourselves time to figure out a strategy. Don't let them rush you into this or you'll regret it.*

"Can we go inside?" Detective Heath said.

"Sure." Julian moved aside for him.

When Armando tried to follow, the detective stopped him. "Wait here, please, Mr. Reis." He glanced at the truck. "That's enough cleaning for now. I'll have my officers bring out a chair if you'd like to sit."

"Don't need a chair." Armando glared at them.

The detective finally glanced at Cassie. "You should go home, miss."

Her eyes went to Julian for confirmation. He nodded and said, "Call you later."

Trying her hardest to keep her expression unconcerned, she made her way past them to her car.

4

———

Cassie drove home to wait. She really didn't know what else to do. Her mother had left a note on the kitchen counter saying she was at Mr. Harrington's house. *Good*. Cassie had not been looking forward to facing a barrage of questions from her.

Needing an activity to fill her time until she might hear from Julian again, she went to her studio in the barn. She set up her palette and easel to continue work on a painting she'd begun during winter break. It was the image of a woman with wind-whipped hair leaning over an as-yet-unnamed gravestone while dark clouds gathered overhead. The subject of death now seemed prescient.

Outside, the weather was starting to resemble what was depicted in her painting. A rare June nor'easter had been forecast for tonight, and already the wind hissed through the cracks in the barn, and light rain pattered on the roof.

Several hours must've passed before she heard his footsteps. Julian came rushing into the building, his hair and jacket damp, his expression wild. She lowered her paintbrush. Part of her wanted to run to him, but the other part was filled with resentment and suspicion. She remained in place.

But Julian, not noticing her reticence, swept her into his arms anyway. He kissed her hair, her cheek, her lips, and even her hand. "I'm fucked."

She drew back. "Tell me everything." She meant it, too. She was ready for him to pour out every bit of the truth to her, however much it might hurt to hear it.

"The cops are getting a warrant to search our house."

"I'm sure there's nothing to find. Why you? Why your house?" *Explain to me why you were with her at Thorne Cove last night*, she wanted to say, but held back.

"I don't know. They're not telling us anything."

You're lying. You were with her and somehow they've figured that out. This was the point when her heart hardened against him. He was so determined to keep the truth from her, it made her question whether she'd ever really known him at all.

She kept up the façade of believing him. "It should be easy to prove you had nothing to do with it. You were out with your friends last night."

Guilt flashed in his eyes. "We didn't stay out very long. I left them around ten and went home. I wanted to see you, but I couldn't stay awake. Problem is, I'm screwed without an alibi for later in the night."

"What about your father? Wasn't he home?"

"He was sleeping. Didn't even hear me come in. You know how he is."

This much was likely true. His father never seemed to hear anything after he went to his room for the evening.

"Even if he wanted to lie and say he was awake and we were watching TV or some shit like that, it wouldn't matter. He'd say anything to protect me. Any parent would."

"I guess," she said, though she imagined there might be parents who wouldn't.

"So I'm asking... and it's totally okay if you say no... I'm asking if you'll be my alibi."

She had guessed this was coming and still it made her insides tighten. "You want me to lie for you?" Because that was exactly what he was asking. And she wouldn't have minded so very much if she didn't know there was something essential he was holding back. She would've happily lied for him if she didn't know for a fact he was at the cove last night.

He could've said something... could've explained why he'd needed to meet with Teresa... even if the explanation was that he'd fallen in love with her. At least then Cassie wouldn't think he was a liar as well as a cheater.

"I'm sorry. I wouldn't ask if I wasn't desperate. You know? But it's okay if you don't want to do it."

"Didn't the police already ask where you were last night? And who you were with? You can't change your story now, can you?"

This stopped Julian dead. She had called his bluff, apparently. The stuff about *it's okay if you don't want to do it* was coming too late.

"You're right... I already told them you were with me. I had to come up with something on the spot. Christ, they were making me sweat. But I really mean it, if you don't want to lie, you don't have to. I'll go back and tell them the truth. I'll just say what I said to you: I was afraid they'd never believe me if my father was the only one who could vouch for me."

She was not about to point out that this too was not the truth. It left out the small matter of his actually having met Teresa at the cove. These reassurances of Julian's were meaningless. Either she would lie for him, or she would not, and if it was the latter, he would definitely have to come up with another story. Or tell the truth.

"What exactly do you want me to say?" she said.

"That you came to my house after I got home, around 10:15 or 10:30, it's okay to not be quite sure. That you stayed with me nearly till dawn."

"I could tell them I took my bike so Mom wouldn't wonder where I'd gone in the car when she got home."

"Yeah, definitely, the bike. They asked me how you got to my house and I said I didn't know." He pulled her close again. "I knew I could count on you."

The words stung. Partly because she wasn't certain he could count on her. And because she didn't know if she could count on him ever again.

"I need to go," he said. "The cops told me not to leave the house. I gotta sneak in there before they come back."

"Cassie?" Her mother's tremulous voice made them jump back from each other.

Standing at the barn door, her mother wore a raincoat with water dripping from the hood. She stared at Julian, and it was not a good stare. Her gaze shifted to Cassie. "I need to talk to you."

"Hi, Mrs. Moran. I was just leaving," he said. Then to Cassie: "Call you tonight." He hurried past her mother, who was looking daggers at him now.

"What is it?" Cassie said.

Her mother checked behind her, waiting till he was out of earshot. "The police just called. They're sending someone over to ask you some questions."

"What about?"

"They wouldn't say. But word's getting around Julian might be involved. The police were at his house today."

"He didn't do anything," Cassie said.

Her mother grasped her arm as she tried to leave the barn. "I want you to tell them the truth. If he's involved, you can't protect him. You mustn't try to protect him."

Cassie gave her an angry look, taking back her arm and continuing through the rain toward the house. Steeling herself for the next part.

5

Cassie had not actually told Julian she would lie for him, and she still hadn't made up her mind. If he turned out to be the killer and her lie saved him, or if he was innocent and her telling the truth convicted him... in either case she would never forgive herself. Damned if you do, damned if you don't.

The police were due to arrive any minute. She felt like she needed someone or something to help her come to a decision, but she simply had no time. There wasn't any point in discussing it with her mother, who'd already made her opinion clear. Cassie was to tell the truth no matter what.

Grant Wolcott came to mind. He'd asked her if she was still seeing Julian and seemed surprised when she said she was. Maybe he knew something about Julian and Teresa.

She darted up the steps to use the extension in her mother's bedroom where she could speak privately. She'd never gotten an extension in her room, much to her unhappiness in high school. Pulling out the directory from under the phone, she scanned through it for the Wolcott's number, but there wasn't a separate listing for the guesthouse.

With little time remaining, she called the main house. It must've been a maid or housekeeper who answered and gave her the number for the cottage. She banged down the phone and dialed again.

Outside, a car door slammed shut. The police were here, she was out of time.

"Hello?" Grant said on the phone.

"Grant? This is Cassie Moran." She kept her voice low as the doorbell rang and her mother went to answer it. "I have to ask you something. You seemed surprised when I said I was still with Julian. Was there a reason for that? Do you know anything I don't know?"

He went silent for a minute. Meanwhile, her mother called up from downstairs. "Cassie, come down please!"

She cupped the phone and shouted toward the door. "I just got out of the shower. Be there in a sec!" Her mother would know she was lying, but wouldn't tell the police.

Grant was speaking again. "I didn't want to say anything. It wasn't really my business. But yeah, I saw him with Teresa Patterson a couple weeks ago. At Thorne Cove, in fact. They were making out."

Her mouth grew dry. Though their cars parked at the cove had been damning, this was the first eyewitness account that confirmed their relationship.

"It looks bad for him, I know," Grant said. "But I can't believe he had anything to do with what happened. I'm sure you feel the same."

"Of course," she whispers. "Hey thanks, I gotta go." She felt like she'd been hit by a truck. Until now, she'd been able to maintain a smidgeon of doubt. Like, maybe that hadn't been Teresa's car at the cove. Or maybe it was, but someone else had borrowed it. Or maybe it was her car, and she was the one who'd driven it to the cove, but it was just a coincidence Julian stopped there at the same time. He always liked late night swims.

But now she knew for certain they really had been seeing each other. No matter how hard she tried to make excuses for him, she couldn't anymore.

"Cassie! Officer Brooks is waiting to speak with you!" her mother shouted.

"Coming!" Dread filled her as she made her way down the stairs.

A young man in uniform, probably no more than twenty-five, stood in the hallway. On seeing her, he smiled and extended his hand. "Hi Cassie. I'm Officer Brooks." She could understand right away why he'd been picked to come talk to her. His handshake was firm and reassuring. His voice conveyed warmth; his face was wholesome. He looked like the boy scout who helped grannies cross the street, all grown up. She liked him instantly.

"I remember your dad," he said. "He coached my Little League team for two years. What a nice man. I didn't have much talent for the sport, but he made me feel like I really made a difference on the team."

"Thanks, yeah, he was like that." If she wasn't already feeling like this guy was on her side, this would've been it. How could she feel hostile toward someone who admired her dead father?

He turned to her mother. "Mrs. Moran, I'd like to speak to her privately if that's all right."

Cassie's mother looked at her. "Is it okay with you?"

She hesitated before nodding. Since she was over eighteen, the officer could probably insist if he wanted. She wasn't a child who required a parent present.

They went into the kitchen while her mother headed upstairs to her room. "Do you want something to drink?" Cassie said.

"No thanks. Have a seat."

She poured herself a glass of water while he got out a notepad. They settled at the table. "This shouldn't take very long. I want to reassure you that you're not a suspect here. We just need to corroborate someone else's statement with you."

"All right."

He grew somber. "I'm sure you must've heard what happened to Teresa Patterson."

She nodded, not trusting herself to speak.

"Well, in the process of investigating the case, your name came up. So I'm going to ask you to tell me your whereabouts last night. Is that okay?"

Her hands were starting to tremble. She clasped them together under the table. "Sure."

"But before you start, I want to say something. I know what it's like to be your age and maybe in love, right? Not so long since I was the same age. And I know what it's like to want to protect the person you care for."

He paused and scratched his chin. "But the fact is, it's always, always better to go with the truth. If the person you want to protect is innocent, the truth is their best defense. It may not always seem that way, but trust me on this. When someone is lying, it's generally easy for us to figure out. But it leaves us thinking, why did she lie, right? So the person she's protecting might be innocent, but we're left wondering if they're guilty because of the lie.

"On the other hand, if the person you want to protect is guilty, you definitely don't want to lie for them. In this case, the guilty person has committed murder. I'm sure you don't want a murderer to get away with the crime. People who commit violence of any sort will commit violence again. Believe me, I've studied this. You don't want to feel responsible for anyone else getting hurt or killed in the future.

"And lastly, think of Teresa's family. There's nothing worse than losing a child, or a sister, and knowing the killer got away with it. Her family deserves justice. You can help them just by telling the truth.

"This was my long-winded way of asking you to tell me where you were last night starting at around seven p.m."

She had never been so torn regarding any decision before. She hated Julian for putting her in this situation. But he was also the sun and earth and sea to her. Could he possibly have killed Teresa, or any woman? Although he'd cheated on her, she still couldn't believe the boy she knew so well might've murdered someone.

She was aware her hesitation to respond made it increasingly clear she was considering a lie. An unconvincing lie would be worse than not lying as far as Julian's situation was concerned.

Grant's words echoed inside her and hardened her heart: *I saw him with Teresa Patterson.* Still, when she opened her mouth, she wasn't certain what would come out of it until the words began. "I was home alone till about eleven last night. Then I went out on my bike." She explained how her mother had gone straight to bed after returning from the party.

"Is there a reason you didn't take the car?"

"I like riding at night." She added the part about her mother possibly getting worried if she heard the car start.

"Okay. Where did you go?"

"I took Ocean Avenue, planning to go to Julian's. I wanted to avoid traffic. But on the way..." Here was where she hesitated. She swallowed a lump and blurted out the rest. "I saw his truck parked along the side of the road. Right before the turnoff to Thorne Cove."

"Are you certain it was Julian's truck?"

"You know how there's a lobster painted on the back? I did that."

"Got it, okay. Please continue."

"I slowed and looked down the lane. I saw another car I thought I recognized. A rusty green VW Bug. I wasn't sure, but I thought it was Teresa's car."

"She does have a vehicle of that description. Did you see the license number?"

She shook her head. "It was dark. And it wouldn't have occurred to me to even look at it."

"Okay. You saw the car. Do you know what time it was then? Did you check your watch?"

"I wasn't wearing one. I think it was a little after eleven."

"Fair enough," he said. "Looking down the lane, did you see Teresa or Julian?"

"No. Neither one of them."

"Did you go to the cove?"

She shook her head again. "I turned my bike around and went home."

"Was there a reason you didn't go look for Julian at the cove? I mean, you were on your way to see him anyway."

She blew out a heavy breath. "Well, it was because of Teresa's car. It made me think he was going to meet her. It made me upset. That's why I went home."

"So you didn't see her there either?"

"No. I saw Julian's truck and Teresa's car, then I turned around and went back home. That's it."

"Did you have any other reason to suspect Julian was seeing her?"

She considered saying what Grant had just told her on the phone. But she decided against it, mainly because this wasn't knowledge she had at the time. "I saw her hanging around near Julian's house yesterday morning. And he acted a little funny, like he wasn't sure about us... our relationship. I thought it was strange he would've planned a night out with his friends on the day he knew I'd be back from college."

"Is there anything else you'd like to tell me?"

Her eyes filled with tears. "Officer, I can't believe Julian would ever hurt anyone. I've dated him for years and he's always been as gentle as can be. He could never kill a person. He's innocent. He has to be."

After finishing his notes, Officer Brooks stood and offered her a tissue. "Thank you for telling me the truth, Cassie. I hope you're right about Julian."

As soon as he was gone, her mother returned to the kitchen. Cassie wept hot tears on her shoulder.

6

After betraying the boy she loved, she could think of nothing further to do. Her mother wanted her to talk about it when she was done crying, but she turned away from her, went up the stairs, crawled into bed, and pulled the covers over herself. This was no more effective in erasing the horror of the last twenty-four hours than if she were a turtle drawing her head inside her shell.

The weather was going downhill fast, mirroring the day's events. The wind wheezed through narrow gaps in the windows. Rain pelted the glass. Branches beat the side of their house.

Her thoughts settled into two distinct camps that lay siege upon each other. In corner number one she reassured herself she'd done the right thing in telling the truth. If her boyfriend was a killer she would not—must not—protect him with a lie.

But corner number two did not believe Julian capable of hurting anyone, let alone murdering them. Therefore she should've lied to save him from the appearance of guilt that would surely be used against him even if he were innocent.

A knock put an end to the debate and caused her to poke her head out from under the sheet. Her mother opened the door without waiting for a reply. "Officer Brooks just called. He wanted to know if Julian came here after he left."

"They don't know where Julian is?"

She shook her head.

Cassie sprang from the bed and crossed to the window. Darkness had settled in, but the front house lights illuminated sheets of rain ricocheting off the roof of their car, and the maple sapling bent so low by the force of the gale, it looked like it would snap. "I have to go."

"Stay here, Cassie. It's a nor'easter out there."

"I'll be careful." She slipped into her sneakers and dashed past her mother, trying to ignore her stricken expression. Downstairs she paused to find the car keys under the newspaper on the counter.

Few other motorists were foolish enough to be on the road. She drove too fast into a deep pool and nearly slid into a ditch before connecting with the solid surface again. When she neared Julian's house, she glimpsed police cars lined up out front. She parked in the first stretch of empty space and the rain drenched her as she rushed along the sidewalk, splattering through puddles. Officer Brooks was in his squad car but he nodded to another cop to let her into the house.

Julian's father emerged from the kitchen, walking with bent shoulders and a shuffling step. Seeing Cassie, he said, "You gonna catch your death of cold." He disappeared into the back and returned with a towel. "Dry off."

"Where is he?" she said.

"He took the boat." His eyes glistened as he shifted his gaze to the window. "They called the Coast Guard."

Her arms started shaking and she pulled the towel tight around them. "Why would he do that?"

Armando lowered his voice. "My boy lost hope. The cops searched, said we had a knife missin' from our set in the kitchen. The murder weapon, they said. We told them anyone coulda taken it. When do we ever lock our doors?"

The image of Teresa with a bloody knife wound made her shudder. "What can we do?" she said.

"Wait. And pray. Never helped me before but maybe God in heaven been savin' up for this." Armando crossed the room to where a photograph of Julian's teenage mother rested on the mantle. She had only been seventeen when she died. He kissed the tips of his fingers and pressed them against her face before lifting the rosary that hung over the frame. Holding it, he lowered his head, muttering words in Portuguese.

Cassie stared through the front window at angry waves crashing against the sea wall across the street. If she'd thought her prayers would make any difference, she still would not have been able to decide whether to pray for his escape, or for his safe return into the arms of the police waiting to arrest him.

PART TWO: WITCH

CASSIE (AGE 26)

7

Cassie rides her bike back from work on one of those rare June afternoons when the sky is blue, the breeze light, and the humidity low. This perfection of elements brings on a feeling close to happiness.

As usual, Gio begins meowing before she opens the door. When she walks in, he tangles himself between her legs, immediately under foot. She wishes she could believe her mere presence fills him with joy, but clearly the amount of attention she receives depends on how urgently he requires her services at the moment.

After putting away her purse, she feeds the poor starving beast. He gulps down his food in chunks with an enthusiasm she envies. How much simpler life would be if the highlight of everyone's day was merely dinner.

Her cat follows her out the back door and plops on the brick patio to clean himself, while she arranges the lawn sprinkler and turns it on. A few drops reach Gio, causing him to leap backward, shaking off his fur while throwing her an affronted look.

She unravels the hose to water the rhododendrons, which are looking wilted. They've had two weeks without rain and she's trying her best not to let anything die on her watch. Her mother has been more than generous, leaving the place in her hands when she moved to Florida last year. Cassie only has to cover taxes and utilities. The house and the old red barn could both use some repairs, which she plans to do after she saves up enough money.

When she's finished with the plants, she brings in the mail—bills and catalogues—and tosses it into the pile on the table by the door. For dinner, she cooks herself brown rice and stir-fried veggies with cheese. Simple but healthy and it generally tastes good enough, depending on which vegetables she happens to have on hand. By the time she brings her meal into the family room to eat in front of the nightly news, Gio has positioned himself at the foot of her chair, ready to snatch falling particles. He carries inside him a deep well of hope that never dries out.

Since it's June, she still has an hour and a half till sunset after she's finished doing the dishes. Gio trots after her to the studio in the barn, and curls into his cozy bed by the door while she gets out her supplies. She uses acrylics because they're easier to clean than oils, especially when her cat manages to spread wet paint all over himself.

Currently on her canvas she's depicted a woman with long auburn hair walking into the woods. Over the past few days, the painting has taken on more and more of an ominous feel, she's not sure why. Maybe because the forest is growing darker, and the branches of the trees are starting to look like the arms and hands of skeletons. The woman faces away from the viewer, something that's true of all Cassie's work. She loves the mystery of it, letting you imagine what her face might look like.

When the sun dips low and the sky turns crimson, she calls Gio, who has disappeared and is probably hunting mice in the bushes. He comes right away, not wanting to be left behind, even though he can return whenever he wants through his cat door.

The phone rings before they're inside, and she's pretty certain she knows who it is. Grant Wolcott. He moved back from Philadelphia a month earlier, after earning his MBA from Wharton and then working at an investment firm for several years. Since his return, they've had coffee a few times, though she has mixed feelings about renewing their acquaintance. This is why she doesn't rush to answer. However, since it's still ringing when she finally reaches the kitchen extension, she decides to pick up.

"Hope I'm not calling too late," he says.

She can't tell if he's being serious or not, and it makes her wonder if he knows what a pathetic life she leads. If he'd called twenty minutes later, he really would've been too late.

"It's fine, I was just painting," she says.

"Good. I was wondering if you want to go out on the boat with me tomorrow. Do some fishing, go for a swim, putter around the coast. Whatever you like."

Until now she'd forgotten tomorrow is Saturday. She racks her brain for an excuse because this sounds like a date and she hasn't dated anyone in a long time. She's not sure she wants to start up again, particularly not with Grant. It isn't that she has anything against him, but she's afraid being around him will bring back all the memories.

Still, the weather is supposed to be beautiful again tomorrow and she suddenly misses being out on a boat larger than her canoe. Before she can stop herself, words are coming out of her mouth: "Sure. Forget the fishing. The rest sounds good." They agree on a time before hanging up.

She stands by the phone a moment longer, hoping she hasn't made a mistake. It's just a boat ride, she tells herself. It's not a promise to get married and bear his children. It's not even an agreement to have sex with him.

Before going to sleep, she watches a dumb sci-fi movie with aliens. Probably because the meteorite that fell behind her hedges also came from outer space, she's reminded she still hasn't done anything about it. If she does decide to contact the science museum, it will have to wait till Monday now.

Recalling the way the thing sparked her, she checks her arm. It's only been a day, but the mark has disappeared entirely. There isn't any pain when she touches it either. Clearly it wasn't anything to be concerned about.

Gio follows her to bed and snuggles beside her. Her thoughts turn to Julian, as they often do. She remembers their night together before she left for college. One of their last happy moments.

She thinks she's about to drift asleep when suddenly her head heats up like a match was lit inside it. Sweat pops out of her forehead and the back of her neck. She opens her eyes but sees only blackness. The bed seems to drop out from under her and she's falling, falling, falling into a limitless void.

8

———————

Cassie's body jolts as it settles back on the firm surface of the bed again. The burning sensation in her head subsides. Her vision returns but she can't believe what she sees.

It isn't her bed, or even her room. She's wrapped in Julian's arms, lying on his bed, in his room. It has to be a dream, yet it feels exactly as if she's awake and living in the moment.

"Cass?" Julian's breath tickles her ear, his voice soft and low as she remembers it.

She's afraid if she looks at him her heart will explode. She's afraid if she doesn't, the dream will end and he'll disappear.

"You okay?" he says.

She doesn't say anything because this isn't real. But when seconds pass without any change in her perceptions, she lifts her face to him. His rich brown eyes filled with concern make her lose it. Tears gush as she draws back from him, at the same time grasping his shoulders and shaking as hard as she can. The sheet falls down, exposing her nakedness, which she assumes is all part of the dream.

"Why, Julian? Why did you do it?" She continues to cry out *why* in a frenzy, not even knowing whether the question is *why did you cheat* or *why did you kill her*?

Julian's arms fold around her and hold her tight until she calms down, gulping in air. "Do what?" he says in a gentle voice. "What did I do?"

"You didn't love me enough." Her answer is petulant, like a child pouting to her mother. It doesn't begin to encapsulate an answer to his question, but she doesn't want to get into it when this is only a dream.

"That isn't true." He kisses her hair. "You're feeling bad because you're leaving. But I'll be here when you get back. You know? Waiting for you. Nothing's gonna happen to us."

A bitter laugh gets stuck in the back of her throat at the irony. She pulls up the sheet to cover herself and wipes her eyes with it. "I've never had a dream as real as this before."

"Dream?" His head tilts the way it always did when he was puzzled. A movement that endears him to her.

"Either that or I'm losing my mind." She presses her hand against his cheek. "Your face is warm. I've never dreamt with all my senses before." She sniffs the air beside him. "There's mint on your breath. Your clock is making a buzzing noise. I'm seeing details I don't even remember, like the way it's torn at the corner of your Jethro Tull poster."

"Don't joke. Not tonight." When he rolls over and stands up, she's shocked to see he's naked too. It makes sense though. On this night long ago, they made love. But since when did a dream make sense?

He pulls on cotton pants before retrieving a small box from his desk drawer. "Got you something." He takes her hand and places it on her palm.

She shifts her gaze between the expectant look in his eyes, and the box, feeling compelled to play along. Of course, she knows what the gift will be, but when she opens it, she acts surprised just to please him. "Thank you," she whispers, holding back more tears.

He takes out the silver band and slips it on the third finger of her right hand. "It's not good enough to be an engagement ring. But it's my promise to be faithful."

"Don't make promises you can't keep." Though he deserves this rebuke, she regrets it as soon as she sees the hurt in his eyes.

"You don't believe me?"

"It's going to be hard."

"Will you be faithful to me?"

"Always," she says.

"So will I." He sits beside her, resting his arm on her shoulder. She remains perfectly still, not wanting anything to interrupt the dream.

"Don't be sad. Only three months till Christmas. You'll be back in no time," he says.

It feels so real she almost wonders if everything that's happened since this day is the actual dream from which she has only just awoken. A sharp urgency fills her.

"Run away with me," she says. "Tonight. We'll go somewhere else, start a new life together."

"You don't mean that."

"I do. I've got some money. It'll hold us till we find work."

Julian is silent. He must think she's lost her mind. Then he says, "You're going to college. You can't give up on that."

"I'll give up anything so we can be together. I will." Again that stubborn, childish note in her voice.

"I can't leave my father. He needs my help on the boat."

"He'll have to hire someone when you go to the conservatory."

"That's at least a year away, if it even happens. I need to save up more money first." His eyes light up with excitement as he gets on his knees in front of her. He places his hand under her chin and makes her look at him. "Ask me what my goals are."

"Why don't you just tell me?"

"C'mon."

"Okay. What are your goals?"

"Number three, make a living even if it means I have to keep catching lobsters."

"What's number one?"

"Getting there. Number two, become a world-renowned pianist. I don't know if I can support myself that way. That's why I need number three."

"If you're world-renowned, someone ought to pay you," she says.

"And number one... make Cassie Moran happy."

She lowers her forehead to his shoulder. "You really mean that?" This is her mind playing with her, saying what she wants to hear.

"You and me forever, Cass." He taps his heart with his fist. Then he's back on his feet. "You should go now. It's late."

In her memory, she was the one to say it was time for her to go. But dreams don't follow scripts, she reminds herself. On this night— their last before she left for Syracuse—they only made love once, but what's to stop them from doing it again inside her dream? And if they do, will it be as achingly beautiful as it was the time before?

But he's handing her clothes to her and she lets the moment pass. After she dresses, he takes her hand and they tiptoe down the stairs. They don't want to wake his father, sleeping in his room at the back of the house.

The front door creaks when Julian opens it, exactly as it did that night. Then and now, Armando does not get up and she remembers feeling sure that even if he were awake, he would have no intention of disturbing them. They go out to the front yard where Julian wraps her in his arms and kisses her again. "Don't let me go," she whispers, clinging to him. He pulls back a bit but she refuses to release him.

It's no use, though. Her head grows hot as her vision blackens. Julian's fading form leaves a hollow space between her arms.

9

———

The morning after her vivid dream, Cassie wakes at nine feeling well-rested. She supposes that means the sequence flashed by in a second of dream time, and she spent the rest of the night sleeping deeply.

Still, the experience has left her unsettled. When she climbs out of bed, she unearths the box of Julian mementos from her closet for the first time in several years and opens it up. She digs through its contents till she finds the silver ring—now tarnished—and puts it on. Its size, its weight, and the way it fits her finger are exactly what she remembers from the dream. How did her subconscious recall it so accurately?

Gio is meowing, the sign that breakfast is past due. She replaces the ring, goes downstairs in her pajamas, and prepares him a mixture of canned food and kibble. She makes scrambled eggs for herself and places the morning newspaper before her on the table, hoping it will keep her from dwelling on how disturbing it was to experience that night with Julian again in such rich detail.

The front page includes an article on the meteor shower, and she skims it to see if anyone else reported finding one or receiving a spark from it. No one did.

None of the other news catches her interest, no matter how long she stares at the headlines. Considering the day ahead of her, she regrets agreeing to join Grant on his boat. She's quite sure she won't make good company while she's still trying to wrap her head around what happened last night. On the other hand, getting out of the house may be the best way to force these troubling thoughts from her mind.

Upstairs, she puts on her newest bikini and models it in front of the mirror. Her thighs look flabby, but what else is new? It's best if she's not overly beguiling anyway. After covering up with her favorite sundress, she brushes her hair and considers a ponytail. Better to leave it loose since she'll be swimming, she decides. She applies pale lipstick and eye shadow though it'll get washed away soon enough. Not that she's trying to wow him with her looks, but it seems more respectful to put in at least the minimum of effort.

Before leaving she reminds Gio to be a good boy. A few days ago, he was not a good boy when he dragged a small dead bird into the house through his cat door. She doubts he learned his lesson, though.

Since today's forecast promised the same clear skies and not-stiflingly-hot temperatures as yesterday, she takes her bicycle. Passing through the small downtown, she notices a new shop called "Broom Witch Antiques," an obvious play on the town's name of Brumewich.

Though many make fun of it, Cassie loves their town name. *Brume* means *fog* or *mist* and does not refer to a device used for sweeping (or flying across the sky). *Wich* is just a common ending for towns in New England. But people think of witches when they see the name. It's understandable, given Massachusetts' sordid history of persecuting innocent women for no good reason whatsoever.

In fact the idea of witchcraft has always intrigued her. As a child, she constantly drew herself as a witch. She would be soaring across the sky on her broomstick and striking the people below with her lightning spells. These would never permanently harm anyone but might turn them into a bug or a snake for a little while. Or she might cause a person's hair to turn green, or their hands to sprout a sixth finger, or their heads to face their backsides. She had nice spells too, that would help an awkward or homely girl or boy to find friendship and love. Spells that changed bullies into saints and struggling students into future Einsteins. Her witch fantasy gave her the sensation of power and maybe that was all it was ever about.

Drawing near the Wolcott manor, she can't help marveling again at its perfection. Of course, with that kind of money, they can afford to keep the place up. If the paint peels in one spot, reason enough to have the whole mansion redone. As opposed to her house, where they had to wait till the paint hung in ragged patches all over before calling every painter in the area to try to get the best price.

She follows the driveway to the guesthouse entrance. Grant has been staying here since his return from Philadelphia. Most twenty-nine-year-old men would not want to be living back home with Mommy—his father passed away five years ago—but he'd have to pay a fortune in rent to get something half as nice minus all the amenities. She doubts his mother charges him anything, though one never knows with the rich. Sometimes they're far stingier than those who have nothing. She imagines that's how they become those-who-have-everything.

Grant calls to her from the dock. As she approaches along the path between the two houses, he pauses to watch her. "You look pretty."

"Thanks." She always feels awkward when anyone compliments her. If she says something nice in return, it comes across that she's being polite, not genuine. Instead, she changes the subject. "Is this new?" She nods at the shiny white-and-blue Boston Whaler, just the right size for vrooming along the coast with a few friends.

"We've had it a while," Grant says.

She's noticed he likes to downplay their wealth and she likes that about him. His mother, on the contrary, never lets anyone forget her money places her well above them in the town pecking order.

Before long they untie from the dock and head out along the channel toward open water. "Where are we going?" she asks, not that it matters. It's enough just to be out on the water, with the sun heating her and the fine mist on her face.

"I thought we might go by the lighthouse. It's high tide." He says this because Farer's Light marks Farer's Ledge, a cluster of black rocks situated just below the surface of the ocean some distance from their shore. The ledge sank many ships in the mid-1800s, before the lighthouse was built. At high tide, though, they can motor over the rocks safely.

"Sure. I haven't seen it up close for a while," she says.

But when they draw near the base of the lighthouse, she feels uneasy. It's an enormous granite structure that looms eighty or ninety feet straight out of the ocean. A ladder runs up the side of it. The part she doesn't like, though, is seeing the rock underneath them, hovering like a massive sea creature preparing to rear up its monstrous back.

When she turns toward Grant, he's looking at her like he's trying to figure something out. But he shifts his gaze quickly, not liking that she's caught him staring, apparently. "When I was a kid, my friends and I used to climb the ladder and jump off," he says. "You ever do that?"

"A few times. I was scared to death looking down from the jumping point, but somehow I managed it."

"A rite of passage."

"Can't call yourself a Brume-witch till then."

He gives her a crooked smile. "I never called myself that."

"What do you say then? Brume wizard?"

"Better," he says.

She's distracted thinking about the time she and Julian took his father's lobsterboat out here. They went up the ladder and got into the lighthouse through a door with a broken lock. Then they made love on an old chair. Later they laughed about it, saying it was the start of crazy places they would have sex. A lighthouse was their first and later it would be a train or an airplane and then maybe they'd do a love-making tour of the national monuments. They went on quite a while thinking of unusual places to do it. As it turned out their list never grew longer than *a lighthouse.*

After a swing round Farer's Light, they go near the beach closest to the harbor and anchor for a swim. Grant dives in while she tests the water with her toe, hanging from the ladder. "How is it?"

"Like there could be ice cubes floating around in here." He swims hard away from the boat and she watches the water ripple over his shoulder blades. She thought he was scrawny in high school, more of a bookish type, but he's grown muscles since then. His father was a tall, distinguished-looking man. Some people called his mother a beauty, but she never saw it. Money buys good opinions along with everything else.

Grant returns and splashes her, making her scream. "Chicken!" He dives down and goes under the boat.

She jumps in. The water feels even colder than she expected and she shoots back up, gasping. She launches into a crawl to warm herself. Grant catches up and they race toward the beach. When they can nearly touch bottom, they pause and tread water.

"I suppose you need to be a Brume witch or wizard to get into this ocean," he says.

"Our blood must run cold."

She's starting to feel a connection to Grant. This is their heritage... creatures of the sea, guardians of the coast, witches and wizards of the east. They'll always be of Brumewich.

Wondering if he feels the same, she asks: "Why did you come back from Philadelphia?"

"Why did you come back from Syracuse after college?"

"I asked you first."

His pale eyes look at her in a way that makes her spine tingle. "You know the answer, Cassie." He flips back into the water and swims toward the boat.

10

____

When they get back to the dock Grant asks if she'll have dinner with him. She says she's tired and wants to go home and clean the saltwater off her. It's a lame excuse, but he knows her well enough not to argue. In fact, because he's been nice and hasn't pressed her, she gives him an opening by suggesting they do it another time.

Her evening is a repeat of the night before, and the many nights before that. A simple, nutritious dinner. Two hours working on her painting. Back into the house to cuddle with Gio while reading an Agatha Christie novel. After twenty-five pages, she remembers she's read it before and puts it away.

She's tired yet almost afraid to go to bed. She doesn't want a repeat of last night's photo-realistic dream. On the other hand, she can't simply give up sleeping from now on.

When she does finally slip under the sheet, she tries not to think of Julian at all. This works about as well as one would imagine. She finds her thoughts flooded with memories of him, and before she knows it, she's picturing the day she came home from college for the Christmas holiday.

It happens the same as before, with the inside of her head feeling as if it's boiling over and her vision darkening. Seconds later she gets the tumbling sensation. When she can see again, she's standing on the staircase in her house, about to lose her balance. With one hand, she lunges for the bannister, at the same time banging her leg with the suitcase on her other side.

It's every bit as real as last night's experience, which she hesitates to even call a dream anymore. It was more like a strange sort of time travel, during which she relived an event that happened in the past. But she doesn't have time to analyze it now.

Something metal bangs in the kitchen. She's about to call out "Gio!" when she remembers he isn't even born yet. It has to be her mother. The aroma of Christmas cookies baking in the oven reaches her, waking a gnawing hunger inside her.

She knows exactly when this is. She's just returned from her first semester at Syracuse. She rode back with Sarah and her father, who live in Ruford. Cassie's mother greeted her at the door upon her arrival, before quickly disappearing to tend to the cookies.

"Everything all right, honey?" Her mother peers out at her from the kitchen.

The urge to hug her mother fills Cassie, but she holds back, though she hasn't seen her in six months. It isn't just that she's missed her. This seven-years-younger version of her mother looks so different. Her skin is smoother, her figure thinner, and her hair is still its natural chestnut color. Cassie aches a bit inside thinking how time takes its toll, and how quickly people age.

Again she wonders how all the details are right in this dream or whatever-it-is, including the way her mother would've looked seven years ago.

"I thought I was dreaming," Cassie says.

Her mother smiles. "It must feel like that, coming back home after your first time away." The timer buzzes and she spins around to deal with the cookies.

Cassie continues up the stairs and deposits the suitcase on her bed. Turning on the overhead light, she glimpses her own reflection in the mirror. Last night in the semi-darkness at Julian's house, she had no chance to see what she looked like. Curious, she peers into the glass and is taken back to the era when her dirty blond hair was straighter and fell more than halfway down her back. These days, she's keeping it a little shorter with more of a Stevie Nicks look— bangs and unruly curls. Along with the differences in hair, this girl she's staring at in the mirror has fuller cheeks and whiter skin than her waking self, currently sporting a decent tan. The paleness, however, is consistent with this dream taking place in winter.

Once again, her dream has gotten every detail right. In fact it's nothing like a dream, but exactly what she'd expect if she traveled through time. Except... if she jumped into the past, wouldn't there be two of her now? Time travel in science fiction stories had people running into their younger or older selves. This would create a paradox so confusing she could never quite wrap her head around the explanation. But that was how it was supposed to work. In this case, though, she *is* the younger version of herself. If it's time travel, it's for the mind only. She left her future body at home.

When the doorbell rings downstairs, her mother gets it. A second later she shouts up, "Cassie, Julian's here!"

She closes her eyes and breathes in slowly to calm herself. *It's just a dream.* Except it's nothing like a dream.

Her feet move her to the top of the stairs. Julian looks up from the bottom with particles of snow on his wool beanie and light reflecting in his eyes. This is all it takes. Excitement overwhelms her and sends her flying down the steps into his arms. "I missed you so much," he says into her ear.

"Missed you too." It's true, even counting last night's rendezvous. Part of her wants to drag him back upstairs and into her bed, but it would be awkward with her mother in the kitchen making them cookies.

"How was it?" Julian says.

"How was what?"

He laughs at her. "Um, that place you were. What's it called? College?"

She's already forgotten she's just come from there on this day in the past. "Oh let's not talk about that." Through the front window, she glimpses white powder settling on the driveway. "Let's go outside." She tells her mother they're going for a walk as she throws on a coat, mittens, and a hat. Aside from gloves, Julian has only his jean jacket over a sweater, but this is typical of him. A true child of New England, he was never one to get cold or hot but somehow his internal temperature always balances between the extremes of winter and summer.

Before leaving, she ducks into the kitchen to grab four warm cookies, handing two to Julian. After scarfing them down, they go to the barn to fetch the toboggan, which he pulls along the slick road on their way to the sledding hill. They pass the haunted house, which is what they used to call the Quinn place. A heavy dose of nostalgia hits her to see its broken shutters, cracked glass, and peeling paint. A few years after this, someone will buy the house and modernize it, destroying its mystery and allure.

Julian pretends to stop for something and next thing she knows, a snowball smashes into her shoulder.

"You're gonna pay for that, Reis." She dashes to the nearest snowbank and scoops up a handful, patting it into shape. When she turns back, he's coming at her, but she gets him right in the side of his head.

"Oh, you wanna play dirty?" he says, aiming one at her neck. When it hits, the icy particles get under her collar and set off something inside her. She gathers an armful of snow and runs at him with it, knocking him backward into the snowbank, jumping on top of him, and pressing it hard into his face. He's choking, trying to push her away, when she realizes she's gone too far and rolls off him. "Sorry."

He sits up, picking the snow off his face. "What was that about?" He's more confused than pissed, as she can tell from the tilt of his head.

"I didn't mean it." Though actually she did mean it. When it comes to her feelings about Julian, there's something dark and unpredictable lurking just beneath the surface inside her.

"This is me. I know you," he says.

"Okay, I was angry."

"A little snow never set you off like that before. C'mon. Tell me."

She has to remind herself it's a dream. "You make me want to love you, but it isn't real. I don't know you, not really. I can't trust you."

He leans forward, takes her chin with his gloved hand, and turns her face toward him. "You can trust me. Always. I swear it."

His eyes convince her. Despite everything that will happen, she finds herself nodding at him.

"You and me forever, Cass." He taps his heart with his fist like he did before at his house.

She nods again.

"Come on then." He pulls her up into his arms and they continue to the hill, where no one else is around due to the late hour. By the light of a lonely streetlamp, they shoot down the slope over and over, taking turns who's in front and who's in back holding the other tight around the waist. At last, overwhelmed by exhaustion, they crash and spill out of the toboggan. They lie where they fell, making snow angels and sticking out their tongues to catch the falling flakes, until Julian gets on top of her and kisses her with his cold wet lips. She's filled with a sensation of lightness like she hasn't felt since before the murder.

As her head starts heating and spinning, she cries out and clutches him harder, but nothing she does can stop this perfect moment from ending right now.

11

―――――――

As on the previous night, Cassie recalls nothing further till she wakes in the morning. Sunlight streams through her window and Gio is standing on her chest meowing into her face. Feeling slightly less rested than she did yesterday, she gets up to feed him.

While he eats, she sits at the kitchen table thinking. Two experiences now, each as lifelike as the other. *What's happening to me? Am I losing my mind?* She can't call it dreaming anymore. Dreams aren't precise re-creations of the past.

Time travel. She can't believe she's even considering this, but no other explanation fits. Each occurrence was exactly as if her consciousness had left her present self and leapt backward in time, landing inside her past self.

However, she's not simply reliving events as they played out then. She can change them; she can act differently than she did the first time. The others—Julian and her mother—behave according to how she remembers, though they also vary from the script when prompted by her.

It's too soon—way too soon—to start wondering if she can change the past, and if those changes will propagate to the present. Would she even know that things were different if those changes became her new reality? She shuts off that line of thinking before her head starts to hurt.

As crazy as this idea sounds, she tries to consider it rationally. Something changed in her two days ago. Her gaze shifts to the window as she recalls the meteorite. The mark on her skin hasn't returned; everything looks and feels completely normal. But a horrifying thought occurs. What if a microscopic alien got inside her and is moving her around through time? She folds her arms tight across her stomach, trying to quell the notion.

The arrival of the meteorite is the only unusual event she can remember happening before her dreams began. Feeling she ought to take a closer look at it in the daylight, she rises and heads for the front yard. Her queasiness increases as another idea comes to her. Maybe it only pretended to be a rock. Maybe it has now wandered off to hide in her house and later emerge in a much more frightening form when she least expects it. Like the baby in *Alien* that grew into full-sized monster in no time at all.

Relief floods her when she peers behind the hedge. The rock is still a rock and hasn't moved from where she left it. She's about to pick it up when she decides she's not being nearly cautious enough. Returning to the house, she fetches her wool jacket, oven mitts, and a cardboard box. Anyone would think she was nuts armoring herself like this to pick up a little stone, but she doesn't want to be sparked again. However, nothing at all happens when she places the meteorite in the box.

She doesn't want the thing inside the house with her, but she thinks she's okay with storing it in the barn. Sticking it on a shelf in the back, she covers the box with a heavy piece of wood. *Try climbing out of that.* But if it really is an alien that somehow arrived here from light years away, she doubts her little box is going to stymie it.

12

Because it's Sunday and she may be losing her mind, Cassie is spending the day painting. If she truly is going batshit crazy, she ought to be able to come up with something great or at least unique and memorable. She believes a fine line exists between creativity and insanity. Like Van Gogh with the ear, and Munch who painted the screaming woman. She doesn't know if Munch was nuts or not, but the brain that envisioned an image like that could not exactly be stable.

It's the third cloudless day in a row, but unlike before, it's become uncomfortably hot and the humid air is stifling. Her T-shirt and shorts are sticking to her. She has the sliding barn door fully open to try to catch a breeze, but hasn't felt any yet. She adjusts her position so at least she won't be standing in the sun.

After staring at her painting of a girl in the woods for several minutes, she realizes she's not in the mood for it. She takes it down from her easel and sets it aside before going to the shelf where she stores the records and tapes she likes to listen to while she's working. As she flips through, her eyes are drawn to Julian's recording of *Rêverie*, which she hasn't played for a long time. Before she can talk herself out of it, she snatches it up and inserts it in the cassette player.

The haunting notes wash over her as she takes out her charcoal and begins sketching. Her hand moves with a surge of energy, and the image of Julian's face that's stuck inside her head starts to form on the paper. Letting her instincts take over, she works like a speed-chess player, drawing whatever snaps into her mind without hesitation.

She's on her third sketch of Julian and fourth time playing the song when a rustling sound by the barn door makes her start and look up.

"Hey Cassie." Grant is leaning against the frame, looking so comfortable she wonders how long he's been there. It's disconcerting that he might've been watching her mad creative frenzy. Immediately she reaches over and shuts off the cassette player. She's not sure he'd have any idea that was Julian playing the piano, but he might.

Worse, she can't let him see these pictures. He'll think she's obsessed with someone she should've jettisoned from her brain years ago.

"Oh hi. You took me by surprise. Did you try to call first? Usually I hear the phone from here." This is a lie. Especially if she has music on, an ambulance could pass by with its sirens blaring and she wouldn't notice. But she's babbling, trying to divert his attention while she closes her sketchpad.

"I hope I didn't frighten you." He doesn't answer her question, which she assumes means he didn't call. *Why would he?* By now he must know her well enough to understand he has a better chance of seeing her if he simply arrives at her door, rather than asking her permission first.

"Can I see it?" He nods toward her sketchpad.

"Too soon. I only just started it. Still needs a lot of work."

He steps toward her. "That's okay. I bet it's better than you think." He reaches toward her pad.

She presses her hand down on the cover. "No really. I'll be embarrassed." She turns toward the canvas she set aside. "Can I get your opinion on this?"

But when she looks back, she finds he's seized the sketchpad and lifted its cover. As he stares down at Julian's face, his grip tightens on the paper and his jaw goes rigid.

"I asked you not to look at it," she says.

"Why in hell would you draw him?" His voice scratches.

She takes back the pad. "It's none of your business."

He tries to play down his annoyance. "You have to admit, this is strange."

"I knew you'd react like this."

"Okay. Sure. I guess I shouldn't have insisted."

Since he's being reasonable now, she softens. "I've had some disturbing dreams lately. When that happens, I need to draw to get it out of me. It's a form of therapy."

"What do you think is causing them?"

She shrugs, not about to bring up the meteorite that sparked her. "Bad memories." Another lie. The memories she's been having are the good ones.

He glances around the barn. "Maybe you ought to get out more."

She gives him a half-smile. "Maybe."

He's sounding more relaxed again. His eyes go to her canvas and she moves aside to let him have a full view of it. Her anger over his seeing the Julian picture is subsiding. He seems to understand now.

He takes a moment to really look at her painting. "Nice," he says.

She's glad he doesn't gush. Gushing never sounds sincere to her.

"I like the colors," he goes on. "And the trees are quite good. Not that I'm any judge. But those branches. Wow. I wouldn't want to walk through that forest."

She uses a damp cloth to wipe the charcoal off her hands. "Thanks."

"Have you tried getting your work into galleries?"

"I don't think it's good enough."

"You won't know unless you try," he says. "My mother could help you. She has a lot of connections."

"I wouldn't want her to feel obligated." She can't imagine her wanting to promote the work of a local-bookstore-clerk-who-hasn't-even-been-to-art-school to her New York art scene friends.

"Don't be silly. Let me know if you want me to talk to her about it."

"Sure," she says. "So, what's up? What brings you here?"

"A little surprise." He leads her outside to where he's left a cooler, a picnic basket, and a vase filled with a mix of summer flowers on the ground. He hands her the vase. "From our garden."

"Thank you." They smell like a spring day. His thoughtfulness touches her.

"Are you hungry? I brought us a picnic."

"Starved. You're really spoiling me. I could get used to this treatment."

"I hope so."

They carry everything to the table on the brick patio in the back and lay the food out.

"Not being sure what you liked, I brought everything," he tells her.

There are cold cuts, sliced cheeses, lettuce, tomatoes, mayo, mustard, white bread, whole wheat bread, strawberries, raspberries, and grapes. And beautiful China plates for setting it all out.

"Wine?" He pulls a bottle of white from the cooler, and two glasses from the basket.

"Remind me to have you plan all my picnics from now on." Actually, she considers it likely his mother's staff prepared everything, but she's decided to play nice and give him all the credit.

He pours their drinks and they assemble their sandwiches. They arrange themselves with a view of the water, watching a canoe floating by in the distance.

Though Grant has impressed her, she's suspicious as to why he would try this hard to do so. She feels a little like Groucho Marx, who refused to join any club that would have him as a member.

"I thought you would return from Philadelphia married to an heiress," she says.

"Is that what you think of me?"

"I don't mean it in a bad way. I was thinking of someone beautiful and classy, like Grace Kelly."

"I dated a few women. But I didn't fall in love with anyone. What about you? I didn't expect you to be single when I got back."

"I like my independence. I'm free as a bird here. No one to clean up after."

"You have a funny way of looking at things. Not all men are slobs. Not all of us expect our girlfriends or wives to clean up after us."

"No, you have servants for that." Maybe she's being too hard on him. But he's the one who keeps pushing this relationship, or whatever it is between them. If it's going to happen, she wants him to understand what he's in for before it even starts.

"I can't help that I was born into a rich family."

"You're right, I'm not being fair. The rich have their own challenges. Kids that end up unemployable. Alcoholism and drug addiction. At least that's what I've heard. But you're obviously doing well for yourself."

"Thank you for setting such a low bar it makes me look really accomplished."

She laughs, pleased to see he's a good sport and has a sense of humor. "I did mean that about valuing my independence," she says.

"I get it. We're alike in that. I'm only staying at the guesthouse till I find a place of my own. Aside from that, I'm not relying on my mother for anything. I have a good job; I support myself."

He pours more wine into her glass. She's starting to feel it; she doesn't drink alcohol often.

After setting down the bottle, he glances over to the cemetery located just beyond the barn. "No wonder you have nightmares, living next to that," he says.

"It's never bothered me. In fact it's amazing. Have you ever looked through it?"

He shakes his head. "My father isn't buried here. He's at the one on Cedar Street." They had two in town.

She takes his hand and pulls him up. "C'mon, then. You can't live here and not know who's been here before us." She leads him a short way down the road to the entrance. It feels nice enough holding his hand she begins to wonder if things could work between them. But she lets go once they get on the path that winds among the gravestones.

She shows him the Yateses and the Browns, the Thompsons and the Marshalls. These names are still ubiquitous in Brumewich. She shows him those who died in the early 1700s, and others during the next two centuries. She leads him to the angel carvings, the site of the soldier who received the Medal of Honor in the Civil War, and the monument to ninety-three souls shipwrecked on Farer's Ledge in the mid-1800s. "I can't believe you've never been here," she says more than once.

The last place they visit is the one most dear. "Look, my father has a view of the harbor. I like to sit here with him."

They get down on the grass and rest their backs against his headstone. Some people think it's disrespectful to sit on a grave, but Cassie knows her father would approve. Grant's shoulder presses against hers while they watch the birds glide over the glassy surface of the water.

Clouds have darkened the sky by the time they get up to leave. On their way to the gate, she leads him along a section of the path they haven't taken yet. However, as they near one of the newer gravesites, she realizes her mistake. She hopes he doesn't imagine she brought him here on purpose; it's bad enough he caught her obsessing over Julian earlier in the day. But she can't turn back now without making an issue of it.

Cassie can't help looking at what's written on the stone as they pass by: *Teresa Patterson. Cherished Daughter. Beloved Sister*. Nor can she keep herself from sneaking a glance back at Grant to see his reaction. He wears a frozen expression, staring at the writing. But then his hard gaze swings in her direction. She could swear his thoughts are exactly what she feared... that she took him past this particular gravesite intentionally. And he's not happy about it. Not at all.

Later she helps him gather up the picnic things which unfortunately have attracted ants. She wonders if he's expecting her to ask him to come in and stay a while, perhaps even spend the night with her. But she can't do it, not just because of the uncomfortable look he gave her. There's also the chance she might time travel again in spite of herself, and it would be awkward to wake in the morning with Grant beside her and her thoughts full of Julian.

He seems like himself again when he pauses after opening his car door. "Can I take you to dinner tomorrow?"

"Sure," she says, grateful for their mostly pleasant afternoon. "I'd like that." It gives her another day to delay making any decision about him.

13

———————

After Grant leaves she starts a jigsaw puzzle. She chooses a picture of skaters on a frozen pond hoping the winter scene will remind her what not-dying-of-the-heat feels like. It's even worse inside than out because their house has no air conditioning. She turns the fan on full blast, but it's just like a furnace blowing sweltering air into her face.

While putting together the edge pieces, she broods over whether she can really travel through time. It seems unbelievable, but she can't deny the evidence of her senses. The only other explanation is that she's lost the ability to distinguish fantasy from reality.

She considers the latter possibility first. *What if my mind has turned to mush?* She would need professional help in that case. She'd have to go to a psychiatrist and get a diagnosis. If she's suffering from hallucinations, the doctor will no doubt want to start medicating her. And if he believes she's a danger to herself or others, he'll want to commit her to an asylum. He would probably need her permission for that. Or her mother's if they judge her too far gone to make rational decisions anymore.

What if, on the other hand, she's truly gained the ability to go back in time? If she tells that to any medical professionals, they won't believe her. They'll order the same treatment for her as if she really has gone mad.

Obviously, she's rooting for time travel over mental illness as the explanation. She decides it's too soon to share her story with anyone. She needs to understand more about how it works first. Maybe after that she'll have a better idea regarding whether it's happening or not.

If it's real, she should be able to change the past. That ought to be something she can put to the test. On the other hand, she wonders if she's being completely irresponsible. There could be thousands of repercussions she can't possibly anticipate. But maybe they'll be good repercussions. Maybe the changes she makes will transform the world into a better place. This sounds like a whole lot of wishful thinking, however.

What it comes down to is that she can't resist. For whatever reason, this power has fallen on her shoulders, and it's up to her to discover its limits. It isn't something she can discuss with another person. The decision is hers alone.

She'll test her abilities tonight. She's already thought about what to do, and ever since it entered her head, she hasn't been able to think of anything else. She *must* do it.

It's all she can do not to jump into bed immediately, but it's too early, the sun hasn't even set. She takes a cold shower and soaks her hair to cool herself. She thinks about eating something, but since she's still stuffed from the afternoon feast, nothing sounds appealing. Instead, she flicks on the TV and switches channels till she finds a boring-sounding documentary. Gio hops onto her lap and they watch it together, although the heat from his small body has perspiration emerging from all her pores again.

After the show ends, she goes up to bed. This time she turns her thoughts to her father, not Julian. Though it's painful to recall, she focuses on their last conversation. Before long she feels the familiar sensations that indicate she's about to tumble into the past.

When her vision clears again, she's in the kitchen staring at her father. Seeing him standing before her—*alive*—fills her with confusion and remorse. But also joy to have this chance to be with him again. Her emotions are so overwhelming her knees buckle and she grabs the edge of the counter to steady herself. Because he never got the chance to age beyond this day, he looks exactly as she remembers him. Pale freckles and sand-colored hair held flat by a generous application of gel. Gentle brown eyes that never looked stern, no matter how hard Cassie provoked him. Like tonight.

She rushes into his arms, startling him. He pats her back. "What's all this? A second ago I was ruining your life."

In reality, that was the last sentence she spoke to him. *You're ruining my life.*

She can change that now. "I didn't mean it, Dad. Forgive me. I love you so much." Her voice sounds girlish. She's her fourteen-year-old self—shorter, and with smaller breasts.

He kisses her cheek. "I know you didn't mean it. Love you too." When he draws back, she notices the crisp blue suit he wears. He's going to Boston for a mandatory event organized by his company. "Take care of your mother, okay?"

This sentence, which she never heard him say then because she stormed away after telling him he was ruining her life, feels prophetic. Actually, he's only asking her to take care of her mother *tonight*. She's upstairs in bed with pneumonia. If she had been well, Cassie and her father would never have gotten into a fight.

She was upset because her father insisted she stay home and watch over mother. If her condition worsened the doctor would need to be called. But Cassie thought her mother was already on the mend, and she was convinced life as she knew it would be over if she didn't get to the party she'd been anticipating for weeks now. She'd only just begun dating Julian and was certain he'd switch his attentions to another girl if she didn't show up.

On this night, she stomped upstairs to her room, slammed the door, threw herself on the bed, and wept for half an hour. Her last actions before her father went to his death. On his way home from the event, a drunk driver traveling in the wrong direction on the freeway smashed into his car. The drunk driver survived but her father did not.

"Don't go, Dad," she says.

He takes out his wool cloak from the front closet. "That's enough, Cassie. You can skip one party and your social life will survive."

She follows him. "I don't mean that. Forget the party. I'm not going anyway. But you need to stay home. Mom needs you. I need you."

He hesitates, surprised by her tone. "I have to go. You can keep an eye on Mom." He kisses her forehead before putting on his coat.

"Please don't go. Please. For me. I'm begging you."

"This is too much. You're being ridiculous." He opens the front door.

"Wait. I have to tell you something. If you go, you'll die in a car accident. I know this for a fact."

"You have a crystal ball? This is over the top even for your imagination." He goes outside.

She considers telling him about the time travel, but knows that won't work either. He's not going to believe it for a minute; he's still thinking her objections are all about the party. She racks her brain for a solution as he pulls the door closed behind him.

I can't let him go. Frantic, she rushes into the kitchen and grabs the knife he uses to carve the turkey at Thanksgiving. There's no other way. Cringing, she lays its edge on her wrist. Outside, the car door bangs shut. He'll be gone in a few seconds. She closes her eyes as she slices into her own skin. Blood spurts out. It's more shocking than painful.

Cassie bursts out of the house and sprints in front of the car, forcing her father to slam on the brakes. Still holding the bloody knife, she raises her wrist to show him the damage. The engine shuts off, the door flies open, her father runs to her side. "What have you done?"

"Come inside. Help me bandage it."

"You need a doctor. Lie down in the back." His voice is thick with equal parts anger and panic. She follows his instructions while he fetches a towel from inside. He wraps it tight around her wrist before getting back in the driver's seat. "I'm taking you to the emergency room."

"Okay, Daddy. I'm sorry." She's his little girl who misbehaved again.

He tries to be stoic, but his anxiety shows in the way he swerves out of the driveway and guns it down the street. It would be tragically ironic if they're killed in a car crash that results from the action she took to save him from getting killed in a car crash.

This thought makes her wonder if it's possible for her to die while she's time traveling. "Dad," she says quietly. She's beginning to feel light-headed from the blood loss.

"What is it?"

"You're the best father in the world. I was incredibly lucky to have you."

Before he can reply, she feels the signs of being drawn back to the future. *No.* She doesn't want to leave him, not without being certain she's saved him. But there's no stopping the pull of her own time.

When she wakes in the morning, she springs up, scaring Gio. Her heart fills with hope as she bounds to her window and looks out to see what might've changed. Her car and bike are in the driveway, exactly where she left them.

With a start, she remembers her wrist. It's normal again, uncut and unbloodied.

"Dad!" she shouts. If she altered history, he might be here now. Maybe she and her parents are still living all together in this house. "Dad!" she cries out again.

Gio is too startled to meow for his breakfast. She races from room to room, but everything is just as it was before she went to bed last night. Still there's a chance. If her father is alive, he will likely be in Florida with her mother. She considers calling, but doesn't know what she'll say if her mother answers. *Remind me, are you down there with Freddie or my resurrected father?*

There is a way she can tell for sure, but she hesitates. Part of her prefers to bask in the uncertainty. Is this what Schrödinger's cat is all about? As long as she doesn't look for proof of his death, he's still alive for her.

When she goes downstairs, she pretends he's in the kitchen with her, and chatters to him while she feeds Gio and makes herself a poached egg on toast. She's sure he would've loved her cat.

But after breakfast, she decides it will only make her sadder the longer she keeps up this pretense. She walks to the cemetery. On her way up the hill, she visualizes her father's section without his headstone. She keeps her eyes averted from his spot until the last possible second.

His grave is right where it's always been. At this point she was sure of it. Still, with her stomach closing in on itself, she kneels at his stone and reads the date of his death in case she might've saved him that night only for him to die of something else in the years since then. But the date is unchanged, and she knows her actions had no effect on the course of their family history.

She presses her forehead against the cool granite. Oddly, she finds comfort in having gotten to relive that night. To have taken back the terrible words she spoke. To have witnessed the love that moved him into action to save her, his only child. Not even scolding her for the craziness and irresponsibility of putting him in that position. She truly could not have had a more wonderful father.

Her leap back in time failed the most basic test. History wasn't changed. *Strike one point from time travel and add one to mental illness.*

She's still not ready to go to a doctor. She vows to keep her thoughts empty before falling asleep from now on. She'll count sheep or fish or something. She doesn't want to visit the past anymore. She doesn't want to relive these painful moments without having the power to change them. The disappointment is too overwhelming, not just because of her failure to save her father. His death isn't the only tragedy she wishes with all her heart that she could change.

14

Despite the emotional trauma of last night and this morning, she makes it to work on time. She's minding her own business stocking new general fiction books on the shelves when Trish comes over.

"Did you have a good weekend?" She says it like she's hinting she knows something.

There's a lot Cassie could say about her weekend, none of which she wants to share with Trish. "It was nice." She picks up another book and scans for its location.

Trish follows her. "My friend Debbie saw you with Grant Wolcott on his boat Saturday."

"Like I said, my weekend was nice."

"I can't believe you're dating him."

"Why not?"

"No, I mean it's amazing. He's so rich. And good-looking. Everyone wants to go out with him."

"Do you want to go out with him?" Cassie says.

"I'm engaged, in case you've forgotten. Otherwise, yes."

"Well don't get too excited. We're just friends."

The manager calls Trish, who's supposed to be manning the cash register.

"Don't be an idiot," she whispers. "Snag him while you can." She hurries back to her post.

Cassie isn't sure if this information makes her more interested in him or less. She's always been contrary that way. She doesn't usually want the things everyone else wants. On the other hand, she's rather competitive and wouldn't mind being the "winner" when it comes to Grant's affections.

With Trish busy, she has time to think again. The evidence is pointing more and more toward her having a screw loose. Her night-time adventures seem absolutely real to her, but there isn't any way they could be. No one has ever proven that time travel is even possible. Most likely these delusions are the result of her withdrawal from human society. She sees few people other than co-workers and customers at the bookstore. Her mother and Freddie no more than twice a year. And now Grant. That's about it. Maybe her fragile subconscious can't take the isolation anymore, so it's choosing to relive past events.

She thinks it might be time to talk to a therapist or psychologist. Someone whose job requires them to keep her ramblings confidential. She decides to look them up in the Yellow Pages when she gets home tonight. It would be better to get a recommendation from someone, but she's not comfortable revealing her need for psychological help.

The workday passes quickly, and she goes home to shower and change for her date with Grant. Feeling some anxiety about seeing him again, she considers calling and canceling. Actually she's surprised he's not the one canceling after having found her drawing pictures of Julian. If she were him, she'd be running for the hills at this point.

But she reminds herself she needs to work on her mental health issues, and human contact is a necessary first step. "Do you agree, Gio?" she says to her cat. He licks his paw. *Sure, talking to the cat is a great way to demonstrate how normal I am.*

Grant arrives in his BMW and approaches the door just as she walks out from the house. He's dressed nicely in slacks and a form-fitting button shirt, no suit or tie thank goodness. She's wearing a blue silk blouse over black leggings, and her long gold earrings. From his look it appears he likes what she's done, but he doesn't comment. She guesses he's starting to understand it's better to keep quiet and avoid making her feel self-conscious.

"Is Giovanni's okay?" he says.

"I love that place." This is true, though she's never been there on a date. The last time she ate at Giovanni's was with her mother and Freddie.

He opens the car door for her like the gentleman he is. She would've been fine getting it for herself, but knows he's been trained this way and she's not about to make a big deal out of it. She's troublesome enough without door-opening debates.

Giovanni's is in Ruford, the seaside town to the east of Brumewich. The waiter leads them to a prime view spot that still manages to be intimate with candles and a red tablecloth. The sun is low on the horizon and soon enough they'll get to watch the sky morph into shades of coral over the water. She's already starting to feel better about the date.

She orders the sole and he gets lasagna. They share a bottle of Chianti after she assures him she's perfectly happy to have red wine with fish. Anyone who grew up drinking Boone's Farm accompanied by Cheetos at high school gatherings is not in any position to dictate the rules of fine dining.

Grant wisely leads the conversation away from anything personal. They talk about art and history and literature and cats. He's playing it safe, because if they speak about their lives growing up in Brumewich, they may enter dangerous territory.

After they've gotten back to his car, he turns to her. "My place for some after-dinner drinks?"

The invitation is tempting. She knows what after-dinner drinks really mean, and part of her wants it. Aside from her recent dreams, it's been a long time since she let a man touch her. But she's still uncertain if it should be this man.

"Sorry, I've had enough to drink," she says. Again, he scores points by not arguing with her literal interpretation of his question. When they reach her house and she says good night, he leans forward and kisses her lips. Though she likes the feeling, she doesn't linger. "Thanks, I had a good time."

"Me too." He doesn't spring out of his car to get the door for her, sensing that would be too much and not at all her style. He does wait until she unlocks her front door and lets herself in, before backing out of her driveway.

Several hours later when she settles into bed, she tries to keep her mind blank to prevent herself from wandering back in time. It seems like it would be particularly unfair to spirit away and visit Julian, after having rejected Grant's overtures. However, trying not to think about Julian only makes her do the opposite. Immediately her brain fills with all sorts of memories she struggles to push away.

Worse, she's already having second thoughts about her plan to swear off time travel. Despite her having renounced it as recently as this morning, the desire to revisit past events fills her. There are mysteries waiting to be unveiled. She may not be ready to face them yet, but neither is she prepared to abandon the possibility of doing so.

What's bothering her most is the uncertainty. Are her time jumps real, and if so, why can't she change history? Does she enter an alternate universe when she goes back? Or a parallel timeline? None of this really means anything to her; they're just words she's read in science fiction stories. It's all too complicated and given that she earned a D in physics, she has little hope of ever understanding it. She has to accept the power she has without trying to explain it.

However, she needs to know if the information she gathers during time travel is true, as opposed to being imagined inside her head. She comes up with a way to test this using Grant, if she can manage a jump back to the very recent past. Closing her eyes, she concentrates on their dinner this evening, picturing the end of it because she doesn't want to repeat it all again. Rehashing the same topics would bore her to death, nor does she have the appetite to stuff in a second meal.

But she doesn't see the harm in a reprise of that luscious molten chocolate cake she split with him. Soon she's spiraling back in time, where her present consciousness plops into her five-hour-younger self. She's getting better at landing, but still manages to drop her fork —full of a precious bite of the amazing cake—onto the floor.

"Oops."

Grant, ever the man-in-charge, signals for a waitress to clean the mess. It's such a classy place, the waitress even offers to replace their entire dessert free of charge. It takes all Cassie's willpower to refuse this.

Time for her to get to the point. She puts a musing look on her face and says, "Who was the first girl you ever kissed?"

Grant's expression transforms, and not in a good way. He almost looks like he did when he discovered her drawing Julian portraits. "What difference does it make?"

Maybe he's just confused because up till now, they've been avoiding personal topics. "What's wrong? Is it a big secret?" she says in a teasing tone.

He seems to realize he's overreacted. "Of course not. You wouldn't know her anyway."

Being privileged, he went to boarding school while she attended Brumewich High School in town. "Hey, I hung out with some kids who went to private school," she says. "I know this one girl who had a big crush on you and boasted you were her first kiss."

"Who's that?"

"You first." She scoops up the remains of her cake and savors it.

"Sure. It doesn't matter. Her name was Marcia. Marcia Williams. Her family moved away when she was in the middle of high school."

"Williams. I think I remember her. Brown hair?"

"Blond. We dated for a few months, until the summer. Then she was gone."

"Marcia, huh?" she says thoughtfully. "Sounds like a private school girl." She smiles to let him know she's only kidding. One thing is true, she's never heard of her before.

"So who was the girl with the crush on me?" he says.

"Oh I can't tell you that. What if you prefer her over me?"

He clearly likes this response. It's the first time Cassie has indicated she's pleased about his interest in her.

When they get in the car and Grant asks her if she wants to go back to his place, she surprises herself by agreeing this time. The truth is, she has a kind of superpower right now, an ability to try something out without anyone being the wiser. If they make love during time travel, he won't remember—won't know—that it happened. If nothing sparks between them, she can drop him without bruising his ego. Or if it goes pretty well but she still wants to take her time and not rush into a relationship, she can keep him hanging on in present time.

Grant brightens immediately at her response, confident they'll end up doing the deed tonight. When they arrive at his house, he pours her sherry—the nectar of the rich—and they sip it on the deck watching the moon rise over the water. She's glad she came if only for this.

Later, when he draws her into his arms and kisses her, it feels nice but not electric. Maybe she's not ready; maybe there's not much connection between them. She decides she doesn't want to half-ass this thing, even if it's something he won't remember. She'll remember, and she'd rather wait till they have a greater chance of success.

"I should go," she says, pulling back from him.

"Really?" He tries to kiss her again, but she turns away.

"Sorry, I'm just not ready."

A sore-loser expression flashes across his face, but he quickly masks it. "Sure, I'll take you home." The temperature of his voice has definitely lowered a degree or two. She can't really blame him, but still thinks he should be dealing with this better than he is. This test has not shown him in the best light, though she's not ready to cast him aside yet either.

During the drive home, her consciousness somersaults back to its own time.

15

Cassie asked Grant for the name of the first girl he kissed because it was something she didn't know. This morning, back in real time, she's dying to confirm the answer. If it's the same as what he told her during time travel, then it must be real. It will mean she's truly able to cast her mind backward and relive past events. She can't change history, but she can learn things she didn't know before.

Needing an excuse to drop by and see him, she hits on the idea of bringing one of her paintings to show his mother. After all, he suggested she might be able to convince her posh gallery friends to help Cassie, though no doubt he'll be surprised when she actually takes him up on the offer. *Why not?* God knows she can use all the help she can get. But almost certainly, his mother is not going to show Cassie's work to her snooty acquaintances. The last thing she wants is to give them the impression she's a lousy judge of art.

Still, Cassie's pride motivates her to spend time picking out a painting she hopes won't shame her completely. Eventually she decides to go with a stormy seascape. It's a little cliché, but she feels like she managed to do something special with the water and the clouds.

After she gets back from work, she allows another hour for Grant to commute home from Boston before she drives over to his place. He's clearly surprised she took him at his word and brought a painting for his mother to pimp for her. It amuses her, in fact, to hand it over and watch him try to appear thrilled about it. "Hey, this is great. My mother will love it." He sets it down by the door. "Can you come in?"

"Sorry, I have to get back." As usual, she keeps things vague. "Before I go, though... I know this is silly, but I've got a question for you. Who was the first girl you ever kissed?"

Like it did in the restaurant, his expression darkens. She gets a creepy feeling inside, maybe because this is the second time watching his face transform.

"What difference does it make?" he says like before.

She wants to get this over quickly. "What's wrong? Is it a big secret?"

Again, he gets control of himself though he still doesn't look relaxed. "No, but you wouldn't know her anyway."

"Hey, I hung out with some kids who went to private school. I know this one girl who had a big crush on you and boasted you were her first kiss."

"What's her name?"

"You first."

"Okay. It doesn't matter. She was Marcia. Marcia Willis. Her family moved away when she was midway through high school."

"Willis. I think I remember her. Brown hair?"

"Blond. We dated a few months, until summer. Then she was gone."

"Marcia?" she says. "Sounds like a private school girl."

"So who was the one with the crush on me?" he says.

"Oh I can't tell you that. What if you like her better than me?"

He gets that pleased look again.

As she's leaving, it occurs to her he never asked who her first kiss was. Not last night or now.

She's sure it's because he knows the answer is Julian.

16

———————

It all comes down to Julian. Nothing will ever change until she solves the puzzle of him. And now through some miracle she has the means to do it.

After speaking to Grant, she's convinced the time travel is real. The proof lay in how well his past and present responses matched. It was true they varied a bit, but she believes that's because the situation wasn't identical. Someone could ask her the same question three different times, and depending on her mood, she could phrase the answer in as many different ways. That was how it was for Grant: the same answer, slightly different phrasing.

Except there was the little matter of Marcia's last name—*Williams* vs. *Willis*. It makes Cassie think he made her up. If she invented a name, she'd probably use different variations of it every time the subject arose, because there would be no *real* person to remember. Still, it was strange for him to lie about something so unimportant.

Back home, she takes out a notepad and pencil before settling into the comfortable recliner in the family room. Gio tries to climb onto her lap for some petting but she nudges him aside. Thinking over all she's learned since *the change* began, she makes a list:

The Rules of Time Travel

- Current me goes back in time to occupy younger me.
- I can choose when and where by concentrating on it.
- It only happens when I'm relaxed, nearing sleep.
- The time jump ends when I reach a similarly relaxed state or finish what I set out to do or learn.
- The past plays out as it did unless I do something to change it.
- These changes don't affect my present reality.
- I can witness what truly took place as long as I don't interfere.
- Injuries I receive in the past are gone in the present.
- Unknown: If I die in the past, does it prevent my mind from returning to the present (leaving me brain dead)?

It's important to consider what she hopes to accomplish by witnessing the past. She can't change the course of events no matter how much she may wish it. If she discovers the truth is not what everyone believes, she can't bring back proof, nor can she bear witness in a court of law without a rational way of explaining how she came by the information.

Therefore if she does this, she does it for herself alone. She does it to satisfy her own unrelenting need for the truth. This will have to suffice.

When she's finished going over the list, she sketches a picture at the bottom showing a witch in pointed hat seated on a broomstick. The meteorite brought her the powers she's coveted so long, but instead of flying through the air, she'll fly through time. She's become the witch of her imagining.

PART THREE: WARRIOR

CASSIE (AGE 26)

17

Yesterday, for the first time since Cassie gained the power to travel through time, she slept through the night without going anywhere. She isn't sure why. She suspects it might be related to her own uncertainty regarding the next step. Maybe *uncertainty* is the wrong word. *Dread* is more accurate.

She needs to be more focused and determined today. This power may only be temporary. Given what didn't happen last night, she might have already lost her ability. But she isn't ready to give up.

This morning she called in sick and told Maggie she expected not to make it in tomorrow either. Assuming she's successful, whatever she sees will take its toll, and she won't be able to waltz into work and act as if everything is normal. Not for some time. Already she's noticing a difference in herself. Lately, she doesn't have much appetite. For breakfast she drank half a glass of orange juice and ate dry toast. Her stomach couldn't take any more. She's also popping aspirin every few hours to relieve the pulsing sensation inside her head that began yesterday.

She resolves not to answer the phone during the day in case it's Grant. She just hopes he doesn't come by the house to check on her.

It seems unlikely he'd take time away from work to do that, but to be extra safe, she doesn't even go into her studio to paint. Instead, she stays inside and does sketches of Gio to occupy herself.

Around mid-afternoon, she's in the family room listening to Chopin on the record player and attempting to reread *Wuthering Heights*, when her eyelids begin to droop. Seconds later, the doorbell startles her awake. She doesn't want to speak to anyone now, particularly not Grant, but the music is a sure sign she's at home. Still, she decides not to answer. Hopefully whoever-it-is will quickly give up and leave.

But the ring turns into a series of sharp knocks, followed by a woman's raised voice: "Cassie? It's Helen Wolcott. Are you there?"

Grant's mother? This is surprising. She wonders what the woman could want with her. *Your painting is brilliant, have you got any more?* Ha, Cassie knows it isn't going to be that, but still, her curiosity is too much for her. "Coming!" she calls out, hurrying to the door, pretending to be out of breath when she reaches it. "Sorry, I was upstairs," she says, letting Mrs. Wolcott assume she must've been in the bathroom.

The woman has accompanied her stiff new frosty-haired perm with a white linen suit, of all things, making Cassie wonder how on earth she keeps it clean. "Hello, dear," she says. "May I come in?"

"Um sure, it's kind of a mess though."

Mrs. Wolcott presses past her and glances around. In fact it's neater than usual, but Cassie is assuming the woman's standards are much higher than hers, given that she has trained staff to take care of such things.

"Could you please lower the volume?" Mrs. Wolcott expresses this as a demand, not a question. Cassie decides to turn the record off rather than guess what level she considers quiet enough.

"Can I get you something to drink?" Cassie says, hoping Mrs. Wolcott doesn't ask for coffee, since she's hoarding the little bit she has left to avoid a trip to the store.

"It's too late for coffee and too early for tea." Following this pronouncement, Mrs. Wolcott walks straight into her living room and across to the sliding glass door looking out toward Inner Harbor. "You have a pretty view here." She glances back at her with a judgmental look, as if questioning the right of someone at her low economic status to be situated right next to the water.

"Would you like to sit down?" Cassie says.

"Goodness no. I've been sitting all morning at my desk."

"All right." Cassie stands awkwardly, thinking it would be rude to sit while Mrs. Wolcott stands, as if she's the Queen of England. Meanwhile the woman stares down her nose at her humble home.

Mrs. Wolcott's eyes stop on a small painting Cassie did of her father. "Yours?" she says.

"I did it when I was thirteen." She doesn't want her to think that's the best she could do right now.

"Interesting portrait. You're not without talent," Mrs. Wolcott says, condemning her with faint praise. "I can recommend a teacher. Harry Feingold in Boston. He's brilliant."

"I doubt I could afford him," Cassie says.

"Perhaps you could allow me to help you with that. If you work hard for two or three years under Harry's tutelage, you might reach a level of accomplishment that would not embarrass a gallery owner to display. I have a particular place in mind."

Until now Cassie hasn't dared consider making a career out of her art. As condescending as Mrs. Wolcott is, she's offering hope that it might be possible someday. On the other hand, Cassie can't help wondering if Mrs. Wolcott is only encouraging her at Grant's request. She fears this may all be a performance unrelated to her talent or lack thereof.

"Unfortunately," Mrs. Wolcott continues, "if I'm to champion your work in the local art scene, there must be no connection of any sort between us. My reputation for identifying talent would disappear if I began promoting anyone with a close connection to our family."

Cassie almost snorts. It's the opposite of what she thought. Mrs. Wolcott hasn't come here on Grant's behalf, but for her own selfish reasons. She's judged Cassie unworthy of her son.

"Are you saying you can only help me if I stop seeing Grant?" Cassie says.

"I'm glad you understand." But Mrs. Wolcott's bullying has the opposite effect of what she intends and increases Cassie's interest in Grant several fold.

"It's a shame. I could've used your help. But I'd rather keep dating your son."

Mrs. Wolcott's eyes narrow at Cassie. "It won't last. You're a pretty diversion right now. When he's ready to marry, he'll pick his own kind."

"What kind is that? Rich? Socially connected? Arrogant?"

The woman shakes her head. "His kind is determined and ambitious. Highly educated. The type who will break barriers and become a leader in business or politics." Her heels click against the floor as she goes into the hall.

Cassie is trying to think of a powerful comeback, to prove her education at Syracuse was as good as anyone's, but her brain isn't quick enough. Sadly proving Mrs. Wolcott's point.

"Trust me, you won't last long with him," she tells Cassie on her way out. "Why let yourself get hurt?"

Cassie follows her to the front stoop and stands with her arms crossed over her chest, watching the annoying woman drive away in her *car-that's-worth-more-than-I'll-earn-in-ten-years* and thinking what a clever retort she'll have waiting for her if she ever comes back.

But when she turns back to the house, she almost laughs to see the painting she gave to Grant propped up by the side of the door. She brings it inside, musing that Mrs. Wolcott's visit has only made her think better of him. It's a miracle he ended up a decent man after having such a mother.

Dealing with the woman's nonsense has exhausted Cassie. She sits back on the recliner, meaning to take a ten-minute nap. Gio claws his way up the back of the chair though he knows that's strictly forbidden, and settles down to sleep beside her head.

Interestingly, Mrs. Wolcott's visit has increased her motivation to get on with things. To learn the truth and finally close that chapter of her life. Therefore, as she tries to relax, her thoughts focus on the night of the murder. A few minutes later, she drifts away from this time, feeling like she's spinning through darkness.

18

―――――――

Cassie's time jump sends her back to her own room, just after sunset on the night of the murder. She panics at first, thinking she may be too late, but a glance at the clock shows she has sufficient time to get where she needs to be.

Setting aside the sketchpad that kept her occupied this night, she checks her mother's room to confirm she hasn't returned from the party yet. Cassie needs to leave immediately to be sure not to run into her and avoid questions about where she's going. Drunken Freddie might also want to chat about how much his daughter is dying to be friends with her. She can't afford these delays.

Downstairs, her hands shake as she reaches for the keys, showing how nervous she is already. At least she manages to set out in her mother's car without encountering anyone. Driving to within a quarter mile of Thorne Cove, she turns down a side street to park. She doesn't want to risk Julian recognizing her mother's Datsun along the main road. If he thought she was in the vicinity, he might freak out and cancel his date with Teresa. Cassie can't allow that to happen. For her to witness the truth, events must unfold exactly as they did then.

She walks the rest of the way, diving behind trees twice to avoid the headlights of passing cars, even though Julian and Teresa would likely be approaching from the opposite direction. Fortunately, neither of them has arrived by the time Cassie reaches the cove.

Her apprehension increases as she scans the shore and realizes a beach must be one of the worst possible places to spy on someone. There isn't anywhere to hide that's within listening distance. She'll have to settle on the cottage located just beyond where the sand ends. She's pretty certain the owners had not arrived for the summer yet when the murder occurred; otherwise, it probably wouldn't have happened at all. At least not here.

Sure enough, the cottage is dark and the windows shuttered, clear signs it hasn't been opened yet for the season. She kneels behind tall marsh grass along the far side. A bright half-moon lights the shore tonight, giving her a clear view. She doubts she'll hear anything they say, but it's essential she remain out of sight. If they glimpse her, events will be altered and her coming will be for nothing.

She rubs her hands together, trying to get a grip on herself. Despite the warmth of the night, her arms are trembling. The full weight of what she's come here to do is hitting her now. She is about to watch one human being kill another. She's never seen anyone die of anything before, not even old age or illness. The worst she's witnessed is two people who were already dead: her father, and the grandmother of a friend at a Catholic wake. Not the same thing at all.

Worse, she'll have to refrain from screaming or calling out a warning. She can't allow herself to intervene. Anything she might alter here and now will have no effect on the future, she reminds herself. However, there is one change that will return with her to her own time. She'll know something she could only guess at before. She'll know what happened here on this beach tonight.

Waiting isn't easy. The air has grown still and humid. Her skin is damp, her hands clammy. Already she feels as soiled as the act she's about to witness. Moreover, mosquitos are beginning to find her. She should've thought to spray on repellent before she left the house. When they sting her, she has to repress the urge to slap at them. She can't afford to make a sound now.

Her breath catches at the sight of Teresa walking along the sand from the road. She looks ghostly in a diaphanous white dress that billows around her legs. Her long black hair falls loosely down her back. A beach bag is slung over her shoulder and her feet are bare. It eats into Cassie seeing her like this—how could she have ever hoped to compete? Teresa's hips sway as she crosses the beach to the rocks. No question she's fully aware of the effect she has on men.

Teresa lays down her bag and to Cassie's shock, lifts off her dress, exposing her naked body. She's not even wearing underwear. Then she slowly enters the sea until it reaches her waist and dives under.

Cassie shifts her gaze to the other side, and soon Julian appears. At the sound of Teresa's splashing, he turns toward the water. For one gut-stabbing moment, Cassie wonders if she might have to watch them making love. A powerful urge to run away fills her, until she realizes they couldn't have done that. If they had, there would've been undeniable proof that Julian had been with her tonight.

Teresa swims back toward shore and emerges from the water. She doesn't try to cover her body, nor does she walk into Julian's arms. Instead, she gets a towel from her bag and wraps it around herself, tucking it to hold it in place.

Oddly, Julian is keeping his distance and appears to be averting his eyes from her nakedness. He doesn't act like a man in love. Or even a man in lust.

There's something of defiance in her movements, making Cassie wonder if they've recently fought. Maybe it was about her. She wants to believe he's told Teresa it's over between them because she's come back from school. But then there's no explanation for this meeting.

They continue to stand apart. There's no touching or kissing for Cassie to have to endure, *thank god*. She hears them without being able to make out the words. Julian's voice is harsh. Teresa's is softer but seems dismissive. They speak for several minutes while Cassie strains to listen. She's on edge, afraid of when it's going to happen. But as far as she can see, he has no weapon. He's wearing a t-shirt, shorts, and sandals. There's no place to hide a knife on his person. Maybe he left it nearby.

When they finish talking, Teresa takes out a cigarette from her bag and lights it up. He walks away from her, looking unhappy but not in any sort of murderous rage. Still, this must be when it happens. Maybe he'll get the knife from the truck and return. Cassie braces herself as he reaches the road and she no longer can see him.

Teresa is in no hurry. She leans against the rock nearest her, slowly smoking her cigarette. Looking more than ever like an actress in some film; she clearly has a flair for the dramatic. She gazes at the water, the moon. It's weird, but Cassie almost begins to admire her. She's a woman comfortable with her own sexuality. A creature of the senses. She isn't the sort to worry about her makeup, or manicure, or a rumpled dress. She trusts in her allure regardless of these considerations. Soaking her hair in the water didn't bother her at all. There's something completely natural and almost feral about her.

Cassie notices the silhouette of Julian returning. At least that's what she thinks at first. But when he draws nearer, she sees it isn't Julian at all.

It's Grant Wolcott.

Her stomach clenches and she fights the impulse to retch. Grant's arrival launches a million questions. *How can this be? Why is he here? What does he have to do with Teresa?*

She hasn't seen him yet, because her face is turned the other way and he's made some effort to be silent. Cassie glimpses the shape of a knife in his hand. It appears he's wrapped a red cloth around its handle to avoid getting his prints on it. She can't doubt his intentions any longer, though she has no explanation.

Teresa notices him when he's within ten feet of her and blows smoke toward his face, looking unconcerned. Cassie thinks she says Grant's name. But it doesn't appear Teresa has seen the knife.

He continues toward her with relentless steps and raises the blade. Her face is confused. It happens so quickly she doesn't have time to react—to scream or back away. But then, the rock is right behind her, leaving her with no place to go.

In a second, he's closed the distance between them and thrust the knife into her heart.

Cassie claps her hand over her mouth, struggling to hold in her own cries. Tears stream down her cheeks. Teresa appears to die immediately; at least she doesn't suffer. Grant lets her body fall to the ground as he draws out the knife. He stares down at her, his face twisted with a shocking combination of malice and triumph.

He looks up like he's suddenly remembered there could be someone watching him. His gaze sweeps past the cottage and seems to pause on the side where Cassie is hiding. A shiver runs through her.

In her effort to see, she may have raised herself too much above the marsh grass. She lowers her head, though that may be worse, he may have spotted her movement. But he doesn't appear to have noticed anything. His gaze moves on.

Seemingly satisfied, he crosses the sand back to the cove entrance, leaving the scene of the crime. Cassie waits a few minutes longer to be sure he's really gone, before rising and approaching Teresa's body. She's not even sure why she's doing this. It's unlikely she'll find any sort of evidence that wasn't uncovered by the police. She thinks... she thinks it's simply that she needs to pay her respects.

Cassie kneels at her side. From her face alone, she doesn't look like a victim of violent death. Her eyes are closed and she appears to be sleeping.

"I would've saved you if I could," Cassie whispers.

A shell cracks behind her. She whirls around to find Grant racing toward her, the knife gleaming in his hand.

She springs up and tries to run back the way she came. It's like a nightmare where she's struggling to sprint but instead her feet drag like she's moving in slow motion. He's faster and she hears him gaining on her. Her mind spins to come up with a defense but draws a blank. He leaps at her, slamming her body from behind, knocking her down. Her head smashes sideways against the sand. He pins her under his weight, and she braces for the thrust of the knife.

But he must've dropped it so his hands would be free for the tackle. His left one wraps around her neck from behind, while the other grips her right arm.

"What are you doing here?" he says.

"Let me go!" She closes her eyes, visualizing her return to the future. *Go back, go back,* she tells herself, terrified she won't be able to end this time jump before it's too late.

He bends her arm backward, making her cry out. "Answer me."

"I came to find out if Julian was meeting her here." Inside, she's still screaming, *get out of here. Go back, go back.*

"Jealous?" he says.

"Of course I was. Now let me go!"

"You know I can't do that. Not after what you saw."

"Why did you do it?"

"No one betrays me and gets away with it."

While he talks, she feels underneath her body with her left hand. Maybe she can find something sharp. A rock or a shell. "I didn't know you were seeing her."

"Nobody knew. We were keeping it quiet. But then I found out she had that stinking, lobster-chasing, Portuguese son of a bitch on the side."

"I wanted her dead as much as you. I won't tell anyone."

His hands tighten round her neck. "I always liked you. I don't imagine that's any consolation."

She can't breathe. Her mind claws for her own future with frantic desperation. But she stays right where she is, struggling to break free of his chokehold. He's too strong and he has her from behind. The force of his body restrains her.

Panic fills her. Her lungs feel like they're on fire. Her mind is going blank. Her vision clouds with a thousand pinpricks of light. Like the meteor shower that brought her here.

19

Cassie sucks in air and breaks into a coughing fit at the memory of what just happened. She's back in the present. The demon who would've killed her, gone. When she rubs her neck, she finds nothing wrong with it. No pain or bruising. The burning in her lungs has disappeared. There's no remnant of what might've happened seven years ago, but actually didn't.

Instead the scars are emotional and psychological. She'll never forget the sensation of his hands around her neck, crushing her windpipe. The feelings of panic and powerlessness that overwhelmed her. If it weren't for time travel, she would've died.

She's still not certain whether her death in the past would cause her to die here, because she's pretty sure her consciousness traveled back before dying. With her oxygen cut off, she must have passed out, and that could've triggered her return.

She pushes these considerations aside as her thoughts turn to the murder. All this time, she wanted to believe in Julian's innocence, but found it impossible to dismiss the evidence against him—because she'd seen both their cars parked at the cove with her own eyes. His motive had always been unclear, though. Did Teresa anger him by threatening to tell Cassie he'd cheated on her? Or did he harbor a twisted, violent nature she'd never once observed during all their time together? These were the sorts of questions that haunted her for years.

Regarding Grant... incredibly, she never considered him before. Yet now that she knows the truth, it feels as if nothing could've been more obvious. How could she have been so blind? When she called him before talking to the police, he played on her jealousy, telling her he'd seen Julian and Teresa kissing. And just Sunday, in the present, when he saw her drawings, he became stiff and cold. The look in his eyes frightened her, the same look he got when they walked past Teresa's grave. Now she understands. His guilty conscience made him think she'd brought him there on purpose.

It's possible he believes she knows something. Maybe he's dating her for that very reason. To find out if she's a danger to him. To do something about it if so.

A sudden noise makes her start. She glances around at the dark corners of the room, looking for Gio. It could've been the sound of him going out through the cat door.

Grant hides his contempt for the working classes well. It must've come from his mother. She made it clear today she didn't want him dating riffraff like Cassie. Teresa was even lower on the socio-economic scale. After high school, she never even went to junior college. Her mother was a bus driver and her father worked as a custodian. That must've been why Grant wanted to keep their relationship secret. It would've put him on the fast track to losing his inheritance.

To take that risk, he must've been obsessed with her. *Good god.* Cassie has a sudden realization. What a blunder, asking him about his first kiss. It was Teresa. It must've been. Because she's certain his answer was a lie. They could've had an on-again-off-again relationship for years. Between her clumsy questioning and the visit to Teresa's gravesite, he's probably convinced she has doubts about him.

She can only imagine his pathetic horror when the girl he has elevated with his attention chooses the lobsterman's son over him. Grant, a man who has wealth, breeding, the finest education money can buy, and at least one ancestor who crossed the Atlantic on the Mayflower. To be cast aside in favor of someone who plucks giant sea bugs from the ocean for a living. His pride obviously couldn't accept this. Better to kill her before anyone finds out, and make sure the usurper takes the fall for it.

Cassie is still stretched out on the recliner where she fell asleep, but time has passed and the room has grown dark. She checks her watch to find it's nearly nine in the evening. Gio must've meowed for dinner earlier, before giving up to forage for mice instead. She can't blame him.

When she leans forward, pain shoots between her brows and she fumbles for the aspirin bottle beside her chair. At the same moment, a soft knock comes at the front door. She freezes in place, praying whoever is there didn't hear the rattle of the pills.

"Cassie?" Grant says from outside in a low voice, probably meant to be soothing but instead it makes her skin crawl. Immediately she remembers him on top of her, his hands clutching her throat. She knows he's capable of killing her.

I can't face him now. I can't face him ever again.

He shakes the knob. She carefully lowers the aspirin bottle, holding her breath, dreading that she may have forgotten to lock the door. But thankfully it doesn't come open. He tries once more, pushing against it, to no avail.

She doesn't dare move an inch in case he hears her. She'll stay where she is until enough time passes that she's sure he's gone. Meanwhile she struggles to calm herself. He might be suspicious, but he can't be sure she knows anything. He has no reason to want to harm her.

She's still waiting for enough time to pass when another sound brings with it the icy chill of terror. The glass door in the living room is sliding open. She curses herself for forgetting to latch it. *What now?* He'll check the house for her. There's nowhere to hide in this room, and he'll see her if she crosses the hall.

"Cassie? It's me." His footsteps tap against the floor. Sticky sweat gathers at the back of her neck. She doesn't know how she can deal with him now. She literally just watched him murder Teresa Patterson, and witnessed the shadow of his malignant soul in his face. She's likely the only living person who knows what he did.

But she has to say something. If he reaches her before she speaks up, he's going to know there's a problem. She can't have him interrogating her. She needs to convince him everything is fine.

"In here," she forces herself to say. Her voice is tremulous. "You better not come in. I'm probably contagious."

His dark silhouette fills the doorway. Where once he might've been a reassuring presence, now he's the opposite. She wants to crawl into the lining of her chair and disappear.

"I'll take that chance. Are you all right?" He turns on the overhead lamp.

She blinks, feeling completely exposed in the stark light. She must look a wreck. It takes all her strength to keep from screaming as he approaches and places his wrist on her forehead. Her stomach roils and she thinks she might throw up.

"I don't believe you have a fever."

"No. It's my stomach." This is true, thanks to him.

"Why didn't you answer the door?"

"I was napping here. I didn't hear you till just now."

He kneels beside her and looks into her eyes, while she struggles to mask her revulsion.

"Did you go to the doctor?" he says.

"Yes," she lies. "He said there's not much I can do. It's some sort of a bug. I have to let it run its course."

He's quiet for a moment. "Why haven't you been answering your phone?"

"Sorry. It's an effort to get to it, and I just haven't felt like talking. I've been sleeping a lot. The doctor said that would be best."

"You could at least have called me. I've been worried about you."

"I'll be fine. In a few days." *If you leave me alone—forever.*

"Is there anything else?" He rests his hand on her arm. The hand that thrust a knife into Teresa. "Have I done something wrong?"

You've done the worst that one human being can do to another. The accusation nearly spills out of her. She clenches her teeth to hold it in. "Of course not," she somehow manages to say.

The silence falls heavy between them. Finally, when she can take no more and is at the brink of crying out for mercy, he straightens. "Okay then. Call me tomorrow? Just so I know how you're doing."

"Sure. I will."

"Can I get you anything before I go?"

She's afraid her "no" sounds harsh and shrill, but he accepts it. He leaves the room and lets himself out the front door, moving at the same measured pace.

She's struck by the sickening thought that he isn't going to go at all. That he will just make the sounds of the door opening and closing, but he'll remain in her house, spying on her, lying in wait until she falls asleep again.

For this reason, she gets up and crosses the hall to look out at the driveway. Relief washes over her as he gets into his car and drives away.

She locks and bolts the doors, front and back.

20

After Grant leaves, Cassie feels weaker than ever. She drags her feet to the kitchen to see what there is to eat. Gio is back and meowing so she tends to him first. Only one can of cat food left, and not much kibble either. He wolfs down the contents of his bowl without missing a crumb, before disappearing out the cat door to do his business outside.

It's harder to find something for herself, partly because nothing sounds appetizing. She warms up a can of tomato soup she finds in the back of a cupboard and sprinkles it with parmesan cheese. The orange juice is gone and normally she wouldn't have caffeine this late, but since time no longer seems like a rigid concept anymore, she goes ahead and makes herself coffee.

She eats slowly, trying to process everything that's happened. For seven years she's wondered if Julian really could've committed that crime, and now she finally has the answer. But her feelings are all over the place. She should be comforted by the realization that she didn't have such poor judgment as to fall head over heels with a boy capable of coldblooded murder.

But she's not comforted. Not at all. Because Julian was innocent and she should've lied for him. Should've trusted him and done what he asked of her.

Ironically, the one person she might've turned to in this moment of existential crisis is the actual killer. *Thank god I didn't fall in love with him.* Her instincts were telling her something was wrong. Now she loathes him with all her being.

Part of her, the exhausted part, wants to give up. Move away from this cursed town, as far as she can go. But the other part is filled with rage and wants to act. That part dominates.

Grant got away with murder. A person capable of killing a human being can do so again. *Fuck, he would've done it to me.* Which means she has a responsibility now; she can't simply walk away from this. She was granted a special power—how or why she'll never know—but she must use it to expose him. To make him pay for his crime. To prove Julian's innocence. To ensure Grant never kills again.

She needs to return to the day of the murder. She'll go earlier and track Grant's actions. He must've made some mistakes. There has to be evidence, even if it's disappeared in the seven years since then. She won't give up till she learns something she can use against him.

Finishing her meal, she feels energized again. Maybe it's just the caffeine. Or more likely, adrenaline. What she's about to do frightens her, but it also invigorates her.

On the morning before the murder, Cassie-from-the-future arrives in her kitchen just as her mother is getting off the phone with Mr. Harrington. This time she asks to use the car to drive to Julian's, though that isn't where she plans to go. Her mother agrees before heading outside to weed while the weather is still relatively cool.

Cassie is about to leave when an idea occurs. She goes upstairs to use the phone, so that her mother won't overhear the conversation if she comes back into the kitchen. Before dialing, she grabs a shirt her mother left out on her dresser and covers the receiver with it. She's counting on Grant not having heard her voice for more than a year at this point in time, but to be on the safe side, she plans to disguise it as well as she can.

After the phone rings four times, she gets hopeful that he's gone out, which will make this ruse unnecessary. However, at the fifth ring he picks up.

"Hello?" There's a tinge of annoyance in his tone, making her wonder if she woke him.

"Wolcott?" Talking through the shirt, she keeps her voice low and gruff, hoping he won't even be able to tell if she's a man or a woman. She calls him by his last name because it seems like a guy thing to do.

"Who's this?" Now he's definitely annoyed.

"Teresa is hiding something from you. Meet me at the skating pond now if you want to learn more." The skating pond is a Brumewich landmark, located close to downtown. A grassy area surrounds it, where two people planning to meet could easily spot one another.

"What the hell? Who are you?"

"You'll find out soon enough." She hangs up. Assuming he doesn't dismiss her call as a prank, he should be leaving right away. She's counting on his wanting to learn who knows the secret of his relationship with Teresa. She rushes downstairs and to the car, waving goodbye to her mother on her way.

When she's fairly close to the Wolcott estate, she parks on the opposite side of the road. She's not concerned about Grant possibly seeing her mother's car. He would not have any idea what it looks like.

She waits until the street is clear of traffic before darting to the other side, where she clambers over the stone wall onto their property. The wide lawn in front of the mansion is bordered by a dense thicket of trees on both sides, and she uses their cover to approach the entrance to the guesthouse.

She's encouraged seeing no car parked in the driveway, though it's possible Grant keeps his BMW in the four-car garage attached to the main house. Still, there's a decent chance Grant took the bait. To be sure, she pauses for a moment behind a pine tree and peers through the windows. After a moment or two of not glimpsing anyone inside, she decides she better make her move before he gets impatient waiting for a mysterious stranger at the skating pond and comes back home.

She dashes from her tree to the main door and tries it. *Shit*. These rich folk don't believe in the town mantra of unlocked doors, apparently. She checks all around for a spare key: under the mat, inside a planter, above the door frame. It's not in any of the obvious places, and the unobvious ones will take too long to search.

Ducking back under the cover of trees, she makes her way to the rear of the house. From there she must briefly pass into the open again; she prays no one is watching from the main house. But she's in luck, he's left one of the French doors ajar, probably to catch the cooling breeze coming from the ocean this morning. She slips inside.

Her plan is to search the place. There might be something—a note, a picture, a gift of some sort—that ties him to Teresa. She does a quick scan downstairs, thankful for the lack of clutter. But it seems unlikely he'd leave any secret items on the first-floor level, where visitors might easily stumble upon them.

She heads upstairs and into his bedroom, where the elegant design and stunning water view dazzle her. His furniture is all matching maple in a simple, beautiful Shaker style. He's a monster with excellent taste. As quickly as she can, she checks the drawers in the dresser and bedside tables. The most surprising discovery is how neatly he folds his clothing, including his socks and underwear. His closet is so well-organized —suits and dress shirts perfectly pressed, ties hung in order of color— that she has to wonder if a housekeeper has done all this for him.

The one other bedroom upstairs has been converted into a study. It looks like the office of an Ivy League professor, with a ponderous desk of polished mahogany, and two walls covered by floor to ceiling bookshelves. They're filled with thick leather volumes that might've been printed a century ago. She can't resist sitting for a moment in Grant's padded chair, mulling over his hypocrisy. He plays down his wealth while basking in the spoils of it.

Moving on, she searches the desk, and in the second drawer on the right, she finally finds something that makes her tingle with excitement. A ring box. Inside, there's an engagement ring featuring a brilliant diamond that sparkles beautifully when it catches the light from the window. She takes it out from the box to get a better look, and notices etching inside the platinum band. Holding it closer, she reads, "*G.W. & T.P.*"

She needs a moment to absorb this. Grant was going to ask Teresa to marry him. Their relationship had actually gotten that far without anyone guessing. She's beginning to understand the depth of his disappointment now. Not that there is remotely any excuse for him. But he must truly have desired Teresa if he was prepared to raise up a member of the proletariat to his elevated sphere.

As she's putting back the ring box in the drawer, she discovers a receipt that had been hidden underneath it. From this she learns the ring came from Dorn Jewelers in Boston, and its value is even greater than the outrageous amount she imagined.

Suddenly she hears the door come open downstairs. Her shock at discovering a ring distracted her; she should've been listening for the car. Now she's trapped up here.

Noises come from the kitchen, like Grant is taking out dishes or something. She replaces the ring and receipt in the drawer, but when she tries to close it, the wood makes a scraping sound that could be heard beyond this room.

All movement downstairs stops abruptly. Knowing he's listening causes her leg muscles to tighten, anticipating her need for escape. He's probably figured out the phone call was just to get him away from the house.

She ducks down behind the desk, listening to his footsteps coming up the steps. She doesn't think he can see her from the door, but if he enters the room, he'll quickly spot her.

He goes into the bedroom first. She hears the closet door open and close. Her heartbeat races as she struggles to recall if she left everything in that room the way she found it.

His feet rap the tile when he enters the bathroom from the hall-way. Metal shrieks as he rips the shower curtain open. If he's checking the bathtub, he's going to look around the desk too. Though she doesn't believe he'd try to kill her over this, the possibility of his finding her has her shivering in terror. She can't erase the feeling of helplessness that overwhelmed her when he pinned her on the beach.

His footsteps pad along the hall carpet, growing closer. They pause at the entrance to this room.

A sharp rap sounds on the door downstairs. Seconds later Grant thumps down the steps. He may think the person knocking is the same one who called and sent him on the wild goose chase.

She breathes again, and carefully finishes closing the drawer that holds the ring. With luck, his glance into the study will have satisfied him that no one is upstairs.

"Mother," he says after opening the front door.

Her reply is muffled.

Cassie decides she needs to get closer. It's important she hear their conversation. Despite the risk of her movements being overheard, she tiptoes across the Persian carpet and slips behind the office door to listen.

"Is anything wrong?" Mrs. Wolcott says.

"I don't know. Someone's idea of a joke. Do you want some coffee?"

"No, thank you."

Too late for coffee, too early for tea, thinks Cassie.

It sounds like he's making it for himself. "Is Dad okay?"

"This morning he couldn't remember my name. But that isn't what I came here to speak to you about."

"If you're going to try to talk me into asking out Diane Perry again, this isn't the time."

A chair scrapes against the floor. "I don't care if it's Diane or another girl like her. But it can't be Teresa Patterson."

"What are you talking about?" he says.

"I know you're seeing her. Your back patio is quite visible from the house."

Fortunately, she must not have been looking out the right window when Cassie arrived, or she would already be busted.

"It's none of your business, Mother."

"Isn't it? You stand to inherit a fortune. It's the responsibility of both of us to ensure you don't marry a woman who's likely to squander it."

"You don't know anything about her. Just because her family is poor doesn't mean—"

"Has she been to college? Does she have any talent beyond working in a department store?"

"She can't afford college. But she's smart."

"Really? Shall we put that to the test?"

The coffeemaker makes percolating noises. "I think you should leave."

"There's one other matter," she says. "I wasn't going to tell you if I didn't have to. Because it's hurtful. But you leave me no choice."

Cassie pictures the hard look in Grant's eyes.

"This morning I drove past the Reis house," she continues. "I saw Teresa letting herself in like she had the run of the place. Don't you think it's odd they're on such terms she feels comfortable doing that?"

A cupboard is banged shut.

"Now the Reis boy, he would be a good match for her. Quite handsome too."

Something shatters, a cup or a dish.

"I'll leave now," she says. "That's all I wanted to tell you."

And it was a mouthful. Cassie didn't know Teresa had gone inside Julian's house. But it explains why she was lingering nearby. She must've come back out right before Cassie arrived.

The front door opens and closes downstairs. More crashing noises come from the kitchen. He's in a fury, she can tell. *God help me if he finds me in this mood.*

A moment later she hears the phone dial. After a pause, Grant says, "Hey, it's me."

Teresa? She thinks so. If only she could hear her side of the conversation.

"You want to have dinner tonight?... Yes, a real restaurant. I'm sick of hiding. I don't care what my mother thinks." His voice grows strained. "You've been going out with friends a lot lately. Fine. Come here later?" Even Cassie can hear the underlying anger in his tone now. "Forget it then. Call me tomorrow."

Teresa has put him off for tonight. No surprise to Cassie. She already knows Teresa is planning to meet Julian at Thorne Cove.

After he hangs up, an eerie silence follows. Cassie holds her breath, wondering what's brewing inside his head. Petrified he might continue his search of the house.

His feet clack across the hardwood floor. What sounds like a closet door is opened. There's the clanging of metal against metal. Then more footsteps toward the back of the house and out to the patio. The place grows quiet.

This might be her only chance to sneak away. But first she needs to verify he won't see her from wherever he's gone. She steals across the hall and peers out the window.

Grant is hunched beside a stately old oak, swinging a golf club over and over, slamming it into the tree, gashing its poor trunk. She's not certain whether he's picturing Julian or Teresa or alternating between them.

She bounds down the stairs, out the front door, and into the grove of trees. But glancing back at the mansion, she's astonished to see the Reis' Chevy pickup parked in the driveway. *What on earth is Julian doing here?* This development is completely unexpected. Did Mrs. Wolcott call him to give him a talking-to? Or maybe it isn't Julian at all. It might be Armando delivering lobster for an upcoming party.

Whatever the explanation, it could have relevance, and she needs to find out what it is. Ducking back down to the street, she takes the sidewalk to the main entrance. This time, like a legitimate visitor to the estate, she follows the walkway to the front door and rings the bell. She doesn't expect Grant to come over and disturb them. Not in the state he's in.

22

───────────

While Cassie waits at the grand entrance to the Wolcott mansion, piano music drifts toward her from an open window. Even if there were no lobster truck parked in the driveway, she would know it was Julian playing *Rêverie.* The song, with its ethereal refrain, makes her chest ache inside.

A middle-aged woman who is probably the housekeeper answers her ring. "Can I help you?"

"I'm Cassie Moran. I've come to see Mrs. Wolcott."

"Is she expecting you?"

"Yes," Cassie lies, hoping to expedite this process.

The woman hesitates but apparently decides it isn't worth checking with her employer first. "Follow me." She leads Cassie through a dark hallway that opens into a magnificent ballroom filled with natural light from the enormous windows overlooking the ocean. The room's centerpiece is a grand piano, where Julian plays Debussy's masterpiece with his head bent over the keys and his eyes nearly shut. The way he always plays.

Mrs. Wolcott is seated with a newspaper open in her lap and a pencil in hand, most likely working on the crossword. Beside her, Mr. Wolcott, who has dementia, stares at nothing in particular.

"Cassie Moran is here to see you, Mrs. Wolcott," the woman announces before leaving the room.

Julian stops playing and looks up at her in surprise. Mrs. Wolcott raises her eyes from the paper without showing any great interest in the new arrival.

"I apologize for disturbing you all, but I, um, I need to talk to Julian urgently. His father sent me," Cassie says.

Julian shoots to his feet. "Is he all right?"

"Yes, but can I talk to you privately?"

Mrs. Wolcott waves a bored hand toward the patio. Julian leads Cassie outside through the French doors. She glances in the direction of the guesthouse, wondering if they might see Grant still swinging his golf club, but fortunately the place isn't visible from this location.

"Your father's fine. I just wanted to ask what you're doing here," Cassie says in a low voice.

"What are *you* doing here? I thought you were coming over this morning."

"Sorry, I've been busy. I was planning to come by this afternoon."

"I missed you, Cass." It surprises her to hear the rebuke in his tone. She'd almost forgotten they haven't seen each other in six months at this point.

"I missed you too. But right now, I'm wondering why you're here. Do they pay you for this?"

"In a way. Four or five months ago, she found me an incredible new teacher in Boston. When I said I couldn't afford her, she said she'd cover it if I would just come by the house now and then to play for Mr. Wolcott."

"He likes your music?"

Julian shrugs. "He never shows any sign of it. But she says he used to love classical piano. Maybe he's still enjoying it even if he can't say so."

"Does Grant ever come here and listen to you play?"

Julian makes a face. "Grant? One time he walked in and left immediately. I don't think he likes me much."

All she can think is that was nothing compared to how much Grant must loathe him now.

"I'll make an excuse and leave with you," Julian says.

"No." Again she sees the hurt wash over his face. "I'm sorry, but I promised my mother I'd pick up some things at the grocery for her. I'll come by your house later."

He swallows his disappointment and kisses her lightly on the cheek. Inside, he returns to the piano and starts from the beginning. Cassie wishes she could stay and listen. The grand piano highlights Julian's talent in a way his little upright can never approach.

"Please remind your mother I need to receive her clothing donation by this evening," Mrs. Wolcott tells Cassie on her way out.

After reaching her car, she breathes in deeply a few times to settle herself. As difficult as this has been, she's glad she forced herself to search Grant's place. She's gained important information. She knows for certain he will lie to her tomorrow, when she calls him before she's questioned by Officer Brooks. He will tell her he saw Julian and Teresa making out at the cove two weeks earlier. But clearly, judging from his attack on the tree, Grant first heard about their relationship today from his mother.

Secondly, Cassie discovered the ring and she knows where it came from. If the store has kept records for seven years... well, it's too soon to get hopeful about that. She's not sure how useful it will be. Buying someone an engagement ring is no proof of murder.

Lastly, she has to wonder if Mrs. Wolcott, following the murder, will come to suspect her own son. Because she's the only one who knows he has a motive.

23

——————

Cassie has one remaining task to perform before the killing takes place tonight.

She drives across town and over the railroad tracks to where Teresa Patterson lives on the right side of a tired duplex. Cassie spots her seated on the sidewalk in front of her home, playing jacks with a boy of eight or nine. The resemblance between them reminds her that Teresa had a little brother. *Beloved Sister* it says on her headstone. The thought pinches Cassie's heart.

Continuing past them, she turns the car around at the next intersection and returns to park several houses down from the duplex. She remains in the car, watching the siblings play. They're so intent on their game, and so completely at ease with one another, neither one notices her. Now and then, Teresa ruffles his hair or kisses his cheek. They laugh a lot, particularly when she pretends to try to get away with cheating. It appears she helps him to win at the end.

What Cassie sees moves her. She's never even considered who Teresa was as a person, aside from being the girl who stole Julian's heart. Until now, she never wondered about her talents and skills, her hopes and dreams, or her friends and family members. Most likely they'll grieve for the rest of their lives, especially this brother of hers. Just like Cassie will never stop feeling the pain of her father's loss.

Before long they gather the jacks and climb into Teresa's car. She's working at Filene's this afternoon—Cassie knows this—and must be planning to drop off her brother at their parents' house on the way. Cassie keeps her face lowered as Teresa checks her rearview mirror, backing out of the driveway.

After the car turns the corner up ahead, Cassie goes to the door and tries the knob, though it doesn't surprise her to find it locked, given that Teresa lives alone. She checks all around for a spare key, and this time she gets lucky and finds it under a conspicuous rock near the steps. Glancing around to make sure no one's watching, she lets herself in.

It's a small place, just a sitting room, table area, tiny kitchen and a half-bath downstairs, two cramped bedrooms and a closet-sized bathroom upstairs. It seems clean enough, but messy. A couple jackets and a blanket on the couch. Some wrappers and an empty beer can on the coffee table. Dishes in the sink and so on. She does a quick check downstairs, not expecting much. If Teresa was dating two guys they might drop in sometime and she wouldn't want them seeing photos of each other.

The main thing she learns in the sitting room is something she never would've guessed about her. Teresa likes to knit. On a side table, she's left out a pink mohair sweater in progress. And inside the front closet, there are hats and scarves of various styles, colors, and types of yarn. She has a flair for this. Unlike Cassie, who's always been terrible at knitting because her attention wanders and she lose stitches.

Continuing upstairs, she glances in the medicine cabinet, not surprised to find a packet of birth control pills. Sensible girl to be doing her best to avoid pregnancy at a time when she might be unable to name which man was the father.

She moves on to the spare bedroom, which holds a spindly chair, a rickety desk, and a bookshelf filled with fashion magazines. It occurs to her this "study" is the exact opposite of Grant's. In some ways she agrees with Mrs. Wolcott: they seem like such a mismatched couple, it's inevitable things wouldn't work out between them. If only Grant could've accepted that.

She riffles through the drawers but they're mostly empty save for the usual stuff like pens, paper, a stapler, and scissors.

Finally she's in Teresa's bedroom where she hopes to find something, anything, that ties her to Grant. Maybe he gave her a piece of expensive jewelry, but the police had bigger clues so they never traced it. This could be more important than the engagement ring, which he probably returned to the store, where they would've removed the engraving that provided evidence it may have been intended for Teresa. That would still be an assumption based on initials alone. But if he'd given her something else, and if her brother now had it, maybe it could be traced to the same place where he bought the ring. If they had a receipt showing his name, this would establish their connection.

A search of her one bedside drawer turns up a few loose photos of her and her little brother. One of her parents, or at least Cassie assumes that's them. No pictures of Grant or Julian. Moving on to the dresser, she finds a large jewelry box in Teresa's top drawer and sorts through its contents. She's no expert, but it all looks like costume jewelry to her. Nothing one couldn't find in a J.C. Penney catalogue. Not the sort of thing Grant would buy for her, or if he did, it wasn't special enough to be traced back to him.

She does a quick sweep of the rest of the dresser, starting to feel like this visit has been a complete waste of time. However, at the very back of the bottom drawer, her fingers poke a small box. She snatches it out with a surge of excitement, thinking *this is it, this is what I've been waiting for.*

A necklace is folded inside: a smooth silver disc on a silver chain. The shape of a heart is etched on the disc, along with the words, "Adoro-te."

The adrenalin drains from her and she has to sit down. When she squeezes the necklace inside her fist, it feels like it's burning into her flesh. She flings it across the room.

The language is Portuguese. Julian has said those words to her before. But he never gave her jewelry inscribed with it.

She wishes with all her soul she'd never come here.

24

——————

When Cassie wakes in her own time, it's mid-morning and poor Gio is beside himself with hunger. She feels like a terrible cat-mother.

She empties out the last of the kibble in Gio's bowl. It's a meager amount. As for her own meal, the fridge is mostly empty and the cupboards are nearly bare. She can't avoid a trip to the grocery store any longer.

In the middle of getting dressed, she hears the phone ring and decides she better answer it to avoid more visits from anyone checking up on her. It's Maggie, her boss from work. Cassie makes her voice thick and hopes she sounds deathly ill, even though she considers it unlikely she'll still have a job at the end of this. She refuses to let herself worry about it; there's too much else at stake right now. And it isn't a lie that she's feeling ill. Her head aches, her face is wan. If she doesn't finish this soon, it may finish her.

After hanging up, she pops two more aspirin and heads out to the car. The phone rings again inside the house, but she doesn't have the energy to run back and answer it. Whoever is calling, let them assume she's busy throwing up in the bathroom.

She drives to the least popular market in town, hoping not to see anyone she knows. Once inside the store, she races through the aisles, putting little thought into what she's buying, just trying to finish quickly. She fills her cart with cat food, eggs, bread, dairy, fruits, and veggies. There's a line at the register, but no one appears to recognize her. She breathes a little sigh of relief once she's back in her car.

At home, she takes two bags from her trunk, leaving the kibble and one more bag for a second trip. With both arms full, she reaches out her hand to insert the key into the knob. This is when she discovers the door isn't locked.

She hesitates. Didn't she lock it on her way out? She's pretty certain she didn't bother with the bolt, which would've required the key. But locking the knob only meant turning it on the inside before shutting the door after her. She thinks she did that.

On the other hand, it's true she forgets to lock up now and then. Her mother used to scold her for it sometimes. This is probably one of these occasions.

Kicking the door inward, she steps inside and sweeps the house with her gaze. Everything appears just as she left it. If someone had broken in, they probably wouldn't worry about making a mess. She waits a moment longer just listening, but the place is quiet.

Continuing into the kitchen with the bags, she begins to unpack them. But seeing the canned cat food reminds her Gio ought to be under foot right now. He usually greets her when she arrives, especially when she's carrying anything. Always hopeful of a meal.

She uses the electric opener on the chicken with gravy. Normally, its sound has the same effect on Gio as the buzz of an oven timer on a human being, drawing him instantly to the kitchen. But this time, he still hasn't appeared after the can snaps open.

She fills his dish and sets it on the floor before going to the hall to listen again. Nothing at first. Then a muffled meow.

"Gio?" she calls out.

He meows again but still doesn't come. She follows his faint cries to the family room, and from there, to a closet where games are kept. When she opens the door, he leaps out from a shelf but doesn't race off to his food. Instead, he stays close like he wants her protection.

How did he get shut in here? She bends to pet him while looking back at the doorway, feeling a tingle at the back of her neck. Someone did this to him. Someone who wanted him out from under foot.

A floorboard groans somewhere in the house, causing the tingle to race down her spine. At the same time, an idea flashes into her head. Turning back to the closet, she gets out her father's favorite baseball bat, a 1962 Louisville Slugger.

She returns to the hall with silent steps. The front door is still ajar as she left it when she came in with the bags. Could the intruder have run off? She glances out the opening without seeing anyone.

Gio slips past her feet and goes to the kitchen now, unable to resist the scent of his food any longer. Continuing from room to room, Cassie checks all around until only the second floor remains. She hesitates at the bottom of the steps, frightened at the thought of being trapped up there by the intruder. Maybe she should call the police, except she's not sure she wants them coming here, asking questions. There are too many inexplicable aspects to her life at the moment.

She steels herself and goes up the steps, glancing quickly into each room, holding the bat ready to swing. Seeing no one, she does a more detailed search. Inside the closets, behind the shower curtain. No one.

She returns to her own room for a more careful examination. The second drawer in her dresser is crooked and not quite closed. This happens when one doesn't know the trick of holding it with both hands and lifting up on the left. For Cassie, it's just instinct to close it the right way, because she's done it so many times.

She notices other small changes. A sketchpad turned down when she believes she left it face up. In the closet, her Julian box is not quite in its place. Dragging it out, she checks inside but nothing appears to be missing. This was no thief, though. A thief would not be so neat. A thief would steal anything they could pawn, even things of small value, like the earrings and silver ring Julian gave her. As far as she can tell, nothing has been taken from the house.

One more thing occurs to her and sends her rushing back down the stairs into the family room. She has left her list of time travel rules in a drawer. It's still there, and doesn't appear to have been moved. But she can't be certain. Likely if he saw it, he'd consider it the ravings of a lunatic. Maybe that would be all right. He might underestimate her.

This must have been Grant. Maybe he was the one who called as she was leaving for the store, trying to confirm whether she was home. As far as she knows, no one else has a motive to search her house. He wants to know if she has any sort of evidence that could be used against him. It's unlikely after all these years. He must believe if she had solid proof, she'd have brought it to the police long ago. But clearly the possibility is eating away at him. He might've hoped she kept a journal where she had written down her thoughts. *Ha*, the only thing in writing is the insane time travel list.

He may not have had a chance to search anywhere other than her bedroom. Most likely her arrival interrupted him. It gives her a chill thinking he must have crept down the stairs and slipped outside while she was getting Gio out of the closet. Thank god he didn't hurt her cat.

She fetches the remaining groceries from her car, and bolts her door when she's back inside. At least Grant ought to stay away for the rest of the day now. This makes everything all the more urgent. With him becoming more reckless, she needs to finish her fact-gathering as quickly as possible.

Though it broke her heart to find that necklace from Julian in Teresa's bedroom, she's aware her hurt feelings are insignificant compared to the much larger issue of exposing Grant as the killer. For this reason, she returns to her bed immediately following a quick lunch.

However, she lies on the sheets so ridiculously awake, her eyes won't even stay closed. No matter how hard she envisions the time where she wants to land, nothing happens. It appears she'll be forced to wait till night to continue.

Just as she gets up, though, she remembers something that may be useful. She still hasn't packed away the things her mother left behind, though she's been meaning to do it for months. Her mother used to take the occasional sleeping pill until Freddie talked her into giving them up. Cassie is pretty sure she noticed a bottle in her bathroom not long ago. Checking it, she finds a few tablets remaining. With luck, she won't need more than this.

25

It's dinnertime on the day of the murder. Cassie is in mid-bite landing in her nineteen-year-old self. Right away she feels the difference. This young body of hers has a strength and energy the older one is currently lacking.

The sounds of her mother getting ready for her big date come from upstairs.

She finishes her meal, since this version of her seems to be hungry, before going upstairs to change into her spying clothes. Simple dark t-shirt and jeans. Ankle socks, black sneakers. They're the quietest shoes she has.

At this point, her mother shouts to her from the kitchen, asking if she'll bring the box of used clothing to the Wolcott's house. Cassie yells back, *sure*, even though she has no intention of going there this time. They exchange shouted goodbyes when Freddie arrives. Thankfully the two leave quickly.

Cassie thinks about bringing her polaroid camera tonight. How amazing it would be to unearth incriminating photos in the future. But she's well aware her actions here don't change anything, nor can she carry photos with her when her consciousness swoops back to her present-day self. These limitations make her job a thousand times harder.

After the lovebirds have driven away, she returns downstairs and gets herself a cup of coffee. She must be as alert as possible tonight. When the sun finally lowers, she leaves on her bike. She's not sure when Julian will be setting out from his house, but she needs the cover of darkness to be sure no one notices her. It's past nine when she reaches the next street over from his, where she ditches her bike behind a play structure in someone's yard.

Approaching Julian's place, she's glad to see the truck gone. She knows now he probably did meet his friends before going to the cove. At the time she thought he hoped they would provide his alibi. Now she thinks he simply wanted some part of his excuse for not seeing her tonight to be true.

Light glows from the front windows. She peeks through the glass and sees Armando seated in the corner chair next to the lamp. His head is bent over a bound notebook in his lap, with his hand poised above it holding a pencil. After a pause, he writes something on the page.

She's filled with curiosity. Did Armando keep a journal? She never saw evidence of it before, but then, as a teenager, she barely noticed him. He was a parent, after all, even if a young one. Who ever paid attention to what their friends' parents were doing?

She has to wait for him to finish and leave the room. Hopefully, no one will pass in the street and notice her lurking outside the Reis house. To be sure, she slips around the side, avoiding the windows, and ducks down behind the trash can. It doesn't take long before the light in the main room is shut off, and a different light comes on in Armando's bedroom window at the back.

Soon that too is extinguished. She waits another ten minutes or so for good measure, to be sure he's fallen asleep, before returning to the front and letting herself in. She had been planning to go directly upstairs, but it occurs to her Armando's journal might possibly hold some clue to Julian's behavior. At first it appears he took it to bed with him, until she checks the drawer in the table beside the chair and discovers it tucked inside there.

Cassie brings it to the window to read it under the light from the street. But when she flips to the first page, she finds he has written in Portuguese. *Duh.* She wants to kick herself for not thinking of that. His English is fine but he would naturally feel more comfortable writing in his native tongue.

However, before closing the book, she notices how the words seem to be written in stanzas. It's poetry, she realizes with a shock. Skipping ahead to scan more pages, she discovers a series of what appear to be poems identified by neat titles at the top.

She smiles to herself. All this time she thought he did nothing but catch lobster by day and watch TV by night, and here he was writing poetry. He must have the soul of a romantic and she'd had no idea. So much for her powers of observation.

Toward the end of the book, a title strikes her eye: *Para Teresa.* She knows enough to guess it means "For Teresa."

Confusion fills her. Why would Armando be writing poetry for Teresa? Could it be some other Teresa? Or maybe he wrote this for Julian to use, helping his romantic pursuits like a fatherly Cyrano de Bergerac. If that were the case, though, why had Cassie never received a poem from Julian? Other than a purposely inept one he gave her on Valentine's Day one year, beginning with the ridiculous "Roses are red, Violets are blue" and going downhill from there.

The sound of a snore from the back room breaks her reverie. She has things she has to do, and since Armando is apparently asleep, she must get to them. After quietly restoring the book to its place, she slips upstairs, avoiding the steps that groan under a person's weight, amazed she remembers which ones they are. It surprises her to find Julian's door shut because he usually leaves it open. She wonders if he might be home, but then who could've taken the truck?

The room is empty as expected, though. She turns on his lamp so she can look around, and immediately notices a folded note on the bed. The paper looks like it's been crumpled, reminding her of Julian's confusion when she arrived at his house this morning. The way his fist tightened around something, and how he shoved it in his pocket like he didn't want her seeing it. She opens the note now and reads: "Meet me at Thorne Cove at 11. Teresa."

She swallows hard. Here it is, the reason Teresa came to the house. She must've dropped off the note before Julian got back. That and the stupid heart-shaped cookie Armando claimed for himself to save his son from discovery.

She hears noises downstairs, like someone's coming in. It could be Julian—or another person. The stairs creak loudly. Whoever it is doesn't know which steps to avoid. With no time to lose, she flies into the closet and closes the door except for a crack she can spy out of.

Julian's door opens slowly. She only has a limited field of vision, but as the man enters the room, she glimpses enough of him to tell it's Grant. This is what she expected, but still her heart beats wildly. She hears paper crinkling as he picks up the note. After he reads it, his hand closes over it, squeezing tight like he wants to make it disintegrate. He blows out a sharp breath before leaving the room and returning down the stairs.

She waits a few moments longer before coming out. The first thing she notices is that the note is gone. He didn't throw it in Julian's wastebasket, so he must've taken it with him.

Tiptoeing to the hall, she looks down the steps. Grant is just leaving, pulling the front door shut behind him. She crosses to the storage room upstairs and keeps herself hidden as she peers out from the side of the window. Grant has paused near the entrance as he inserts a long knife into his backpack. He draws on the pack while rushing to the side of the house. She can't see what he's doing there. He returns shortly, grabs the bike he left near the truck, and pedals away.

Recalling Armando telling her the murder weapon came from their kitchen, she hurries downstairs to check the butcher block that holds their cutting and carving knives. Sure enough, there's an empty slot that looks like it held the largest of them. Here is proof that Grant has already made up his mind to kill her and frame Julian. Proof that he's acting with cold deliberation, perhaps from the moment he read the note and knew where he would find them together. Later, he'll be sure to leave the knife where it will be found. When they search the Reis house, police will easily match it with the set. When that happens, Julian will lose all hope of proving his own innocence.

She goes out the front door and around to the side, wondering what Grant was doing there. Opening the lid of the garbage can, she discovers the crumpled note where he placed it inside. Tomorrow when the police come with their warrant, they'll find it and might wonder how any killer could be stupid enough to cover his tracks so poorly. But with all evidence pointing to Julian—including Cassie's eyewitness account that places him at the cove at precisely the right time—they'll still be convinced of his guilt.

Filled with an impotent rage, Cassie leans against the clapboard, pressing her hands hard against it. Teresa's killing is the greatest horror, but the calm way in which Grant has set this trap for Julian is nearly as monstrous. He'll destroy two lives without flinching.

Before long, she recognizes the noise of Julian's truck as it approaches from the street and swerves into the driveway. Its door comes open and is slammed shut. A bang follows Julian's entrance into the house. She resists the urge to go to him, warn him, tell him everything she knows. Because it won't change anything.

Gazing up at the light from his bedroom window, she wonders if he's noticed the note is gone. If so, he probably doesn't think much of it. He may believe his father found it and threw it away. A moment later, his light goes out. Julian has no idea regarding the tsunami that will overwhelm him tomorrow. Probably he'll even sleep soundly tonight, despite his apparent irritation with Teresa.

One thought continues to nag at her. Armando's poetry. *Para Teresa.* Why would he write such a thing? A new idea is taking hold inside her. She might never get another chance to find out if it's true. Despite the resolution she made only minutes earlier, not to disturb Julian, she returns to the front of his house and enters again. She glides up the stairs to his door, where she knocks lightly and whispers his name.

Seconds later the door is flung wide. He gathers her in his arms. "How'd you know I was dying for you to come?"

He tries to kiss her but she resists and makes him sit beside her on the bed. She says what she should have said to him seven years ago. "I know you went to see Teresa at Thorne Cove. I saw your truck."

"And you thought...?" He slips one arm around her waist. "You couldn't think... Cass, I wasn't cheating on you. I never have."

"She has a necklace. It says 'Adoro-te.'"

"Does she? That doesn't surprise me."

"She left a note for you to meet her." All the accusations, gushing out of her.

He glances around for it. "Were you here earlier? I left it on my bed."

"It upset me to see it. I threw it away." It won't help to tell him anything about Grant.

"But it wasn't for me. She left it for my father," he says.

His father. *Para Armando*. Then perhaps it's true, Cassie thinks. Like his son, the man had an undeniable appeal to women. The same shiny black hair and muscular physique. He had a roguish charm and appeared younger than his age. His devotion to Julian was evidence of a warm heart.

"I found it in his room this morning. I took it away without telling him," Julian says.

"Why would you do that?" This part makes no sense.

"He's been quietly dating her since before Christmas. But last week, I saw her with Grant. Figured she would dump my father. I didn't want him getting hurt."

"Don't lie to me." She's lived with a different belief for so long, it's a struggle to wrap her head around this new information. But then she remembers what she saw the night of the murder. His eyes averted from Teresa's naked body. He never touched her. He kept his distance.

"I swear it's true. I went there to tell her to leave him alone," Julian continues. "To ask her to find an excuse to let him off easy. But she said she was breaking up with Grant. She loves my father. Can you believe it?"

"I can, actually." Teresa probably had begun to sense the corruption inside Grant. As Cassie has.

"You wanna know something? I've been an ass. I didn't just go there for my dad's sake. I wanted her to break it off with him for my own selfish reasons. You know why? Mrs. Wolcott. If Grant finds out he got dumped for a Reis, I can kiss my piano lessons goodbye. And she promised to help me get into the conservatory. But he's gonna be so pissed, he probably won't rest till he gets her to totally sink my chances of a career."

Oh he's going to do so much worse than that. Cassie lays her head against his shoulder.

"Screw them," he says. "I want my father to be happy."

"Why didn't you tell me before?"

"It was his secret. Him and Teresa. You know? Didn't think it was mine to share."

"It would've made all the difference." Her heart is shattering. If she'd known, she would've told a thousand lies for him. But instead she was petty and jealous and suspicious.

"I would never cheat on you," he says.

"It was Armando all along?"

"I swear it."

She closes her eyes, drowning in regret. A fire starts inside her head and takes her away.

26

———————

It's early evening when Cassie returns to the future. Her first thoughts: *Julian never cheated. Armando was in love with Teresa.* She pushes them back, refuses to let herself think about them. Otherwise, the revelation will overwhelm her and she'll never complete what she set out to do.

She feels a weird combination of exhausted and sleepless. It's essential she finish this thing soon. Just one more trip, she thinks. One more trip to allow the final chapter to play out.

After making herself an omelet, she sits in the kitchen to eat and consider her next move. So far, despite what she's observed of Grant's actions, she doesn't know how to prove he's the killer. She can only imagine Officer Brooks' reaction if she skips into the station, reveals everything she knows, and tells him she discovered it all through time travel. Oh, that would go over well. Especially since there's such an obvious rational explanation for how she knows details that were never publicly revealed. *She knows because she's the killer herself*, they would say. Murder by reason of insanity would no doubt be the verdict.

But she's come this far, she refuses to give up now. There's more to learn on the day following the killing. Maybe she'll find out Grant made a mistake she can somehow use against him. She has to try.

Every second she delays brings her closer to the time when Grant will come back to her house to check on her. She can't bear to look at him right now. She needs to get through all of it, and then she'll sit back and figure out a plan. If a plan is even possible.

The unpleasant smell of an old sock hovers in the kitchen, and it isn't her omelet. *It's me*, she thinks after sniffing around. She hurries upstairs to the shower, a place she hasn't visited in several days, and peels off her clothes. Her hair is greasy and her skin sticky. But when the warm water pours over her, no matter how hard she scrubs, she can't remove the feeling of violation that's enveloped her.

Putting on a clean outfit makes her feel a little better. She goes outside and collects the newspapers that have gathered, plus the mail that's overflowing from the mailbox. She would've done that when she returned from the supermarket, but the signs of an intruder distracted her. She glances through the bills and decides she has a few days to take care of them. Lastly, she rechecks that all the doors and windows are secured. It's possible Grant has already learned how to pick locks, but at least she has to do what she can to try to keep him out.

She's ready now. To guarantee she'll be able to sleep, she takes another of her mother's pills. Closing her eyes, she concentrates on the day following the killing, shortly after Officer Brooks' departure.

When she lands, she's in her bedroom weeping. She stifles a sob and goes to the bathroom to blow her nose and clean her face. Nothing she can do about her swollen eyes. Checking the time, she hopes she hasn't cut things too close.

She tries not to think too hard about her next step, or she might lose her resolve. It's essential for her to observe what Grant is doing in the aftermath of the killing. Most likely he's spending the day covering his tracks in every way possible. She can't do anything with destroyed evidence, now or in the future, but knowing what he's done, understanding what he believes to be incriminating, still might help her when it comes to formulating a plan.

When Cassie comes downstairs from her room, she finds her mother in the kitchen preparing to fry up some chicken.

"I have to go out," she says. "I'll need the car."

"Have you seen the weather?"

She looks out the window, where wind-driven rain beats against the glass. "I'm not going far. I'll drive carefully."

Her mother breathes out heavily. "Honey, you know you can't go see him. You have to stay out of this."

"I'm not going there. I'm going to see Shawna." She was Cassie's best friend in high school. "I really need to talk to a friend right now."

"At least eat some dinner first."

"I have to go right away. The weather is only supposed to get worse."

Her mother sighs again. "Fine. Drive carefully. Don't slam on the brakes. During the last nor-easter, Mrs. Lindley slid all the way down—"

"I know, Mom." Cassie takes the keys, grabs her rain jacket, and hurries out before the permission is withdrawn. She would've gone with or without her mother's consent, but it feels better this way.

Outside the storm is as bad as she remembers, and the sky is growing dark. At least not many drivers are stupid enough to be on the road. Her windshield wipers are swiping back and forth at full speed, but it's still difficult to see anything. She turns a corner and confronts a thick branch on her side of the road. No choice, she has to brake hard, and her car swerves left. A jeep coming the opposite way screeches to a halt barely in time to avoid hitting her.

She backs up, and after the other car passes, manages to get around the branch on that side.

Down the street from the Wolcott estate, she parks at the curb and hurries up to the house, splashing through puddles in her sneakers, wishing she'd remembered to put on boots. Like before, she sneaks among the trees till she's close to the guesthouse.

What she sees upon approaching shocks her. Julian is here, rattling the doorknob and shoving against the door. When he can't get in, he doesn't do the sensible thing and check around back.

Instead he hurls a rock through one of the glass panes. Once it shatters, he covers his hand with his sleeve and reaches through to turn the knob inside. He leaves the door ajar behind him when he goes in. Shutting it doesn't matter when it's obvious there's an intruder inside.

So Julian knows... or suspects. Another piece of information Cassie never had. This new knowledge forces a change in her plans. The question is, should she reveal herself to him? Her mind says it isn't a good idea, but her heart drives her forward into the house.

He's already upstairs. The sound of drawers being yanked out and thrown on the floor come from the bedroom. He's frantic, searching for evidence against Grant. She races up the steps to join him.

"Julian, it's me," she says before entering, in case he thinks she's Grant and is preparing to bash her over the head with something.

He looks up from the mess of Grant's possessions he's made on the floor. "Cass?"

"Julian, I'm so sorry. I couldn't lie for you."

He doesn't look surprised. "It's all right. I shouldn't have asked you."

"I'll help you search."

"You believe in me? Even after—"

"I know you didn't do it."

"Grant was seeing Teresa," he says.

She resists saying *I know* again.

Julian freezes at the sound of a car outside. "Fuck. He's back. Don't let him see you."

"What are you going to do?"

He doesn't answer, just hurries past her to the stairs. She debates following him, but there's one other thing she wants to check. Going into the study, she searches his desk again for the ring, without finding it this time. She scans the room for another hiding place, and discovers Grant has a safe. Probably it's in there. Maybe it's still in there, seven years later.

"What the hell are you doing in my house?" Grant says downstairs.

There's a loud bang, like someone got slammed up against the wall. She thinks it must be Grant.

"You killed her, you bastard," Julian says.

Grant sounds like he's gagging. "You're crazy. I barely knew her."

"Don't lie to me! I saw you together."

"You're the one lying."

"She humiliated you. Richest family in town and she chose a guy who's got nothing."

A bang like someone's head hitting the wall. "You're gonna confess," Julian says. "You're gonna call the cops right now and tell them you did it."

"Or what?"

"Or I'll kill you," Julian says.

The table bangs and scrapes against the floor. It sounds like Grant escaped Julian's grip. She hears fists hitting flesh and bone. If Grant were not still alive in the future, she would seriously wonder if Julian is about to beat him to death.

"Stop it!" Mrs. Wolcott calls out. Cassie wonders if she heard the commotion from her house. More likely she's been keeping a close eye on her son.

The noises stop. Julian is not really capable of killing anyone, especially with Grant's mother watching.

"Leave my son alone," she says.

"He did it," Julian says. "He killed her."

"My son would never do such a thing. He was home with me. We played cards in the main house. His father sat with us."

One of Cassie's most important questions now has its answer. How far would Grant's mother go to protect him? *All the fucking way.*

An alibi from one's parents shouldn't count for much, just as Julian once said. But this is Mrs. Wolcott. The most influential woman in town. And the toughest. No one likes to cross her. Whatever she wants, she only need make a generous donation.

"The police are on their way," she says.

"You're lying about Grant. He wasn't here." Julian's voice drips with resignation. He knows this visit was ill-considered. But he couldn't help himself.

"Why don't you let the police sort it out?" she says.

It sounds like Julian leaves the house. Cassie looks out the front window and sees him paused outside, staring up at her. There's no point in his waiting. She waves him on, trying to show she'll be all right. He must realize there's nothing he can do to help her anyway. He disappears into the darkness.

Grant and his mother are talking downstairs. She strains to hear them.

"Come with me to the house," Mrs. Wolcott says.

"But the police—"

"Don't be foolish. They're not coming here. I told them Julian jumped you when you were walking home and stole cash from you. Last you saw him he was running away. Now come up to the house and we'll get that cut cleaned up."

Cassie hears them go out and shut the door. After waiting a few minutes, she leaves as well. One thing is clear. Helen Wolcott is complicit. She knows exactly what Grant did. And she'll clearly do whatever is necessary to protect him.

No wonder she didn't want Cassie dating him in the future. Julian's former girlfriend? A very bad idea. What if she became curious about what really happened?

27

<hr>

Outside, the rain whips into her. She moves behind a tree on the Wolcott property, considering her options. She knows what Julian is going to do next. But there isn't time for her to follow after him.

She looks out toward the water, realizing she only has one chance to reach him. Thinking about it will only cause fear and hesitation. Instead she sets off across the lawn and when she reaches the dock, she goes to the very end of it, squinting toward the harbor, searching for any sign of him.

The ocean swells are larger than she's ever seen them. Waves crash against the shore on the other side of the channel. Meanwhile the wind-driven rain pushes against her, soaking her hair and clothes, chilling her bones. The howl of the gale makes her want to clap her hands over her ears.

She sees the lights of the vessel before the sound of its engine reaches her. A desperate Julian fleeing in the lobsterboat. He knows the evidence against him is overwhelming and has no clue how he'll prove his innocence. He probably hopes to gain time by running away. Time to figure out his defense. Time for proof to emerge that

Grant is the killer. It isn't a real plan. Julian isn't thinking straight at this point.

Grant has done too effective a job of framing him. The knife from the Reis kitchen. The note that Teresa wrote. There was no name at the top, but anyone would assume it was meant for Julian. The necklace she was probably wearing when she was killed—*Adoro-te.* Again, it could equally have come from Julian or his father. But Julian is the one who went to the cove. The police know that, of course, thanks to his girlfriend back from college, who has told them that the boy she loves, without a doubt, was there at the time of the killing. If she were on the jury, she'd convict him too.

He's taken the boat because officers have surrounded his house. Even if he could reach his truck, he would not get far in it with police watching the highways, searching for him. Escaping in the boat was the natural second choice for him.

As he passes near the Wolcott dock, she calls out to him. He doesn't turn, probably didn't hear her over the onslaught of rain and wind. She shouts again. "Julian! Over here!"

He looks now and slows the engine. He's close enough she can see his anxious expression. "Go home, Cass!" He waves her away and continues on.

"Take me with you!" she cries.

He stays the course. She can't let him go without her. An insane idea comes to her, similar to when she slashed her wrist. If she hesitates, he'll be too far away, and she'll never get him back. So she steps off the dock into the roiling sea.

Oh my god, it's so cold, so cold. When she rises for air, she's gasping. This might be it; she might die here and now, and never return to the future. They'll find her prone body with her mind erased.

But then Julian looks back and does a double-take. He must've seen she's no longer on the dock. "Cass!" he calls out. He cuts the engine and scans the water, looking for her.

"Here, Julian!" She swims toward the boat, but the swells threaten to overwhelm her.

"Fuck." Julian tosses out a lifesaver. He draws her in, lifts her into the boat. "You're crazy," he says, holding her close.

"Take me with you."

He stares at her, gauging her resolve. The waves rock them dangerously. "I have to get the helm." He takes the wheel and directs them out toward open ocean. She stands beside him, shivering and clutching his arm for balance.

"You can find something warm in the hold. And a lifejacket," he says.

She stumbles down the steps to get below deck. Removing her soaked top, she pulls on a man's sweatshirt she finds hanging on a hook. She grabs two lifejackets, puts one on, and brings the other to Julian. She clings to his side while he steers, and they shout over the blasting wind.

"Guess I should've checked the forecast," he says.

"You ever been out in weather this bad?"

He surveys the mounting swells, his face grim. She takes that as a *no.*

Julian nods toward shore. "I can let you off at the point."

"Only if you come with me."

He throws her a look and holds his course. She wraps her hand around his arm. Heavy rain pelts the front windshield. The wipers slap the glass furiously. The waves loom ever larger. But when she looks at Julian, she's shocked to see an excited glow in his face. Amazingly, the challenge of navigating through this storm from hell has invigorated him. Her, on the other hand... she's struggling to swallow her panic.

Glimpsing the lighthouse through the darkness ahead of them, she says, "What's next on our love-making tour?"

His lips curl into a smile. "The train, after we ditch the boat in Boston."

"Where will the train take us?"

"Maine. Then we'll cross over into Canada."

"We've never done it in Canada."

"There are lots of lighthouses."

"Something different," she says.

"King's Landing, then. New Brunswick."

"Why there?"

"King's Landing? You know."

She laughs because that's the meaning of *Reis*. King. "It's calling your name."

The boat tips port side and she loses her grip. He reaches out to grasp her arm and pulls her back to him.

"You were crazy to come out here in weather like this," she says.

"I'll take it a million times over being locked up in a cell."

"What about Brumewich? How can you leave your home behind?"

Julian taps on his heart. "It's in here. It's always gonna be here. Same as you."

Farer's Light looms ahead. Waves crash with terrible force against its walls. Julian, momentarily distracted, returns his attention to the helm. He fights to keep the boat steady.

"Forgive me," she says.

"Nothing to forgive. Grant caused this. Not you, or me, or my father. Just Grant."

"You're right. He did this. He has to pay. I swear to god, I'll make him pay."

Julian wraps his arm around her waist, pulling her so tight it hurts. "I believe you, Cass."

They're both unprepared when the wave rises up and washes over them. The force of the water tears Cassie from his grasp, dragging her with it off the boat, under the sea. She tumbles downward.

All is lost. She doesn't even want to help herself. She doesn't think she can live with knowing he was true to her, always. She should've known him better. She should've trusted him.

But her instincts do what her mind won't. Her lungs are in agony. *Must get air.* She raises her arms and pulls hard toward the surface. Not even sure if she's headed the right way.

She feels it then. Julian's hand reaching out to her. She grasps it and he holds her tight. Draws her to the surface. She splutters and chokes, struggling for breath.

They both turn at a flicker of light. Another vessel approaches in the distance. Julian pulls her onto the lifesaver he must've taken from the boat. "Hold on!"

But as she clings to it, a swell surges over him. When it passes, he's gone.

She turns to the boat, almost upon them now. It's the Coast Guard ship sent out to find Julian. "Help! He's drowning!" she shouts.

Divers are ready. The boat slows and they jump in. One locks her in a lifesaver's hold. The other dives under the water. A moment later he surfaces with Julian. Her lover's eyes seek hers and grow calm. It's the last thing she sees before her mind drifts away.

28

————————

I t's over. Cassie has learned all she can. Now she needs to regenerate. It's Friday, and she's already begged off work for today. She has till Monday to decide if she wants to return to that job or not.

She's catching up on everything she's neglected, trying to regain some sense of normalcy. Do the laundry. Clean the toilets. Dust and vacuum the house. Pay the bills and balance the checkbook. Shave. Clip her nails. Take a very long shower. Change into fresh clothing. And play with Gio— her sweet, wonderful, adorable companion who still tolerates her unconditionally despite her unintentional neglect of him.

In the evening she gets into bed early, though she's afraid she might time jump in spite of herself. Fortunately, this doesn't happen. Somehow her body understands she's finished what she needed to do. When she wakes in the morning, she feels better rested than she has since the whole surreal experience began.

Her promise to Julian remains foremost in her mind. She's never been more serious than when she swore to make Grant pay. It won't be easy. He killed a woman and got away with it. Though she's now a witness to that act, she's well aware no court of law will accept testimony provided by a self-proclaimed time-traveler. Moreover, she has no physical evidence, unless she counts her knowledge of the ring he bought for Teresa. But it's not proof of murder.

The phone rings after she's eaten breakfast and she feels sure it must be Grant. The thought makes her insides clamp up, but she makes herself answer. She can't avoid him forever, and she'd rather get it over with sooner rather than later.

"Hello?" She tries to sound relaxed, not like someone who's afraid a cold-blooded killer is calling.

"Cassie, hi," Grant says. "How are you feeling?"

"Much better." This at least is true.

"Are you up to having dinner with me this evening?"

Sorry, Jack the Ripper has me tonight. She doesn't say this, though she'd like to. She's hesitating, wondering if a delay of several more days will help her or not.

But then the word, "Sure," slips out before she can stop it.

"Pick you up at seven?"

"That works."

After they hang up, she doesn't move for several minutes while terror builds inside her. What has she done?

29

___

Cassie is in the barn finishing a drawing in pastels when she hears his car drive over the gravel and his door come open and shut. His footsteps create a feeling like ants running up and down her spine. But she has Julian's *Rêverie* playing in the background, and it gives her a measure of courage.

"Grant? I'm in the barn," she calls out to him.

"Hey there," he says, striding into her studio. To anyone else, he probably looks the same as always, but to her, he's taken on a sinister quality. His eyes, a lackluster blue, appear void of feeling. His hands —which she instantly pictures around her neck—are suffused with menace.

She forces herself not to shrink back as he approaches with swift steps, hugs her, and tries to kiss her. She turns her face just in time for his lips to brush her cheek instead.

He draws back to look at her. "Everything okay?"

"Sure." She reaches past him to turn off the music.

"Ready to go?" he says. He may be wondering why she hasn't put any effort into her appearance this evening. She's wearing a T-shirt, jeans, and sandals.

"Wouldn't you like to see my drawing? You were very anxious to look at my sketchpad last time you were here."

He's puzzled by her tone. "Yeah, okay." He shows a distinct lack of enthusiasm, for which she can't blame him. She's sure he doesn't want to see more pictures of Julian.

She leads him to her easel and steps out of the way to give him the full view. It's a sketch of Grant, actually. Standing outside Julian's house. He holds a large kitchen knife that he's about to slip into his backpack. She's witnessed this scene quite recently and was able to hold it in her memory long enough to capture it fairly well. The perspective is hers, from the second-floor window where she looked out and saw him.

"What the...?" he says.

"Do you like it?"

"What the hell is this supposed to be?"

"Can't you tell? I think it's pretty clear. That's Julian's house, in case you're unsure."

"Do you think this is funny?" he says.

"Not funny. Just accurate."

"This never happened."

"Well then, you have nothing to worry about," she says.

"Are you trying to blackmail me?"

"How could I, if it never happened?"

She watches his brain churning. *How do I find out how she knows this without admitting it happened?*

"The picture is a lie. I've never been outside Julian's with a knife. So why draw it?" he says.

She needs to take this further now. "I felt it was time. We've gotten to know each other pretty well over the past few weeks. At least, I feel as if I know you. I've been more distant, but I'd like to change that. You might be surprised to learn we're very much alike."

She's catching his interest now. "I was there the night she was murdered. At Julian's. I was watching you."

Is she imagining it, or does the blood drain from his face? "I was in his bedroom when I heard you come into the house," she continues. "I hid in his closet. I watched you read the note and take it away."

He can't doubt that she's telling the truth at this point. Because he can't imagine any other way she could know exactly what he did in Julian's room.

"I went to the window when you were leaving and saw you put the knife in your backpack," she says. "The knife you used to frame him. Oh, and I also saw you throw out the note in their garbage can."

He struggles to find his voice. "You're making this shit up. I don't understand why. Especially after all this time."

"I told you. We're alike. Well, I don't imagine I could actually have killed her, especially not with a knife. I really don't like looking at blood. I suppose I could poison someone if I had to. But that's neither here nor there. I was glad you killed her. And glad you made Julian take the fall for it. I hated them both for what they did to me." This part of her speech is much harder to get through, but she manages it.

"Have you told anyone about this fantasy of yours?"

"I'm not sure I should answer that question. Are you threatening me?" she says.

"Of course not. But if you mean what you say, and you're really on my side, you wouldn't be going around telling people that I killed someone."

"Probably not," she agrees.

"And what about the police? Did you tell this bullshit story to them?"

"That wouldn't be very smart of me, would it? I'd look really bad for not having said anything seven years ago. I'm pretty sure they could arrest me for withholding evidence. They might even figure I was your accomplice."

This next part is the hardest. She leans into Grant and gives him a long, slow, luxurious kiss. At the end she says, "I've kept your secret all these years. I'm not about to give it away now."

Then, as if this has been the most casual conversation in the world, she adds, "Shall we go now?"

30

____

Needless to say, they don't go. It would've been the most uncomfortable meal since Salome served up John the Baptist's head. Grant says, "Are you fucking kidding me? Dinner's off."

"I get it," she says. "Take your time thinking it over. In the end, I hope you'll understand you can be honest with me. Like I've been with you."

She's never seen anyone gun their car out of her driveway so fast. Buckets of gravel shoot out behind his tires.

Once he's left, she returns to the house and locks up carefully. Having predicted Grant would back out of their dinner date, she ate early and washed it down with a cup of coffee. Now she pours herself a second cup and brings it with her into the family room. It's still early so she switches on the TV to distract herself. She keeps changing the channel because there isn't anything entertaining enough to pry her thoughts from the contemplation of Grant's next steps.

At least Gio comes to her lap and soothes her with his gentle purrs. When the sun finally sets, however, she puts him outside and latches his cat door shut to keep him out of the house until morning.

He'll be fine. The weather is warm, and he knows how to take care of himself. She's only trying to protect him from possible harm. If anything happens.

She gathers a few items she'd like to keep with her tonight and turns out all the downstairs lights before heading upstairs. When she's finished using the bathroom, she gets into her mother's bed without changing into pajamas and turns out the lamp beside her. The house is completely dark now. The coffee has made her sleepless, leaving her with little to do aside from staring up at the ceiling, remembering her vow to Julian.

Eventually, she doesn't know when, she drifts to sleep, until the splintering of glass downstairs wakes her. Her eyes snap open and shift to the clock, which shows 2:13 a.m. She sits up and quietly lifts the phone receiver. She's about to place the call when she realizes there's no dial tone. Her hands tremble. *Fuck.* She hadn't meant to fall asleep. She'd hoped to hear him and use the phone before he had a chance to cut the line. He's been admirably stealthy. No doubt she heard nothing because he came on his bike. A car is much more noticeable and likely to be witnessed. Cassie knows something about that.

It's going to be much harder now.

Slipping out of the bed, she takes the two long pillows she brought up from the family room and places them under the blanket. With a little adjustment, they resemble the shape of a person close enough.

Sounds of falling glass come from the back of the house. He must be reaching in and opening the sliding door. Soon he'll be here.

She reaches under the bed for her father's bat that she placed there earlier. Though she's not religious, she blows a kiss up toward the sky. Knowing how many times his hands gripped this wood gives her courage.

The stairs creak once. Twice. Time is running out. She crouches on the other side of the dresser. He'll need to enter the room fully so she can swing at him. She's practiced the move, though she's no baseball player—a fact that sorely disappointed her father.

She hears the squeak of a door being pushed open. He's checking her bedroom first. Next will come the study and bathroom before he reaches here. She clenches the bat and gets ready. All at once, the room feels sweltering. Sweat oozes out of her pores.

A footstep sounds just outside the door. He pauses to take stock, she thinks. A few seconds later, he moves forward into the room, approaching the bed. Glimpsing him from her hiding place, she sees a loop of rope in his hand. How kind of him not to use a knife. He must've remembered she doesn't like the sight of blood.

He's about to lift off the blanket and discover the pillows. She has to act. Vaulting up, she takes a great swing with the bat, aiming at his head. But two things happen. One, her sweaty grip slips and fails to deliver as fast and hard a blow as needed. Two, he's so much quicker than she could've imagined. Raising his hand, he blocks the impact. She might've hurt his wrist, no more than that.

Knowing she won't get another chance, she drops the bat and leaps past him while he's still staggering. She races toward the stairs as his steps start thumping behind her. "Bitch!" he calls out.

She flies down to the first floor and turns toward the front door, but he's faster, gaining on her. He leaps and tackles her. Flashback to the beach as she crashes to the floor, but this time she fights harder, squirming and managing to turn so she's on her back facing him.

He sits on her, pinning her, pressing her wrists against the hard floor. She struggles to escape, kicking at him, raising her head to try to bite his arm. But then he lifts her right hand and slams it with incredible force against the wood. She screams in agony. The pain is excruciating. She's sure he's broken something.

"If you don't stop moving, I'll do that again," he says.

She grows still, waiting to see what's coming next. Tears leak down the side of her cheeks.

"It won't help you to kill me," she says. "I've told someone else all about you. If I die, she'll know it was you."

"I don't believe you. Who would you tell? You're like a hermit here. You don't have any friends."

"I sent a letter to my mother. She'll go to the police if you do anything to me."

"Your mother," he says. "I don't believe you. No way would you tell her you knew I was guilty and did nothing. You watched me take the murder weapon and didn't even try to stop me. You'd die before admitting that to her."

"Let me go!"

"Sorry. I can't allow you to create trouble for me." He moves his legs onto her upper arms to free up his hands briefly. With swift movements, he takes the rope from his jacket pocket, yanks her hair to lift her head, and slips the rope around her neck. Her head bangs when he drops it, but the pain is nothing compared to the sensation of the rope being tightened around her wind pipe.

Oh god, oh god. She thrashes her body, trying to hide her real purpose. Struggling to force her throbbing hand into her pocket. She would be screaming if she had air. She barely manages to grasp the jackknife and pull it out. But opening it with one broken hand... it isn't working... though she practiced for hours earlier.

As her lungs burn and she starts to lose her sight, the knife springs open. She thrusts it into his ass, the only part of him she can reach. He cries out and loses his grip on the rope. She sucks in air and jabs him with the knife again, this time his belly. He tumbles sideways, staring in disbelief at the blood spewing out.

She wastes no time shoving past him, scrambling to her feet, darting to the door. *Why didn't I leave it open?* It all takes time, snapping the bolt, turning the knob, pulling the door open. Already Grant is forcing himself up. A glance back shows her he's in an absolute rage.

The door swings wide and she vaults to the driveway, heading toward the street, aiming for her neighbor's house across it. She wants to scream but barely a whisper comes out from her scratched and damaged throat.

Grant's steps crunch the gravel in back of her. He grabs her shirt from behind; it tears as she keeps running. He reaches for her arm, his clammy fingers grip her, when lights appear in the distance.

They're headlights from a car turning onto her street. Grant's hands slip away from her. She keeps running, waving her arms, as the car races toward them. The police. They swerve into her driveway, brake hard. The doors fly open. Two men leap out, one who she recognizes as Officer Brooks, the nice man who helped her betray Julian.

They go after Grant, who's now dashing between the house and the barn, dripping blood in his wake. She follows behind, wondering what he's doing, because there's nothing back there but water.

Before they can reach him, he splashes into the harbor and dives beneath the surface. She guesses police aren't prepared for swimming pursuits—with all their heavy equipment they'd sink like boulders. The two officers stop at the edge and call out to Grant, ordering him to stop and come back. When he doesn't, one lights the water with the spray of his flashlight, while the other gets out his gun and shoots. She can't tell if a bullet strikes him or not, but it isn't long before the surface is still as glass and there's no further sight of him.

It doesn't surprise her Grant chose the water. He was of Brumewich after all. The sea doesn't distinguish between wicked and virtuous when it calls its creatures home.

31

———————

Three days later, the sea spits out what's left of Grant Wolcott at Thorne Cove. It didn't want him after all, and was clever enough to send him back to the scene of his unforgivable crime.

After two weeks have passed, Cassie is ready to move on. With her one hand in a splint, she gathers up the mementos of Julian she's kept all these years and puts the sealed box in storage. Briefly she considers throwing it out, but decides baby steps are sufficient for now.

Quitting her job has freed up her time. She's sure Maggie was happy to see her go, though her boss kindly pretended her departure would be a big loss to them. Maggie even offered to give her an excellent recommendation, despite that she's terrible at sales. She can't be bothered to try to convince anyone to buy something they're not already sure they'll love.

As she's brushing off dust and spiderwebs that came of her trip to the attic, the doorbell rings. Happily, the sound no longer makes her want to flee out the rear exit.

It's Officer Brooks. This will be the first time they've spoken since the night he and Officer Fanshawe rescued her. In the light of day, she sees he's changed in the years since Teresa's murder. The worry lines on his forehead and flecks of darkness in his eyes show the toll his work exacts.

She ushers him into the kitchen and offers him coffee, which he accepts. They sit across from each other at the table, him with his notepad and pencil.

"Do you have any questions for me before we get started?" he says.

"No one has told me who called you to my house." In all the madness of that night, she didn't think to ask.

"It was Helen Wolcott."

His answer astonishes her. "Mrs. Wolcott?"

"She told us she was concerned when Grant came home that evening in a fury. He wouldn't tell her what it was about, but she knew he'd been planning to take you to dinner."

"I'm still baffled. How did this lead to her calling the police at two-thirty in the morning?"

He swallows a sip of coffee. "Mrs. Wolcott had hired a man to watch her son."

"Seriously?"

"She wanted someone to keep an eye on him. The problem was, the guy fell asleep on the job. Otherwise we would've been here right away. Because when he finally woke up, he saw Grant's bike was gone, reported to Mrs. Wolcott, and she called us."

"Why was she having him watched?" She's starting to think she must've completely misunderstood the woman.

Officer Brooks lowers his cup. "She suspected he was responsible for Teresa's murder. And since then, she's apparently been tortured by the fear he might kill again. It worried her deeply when he started dating you. Another girl who'd had a relationship with Julian Reis, right?"

With nothing to gain by revealing Armando, not Julian, had dated Teresa, she remains silent.

"Mrs. Wolcott was concerned about his motives," he says. "Did he think you might know something? Could you be a threat to him?"

She wonders if it's much simpler than Mrs. Wolcott imagined. In Grant's eyes, Julian stole the love of his life. Grant's narcissism required he do the same in return.

"I'll be honest," he says. "Mrs. Wolcott often comes across as haughty. But she's clearly a woman of principle. My impression is she couldn't live with herself if her son killed again on her watch."

"I understand. I'm indebted to her. She saved my life." Cassie would not go so far as to call her a woman of principle. She'd been willing to lie for her murdering son. But at least she took action to prevent it from happening again. Her unsuccessful attempt to drive Cassie away from Grant had not been motivated by snobbery after all.

Officer Brooks raises his pencil. "A few things puzzle me."

"Go on."

"When did you begin to suspect Grant killed Teresa?"

When a meteorite landed and granted me the gift of travel through time. No, she doesn't say this. Instead, she weaves a tale that begins with Grant's uncomfortable reactions to her sketches of Julian and an accidental visit to Teresa's grave.

"I decided to test Grant," she lies. "I let on I had a friend who thought he and Teresa had a relationship. I asked if it was true and he angrily denied it. But the most interesting part was how hard he tried to get the name of my 'friend.'

"On another occasion, I led him into a discussion of jewelry. He told me his favorite place to buy gifts is Dorn Jewelers in Boston. So just to test him, I said in a teasing way, I guess one way to find out if you ever dated Teresa would be to ask Dorn to check their receipts."

"Interesting," Officer Brooks says. "We opened a safe in his office and found an engagement ring that came from there. Grant's and Teresa's initials engraved inside."

She nods her head. "It doesn't surprise me." *Since I've seen that ring before*, she doesn't say.

"Grant went ballistic over the jewelry thing," she goes on. "I managed to patch it up, sort of. Meanwhile, I was thinking if he killed her, he must've framed Julian somehow. Grant could easily have taken the knife from his house. You know it was always unlocked, don't you?"

She gets up, removes a drawing from where she left it in a drawer, and shows it to the officer. It isn't the original one she drew, which she destroyed. This one shows Grant leaving the house holding a knife, without details like the backpack. She doesn't want Officer Brooks thinking she must've been there and seen it with her own eyes.

"When I showed this to Grant, I knew from the look on his face that I'd guessed right. This happened on the evening before he attacked me," she says.

"You shouldn't have provoked him," he says. "You almost got yourself killed."

"It was the only way to force a confession out of him."

"He confessed?"

"Oh yes," she says. "He told me everything." It was true he confessed, but not that he revealed everything. She added that to protect herself if she ever slips up and reveals she knows more about the murder than she possible could.

"What good would the confession be if you were dead? Right? You took a terrible risk."

"I did try to defend myself, but as you know, that didn't go terribly well. Still, I also sent a letter to my mother, telling her what I'm telling you now. She would've brought it to you if I was killed." What she told Grant was another half-truth. She'd written to her mother, but there was nothing in the letter about hiding in Julian's house and watching Grant steal the knife.

"Why go so far to prove Grant guilty?" he says, though she thinks at this point he knows the answer.

"For Julian, of course. I did it for him."

32

———————

Cassie's health is restored. She's eating normally again and the headaches and exhaustion have disappeared. She still isn't sure whether these were side effects of the time travel, or the result of her mania to discover the truth and reveal it to the world. In the end, it doesn't matter.

In real life, Julian didn't survive his attempt to escape in the boat. In the past—the real past—she never went to Grant's house, never knew Grant was involved in any way. She never beckoned to Julian from the Wolcott dock, never jumped in the water to make him stop for her. Instead, she waited with Armando for his son who never came home.

The overturned boat was found near Farer's Light with no one onboard. All lifejackets were accounted for in its hold, meaning Julian hadn't been wearing one. It was she, in the altered past, who made him put it on. A man who'd spent his life on boats ought to have known better. Maybe the rush to get away, and the strain of navigating through an unrelenting storm, kept him from taking the most basic steps to ensure his safety. Or maybe it was a choice.

Unlike with Grant, the sea swallowed Julian and kept him as its own.

Armando moved to New Bedford several months later. He said his lobstering days were over, though she's not certain what he planned to do instead. At some point, he must've considered telling the police he was the one in a relationship with Teresa. But it wouldn't have cleared Julian's name. After all, it was Julian who met with Teresa at Thorne Cove, and Julian who fled in the boat. These actions gave him all the appearance of guilt, and nothing Armando might've said could change it.

Cassie is moving to Boston in a few weeks. Her mother and Freddie are coming home to stay. "Florida's too hot in the summer," her mother said. "We can visit in winter."

She isn't certain what she'll do in the city, but it will have some relation to art. Maybe she'll find work as an assistant at a museum or gallery. Or she might pursue a degree in education that will allow her to teach. For the first time, the possibilities intrigue her, and the thought of leaving Brumewich no longer frightens her.

Julian had it right all along. You carry the things you love inside you.

She's about to take one last jump, and then she'll be done. Tomorrow she'll paddle out to the middle of Inner Harbor in her canoe and drop the meteorite into the water. She hopes that will keep her from ever trying to use it again.

After settling in bed with Gio beside her, she spins back to the place of her memory. She's just arrived outside Julian's house on Christmas Eve during her winter break from Syracuse. Snow has covered the yard in a thick, inviting blanket, but she resists the urge to wrap herself in it.

The window by the door is adorned with orange lights in the shape of a lobster. It's been a staple of their Christmas decorations for as long as she can remember. She knocks once before letting herself in.

Armando greets her on his way out. "Where are you going on Christmas Eve?" she says.

He carries a large red envelope and a small, wrapped box. She thinks it must be the necklace etched with the words, "Adoro-te," which he's bringing to the woman he loves. She imagines the poem *Para Teresa* written inside the card.

"It's a secret." He winks at her.

When he's gone, she and Julian sit by the fireplace and exchange gifts. He receives a painting she did of his mother from a photograph Armando loaned her. She gets a handknit hat and scarf that might've been purchased from Teresa.

"Play *Rêverie* for me," she says.

When he sits at the piano, she stands behind him with her arms around his shoulders, leaning into him.

As the beloved melody flows through her like the sea, she presses her face against his neck. After the last note is played, she moves beside him on the bench and he draws her into his lap, holding her close.

She whispers her last words to him. "You and me forever, Reis." She taps her hand against her heart.

The End.

BEFORE SHE WAS TAKEN

THE BEFORE SERIES BOOK TWO

For Kay

PART I

1

———————

Moonlight spills across the frayed mustard carpet to reach Nicki, splayed on her back atop the rock-hard mattress of her bed. The brightness wakes her as she had intended. At bedtime, Mother had lowered the shades, but Nicki had quietly raised them after she left.

The time is three in the morning. Her hands tingle as she rises and puts on her heavy blue hoodie over her pajamas. She crosses to the chair, trying not to look at the yellowed wallpaper with pictures of little girls in pigtails playing on a slide, on a swing set, in a sandbox, and splashing in a baby pool. However much Nicki grows—she turned sixteen last month—it feels like she's forever trapped inside the moments of childhood depicted on these four walls.

She picks up Cinderella, a large stuffed bear with one eye missing, and reaches under her skirt through the hole she slashed into her long ago. With the stuffing removed, the space serves as a hiding place for any cash she manages to steal, and for the treats she saves for Sadie. Nicki removes half of a Hershey's chocolate bar and pockets it before putting on her sneakers and tiptoeing to the door.

With practiced caution, she turns the knob, slips through the narrow opening, and silently closes the door behind her. She pauses to listen to Uncle's gruntlike snores from the room next to hers. It gives her some courage to confirm he's asleep. Unfortunately, she can't be certain about Mother, in the bedroom across the hall, who never makes a sound that can be heard outside her room.

Nicki proceeds to the stairs and descends them with delicate steps, careful to avoid the parts that creak the loudest. She's almost at the bottom and ready to congratulate herself, when the wood groans under her foot. Freezing in place, she listens for sounds of stirring.

After a minute passes without anyone coming, she decides it's safe to continue. Thankfully, the hall and kitchen have linoleum floors that allow her to cross quietly. The drawer, on the other hand, sticks to its frame and makes a horrible noise if she's not careful. She must open it for the flashlight, though, and she manages well enough. She'll worry about closing it later.

She takes a water bottle from the box by the counter before snatching the key to the shed from behind one of the shelves. Some time ago, she discovered where Uncle kept it by spying on him from inside the pantry.

Her last hurdle is the back door, so tight in its frame it has to be yanked open. It makes some noise and even rattles the house a bit, but it's too late to turn back now. She escapes outside and down the steps, where she pauses for a gulp of the brisk air scented with pine. A shiver skips down her spine at the sight of the moonlit trees, lurking around the edge of the property like rows of tall, spindly jailers.

She dashes across the carpet of pine needles to get to the shed, and lets herself in with the key, closing the door after her. Switching on the flashlight, she's careful not to aim it at the bed since no one likes to be woken with bright light in their eyes.

Four-year-old Sadie is curled under the blanket looking up at her. Her hair is matted and there's a dark smudge on her left cheek. She sucks on the tip of her thumb, with a filthy, threadbare rabbit missing most of its stuffing clutched under her arm.

Nicki sits on the mattress beside her and touches her hair. "Hey there," she whispers.

Sadie lowers her thumb. "Hey."

"I brought you a treat." Nicki takes out the chocolate bar.

Sadie sits up and leans against the wall. "Thank you."

"Should we have a tea party?"

Sadie nods.

Nicki arranges the rabbit and a stuffed dog with a monocle on either side of them. Recovering four plastic teacups piled in the corner, she sets them in front of everyone and pours a bit of water into the cups. "Sugar?"

"Yes, two please," Sadie says.

Nicki drops imaginary sugar cubes into her cup and turns to the rabbit. "Becca?"

"One half, please." Nicki provides the high-pitched voice of Becca the rabbit.

Pretending to struggle to break the cube in half, Nicki speaks in an aside to Sadie. "She only wants to make things difficult."

"I heard that," the rabbit voice replies.

"Mr. Fluffernutter doesn't need any. He doesn't like sweets," Sadie says regarding the dog.

"They, hem, interfere with my digestion." Nicki lends Mr. Fluffernutter a deep growly tone.

Sadie places a piece of her chocolate in front of Becca.

"I'd like half of that," the rabbit says.

"No!" Sadie says, laughing.

"Tomorrow let's take Becca to the salon and get her fur done," Nicki says.

"I went there yesterday!" Sadie does the rabbit voice. "Can't you tell?"

"Oh my, and a beautiful job they did too." Nicki winks at Sadie.

"Mr. Fluffernutter should get a pedicure," Sadie says.

"Hem, only if I may get the purple glitter polish," is Mr. Fluffernutter's response.

Sadie sips from her cup. "I want to see my mommy."

Nicki glances back toward the house. "Mother's sleeping now."

"Not her." Sadie makes a face. "My real mommy."

"She's your real mommy now. And he's your uncle."

Sadie shakes her head hard. Her face crumples and tears start to flow.

"Come here." Nicki moves everything out of the way and sits beside her holding the girl's hand in her lap. "You have to be patient. Things that are important take time."

"I miss her," Sadie whispers.

"I know. I'll take care of you. You have to trust me." But even as the words emerge from her lips, she hears the heavy shoes pounding down the back steps of the house and rushing toward them.

2

———

Rebecca hurries toward Dev as he waits for the garage elevator.

"Hey there," she says, slowing abruptly, becoming all casual, like she hasn't been waiting in her white Honda Fit parked near the entrance, watching for his return from work.

He glances back, surprised at her appearance. "Oh, hi. How are you?"

"Great. It's my night off," she says.

"Have anything special planned?"

"Maybe." She tries for an enigmatic smile, which only causes him to look puzzled.

The elevator doors open and he waits while she enters first. Her gaze drinks him in as he presses the button for their mutual floor. A marketing exec at a high-tech company, he's meticulously turned out in dark slacks and a white button shirt that contrasts beautifully with his toffee-colored skin. No jacket or tie because this is Silicon Valley, not Wall Street. As the doors slide together, the sensation of their being alone in an enclosed space causes a prickle of excitement inside her.

"You remember that new wine club I told you about?" she says.

His eyes light up with interest. Since the time some months ago when he passed her in the hall carrying a case of premium California cabernet, she's been aware of his obsession.

"I got my first shipment three days ago. And I know I should let the bottles rest, but I couldn't resist opening the pinot. Russian River Valley. It's amazing." She ought to use more precise descriptors to impress him—*earthy* or *spicy* or *notes of barnyard*—but she's never gotten the hang of that and is certain she'll screw it up.

"Really? Remind me what club this is," he says.

"It's called... wait, don't take my word for it. I'd feel terrible if you joined and didn't like the wine. Our tastes might be different."

"True, I never like the stuff that gets high ratings from *The Wine and Truth Journal*."

"Have you got a minute? You can come try it yourself."

He looks nervous at this point. No doubt it flashes across his mind that his girlfriend might not be thrilled by his interaction with this young, unattached neighbor. But the lure of wine is too strong. "Uh, sure, why not? Thanks."

They spill out of the elevator and he follows her into her living space. "Nice place," he says, glancing around. She's never been in his apartment but she assumes it's exactly the same, other than their decorating choices. Her furniture is only one step up from *college student*, but he shouldn't expect anything fancier from someone earning a pittance as a waitress. Although she does have some inherited income, it mostly goes toward paying the absurd cost of renting a measly one-bedroom unit in Silicon Valley.

The open bottle of pinot noir awaits them on the counter. She takes out two wide-bottom wineglasses and fills them a third of the way. Handing one to Dev, she clinks it with the other. "Cheers." Slipping into full connoisseur mode, she swirls the glass and sniffs the wine before sipping and swooshing it inside her mouth. She closes her eyes and parts her lips to breathe in and let the air open up the wine. Only then does she swallow and look at Dev, whose fathomless eyes are fixed on her.

"Have a seat?" She nods toward the couch, letting him settle there ahead of her. She brings the bottle along with her glass and sits right next to him, pinning him on one side with their arms nearly touching. He looks as if he'd like to switch to a chair, but doesn't want to seem rude.

Rebecca prompts Dev to talk about wine. While he waxes poetic regarding the optimum terroir for cab versus pinot, she wriggles out of the coat she has kept on until now. Underneath, she wears a short, ass-hugging black skirt and a lowcut silk camisole with no bra underneath. Quite accidentally of course, she pushes closer to Dev after tossing the coat behind the couch.

He loses his train of thought and compensates by slurping down the rest of his wine like lemonade on a hot day.

"So you like it?" she says.

"Love it."

It is, in fact, an absolutely delicious concoction that glides over the palette. It took many days of experimentation for her to identify a pinot noir that would be exactly to Dev's taste.

"Let me get you some more." She leans past him for the bottle and gives him a telescopic view of her breasts while she fills his glass. When she's done, she *unintentionally* loses her balance and falls into his lap. He grasps her waist to help her, which naturally leads to her arms wrapping around his neck. He's not the man to resist kissing her now, and the rest follows because, of course, *wine*. Besides, he must be thinking if he's going to get nailed for cheating, he may as well experience the full benefit of it.

The sex ends too quickly, which is both the good and bad of it. It's like the adrenalin rush of jumping off a cliff as opposed to the gentle, euphoric sensation of gliding to the bottom with wings.

They hold each other briefly afterward, while she questions her life choices. Eight months ago, she became a time traveler after being sparked by an unusual rock she encountered off the trail during a hike. At first she thought she was having unbelievably realistic dreams. But before long, she learned she could pick the moment she wanted to revisit simply by concentrating on it. Her time jumps ended naturally whenever she achieved a sense of completion or simply when she could no longer remain awake. She made up a name to describe the process—*mindcast*. Her body stayed home while her consciousness leapt backward to occupy younger versions of herself.

Through experimentation, she found that her actions in the past never changed anything in the present. It was as if an alternate time thread opened up... like there might be infinite possible variations. Mindcasting allowed her to experience some of these variations, without, fortunately, becoming stuck in any one of them. In the end she always returned to what she thought of as *real-time.*

It soon came to her how she could use this power to do things no one but she would ever know about or remember. If she seduced Dev during a mindcast, he would have no idea in real-time. She would have all the pleasure of fucking him, without any of the complications.

It took eleven jumps to perfect the method of seducing Dev. Since then, they had done it seventeen times using this exact scenario. Despite telling herself it was enough, she kept returning to this day like a glutton unable to forgo cheesecake at the end of each meal. Each time, remorse and disgust filled her afterward, but it wasn't sufficient to stop her from repeating the same act on the next night or the night after that. She imagines she's some sort of sex addict, but even more twisted because she craves that extra level of fervor that comes of his thinking this is the first time he's ever touched her in his life.

Escaping before the inevitable moment of extreme awkwardness, she begins her return journey through time. The inside of her head grows hot and her vision fades. But this time, instead of seeing only blackness, she pictures four-year-old Sadie as if through a shroud. An instant later her sister is gone, disappearing as she did outside their house nineteen years ago, when Rebecca was six and supposed to be watching her.

3

When Rebecca wakes in the morning, she gets the sinking feeling she's overslept again. A glance at the time on her phone confirms she should've been at the wildlife refuge an hour ago.

Dammit. Her eyes used to pop open at eight every day, regardless of when she went to bed. But lately a feeling of lethargy has come over her. Since nothing else has changed in her life, it has to be related to the mindcasts. At first, she thought they only occupied a flicker of a second in real-time. Somewhere she'd read that dreams pass that quickly, and she had for some reason assumed her time travel worked similarly. But now she wonders if the mindcasts rob her of as much sleep as the number of hours she remains in the past.

She races through her shower and blasts her hair with the dryer at the maximum setting. Glad for her short cut that dries quickly, she only wishes she had more time to style it. A bit of gel tames it, at least.

After tossing on a cotton top and jeans, she calls Gary. "Hey, running late this morning. I'll be there in forty-five."

"Um, Rebecca, this is like the fifth time this month? Sarah already did a bunch of your assignments," Gary says.

"I'm really sorry. It won't happen again."

"You told me that last week. I think you should take a break, like, get your shit together?"

Get your shit together. That stings. "I'm a volunteer, for god's sake." It feels like he's expecting a lot from a free employee.

"Yeah, no kidding, but we still need to be able to count on you."

"Please give me another chance."

"Let's give it till after the holidays? Call me then if you're ready to commit to a schedule." He ends their conversation before she can protest any further.

She slumps down onto the nearest chair, thinking of the animals she's helped care for since she began volunteering three years ago. Angus the barn owl who loves to be rinsed off with the hose on hot days. Sir Lancelot the gray fox, an expert climber. The Bobbsey Twin bobcats that wrangle with each other constantly. Even Jesse the king snake with his beautiful orange markings. She can't imagine how she'll get through the next two months without seeing them.

Eventually her empty stomach drives her out for coffee and a sesame bagel at Mathilda Café. She settles into her favorite little table by the window, where the bright sunlight warms her. It's diverting at least to watch people passing on the sidewalk, enjoying the Bay Area weather that feels more like summer than fall. When she's finished eating, she too sets off for a walk along the streets of the nearest residential neighborhood.

After several blocks, she notices a white van creeping past a house where children are playing outside. Most likely it's a service vehicle looking for a particular address, but just in case, Rebecca takes a picture of the back of it, making sure to get a clear image of the license plate. She often photographs suspicious-looking cars, and pedestrians who linger too long or stare too intently at houses and the families living in them.

She organizes the pictures by street and date and stores them in files on her computer. If a serious crime or an abduction occurs in the area, she'll bring the photos to the attention of local law enforcement. Once a murder did happen and she got in touch with Freddie, a detective who worked on her sister's disappearance. He took copies of her pictures and later told her they helped in solving the case, though she believed he only said that to be kind.

Rebecca knows her habit is weird and probably won't make a difference. But if it ever leads to even a single success... to a crime being thwarted, a killer being apprehended, or a child being found... it will have been worth any amount of time she put into it. Sadie might've been saved if someone had noticed a suspicious vehicle trolling the streets of Windlake and snapped a picture, or at least made a note of its license.

When she returns to her apartment and downloads the photo of the van, she glances through the other images in her collection. It occurs to her she could make a collage out of them, particularly the older photos that aren't likely to be of use anymore. She would have to blacken any identifying information, like license plates, house numbers, and people's faces. Maybe give it a title, like *Fear and Suspicion in Suburbia* or *Diary of a Madwoman*.

During the rest of the afternoon, she solves logic puzzles, a hobby she's enjoyed since high school. She's always had a knack for them, a skill that must've come from her father, a mathematics professor at U.C. Berkeley. But unlike him, she decided not to pursue a career based on numbers. She decided not to pursue a career in anything, in fact.

She eats the leftover Thai takeout for an early dinner before rushing out to her job at Pythonella, making certain to arrive on time, especially since she's been late for three out of four of her last shifts. After losing her volunteer position this morning, she's determined to hang onto her one actual, paying job.

But as the night continues, she finds her attention wandering. Somehow she writes down the garlic pasta with Cajun cauliflower only to have the customer later insist she asked for the basil pasta with roast chicken. All the ladies in their large group were talking at once when Rebecca took the order. They ought to shush up if they expect to get the meal they want.

Then ten minutes after that debacle, she delivers an order for two to the wrong couple. Worse, they don't notice immediately, causing the food to be left on the table for several minutes before Rebecca is called back. This results in two wasted dinner entrees that can't be re-delivered, and two customers unhappy to have to wait another twenty minutes for their food.

At the end of the evening, Joanna the owner and head chef calls Rebecca into her private office that somehow always smells of rosemary, despite the myriad of scents produced in the kitchen next door. "Got something on your mind lately?" Joanna says.

"No, I'm fine." Rebecca decides her wisest course is to pretend everything is normal.

"So this is the best we can expect from you from now on?"

"I thought I did okay."

"*Okay* is not the way we ever want anyone to describe Pythonella. How many people do you think will eat here, if the reviewer says the food is *okay,* the ambiance, *okay*, and the service, *okay*?"

"I'll try to do better."

"You cost us money tonight."

"Take it out of my tips."

"I doubt you earned the tips to cover it."

This is close to the truth, especially since her distracted behavior has led to stingy rewards.

"I'm going to cut one of your work days. Jaqueline will take Saturdays."

"I get my best tips on Saturdays. How about Thursday?"

"You show me what *outstanding* service you can provide, and we'll see about getting Saturday back for you," she says. "Now go on home. Get some rest. You look like you need it."

It's true she's been a lousy employee. Joanna has every right to cut down her work week. But it hits her all at once how much she hates this job. That clenched feeling inside her stomach isn't coming from the thought of losing a day's work, but from heavy disappointment that she didn't get fired outright.

"I quit," she says.

Joanna raises her eyebrows. "You can't do that. I can't replace you that fast."

"Try Jaqueline," she says before leaving the office and walking straight out of the restaurant, where the crisp night air cools her face and the tension slips from her joints.

It isn't until she's halfway across the parking lot that she notices a small red Kia parked on the right side. She doesn't recognize it as belonging to any of the other employees. The streetlamp above the car illuminates a man in the driver's seat. His profile seems familiar to her and there are marks around his neck. A tattoo. It's too dark to tell if it depicts an eagle with wings spread on both sides. But it might.

A spike of adrenalin propels Rebecca to her Honda. As soon as she's inside, she locks all the doors and checks her rear view. The man is getting out of the Kia. She turns her key, the engine cranks, but the car doesn't start. *Come on, come on*. Checking the mirror again, she glimpses the man stepping in the direction of her car. A second turn of the key, the engine cranks. *Go, go, go*. It finally starts and she throws it into reverse, hits the gas, brakes hard, shifts forward, and careens out of the parking lot, right into the street without checking who's coming. A car squeals behind her and honks as she speeds away.

The man who got out of the Kia had white hair. Bray Reamer's hair was light brown when he was sent to prison. But that was a long time ago.

$$4$$

For the next few days, Rebecca alternates between long walks and working on her collection of math puzzles. Since her mother left her an inheritance that came from her grandfather, a commercial property developer, she doesn't exactly need to race into a new job.

Sadie has begun appearing in her dreams again. When Rebecca wakes, though, she usually can't remember anything that happened aside from having seen her sister. Except for one recent dream, where Sadie arrived at her apartment all grown up, insisting her so-called disappearance was nothing more than a product of Rebecca's imagination.

By the end of the fourth day, she craves another mindcast rendezvous with Dev. It's in her thoughts when she leaves her apartment to pick up dinner from Hola's, and finds herself face to face with Dev and his girlfriend in the hall.

"Rebecca, hi," he says, seeing her approach. "Have you met my girlfriend, Lisa?"

Lisa is a striking woman of Asian heritage, with long sleek black hair and an irresistible dimpled smile. Caught off guard, Rebecca hopes her face reveals no hint of the lust that filled her only seconds ago while she was imagining Lisa's boyfriend having sex with her.

"Oh right, Dr. Sheng, isn't it?" Rebecca says, recalling that the woman has somehow already qualified as a pediatrician though they look the same age.

"Call me Lisa." She flashes her killer smile as the elevator arrives and she and Dev wait for Rebecca to enter first.

"Rebecca works at Pythonella," Dev says.

"Oh, I love that place! Are you the chef?" Lisa says.

"I don't work there anymore." Rebecca leaves Lisa to imagine she might've been the chef. No reason to admit she got fired for failing at a job anyone can learn to do passably well in about two weeks.

"Are you starting your own restaurant?" Lisa says.

Rebecca shrugs. "We'll see." As if this is an actual possibility.

The elevator doors open as Dev tells her, "We'd love to eat there."

She almost snorts, picturing slabs of burnt toast and undercooked eggs artfully arranged on decorative plates. "You'll be the first to know." She rushes past them to the street, but can't resist glancing back. Pressed together, Dev and Lisa stare into each other's eyes with lovesick expressions. They're so ridiculously gorgeous and exotic, they might as well be rehearsing for the role of this year's celebrity golden couple. Rebecca feels like retching.

Seeing them together has effectively destroyed her appetite for sex with Dev tonight. Instead, she spends the evening eating her chicken mole in front of the TV, re-watching the Harry Potter films starting from the first until she falls asleep in the middle of the third.

In the morning she gets a text from her father's wife asking if she's coming to their barbecue this afternoon. They invited her two weeks ago but she never answered. She's about to make an excuse when she remembers she has something she wants to discuss with him. She texts back accepting the invitation before she can change her mind again.

Rebecca and her father barely get along. She used to blame it on his being one of those people who don't connect well with children. Someone who had to be talked into having them by her mother. But then, in the seven years since she left his home at age eighteen, he married for the second time and his twelve-year-younger wife promptly gave birth to two boys—Tyler who's now five, and Kevin who is three. Rebecca has seen the way he dotes on them, nothing like what she recalls from her own childhood.

She's half an hour past the start time when she reaches their house in Berkeley. The shrieks of the boys playing in the backyard draw her to the side gate. Part of her misses this home where she grew up after her mother died. It's early November, and the gingko trees are splayed out like golden sheaves, while the Chinese pistache in the corner flaunts a full circlet of burnished red leaves. Despite the appearance of fall, temperatures still hover in the seventies, typical for California this time of year.

A dog that looks part German Shephard, part Husky, barks and dashes toward her.

"Scratch!" her father calls out. "No barking!"

Rebecca holds out her hand allowing the dog to sniff. "New family member?" she says as her father approaches.

They give each other a fleeting hug. "We got her six months ago," he says. "Has it been that long?" He's wearing his relaxing-at-home uniform, a gray T-shirt and khaki pants with enough pockets to accommodate a small toolbox worth of supplies.

"I thought you never wanted a dog." She spent the desolate nights following her mother's death wishing for one to share her bed.

He nods at his oldest. "Tyler was relentless."

Rebecca waves across the lawn at her father's wife cooking hamburgers on the barbecue. "Hey there, Marie."

"Hi, glad you could make it."

Unsurprisingly, Rebecca detects a rebuke in her tone. Probably for the two-weeks-late response to her text, the half-hour-late arrival at the house, and other offenses Rebecca isn't even aware she committed.

The dog rejoins the two boys, who are tackling each other over a ball. "Hey, kiddos, where's my hug?" Rebecca calls out.

They race to be first to squeeze her around the waist.

"Who's going to toss me the ball?" Rebecca plays catch with her stepbrothers and the dog while her father helps Marie prepare the burgers. Kevin, with a recent buzzcut that makes his head look rounder, says, "Look, Dad built us a treehouse!"

"Oh yeah? Can you show me?" She's seen it before but Kevin is young enough not to remember the last time she came.

He takes her hand and leads her to the tree, while Tyler races past them, swinging up the ladder to be first into the structure. The disappointed Kevin follows with Rebecca behind him. She peers at the two boys seated cross-legged inside. "This is so cool." Envy burns her up inside. All she and Sadie asked for was a rope swing but her father put it off with lame excuses. She forces that remembrance aside, smiling as the boys display the toys that live in the hideout.

"Lunch is ready," Marie says.

Tyler and Kevin jump up and scramble down the ladder as soon as Rebecca gets out of the way. They gather at the picnic table, where the food has already been laid out.

"Where are the hot dogs?" Tyler says.

"You told me you wanted burgers," Marie says.

"I want a hot dog!" He pouts.

"Me too," says Kevin, though clearly his heart isn't in it.

"Well this is what we have," Marie says.

Tyler pushes his plate to the ground and the dog wastes no time in snatching up the meat. "Scratch ate my hamburger!" Tyler looks like he regrets it now.

The parents exchange exasperated looks. "We don't have any hot dogs," Marie says.

"I'll get some," Rebecca's father says.

"No." Marie's voice is sharp. "I know what kind he likes. I won't be long." She leaves right away, clearly anxious to avoid being stuck alone with her stepdaughter.

Rebecca is thinking how fast she would've been sent up to her room with nothing to eat if she behaved like this at Tyler's age. But no one has a harsh word to say to him. The boys shove in handfuls of potato chips before returning to the yard to toss the ball for Scratch, leaving Rebecca and her father alone at the table.

"Beer?" he says.

"Sure."

He opens two cold ones from the cooler and hands one across to her.

"Nice beard," she says. He was cleanshaven last time she saw him. "It's kind of reddish."

"Like this used to be." He rubs the top of his mostly bald head. "You look a little tired. Are you still working at that restaurant?"

"I quit a few days ago."

His thick eyebrows raise up. He never wanted her to be a waitress. "So what are you doing?"

"Nothing, Dad. Absolutely nothing."

"Seriously? If you're not working, you could at least take some classes."

It's their age-old argument. "Classes in what? I'll find another job soon enough."

"As a waitress." He says it exactly as he might say *hooker* or *drug dealer*.

"Maybe. It's a perfectly good profession. You act like it's beneath me."

"If you were happy being a waitress, I wouldn't say anything about it."

"How do you know if I'm happy or not?"

"Tell me, then. Are you happy being a waitress?"

He knows she can't lie to him. She swigs from her beer.

"You were so good at math," he says. "You should do something that challenges you."

"I guess I ought to become a math professor like you."

"Why not, if you have the ability? You'll never know unless you go to college. There's a lot of different things you can do with a math degree."

"It's too late for me."

"Don't be crazy. You're twenty-five. You've got all the time in the world."

"Do I?" She wraps her hands around the weeping bottle. "Do you ever think about her anymore?"

There isn't any question who *her* is. "Of course I do," he answers gruffly.

"Then I don't know how you can…"

"What? Lead a happy life? Maybe you'd rather I acted like your mother."

"That's a terrible thing to say." Her mother had taken pills. It might've been suicide, or it might've been an accident. Either way it came to the same thing.

She lowers her voice. "I think I saw him the other day."

"Saw who?"

"You know. Reamer."

Her father stares at her.

"When I was leaving work, he was in a car watching me."

"Why would he do that?"

"I don't know. Maybe he blames us for the long sentence he got."

"If he did it, he knows he got off easy," her father says. "I'm sure you imagined it was him in the car. He lives in Fresno now."

"Only a few hours to drive here from there."

He takes a long slurp from his bottle. "Are you still seeing that therapist?"

Frustration fills her. "You never believe anything I say. You never have."

"That isn't true."

Kevin wails and she glances back to see him flat on his butt. "Tyler pushed me!" he cries out.

"I shouldn't have come." She stands up.

"You're letting him win, you know," her father says.

"What do you mean?"

"He got two of our family already. Don't let him take another."

"What can I do about it?"

"Everything." He rises and goes to his sons.

5

———————

Rebecca leaves her father's house before Marie returns from the market. She should've known better than to go there. Seeing him just makes the grief resurface. Maybe when her brothers grow older, she can have a better relationship with them, but not if their parents' spoiling turns them into entitled adults.

After returning home, she pours herself a glass of wine and sits on the couch, staring at nothing. Her life is shit. She has alienated the few friends she once had, lost her job that helped pay the bills, and been put on leave from the volunteer work that brought her some happiness. She has a lover who is literally a phantom. Her father and his family will probably want nothing further to do with her following today's performance.

She knows deep down that he gave her good advice regarding college. It could be exactly what she needs to get her life back on track, if only she could motivate herself to get started. But the to-do list overwhelms her. Researching college programs... deciding which career track interests her the most... filling out and submitting applications... and possibly having to arrange a move if the place that accepts her is too far. She can't wrap her head around any of this, particularly the moving part. These days she feels as if she's a rare creature whose travels on earth are not meant to involve distance, but time. All because of the average-looking stone that threw a spark at her. She had thought little of it then, until the mindcasts began. Even now, she can't be certain the two events are related, but her instinct says they are. She wishes she had taken the rock home with her. It would be impossible for her to ever locate it again, particularly since she encountered it off-trail.

She isn't sure how long she sits in a vegetative state before hunger finally drives her to the kitchen. Not feeling like going out or even ordering in, she prepares an English muffin with melted cheese to accompany the bit of leftover Mexican food she still has in the fridge. She opens a fresh bottle of Syrah and drinks two glasses with her meal.

When she eventually gets into bed, she's planning on reading herself to sleep. Instead, her thoughts turn to Dev. What harm could there be in paying him a visit in the unalterable past and seducing him? It's not as though she forces him into anything; he enjoys himself as much as she does.

After ten more minutes of rationalization, she sets her thoughts to the time and day when she always meets up with him. Before long, she feels the familiar burning inside her head, and the dizzying sensation of flipping back in time. She follows the script as usual, pretending to accidentally run into him outside the elevator, telling him about the pinot noir, and inviting him into her apartment. They sit on the couch, drinking, while he drones on about wine production methods.

Part of her wants so much to be with him, especially after the wrenching disappointments of the last few days. But another part is watching as if outside her own body—which is, in fact, a fairly accurate description of her situation, given that her present-day mind has jumped back into a little-bit-younger version of herself.

But just as she prepares to reach over and pour more wine for him—starting the all-important seduction phase of this whole charade—she suddenly feels as if she's in the middle of a poorly written romance novel, with her as the desperate, insecure heroine.

Laughter bubbles out of her, building up, making her whole body shake while tears sprout from her eyes.

Dev is perplexed, maybe wondering if he's the oblivious butt of her private joke. "Um, did I say something?"

"It's just that... the wine... the situation... you... me..." She loses control as her laughter morphs into sobbing.

"Are you okay? Maybe I should go."

It takes a moment for her to manage to speak again. "No, I just... I think I really need someone to talk to."

"You have a girlfriend you can call?"

She shakes her head. "Pathetic, I know. My life is completely fucked up and it's my own fault. It all started when I was six. I'm a terrible person."

"No, you're not. You're very nice." He checks his phone.

"I was supposed to be watching my little sister. She was only four. But I ditched her to play with my friend. Sadie wandered off to the front yard by herself." She has to gulp a few times before she can finish this. "That was the last time I ever saw her."

She's not sure what to expect. She hasn't told anyone about Sadie in years. He's just staring down at his hands saying nothing.

"I still don't know what happened to her. There's a guy... I think he did it. But there was zero evidence. Two years after she disappeared, my mother OD'ed on Ambien."

All she wants is some comforting words and a warm hug. Reassurance that she did nothing any other six-year-old would not do. A pat on her back and a kind voice telling her things will get better.

He gets up from the couch. "Sorry about what happened. I wish I could stay and talk about it. But I'm meeting my girlfriend in a half hour. I have to go."

Her mouth falls open in disbelief. *Meeting my girlfriend...* Rebecca knows for a fact that Lisa is at a conference in Chicago right now. It's why she chose this day.

When he was fucking her, he never had to run off and meet his girlfriend.

He slinks across the room and out the door, pausing only to twist the knife with his final words. "Thanks for the wine. It's not my style, though."

When the door is shut behind him, she takes his glass and flings it at the wall. It shatters into a thousand pieces, dripping wine like blood onto her floor.

6

———————

Rebecca knows what she has to do. She's known ever since she first gained the ability to transmit her consciousness back in time. Fear has kept her from it, though. Fear of learning that Sadie's suffering was even worse than she could've imagined. Fear that she lacks the fortitude to handle the horror of what her sister faced.

But her life has hit rock bottom and she has nothing more to lose. Her father's words ring inside her: *You're letting him win... don't let him take another.* He had been speaking metaphorically about the ways she was failing at life. But he could equally well have been referring to other possible victims. Bray Reamer finished serving his sentence six months ago. What if he took another child?

Nothing was ever proven against him. A year after Sadie disappeared, police arrested him for selling marijuana he cultivated in the backyard of the house he was renting. When they searched inside, they found child pornography. He was selling that too.

He lived a mile from their house and he was the strongest suspect the police ever identified. When he tried to skip bail and escape to Mexico, he was caught and brought back to stand trial for drug and child pornography trafficking charges.

They searched inside and out but never found any evidence of Sadie having been at his house. A whole year had passed by the time of his arrest, giving him plenty of opportunity to obliterate any evidence of her. The FBI dug up the yard and brought in dogs to sniff everywhere, but still nothing turned up. Again and again, they interrogated Reamer without his ever admitting having anything to do with Sadie's abduction. With no confession and no proof, law enforcement had to drop the case against him.

He served seventeen years for his other crimes, but now he's out, and Rebecca is afraid he might be stalking her.

After her morning coffee, she takes down the Sadie box and unfolds the newspaper article in which Reamer's arrest was reported. It contains a bleary, black and white photograph, which she raises closer to her eyes. Could this be the man she saw in the restaurant parking lot? She can't be certain—it was dark and she didn't get a direct view of him.

Though she would much rather not, she tries to commit his face to memory. The odd choice of where to part his hair, too far to the right, almost like he meant to do a combover but he had too much hair for that. The plump nose and thin lips. The tattoo of an eagle reaching from behind to encircle his neck with its wings. That alone should be enough to identify him if he doesn't wear something to cover it up, and hasn't had it removed.

She sets the article aside and opens the photo album. Her mother took many pictures of Sadie from birth to four years, more than she took of Rebecca. Sadie sleeping in her crib... with chocolate cake smeared on her face at her first birthday... half-buried in a pile of leaves... on a sled with their father in Lake Tahoe. There had been videos too, many of them, but these were all gone. Her mother destroyed them, saying that each time she watched one, it was like someone reaching into her chest and pulling out her beating heart, and yet she couldn't stop herself.

Rebecca thinks of this as she comes to the photo of her and Sadie in their pajamas, hugging each other tight with the Christmas tree behind them. It's too much for her and she has to close the album.

You're letting him win. She may not be able to beat him but she could at least mount a challenge. Through some miracle, she has gained an ability that may be unique in the world. It suddenly feels unbelievable that she's waited this long to use it for good. On the contrary, she's wasted it in the worst possible manner.

She'll take the first step today, she decides. This calls for putting a little effort into her appearance for a change. She dresses in her black straight leg jeans, a cream-colored blouse, and her fitted, green jacket. She styles her hair and dabs on lip gloss and eye-liner before setting out in her Honda Fit.

Her hands are clammy against the steering wheel as she drives toward Windlake underneath a solid bank of gray clouds. She expects they'll burn off by noon, as they generally do, though California is in desperate need of rain.

The last time she saw the house she was eight years old. By then her parents were divorced and her father had purchased the home in Berkeley. Her mother showed consideration in choosing to die while Rebecca was with her dad for the weekend. The timing was why she never believed the death was accidental. Well, this and one other reason. Her mother had stopped writing after Sadie was taken, and sometime before she died, she destroyed every copy—electronic and paper—of the one novel she'd completed, which had never been published. It still caused a deep ache inside Rebecca that her mother had chosen to eradicate this deeply personal thing she had created instead of leaving it for her daughter to savor as an adult, as her one remaining connection to her lost mother. At times it was hard not to hate her for what seemed like needlessly cruel and selfish actions, but she would remind herself to blame it instead on the sickness that had come over her mother.

Her father didn't bring her back to Windlake after that, figuring no good could come of Rebecca returning to the place where she'd experienced so much tragedy. He moved her toys, books and clothing to his house, before selling everything her mother owned, placing the proceeds into a trust since she was only eight.

Rebecca lets the GPS guide her to her former home. The freeway isn't crowded at this time, and after a while, she notices a small red car behind her, reminding her of the Kia that was parked at the restaurant. At first she shrugs it off as paranoia, then ten minutes later when it's still following her, she tries to glimpse the person in the driver's seat. But the sunlight reflecting off the front windshield makes it impossible to see inside the vehicle.

The driver maintains the same distance, even when Rebecca reduces her speed. After going another fifteen minutes with the car continuing to shadow her, she takes the next exit. To her great relief, the driver speeds past her on the freeway instead of following her.

Pulling up to a pump at the nearest gas station, she lowers her forehead on the steering wheel. She needs to pull herself together. Plenty of people own red cars, and quite possibly none of them belong to Bray Reamer. Even if it *was* him... she can't let him rattle her. Everything depends on her ability to keep a cool head.

After filling her tank, she returns to the freeway and listens to her favorite wildlife podcast until reaching her exit. The GPS guides her to her former home, but when she pulls up in front, she can't believe it's the place where she grew up, though the address is printed right there on the mailbox.

Before getting out, she leans across the seat to stare through the passenger window. In her memory, their house had wood siding painted gray, and a brown shake roof. Now the building is blue stucco with a red tile roof, white trim and a burgundy door. But the worst of it is, the majestic California oak that once stretched across their front lawn is gone.

Whenever she dreams of her childhood home, it's like a black and white Edward Gorey etching, with curved and crisscrossing branches making a jigsaw puzzle of the house behind them. Though its mood was somber and mysterious, she preferred it a thousand times to this thing it has become, a fourth of July centerpiece in Happy Town, USA.

The neighborhood has changed as well. Two new houses sandwich her old home, where once a weed-infested field surrounded their property. Across the street, a line of identical residences in garish shades has taken the place of a modest ranch house. Goats often grazed in its overgrown front yard.

On the positive side, it's hard to imagine a child being kidnapped here without anyone noticing.

Rebecca emerges from her car and approaches the house. A child in the back lets out the kind of playful cry she and Sadie would make when they ran through the sprinklers. She rings the bell and waits until shoes tap across the floor inside and the door comes open. A harried young mother holding a toddler against her hip looks at her with annoyance. Though it's not even eleven, the woman's eyes already wear a *get-me-out-of-here* glint. But Rebecca pretends not to notice and smiles at the child, causing her to turn away and smother her face against her mother's armpit.

"Sorry to bother you," Rebecca says, "but I used to live here and I was wondering if I could take a quick look inside. You know, for old time's sake."

A boy of about four-years-old walks up behind his mother and latches onto her leg.

"I'm busy, as you can see. I thought you were someone else." After this explanation of why she opened the door to a stranger, she starts to close it.

"My name is Rebecca Danser. My sister and I lived here when we were quite young."

The woman pauses to squint at her. "Danser...? Oh my god. It was your sister who..." She lays a protective hand on her boy as if danger might be lurking nearby.

"That's right. It would mean a lot to me if I could look around."

"Of course, I'm so sorry. Come in." She moves aside for Rebecca. "The realtor told us. They have to disclose that, even though it's been a long time."

"It didn't bother you?"

"It didn't seem that... whoever did it... would still be hanging around here. And the neighborhood has changed a lot. Right? I think it was more rural."

"Yeah, it wasn't anything like it is now." Rebecca hopes she finds this statement reassuring. She follows the woman and her kids into the kitchen, drawn by the heavy aroma of brownies in the oven. Somehow it conveys a feeling of home and family, though her own mother tended to burn everything she tried to bake.

Noticing Rebecca's confusion on glancing around, the woman says, "We're the third owners since your family moved out. All of us remodeled to some extent. I think we did the most. New appliances, cupboards, counters, floors, everything."

"It looks nice," Rebecca says. Like a page out of *House Beautiful*. Not like what she remembers of their old kitchen, where her mother always complained about the peeling floors, one electric burner that didn't work, and the stains on the countertops.

They continue to the room in the back, where their family had spent most of their time.

"New carpeting and paint," the mother says.

Her little boy, growing more courageous, approaches Rebecca. "Do you like dinosaurs?"

"My favorite is triceratops. Do you have one?"

He brightens and bounds up the stairs.

The opening to the backyard has been changed to French doors, but she can still picture her mother at the glass watching as they played outside. Now there's a gated swimming pool and a fancy play structure, but then they had a blow-up pool, a sandbox, and a short plastic slide.

She turns back, about to give up on the idea that there is anything left of her family here, when her gaze shifts to a familiar sight. "You kept the stone fireplace."

"Oh yes, we love it." The mother bounces the baby, who is starting to squawk.

Rebecca drops down on the floor beside it and turns on her phone flashlight. A timer buzzes in the kitchen.

"My brownies." The mother rustles out of the room.

Rebecca finds what she's looking for. *R & S*, their first name initials that they scratched with a sharp rock onto a dark stone on the right side. The *S* is barely legible because Sadie had insisted on doing hers. Rebecca touches the letter, squeezing her eyes shut, trying to picture her sister crouched there beside her as she was on that day.

"Whatcha doing?" The boy runs toward her carrying a box.

She shuts off the flashlight and sits on the floor as he dumps out his toys beside her. "Triceratops." He raises a large plastic specimen.

While he names each dinosaur, his mother brings them brownies and the toddler girl joins them on the floor, preferring to chew on a brontosaurus head. When Rebecca finishes eating, she thanks the woman, compliments the boy on his collection, and leaves the house grateful for this reminder of family connection. Seeing her former home has strengthened her resolve to move forward with her plan, which was exactly as she'd hoped.

She has another visit to pay while she's here, one that's difficult but necessary. Earlier she verified the directions—a right turn at the end of this street, then straight for three quarters of a mile, then a left onto Willow Lane. Reamer's former house sits at the end.

She drives slowly, paying attention to the terrain. The route is mainly flat, with a gentle uphill following the first turn, and a slight downhill preceding Willow. A narrow sidewalk hugs the road on one side for most of the way. A little girl could manage this walk without venturing into the street or tiring too much.

Rebecca parks near Reamer's former rental and gets out of her car to survey the street, which is still relatively undeveloped. A field borders the house on the far side. Overall, the place—recently painted with a new roof—looks much nicer than she remembers. Rose bushes with fresh red, yellow, and pink blossoms line the walk-way, filling the air with their enticing scent. By contrast, the one time Rebecca came to this house, sitting in the back of her mother's car, she thought it reeked of decay. Maybe that was simply a case of her projecting her thoughts onto the smell of the place.

Lost in memory, she doesn't notice the steps approaching behind her until the man is close. "What're you doin' here?" he says in a grating voice.

Her breath catches in her throat as she spins around. Bray Reamer lurks behind her, easily identifiable from the still-vibrant eagle tattoo surrounding his neck. His hair has gone white, as she guessed, and his face is flushed and leathery, with deep lines across his forehead. Compared to her memory, he's gained weight, which only makes him more imposing.

Before she can run, he grasps her arm.

"Let me go!" She tries to pull away but he tightens his grip.

"Why're you here?"

"Why are you following me?"

"You still think I did it," he says.

"You're hurting me!"

He releases her arm. "Want you to know I never touched her. Never kidnapped her. You got it all wrong."

A door opens across the road, and an elderly man steps out, holding his phone. "Are you all right, miss?" he calls out.

"I'm goin' now," Reamer says. "I didn't hurt her. That's not me. Never wanted to hurt anybody."

Rebecca isn't sure whether his remark refers to her or Sadie.

With his head lowered, he speed-walks toward his red Kia, parked near the intersection.

"Should I call the police, miss?" the neighbor says.

She could accuse Reamer of assault for the way he'd gripped her arm. But dealing with the police and providing a witness account will tie up her time. She can't put off what she needs to do any longer. "No, I'm all right," she says.

"You sure? Can't be too careful."

"I'm sure. Thanks for your help."

She waits until Reamer is gone before getting into her Honda. Driving back, her thoughts are full of the encounter. It was incredibly disturbing to confirm he's been watching her... following her even. And yet, the confrontation strengthened her resolve instead of weakening it. With him hanging around, it's all the more urgent she go back in time and find out the truth.

As determined as she is, however, she has to entertain the possibility that if she's killed in the past, that may truly be the end of her.

The death of her former self could prevent her mind from returning to real-time.

Which is why her first action on arriving home is to write a letter to her father. It seems unlikely, but what if her body is still capable of functioning? He might have her connected to a machine to keep her alive. This is the last thing she wants. It would be a complete waste of his money, and might even give him hope where there would be none.

She dates the letter two years earlier so it doesn't appear she was able to predict she might end up as a vegetable. Her instructions are that she is not to be kept alive through artificial means. If she is unable to communicate her wishes or even form a coherent thought, then he must pull the plug as quickly as possible.

She fervently hopes this doesn't happen, because she's not certain she can trust him to honor her wishes. Also, without witnesses, the document is unlikely to be valid in any court of law. But it's better than doing nothing. She signs the letter, *Love, Rebecca*, which is the only reference she makes to her feelings for him. He and she are alike in this way. Stoic but steadfast. Bound to each other forever in grief, though he does a better job of masking it.

With this task out of the way, she makes herself two frozen waffles topped with real maple syrup for dinner. It's what she would request for her last meal on death row.

Later, thinking of Reamer, she checks to make sure she bolted the front door in addition to locking it. He clearly knows where she lives and could easily slip into the building while a resident is coming or going. People are careless about that. The real deterrent is the camera at the entrance. If he didn't care whether he was filmed or not, he most likely would've already broken in instead of following her about in his car. On the other hand, the man didn't appear rational so it's best to take at least the minimum of precautions.

When she finally settles into her bed, she focuses on the day that Sadie disappeared. It takes a long time for her to reach a sufficiently calm state of mind, but at last she answers the call of her six-year-old self, whose childhood ended that day as surely as did her sister's.

PART II

7

———

After Uncle caught Nicki sneaking out to the shed, he and Mother went back to keeping her locked in her room all the time except for meals and bathroom.

With nothing else to occupy herself, she does her schoolwork. She's not allowed to attend school because Mother thinks the other children would be a bad influence. But a few years ago, she begged Mother to buy her textbooks so she could still achieve a high school education and maybe even apply to college someday. At first Mother resisted and mocked her ambitions. But then one day in a used bookstore, Mother happened to spot a few decrepit volumes that were dirt cheap, maybe even free, and she brought them home. After Nicki began doing the lessons, she became less agitated and more cooperative, and Mother came to understand the benefits of allowing her to continue. From then on, Mother and Uncle would pick up textbooks, classic novels, short stories, and essays for her whenever they could find them for practically nothing.

She is highly motivated to excel in all her subjects, because Mother eventually relented and told her she might allow her to apply to college after she turns eighteen—less than two years from now. She longs to be able to leave someday, despite the barrage of warnings from both of them regarding the dangers that exist beyond the confines of their house. Nicki knows little of the world, other than what she's been able to glean from reading, watching old films, and listening to conversations between Mother and Uncle, who both have jobs outside the house.

Today, just as she's cracking open her book on English composition, she hears the turn of the lock in her door. Mother lets herself in.

"Do you have a minute?" Mother, with her breathy, childish little voice, starts many of their conversations this way. It feels like cruel mockery, given that Nicki has all the minutes in the world, with not one single pressing matter to occupy her time.

"Sure." Nicki smiles like she's happy to see her, hopeful to regain her privileges.

Mother sits on the bed. "You've had some time to consider what you did wrong."

Nicki turns her chair to face her. "Yes, Mother."

"You might think I'm too strict, but the rules are there to keep you from harm. You can't be sneaking about in the dead of night. There could be wild animals, and all kinds of dangerous things out there."

Nicki wants to say, *Well, what about Sadie, all alone in the shed? Who is watching out for her?* But she knows this will just make Mother angry, and then there will be months more of lockup.

"I'm ready to give you another chance if you promise not to break the rules again."

"You'll stop locking my door?"

"Yes. Except at night, or when Uncle and I are both going to be out."

"I promise, Mother. I won't misbehave again."

She holds Nicki's gaze a moment longer before rising. "Let's watch a movie."

Nicki follows her into the hall and glances across at the door to Mother's bedroom. Most of the time she leaves it fully closed and locked, but today she's been careless and left it ajar. This could be Nicki's only chance for weeks or months to get her hands on an item she desperately needs that's kept inside the room.

Masking her excitement, she continues down the stairs after Mother, who pauses outside the TV room. "You pick," she says. "I'll get the snacks."

Nicki goes to the bookcase that holds their massive collection of old films on cassette, many of them westerns, including every feature starring Clint Eastwood. They've watched them over and over on their ancient VCR that never breaks down, despite Nicki wishing every day for lightning to strike it. Then maybe she could talk Mother into getting TV service instead, which, according to the movies they watch, every family except hers seems to have.

She picks *The Outlaw Josey Wales* because it's Mother's favorite and that will score her some points. After getting it ready to start, she goes to the kitchen to offer help.

Since Mother likes to pretend they're viewing a matinee at a real movie theater, she always prepares soda with lots of ice, a bowl of microwave popcorn, and a family-sized box of Milk Duds. They carry these to the TV room and when Nicki sits on the couch, Mother settles right beside her, too close as always. She wouldn't like it in any case, but the worst part is Mother's perfume that stinks like the stuff they spray on in summer to keep away the mosquitos. Mingled with the scent of popcorn and fake butter, it makes her food taste bitter. Despite this, she's going to force down everything in her bowl so Mother doesn't get angry and accuse her of being ungrateful.

When Mother finishes eating, she dozes with her head flopped back on the edge of the couch. This is Nicki's chance to sneak into her room, if she can get up without her noticing. Since their arms are still pressed together, she begins a painfully slow process of pulling away. Just at the moment when they're no longer touching, Mother shudders and seems like she's going to wake up, but then she just turns her head sideways and continues snoring lightly.

Nicki moves with practiced stealth as she lifts her weight off the couch and tiptoes out of the room. She hesitates, wondering if she should turn down the volume on the TV, but decides against it. Mother tends to notice any change to her usual settings.

Taking the stairs slowly, Nicki manages them without causing too many creaks. But just as her hand touches the door handle, Mother screeches from downstairs. "Nicki! Where are you?"

Her hope shrivels. "I'm just going to take a pee!" She hurries down the hall to the bathroom, shuts the door and uses the toilet. She'd been holding it in to use as an excuse anyway.

When she returns to the TV room, Mother has paused the film and is giving Nicki her squint eyes. That's how she looks when she's suspicious of something Nicki has done. "Why didn't you go down here?" she says.

"I don't like that toilet. You have to remember to hold the flusher down or it gets stuck."

This reminds Mother it irritates her too. "We need to get your uncle to fix that."

They watch the little bit remaining of the movie together, and then while the credits roll, Nicki gets up and carries the dishes into the kitchen to be washed. Uncle returns home while she's rinsing the glasses.

"You're out of your room?" he says.

Nicki is about to answer when Mother joins them from the hall. "We watched a movie. Nicki, go back upstairs now. I need to talk to your uncle."

"Yes, Mother." She places the second glass in the dish rack and restrains herself from skipping as she leaves the kitchen. Now is her chance, while the two carry on a private conversation they don't want Nicki to hear for some reason.

Still, she hesitates when she reaches the upstairs hall, thinking if she's caught, it will undo everything she's gained from her perfect behavior today. On the other hand, if she doesn't act now, she may not get another chance for a very long time.

The cadence of their voices wafts up the stairs. If she's lucky, the conversation will continue until Mother has to leave. She works nights at JJs Bar & Grill and according to Nicki's watch, that's in twenty minutes. But while her mind weighs the options, her body moves gingerly to Mother's door, pressing it open and slipping inside without a sound.

She's come with a specific purpose. Mother made the mistake of bringing her a collection of contemporary short stories, including one in which the protagonist has to pick a lock using two bobby pins. The author, a master of realism, included detailed instructions.

Mother often uses them to fasten her hair. At first, Nicki thought she would simply ask her if she could borrow some for the same purpose. But Mother has an untrusting personality that makes her suspect any change in behavior, no matter how insignificant. If she had any idea bobby pins could be used to pick locks, she would refuse Nicki's request and keep a careful eye on her supply from then on.

Nicki begins her search with the top drawer of the dresser, though she regrets this choice when it immediately scrapes against its frame. She nudges it closed again, resolving to save it as a last resort. It occurs to her the bathroom is a more likely place for anything to do with Mother's appearance.

It gets all quiet downstairs, giving Nicki a stab of panic, until Uncle says something again. His voice is always louder than his sister's.

She crosses the room, tiptoes into Mother's own private bathroom, and opens the left-hand drawer in the cabinet below the counter. It's crammed with cotton balls, old toothbrushes, scissors, nail clippers, a pin cushion, and other random junk, but no bobby pins. She moves to the drawer on the right.

The conversation in the kitchen seems to waver again, but it might be that Mother is talking and can't be heard.

This second drawer is crowded like the other, but after reaching into the very back, Nicki draws out a clear plastic case filled with bobby pins.

A heavy step lands on the stairs. Uncle is coming.

Having gotten this far, she can't give up. She fumbles with the case but her hands are trembling and it flies out of her grip, landing on the floor with the bobby pins spilled out. She bites her lip to hold back a cry.

Mother must've said something to Uncle. His steps have paused and he's resumed talking.

Nicki gets down on her knees and gathers up the bobby pins, praying she hasn't missed any. She takes five or six and shoves them in her pocket. Closes the case and puts it back. Shuts the drawer.

The stairs groan under Uncle's weight as he continues up them.

Nicki runs, light-footed, to the door. There's no time to cross the hall to her own room; at this point, Uncle may see her from the stairs. Instead, she pushes Mother's door mostly closed, leaving it open just a crack as it was before.

Uncle arrives at the hall where he hesitates again.

Nicki shivers, poised behind Mother's door, listening to the click of the lock being turned on her room because he thinks she's in there. He moves on to his own bedroom and from the sound of it, goes in and shuts the door.

As soon as Nicki slips out, the tap of Mother's feet at the bottom of the stairs reaches her. There's nothing she can do but hope to god Mother doesn't hear her returning to her room. Once inside, she rushes to insert the bobby pins inside Cinderella's rump, setting down the bear only a second before Mother opens her door.

"I heard you come in the room." Mother's eyes squint with suspicion.

"I was in the bathroom." Let Uncle not be called for corroboration since he just walked past and must've seen it empty.

"Again? I didn't hear the toilet flush."

Nicki holds up her hands. "Not to pee. I washed my hands. They were still sticky from the popcorn." It's a terrible excuse since she was just doing dishes a few minutes ago, but nothing else came to mind.

Mother seems to have forgotten. "I have to go as soon as I get changed." She approaches Nicki. "I appreciate your good behavior today." She gives her a squeeze. "Love you."

"Love you too," Nicki says. Once this was true, but now she's no longer sure what she feels for her. When Mother turns the lock again after going out, it's another notch in the coil of anger and resentment that has wrapped itself tightly around her heart.

Looking back at her textbook, she wonders if there's any point in doing the work. Mother isn't ever going to let her go to college. It's just another of her lies.

Rising, she goes to the window and gazes out at the shed. Even if through some miracle she finds a way to leave home someday with their permission, she can't make Sadie wait that long. Someone has to help her now, and there is no one but Nicki to do it.

She will practice with the bobby pins tonight.

8

————

It wasn't possible for Rebecca to prepare for the mind-blowing strangeness of reverting from an adult-sized body to that of a six-year-old. Gaping down at her skinny little self—mostly bare except for a bright yellow bikini—with her matchstick arms, stubby fingers, and short pudgy feet, she fights a powerful urge to flee. Running won't change a thing, nor will it calm her panicked, racing heart.

Water splashes her in the face and she realizes she's standing in the path of the sprinkler.

"Run!" Sadie shouts, herself in a purple flowered suit, waddling through and pausing when she gets beyond reach of the water.

Hardly aware of the soaking, Rebecca turns to the sister she hasn't seen for nineteen years. A mix of grief and joy overwhelm her, blurring her vision, tightening her chest. She wants to go to her, but the length of her stride falls short of her normal expectations, so that she pitches straight over onto her face.

"Becca, what are you doing?"

Becca. No one but Sadie ever called her that. Though her nose hurts, she jumps back up to her feet, aware of a feathery sensation of lightness. "Sadie, come here." Her childish voice sounds all wrong to her ears, high-pitched and lispy.

They meet outside the range of the sprinkler and Rebecca grabs her sister before she can escape, holding her tight. "Sadie… Sadie… Sadie… I missed you… I love you."

Sadie struggles in her grip and lets out a scream. "Mommy! Becca's hurting me!"

The backdoor slams and footsteps approach. "Rebecca, let go of her!" their mother calls out.

Only her presence could've pried Rebecca from her sister. She releases Sadie and watches as her long-deceased mother sweeps her long-missing sister up into her embrace. Her mother makes soothing noises as her gaze shifts to Rebecca and grows hard. "What did you do to her?"

Rebecca stands rooted, mouth open but no words coming out. Her body shakes like she's at the North Pole instead of sweltering-hot California in July.

Their mother lowers Sadie before approaching Rebecca. "What's going on?" Seeing how traumatized her oldest daughter appears, she softens her tone.

"Sorry, Mom," Rebecca squeaks.

"Are you sick?" Her mother glances at Sadie, worried she might catch it.

Rebecca shakes her head and closes her eyes, struggling to calm herself. Her mother pats her shoulder. "It's all right."

When she opens her eyes again, her mother is leaning over her and Rebecca realizes the few remaining photos of her don't do justice to the vitality of her living face. Moreover, until this moment, she hadn't grasped how similar they were. It's a bit like gazing into a mirror, with her mother only seven years older than Rebecca's age in real-time. Their hair is different but the structure of their faces, the shape of their eyebrows, and the lift of their lips on one side in irritation—these are the same.

Her mother is more beautiful though, with golden hair shining in the sunlight, framing her face in soft, natural curls. Her skin is lightly tanned, her eyes dusty green, nose straight, chin firm. She wears a sleeveless lilac blouse and slim jeans. Her gaze softens when it shifts to Sadie, radiating warmth. Her clear preference stabs like a needle through Rebecca's heart. Still, she can't resist clasping her mother's waist with her T-rex arms, the scent of her filling Rebecca with powerful feelings of remembrance and belonging. She isn't sure whether it's perfume or shampoo or something else, only that its smell is a familiar one, minty with the hint of cucumber.

"Sorry, Mom," she says in her childish voice. "Sorry for everything." The *everything* is loaded with meaning for her, meaning her mother doesn't yet understand.

"You're wet, honey." Her mother gives her a swift squeeze before pulling back. "Hey, you're not in trouble. There's nothing to be upset about. Let's go inside."

As they follow her into the house, Sadie approaches and takes Rebecca's hand. She then seems surprised when her big sister grips her back instead of batting her hand away. The real six-year-old Rebecca would have done that. But this Rebecca wishes beyond anything that she could find a way to hold onto Sadie forever.

The family room looks nothing like the one she visited yesterday. Her mother's workspace is positioned as Rebecca remembers it, next to the window where she can keep an eye on the girls playing out back. Her laptop open on the desk looks terribly dated but was probably state-of-the-art at the time. The rest of the furniture, from the plumpy couch to the notched wooden coffee table, is well-worn but comfortable. The stone fireplace that already has their initials carved into it gives Rebecca a feeling of reassurance. Several stains from spilled drinks mark the carpet, and the cream-colored walls sport a few pairs of child-sized fingerprints. Their parents' talk of fixing up the place is destined to come to nothing.

"Is Dad home?" Rebecca asks.

"What? You know he's at work," her mother says.

She does know he was at work this day, but she needs to confirm everything is as it was. Part of her deeply wishes he was here now, only so she could see him again too, before it all happened, and watch the way he interacts with Mom, Sadie, and her. Like with her mother, she isn't sure she can trust her memories of him.

"Get changed. I'll make you lunch," their mother says.

Sadie scampers up the stairs and into their shared bedroom, with Rebecca following at a slower pace, being cautious not to tangle her legs again.

Before returning here, she could not have described her childhood room other than to say it had twin beds. Seeing it now, everything comes back to her. The posters of dragons and unicorns. The coloring books and crayons on the desk she and Sadie shared. The matching midnight blue bedspreads with yellow stars and moons, covered with stuffed animals. She goes to the bookcase and looks at a *Magic Treehouse* novel. It strikes her funny to imagine her interest in time travel beginning with these books.

They take off their bathing suits and put on the clothes they left on their beds. Sadie wears a white tank with a purple unicorn on the front of it, and red shorts. Rebecca dons dark green stretch capris and a mint T-shirt decorated with butterflies.

"Come here, Sadie," Rebecca says, going up to the full-length mirror that hangs from their closet door.

Standing side by side, the girls look remarkably similar, partly because Rebecca is nearly as petite as her sister. Both have pale skin, button noses, and long hair in a nutty-brown shade. Rebecca wears hers loose over her back while Sadie's has been woven into two braids by their mother. Both have hazel eyes, but Sadie's still shine with a wide-eyed wonder that is gone from her sister's. They wear glitter polish on their finger- and toenails, gold for Rebecca and silver for Sadie. Rebecca always chose her color first and didn't allow her little sister to use the same.

Rebecca leans closer to the reflection and stares in awe at her face, so smooth and unblemished. She rubs her hand over her cheek, amazed by how soft it is.

"Lunch is ready!" their mother calls from downstairs.

A minute later the girls are seated at the kitchen table with glasses of milk and peanut butter and jelly sandwiches. Their mother was never creative when it came to meals, and Rebecca estimates they had PB & J at least fifty percent of the time. She hasn't had one in years, though, and finds herself looking forward to it, particularly since her stomach has been rumbling and now feels hollow.

After taking a few bites, Rebecca says, "How is your writing going, Mom?"

Her mother gives her an odd look. Probably it's the first time Rebecca has ever asked her that.

"Fine. Since when do you call me Mom?"

Rebecca is confused for a second before realizing she must've still called her Mommy at this age. In fact, there must never have been a time when she called her Mom. It was only while growing up and listening to her friends talk to their mothers that she started thinking of her as "Mom."

"Do you think you'll find a publisher for your book soon?" Rebecca says. She truly wants to know more about her mother as a working woman. She knows so little about her.

"Since when did you get interested in that?" She gives Rebecca a half-smile, bringing over their lunch. "I don't know. I hope so. My agent is working on it." While they start to eat, she gets out grapes and washes them.

Glancing over, she says, "Sadie, honey, you dripped jam on your pretty shirt!" She wets a paper towel and bends over her youngest daughter, wiping the spot. She kisses the top of her head.

"Why don't you love me as much as Sadie?" The words slip out of Rebecca. This is the only chance she'll ever get to ask her, but she should resist the temptation. If she does anything to change the trajectory of today, she might not get the answers she's looking for. If something she says or does makes her mother take them out instead of remaining home, for example, then she will have ruined everything.

Her mother freezes. "What did you say to me?"

She still has the power to terrify Rebecca. "Nothing."

"I treat you and your sister exactly the same."

"Uh huh." She feels as small as the body she now occupies.

"You've always wanted more attention," she says.

"Sorry, Mom. Mommy."

Sadie just keeps eating her sandwich, wisely staying out of the argument.

"Finish up now," her mother says.

Her appetite is gone. She can't eat the other half of the sandwich. "Can I eat it later?"

"After your nap, then."

Nap. Of course. It was required at that age.

The sisters rinse and dry their hands before running back upstairs to their bedroom. Sadie sits on the floor and begins dressing one of her dolls.

"What are you doing?" Rebecca says. "We need to nap." More accurately, she needs Sadie to nap so she can slip out of the room. If she does that while Sadie is awake, her sister will either try to follow her, or tell on her.

"I wanna play," Sadie says.

"I can't sleep if you do," Rebecca says. "You have to put your dolls away."

She ignores her.

"I'll tell Mom if you don't."

Sadie pouts but gets on her bed, bringing the doll with her.

"Close your eyes," Rebecca says.

Sadie closes them but they pop right back open. She clearly isn't sleepy enough.

Rebecca gets an idea and checks the bookshelf again. There it is, one of their favorites, *Where the Wild Things Are.* She pulls it out and sits beside Sadie on her bed.

"I'll read to you." She leans against the headboard while Sadie lies with her head in Rebecca's lap.

She reads the story slowly and in a soft voice to get Sadie to sleep, while gently smoothing the hair back from her forehead. It doesn't take long for her sister's eyes to close and breathing to thicken. Rebecca looks down at her angelic face, wanting to remember every aspect of it, wishing she could whisk her back to the present. How anyone could get it into their head to hurt such a creature, Rebecca will never understand.

Fortunately, Sadie is a deep sleeper even when just napping. Rebecca slips out from under her, opens her dresser and goes through her clothes till she finds jeans with deep pockets, and a pair of cotton socks. She changes into them before looking inside the closet for a pair of sturdy-looking shoes that will provide the best support. These go on quickly with Velcro closures.

Rebecca then checks the desk drawers for items that might be useful. It takes a minute to find a cheap plastic Aladdin watch that appears to be working. She keeps searching, looking for a flashlight but not finding one. She checks in the top drawer again, which is full of pencils and a few pens. That's when she spots it, a pen that's also a flashlight. She whisks it into her left pocket.

Pausing at the door, she presses her ear against it. Good news, Mom is talking on the phone and will be distracted from the noises Rebecca might make as she wanders about. She opens the door silently and creeps out into the hall. It's necessary for her to go downstairs, but since the lower section is in view of the family room, she gets on her stomach and slowly slithers down. When she reaches the bottom, she sneaks a peek toward her mother, happy to find her facing the other direction. From there Rebecca crawls on hands and knees to the kitchen, a much easier task at age six than twenty-five. Her limbs are so much more flexible than when she's an adult. Overall, she feels as light as the butterflies pictured on her shirt.

She stands when she reaches the kitchen. Somewhere there's a junk drawer that holds what she needs, if only she could remember which one. There are more drawers than she recalls, and each makes noise when she opens it. She starts with the outer ones, which seem a lot more likely to contain stuff that isn't useful for eating or cooking. The first holds waxed paper, aluminum foil, and plastic bags. The second has tape, pens, and notepads. When she pushes it closed, it moves too easily and bangs in the back.

This makes her cringe inside, especially after she realizes Mom isn't talking anymore. She may have hung up; she could be coming into the kitchen any minute now. This might be Rebecca's only chance. She whips open the third drawer, rattling its contents. It has tools, flashlights, matches… and the Swiss army knife. Snatching it up, she shoves it in her pocket, shutting the drawer with her other hand.

"What are you doing?" Mom says.

Rebecca whirls around to find her mother standing in the doorway. How much did she see?

"Looking for the tape," Rebecca says, afraid her childish face is not skilled at masking the lie.

Her mother approaches, narrowing her eyes. "What for?"

"Um… I… um… I drew a picture and wanted to tape it up on my wall."

"You know you're not supposed to do that."

She hangs her head. "I forgot. Sorry, Mommy." Hopefully she won't ask to see the picture.

"Your nap isn't over either. Go to your room. And stay there till I say you can come out."

"But Mom…"

"You heard me."

She knows this mood. There's no point in arguing. But just as she has resigned herself to returning upstairs, the sharp ring of the doorbell makes them jump.

"Oh who could that be?" Her mother is annoyed.

Knowing the answer, Rebecca follows her mother to the front door. Rebecca's friend Mikayla bounces on the doorstep, looking ready for a child photo shoot, with her wavy blond hair in a ponytail and her pink sunglasses shaped like hearts. She wears a crisp pink button blouse, a pink plaid skirt, and pink flip-flops. Her outfits are always coordinated because her mother works in fashion.

Mikayla's mom hovers behind her on the walkway in a designer sundress and white high-heeled shoes. "Camille, would you mind terribly watching her for a few hours?" she says to Rebecca's mother. "My father's just gone to the hospital and needs my help."

Her mother answers politely though Rebecca can tell she isn't pleased. "Oh no, what happened?"

"He's had a small stroke apparently."

"I'm sorry. Sure, Mikayla can stay here."

"Thanks a million. I owe you one." Mikayla's mom walks with swaying steps toward her car, being careful not to get her heels stuck in a crack.

Sadie runs down from her nap just as their mother is closing the front door. Rebecca's punishment forgotten, their mother says, "You can play in the backyard." This is her code for, *stay out of my hair while I work.*

As Sadie and Mikayla dash through the sliding door to the back of the house, Rebecca lingers. This is likely the last time she'll see her mother. At this moment, she wants nothing so much as to stay here by her side and grow up all over again. With the knowledge of foresight, she can make things different in this timeline. She can prevent Sadie from being taken. She can try to figure out how to win her mother's love. The years will pass as their family flourishes. She will not reach the age of twenty-five riddled with guilt and regret, alienated from the one parent she still has.

But it isn't possible. Before long, she'll be drawn back to her own time. There isn't anything she can do to prevent it.

Her mother has already returned to her computer. Rebecca runs to her side and reaches up to kiss her cheek. "I love you, Mommy," she tells her.

Her mother looks startled but not unhappy. "I love you too, Rebecca."

It will have to be enough. The phone rings and her mother turns away, settling into her chair and pressing the receiver to her ear like she expects this to be a long one. Rebecca knows it's a call from the literary agent.

When she emerges from the house, Mikayla hurries to her side. Exactly as she did in the past, Mikayla suggests in a whisper that they ditch Sadie during a game of hide & seek. That this suggestion came from her friend did little to assuage Rebecca's feelings of guilt over the years, probably because she had readily agreed. But now for the first time she wonders what effect this had on Mikayla. Their friendship ended after Sadie's disappearance. Was Mikayla also living a life full of fear and self-doubt? Did she need therapy to get through it? If Rebecca manages to survive this experience, she thinks she'll look her up in the present. Maybe it will help both of them heal. Most likely not, though.

Despite hating herself for it, Rebecca must go along with the plan. But first she wraps her arms around her sister's delicate frame, and kisses the side of her head. "I love you, Sadie," she whispers. When she backs away, both her sister and her friend are giving her odd looks.

"Sadie, we're playing hide and seek and you're it," Mikayla says.

Sensing there is no resisting her, Sadie merely nods before turning away to count.

"You have to hide your face at the tree," Mikayla commands.

Sadie casts her a long-suffering look, goes to the tree, and presses her hands and face against it. "One, two..." She knows how to count to twenty.

The two older girls run away and quietly sneak into the garage through the door at the side of the house. Her parents never park on one side so the kids can use it for hopscotch and other games. She tells Mikayla to draw the hopscotch board. "I have to go outside for a sec," she says.

"Don't let Sadie see you."

"I won't."

Since Sadie will come out to the front on the other side of the house, Rebecca waits next to the garage. She can't go to the yard yet, or the kidnapper might see her and drive away. But she stands on tiptoes to raise the latch and open the gate just a crack to allow her to watch for his arrival.

A minute later, Sadie dashes across the lawn from the other side and checks for Rebecca and Mikayla around the giant old oak tree. From her hiding place, Rebecca hears the noise of a car's engine, followed by its door opening. This has to be it. She slips through the gate to see.

The trunk of the car is raised. She glimpses Sadie inside it, pulling back her hand as the kidnapper slams the trunk closed. The engine is running and the driver's side door left open. He runs back to his seat, slamming the door shut and speeding away from their house.

The scene takes Rebecca's breath away. The horror of it. How fast it all happened. The thought of her baby sister frightened and alone.

But she has kept her head sufficiently to notice a few things. The car was a silver Ford Taurus with its license plate removed.

The kidnapper did not look anything like Bray Reamer.

Despite this, she sets off as fast as her miniature legs will take her down the street, and makes a right turn at the end of it. She has to stick with the plan, because this stranger could be working with Reamer, and might be bringing Sadie to his house this very minute.

9

Annoyed with herself, Rebecca has to stop to catch her breath before she's even halfway there. She doesn't have the stamina of her adult persona, particularly since her half-sized legs must take more than twice as many steps as normal. Plus the constant checking for cars approaching behind her slows down her pace even further. An adult, especially one who lives in the neighborhood and recognizes her, is likely to stop and see what this child is doing away from home all by herself. Or her mother, alerted by Mikayla, might come this way looking for her and Sadie.

The roads are thankfully not busy, but when a car eventually does come along, she has to throw herself behind some prickly bushes that scratch her legs. She huddles there until the car has driven past, breathing in deeply to slow her racing heart before launching into another mad dash. A minute later, a gardening truck heads toward her from the opposite direction. She decides against hiding, which might only attract more attention given that she's already in their field of vision. It's the right decision; the truck continues past her without the driver even glancing her way.

Before too long, she reaches Reamer's street and ducks onto it, slowing to a trot, since at this point, she'll be able to see if the silver Ford comes up or down the road. When she rounds the next corner, she gets a glimpse of his so-far empty driveway. However, it's possible the kidnapper's Taurus is already in the garage.

Approaching, she keeps her eyes on the windows, trying to make out if anyone is inside or not. Seeing no movement at all, she continues to the wooden gate next to the garage, hoping to look inside if it has a window in the back. She has to jump up to reach the latch, but she can't get it to lift. After trying several times, she figures it must be padlocked on the other side. It makes sense Reamer doesn't want anyone wandering into the backyard and discovering his marijuana plants. Or whatever else he's up to.

She looks back at the front of the house. On the far side near the corner, a window is partly open, probably to catch some air on this hot day. Looking down at herself, she realizes she's actually scrawny enough to fit through it, without even opening it further.

Her hands go clammy thinking about it, though. What if she encounters him in the house? She shakes her head, forcing herself to focus on the task at hand. Get inside, find Sadie or any other proof that Reamer has a connection to her kidnapping.

She ducks down as she crosses the front lawn, hoping she's too short to be seen from inside. No one appears at any of the windows. It seems that he's not home, which would be the best possible situation. If so, she can hide and wait for his return, possibly with Sadie and the other man.

When she reaches the window, she glances behind her in case any neighbors are watching. But no one is about. It's a weekday and they're probably all at work. Turning back, she peers into the house at a family room not too different from her own, except everything looks older and more frayed.

She has to pull herself up onto the ledge as the window is a little high for her. The first time she doesn't manage it, but on the second try, she jumps and the momentum helps her body to swing up. She hooks her leg over the sill and slides into the room backward, landing with a thud.

Freezing in place, she listens for the sound of anyone coming toward her. All is silent, though. She sniffs the room, wondering if there could be a skunk nearby, before remembering that's what weed smells like to her. She never did want to smoke the stuff, even as a teenager.

It shouldn't take long to search this one-story ranch house. Crossing the hall to the kitchen and eating area, she looks out toward the back where marijuana plants grow in the open. It's astonishing he didn't get busted a lot sooner.

She continues down the hall past a bathroom to the first bedroom. It looks empty from the doorway but she decides her search must be thorough. The kidnapper might've left Sadie bound and gagged, while he and Reamer drove off to fetch something. Rebecca checks behind the bed, under it, and in the closet. No Sadie.

"Well, well, well, what do we have here? Alice in Wonderland?"

Rebecca yelps at the sound of Reamer's voice. He managed to creep up on her and now his form blocks the door. It's definitely him, with that neck tattoo and the same hulking shape—though he looks much younger than when she last saw him.

He laughs at her. "Need help findin' anything?" His voice is drowsy and his eyes half-lidded like he just smoked weed.

Panic gets her legs moving and she tries to tunnel past him to the hall, but he effortlessly bars her way with one arm before grasping her around the waist and picking her up.

"Ow! You're hurting me!" She struggles to break free.

He carries her to a chair where he sets her down.

"Little Missy, think you can get away from me?"

"Let me go. I got lost. I'm sorry I came here."

He laughs again. "You got lost and climbed in through my window to find your way? I guess the breeze from my backyard been blowin' up your nose."

"It stinks," she says.

His face darkens. "Smells better'n you. Somebody set you up to this?"

She gets an idea. "My friend dared me. But we agreed if I wasn't back in five minutes, she would run home and get her mom to call the police."

"Your friend, eh?" He glances out the front window. "Who's she, the invisible girl? Don't see anyone out there."

"She's already gone to tell her mom."

"I'm the one should call the cops and report you for breakin' and enterin'. Will if you try somethin' crazy like this again. Lucky you picked my house. There's more guns than people in Windlake. Fingers on the trigger faster'n they can see you." He nods toward the front door. "Go on now."

"I can go?" Her voice gets even squeakier with surprise.

"If you don't, I'll just put you to work in the garden."

She jumps up and races away from him, gulping for breath at the sound of him following her. Maybe he's been playing with her and won't let her leave. But then he says, "Sure you know your way back home?"

"Of course I do." She flings open the door and rushes out.

Her thoughts whirl inside her head. She has found not one single indication of Reamer being involved in Sadie's disappearance. Not the Ford Taurus, not the actual kidnapper, not Sadie. If he were the mastermind who organized the plot, he wouldn't be sitting around smoking weed by himself right now. He wouldn't be laughing when little girls broke into his house, nor would he send them merrily on their way.

She has to accept that what she has believed ever since Reamer was first arrested simply isn't true. He had nothing to do with what happened to her sister.

She remembers from her reading about his trial, how his lawyer kept emphasizing his client had *sold* underage porn, but not *produced* it. Reamer had seemed quite remorseful, saying he'd been desperate for cash at the time. He swore he never looked at it, which no one believed. For the first time, she wonders if he was telling the truth. His actions were still inexcusable, but his behavior today showed he was not someone who had it in him to harm a small child.

For years she convinced herself of his guilt because he was all they had. Now she knows differently. It wasn't Reamer at all. It was the man who drove up to their house, snatched Sadie, and threw her into the trunk of his car. He's the one she needs to find.

10

I t's morning, Rebecca is twenty-five again, and her stomach is growling. Minutes after leaving Reamer's place, she tumbled back to the present, because she had learned all she could from that particular time jump.

She treats herself to a large breakfast at her favorite brunch spot. Eggs and hash browns and biscuits and a fruit plate. She has to keep up her strength for the grim task ahead of her.

As soon as she returns home, she goes straight to her computer and writes a detailed account of everything she can recall from her mindcast. The color and make of the kidnapper's car, and that it had no license plate. The unknown man's size—medium height, slim—and his actions. A full description of what happened at Reamer's house, including their conversation. She no longer believes he was involved, but that assessment could change yet again once she gains more information.

Unfortunately, she was too far away to glimpse the kidnapper's face, partly covered by sunglasses and a black baseball cap. Along with these, he wore a plain black T-shirt and blue jeans. No team logos or anything else on the cap or shirt. She didn't manage to see his shoes, but no doubt they were as nondescript as the rest of his outfit.

When she's done, she opens a new window and searches on photos of "serial killers in California." Some are truly horrific, with wild eyes and fascist tattoos like Charles Manson—people you would guess are crazy just by looking at them. Then there are the others, the Ted Bundy types, who look normal, with pleasant or even handsome features. The guy they called the Dating Game Killer, because he was a contestant on that show, where young men or women interviewed prospective dates who were hidden from view, and chose one based on personality, not appearance. Amazingly, the Dating Game Killer was picked out of his group of three, but later, the woman refused to go out with him because she found him "creepy."

When Rebecca limits her search to those who were alive and not imprisoned in July, 2000, the list grows shorter. When she further reduces the field to those no older than forty at the time, few remain. She isn't certain about this, but from her brief glimpse, she thinks Sadie's kidnapper was young.

She expands the search to include convicted rapists and pedophiles, which greatly complicates her job. In many cases only the names are listed and she has to delve deeper to find photos. After six hours of this, she suffers from dry eyes and blurry vision, and the faces have all melded into one amorphous blob.

Her only real hope of identifying the kidnapper lies in a second mindcast. Her brain cries out against it and wants to delay indefinitely. Her heart, though, feels the urgent need to push forward and learn her sister's fate while she still has the ability to travel through time. For all she knows, it could end as suddenly and unexpectedly as it began.

Her heart wins the battle as nighttime approaches. She orders pizza to be delivered and opens a bottle of premium cabernet she has been saving for a special occasion. Unearthing a particularly challenging puzzle, she distracts her brain during her meal.

When she gets into bed, she makes her most effortless transition ever back to her childhood home, arriving at roughly the same time as before. This will allow her to gather the necessary tools again during naptime.

She repeats the actions of the day in listless fashion, determined not to dwell on whether this will be her last visit here to see Sadie and her mother. Her focus must be on setting up the right outcome. After Mikayla arrives, she takes off for the backyard with her and Sadie without looking back. Like before, she hears the phone ringing behind them in the house, and her mother picking up.

But this time, in answer to Mikayla's suggestion to ditch her sister, Rebecca says, "No, that isn't nice. Let's all play hopscotch in the garage." What she should've said nineteen years ago, in other words.

Mikayla likes to be in charge and therefore doesn't give up easily. "Oh, c'mon. You know Sadie's really bad at jumping."

Her twenty-five-year-old self is not about to defer to a six-year-old. "Sadie, let's play hopscotch," she says by way of answer to Mikayla.

Though her friend makes a face, she follows them into the garage, not wanting to be stuck alone in the backyard either.

Rebecca checks her watch, beginning to worry that time is running out. She knows the kidnapper will drive by soon.

"You draw the squares," Rebecca tells Mikayla, in her new role as the boss of them. She hands her a thick piece of chalk. "My mother made some chocolate chip cookies. I'll go see if they're ready."

Mikayla is about to argue, but the cookies shut her up. She loves sweets.

"I'll help you," Sadie tells Mikayla, luckily not mentioning anything about Mom not having made cookies at all.

Rebecca points at some coloring books. "No, you color. Let Mikayla do it." Her friend would balk at Sadie's help.

Her sister doesn't much like the new extra-bossy Rebecca either, but she still does as she says. Rebecca gives her a quick pat on the shoulders since there's no time for any more hugs, before hurrying out to the gate and lifting the latch on tiptoes. She dashes across the yard and around the oak tree to the sidewalk. The street is empty, of course. If anyone had been around, they could've witnessed what happened. The only people who might've seen anything were not home that day. The retired couple who lived across the street had gone to the reservoir to paddle their canoe.

She's not at all sure the kidnapper will take her. He could drive right past her, not interested. Although she and her sister bear a strong resemblance, he might realize she's older. Rebecca is more of a tomboy, especially now with her jeans and sneakers. Sadie is cuter and looks particularly girlish in the little red shorts she's wearing today.

At least the man might slow down enough for Rebecca to get a better look at him. But her goal is to get him to take her, no matter how terrifying the prospect. It's best for her to spend as little time as possible contemplating what she's doing—setting up her six-year-old self to be kidnapped. Her, a little kid with a Swiss army knife, a pen-flashlight, and an Aladdin watch.

A shudder grips her. She could die, and no one will ever know Sadie's kidnapper claimed a third life this day.

To give the impression she has come out here to play by herself, she finds a broken branch and uses it to bat a pebble around. Otherwise, the kidnapper might think she's waiting for an adult to arrive and pick her up.

Her leg muscles tighten as she hears an approaching car. She acts like she doesn't notice, but glimpses the vehicle out of the corner of her eye. A convertible. It continues past her.

When the pebble rolls into the street, she runs to fetch it. The sound of a second car makes her back away and look up. *The silver Ford Taurus.* It stops sharp at the curb, the trunk pops open, and the door flings out. The driver reaches her in several rapid strides. He grasps her around the waist and tosses her into the trunk like she's no heavier than a chicken. She wants to scream but bites down on her lip. She can't allow herself the chance of being rescued without having any idea who he is yet. Anyway, it all happens so fast, before she can even look at him, the trunk is banged down, his door slams shut, and the car bursts forward.

The plan has worked.

11

———————

Within the belly of the beast, Rebecca is bathed in perspiration, lying on some sort of filthy cotton comforter. Darkness blinds her while musty air that reeks of sweat and mold saturates her nostrils.

She knew he was going to put her in the trunk—she watched him do it to Sadie. But it's more harrowing than she could've imagined. Between claustrophobia, the threat of suffocation, and anxiety regarding the kidnapper's plans for her, she has an abundance of things to freak over. Her heartbeat races, and between this and the heat like the inside of an oven, she wonders if she'll survive the trip. Wonders if her sister survived it.

Struggling to hold down the panic, she takes long, slow, deep breaths. At least she can stretch her limbs. As an adult she would be all folded up and her muscles would be cramping.

As the car turns a corner, her body shifts and a plastic bottle rolls against her. She remembers her penlight and flashes it on. Seeing it's water, she opens the cap, glad to hear the click of a sealed bottle though she would've drunk it anyway. She slurps greedily but not too long because it needs to last. It may be a good sign, finding this here. It means he doesn't plan to kill her right away.

Rebecca sprays the light again, wondering if anything else is in the trunk. She nearly whoops for joy on finding a license plate. Finally, a stroke of luck. He must've removed it so it wouldn't be spotted while he drove through her neighborhood. Even better, it has a current California registration sticker, meaning the plate should be legit and traceable. She keeps the light on it while she memorizes the sequence.

Lying on her back, she repeats the number/letter combination over and over in her thoughts. She devises a memory game to help her recall it. No matter what else happens, she must return to the present with that license securely tucked inside her head.

Everything she's found so far indicates this kidnapping was planned. He took off the license plate. He put water and a blanket in the trunk. He removed possible weapons like the jack. He must've been waiting for just the right opportunity to snatch a lonely little girl up off the street.

Naturally, it didn't occur to him that leaving the plate in the trunk might be a bad idea. Few children would understand its significance. Although Sadie knew her numbers up to twenty and could recite the alphabet, she didn't have the presence of mind to memorize anything that wasn't repeated to her many times.

The kidnapper has the radio playing. It sounds like some kind of political commentary, though she can't clearly make out what's being said. Every now and then he responds to it, arguing with the guy on the radio. *Well, how stable could someone be who goes around snatching little girls?*

She isn't sure how much time has passed when the car slows down and gradually comes to a stop. Her small body trembles. If he opens the trunk, it's going to be hard to resist making a run for it if she gets the chance, but she can't leave without learning more about him. The license plate could be stolen from another vehicle and might not be any help at all. She needs to find out his name, or the address of their destination. Preferably both.

The car door creaks as it opens. Footsteps crunch on gravel. There's a beep, and the trunk pops open. She squints at the bright sun behind his dark silhouette but doesn't squirm, wanting to show him she's going to be cooperative. For now.

"You doing okay?" His words come out like he's striving carefully to form them.

She pulls herself into a sitting position, hoping he won't object, and gets her first real look at his face without the sunglasses, which he must've left in the car. On the left side, his eyelid and mouth droop unnaturally, like he has some kind of paralysis. There's a bit of drool at the bottom of his lip on that side. Reacting to her scrutiny, he takes out a cloth handkerchief and wipes it.

Her first instinct is to pity him. If he had this appearance as a child, he would've been ruthlessly bullied. But her heart hardens again almost instantly. *He took Sadie and did who-knows-what to her.* No mercy. No forgiveness.

Her thin, childish voice says, "It's very hot in here."

"Yeah, sorry about that." His "s" is slurred a bit, like a cross between "sorry" and "thorry." He talks slowly, enunciating each word. She thinks the paralysis may have forced him to adopt a more deliberate manner of speaking.

He glances at the water bottle. "You found it. Good." He reaches into a backpack at his feet and puts another bottle in the trunk, along with a bag of generic hard candy.

"Thank you," she says.

He musses her hair in what is meant to be a friendly gesture, making her flinch. "You're a polite little girl, aren't you?"

"I want to go home." She says that mainly because he will expect it.

"We'll be there soon."

This answer surprises her. But he is probably referring to *his* home. Or to wherever he is going to bring her.

"Can I ride in the backseat? I'll be quiet."

"You seem like a good kid. But you have to stay here. Sorry." He reaches past her for the license plate, then kneels and takes a screwdriver from the backpack. Rebecca looks past him at trees, a dirt road.

It appears he pulled off the freeway to this deserted location. He starts screwing the license plate back on.

"But it's so hot, I might die."

He pauses. "I don't think so. Anyway, you can't sit up front so I don't want to hear any more about it."

Not wanting to annoy him, she waits a moment before speaking again. "Where are we going?" She needs to get as much information as she can, in case her trip is cut short.

"You'll see."

"Is it in the mountains?"

"I said, you'll see."

"What's your name, mister?"

"Call me Uncle." He continues with the second screw.

"Uncle who?" Fishing for a name.

"Just Uncle."

Creepy Uncle No-Name. She decides she's not going to call him anything, while dubbing him *Bob* as in the expression *Bob's-your-uncle*, inside her head. "My name is Rebecca Danser," she says, still fishing.

"Is it?" He makes a face like he smells something bad. She'd like to tell him if he wants to experience a truly terrible stench, he should get inside the trunk.

"Well, Rebecca, I expect you to do everything I tell you," he says. "If so, you'll get more candy and other good things."

Like I want your fucking Walmart candy. "What if I don't?" she says because she wants to know what kind of threats he's going to use against her.

"If you disobey me, I'll shut you in a dark room all by yourself. If you try to run away, I'll find you wherever you are and I might have to hurt you."

Fury fills her as she pictures actual four-year-old Sadie sitting here being terrified by him. If she were an adult with a gun, she would probably shoot him right now.

She forces herself not to think about her sister and instead concentrate on the details of his appearance. Of course, the facial paralysis is enough to recognize him if she learns where to look for him in the present. But other details could still be helpful and might give additional clues regarding his identity. He has blond hair in a short cut he might've done himself, a scar just above his right eyebrow, blue eyes, and a ski-jump nose. His eye teeth protrude like someone who never wore braces. And he wears a silver chain around his neck, with a round silver pendant that has the silhouette of a Labrador or similar type of dog etched inside it. Maybe he wears this all the time, or maybe just today. She would put his age at early twenties. He's medium height, thin, even scrawny.

The man has no visible tattoos or piercings, which makes her wonder if he had a strict upbringing in a conservative family, with a father who might beat the crap out of him if he ever did anything to express himself. The neat way he's dressed supports this idea. His T-shirt is tucked into his belted pants, which look like they might've been ironed. He wears clean leather work boots.

His hands reveal a couple of chipped nails, and some dark staining near the fingertips. Like he works in a dirty profession. Factory worker? Farmhand? Chimney sweep?

He finishes with the license plate and stands up. "You need to pee?"

"When will we get to where we're going?" she says, continuing to push for more information.

"You need to pee or don't you?"

She nods, not knowing when she'll get another chance. Before she can crawl out, he takes her under the arms and lifts her from the trunk, filling her with revulsion. He points out a tree close to the car. "You can go behind there. Don't try to run away. I told you what would happen."

"I won't. Do you have toilet paper?"

He scowls. "Just go."

She hurries behind the tree, lowers her pants and squats. It occurs to her, what if this is the exact place her sister went to relieve herself after she was taken? It makes her want to reach out and touch the tree. *Sadie, I'm with you.*

Without paper, she shakes her bottom before lifting her pants. She wishes she could go anywhere but back to that man, back inside the trunk of his car. But she has to follow this through. She has to find out where he's taking her.

When she returns, he lifts her into the trunk and shuts it over her.

12

———

R ebecca had checked her watch when kidnapper Bob stopped the car to put the plate back on. Forty-five minutes had passed since he grabbed her from in front of her house. Ten more minutes elapsed before he resumed driving.

Another fifteen minutes go by before she feels butterflies in her stomach from the up and down motion of a hilly road. Soon they're weaving more frequently from side to side as well, giving her the full rollercoaster experience. These are the indications that they've come to the Sierra Foothills and are headed into the mountains.

She can tell they're no longer on a freeway, because they've paused several times at what feel like stop signs. Fifty more minutes pass before they come to what must be a traffic light. Then two more lights before their speed increases like they're back on the highway. In eleven minutes, she hears the tick-tick-tick of the turn signal and feels the Taurus cut to the right. They slow significantly and follow a windy road until coming to a stop eight minutes later.

Is this their destination? She checks her watch again to confirm it's been roughly two hours total—information she tucks away along with the license plate number.

She hears him get out and a second later the trunk opens. Her eyes accustomed to darkness have to squint up at Bob, who's framed by a mantel of trees behind him. "Is this it?"

"Yeah. You keep quiet now."

She stumbles on weakened knees when he sets her down next to the car, and he has to pull her back up again. Ignoring him, she scans the property for any useful details. It's an isolated, heavily treed lot with a partly crumbling paved driveway. They've arrived in front of an unattached single-car garage, the size of a windowless cabin. On the other side of the driveway, pulled off to the side, a small, old-fashioned pickup truck is parked facing them. Rebecca would love to get its license number too, but to her extreme disappointment, it has no plate in the front.

A rust-brown two-story house with wood siding and a steeply sloped shake roof looms across the short walkway. Once it may have been charmingly rustic, but now it looks dilapidated, in need of fresh paint and repairs. The windows are dark, and try as she might, she can't see anyone through the glass. Most likely he lives alone in a house inherited from his parents, who must've abused him to turn him into the monster he is.

"This way." He grabs her hand with his sweaty palm causing her insides to clench up, and leads her around the side of the house to a clearing in the back covered in leaves and pine needles. She glimpses what could be a stagnant pond on one side. On the other, raised up on a small hill, squats a building that's big for a shed, but small for a cabin.

"Where are we going?" She tries to wrench her hand out of his grip, panic welling up inside her.

"Stop it." He drags her to the building and holds her with one hand while the other gets a key from his pocket and unlocks the door. When they're both inside, he shuts the door behind them and lets go of her.

The inside looks hastily prepared, with a twin mattress on the floor made up with sheets, blankets, and a flat pillow. A child-sized table and chair are propped against the wall. Toys and a few worn stuffed animals with matted fur are piled in a box. A bucket covered by a piece of wood sits in the corner, with toilet paper beside it. *Thanks for your consideration, asshole.*

There's barely enough floor space for them to stand without stepping on the bed. One small window, too high for little-girl Rebecca to reach, provides scant light. She glances around the small area for lamps without seeing any. "Can you turn on the light?" she asks to check this.

"There's no electricity." He moves to go.

"You can't leave me here!" This is real, he's planning to lock her inside, and the thought of being his prisoner, and what he might do when he returns, fills her with dread. Whatever her mind may be, her body is six-years-old and she's completely at his mercy.

"Calm down. I don't want to hear a word out of you." He pauses at the door and perhaps in response to the expression of sheer terror on her face, he says, "I'll be back," as if that could be comforting to her instead of only making things a thousand times worse.

His footsteps recede toward the house and as soon as she hears a door bang shut, she takes out her Swiss army knife. If she has any hope of escaping, it needs to be while she still has light to see inside the shed. But there's no keyhole on the inside for her to use to pick the lock, if she were even capable of doing that. Fighting off a feeling of desperation, she tries to insert her knife between the door and its frame, but the fit is too tight. Throwing down the knife in frustration, she hurls herself against the outward opening door, but it's much too sturdy to be affected by her featherlight body and she only ends up hurting her shoulder.

If she could just get out, she could run down the driveway and possibly get the address from a mailbox, or the name of the street from a sign. This might make the difference between finding him in the present or not, especially if it turns out the license plate belongs to a stolen vehicle.

The window is the only way and she has only one chance of reaching it. She shoves the mattress to the side to make space on the floor before dragging the table to the area below the window, right up next to the wall. The chair is light, allowing even her weak and spindly arms to lift it and place it on the table. She folds her knife and pockets it before beginning the climb from floor to table to chair. Raising herself to a standing position, she steadies herself against the wall while the chair wobbles beneath her feet.

Rebecca reaches the latch and snaps it open. Lifting onto her tiptoes, she pushes the bottom of the glass outward as far as it will go. But she isn't sure whether she can squeeze through the narrow gap she's created.

"Hey!" The man shouts from the house.

Fuck. He must've seen the window come open, and now he's running to the shed. In seconds he'll have the door unlocked and who knows what he'll do to her then.

In her panic to get back down quickly and be ready to jab him with her knife, she loses her balance. The chair slips out from under her feet and she tumbles downward. The sound of the key turning in the lock reaches her at the same instant her head cracks against the floor.

PART III

13

Nicki hunches over the game table staring down at the jigsaw. She and Uncle have been working on it for several days because it's hard. One thousand pieces. Uncle snaps one into a spot she'd given up on. They're nearing the end.

As usual, it's a picture of dogs doing doggie things. This one has a Doberman, a Golden Retriever, and a French bulldog being walked by owners who look like them.

She glances across the table at Uncle with the silver dog medallion dangling from his neck. "If you like dogs so much, why don't you ever get one?"

He answers without looking up. "You know Mother's allergic."

"Are you sure about that?"

He raises one eyebrow. The other doesn't move because of his paralysis on that side. "She wouldn't lie about it."

"Yeah, but maybe she's mistaken. Maybe she happened to sneeze around a dog one time, but it wasn't the dog that caused it. There might have been chrysanthemums or some other flowers on a table nearby. Maybe that's what she's allergic to."

He presses another piece in place.

"You could test it, you know. Get some dog hair, I'm sure it's easy enough to find. Spread strands of it around the house. See what happens."

"That's crazy. She would get so angry if she found out." He dabs his lip with his handkerchief.

There was a time when she would've dearly loved having a dog at the house. But not anymore. Not if things work out the way she hopes. So she's not really sure why she even started this conversation, except that it annoys her how he constantly defers to Mother. His sister is eleven years older than him, and he's used to her telling him what to do ever since he was a baby. But it could be he never challenges her because she's clever enough to let him have his way in the stuff that's important to him.

Footsteps tap down the stairs and Mother appears, ready for work. She always wears a button blouse with a bow that ties at the collar, a straight skirt, nylons, and shoes with sensible heels.

"It's so nice to see the two of you playing together," she says like they're eight-year-old siblings. She bends to kiss Uncle on the side of his head. "Why don't you eat the fish sticks and tater tots tonight? There's carrots to go with it in the fridge." She always has carrots with her fish because she likes dipping them in the tartar sauce.

"Okay," Uncle says.

She comes around the table and pats Nicki on the shoulders. "You be good now."

Nicki ignores her, pretending to concentrate on searching for a piece.

Mother hates not getting a response. "Aren't you going to wish me a nice night at work?"

"Have a good night," Uncle says.

Nicki still doesn't respond and Mother turns away in a huff. "If someone hopes to get back full privileges, someone ought to start being nicer around here." She goes out the door and a minute later, the car starts up.

"She just wants what's best for you," Uncle says.

"Does she?" They've been saying these sorts of things for years, but Nicki no longer believes them.

"Course she does." He wipes his mouth.

"You can finish the jigsaw." Nicki rises. "I've got school work to do." She goes upstairs to her room and works on geometry until Uncle calls her for dinner.

Unsurprisingly, he's prepared the menu ordered by Mother. Nicki neither loves nor hates the meal; she's pretty neutral about everything she eats. It provides nourishment but not pleasure.

"How come we never get to eat hot dogs?" Nicki says, still feeling ornery.

Uncle frowns. "You know Mother doesn't like them."

"Yeah, but how come you and I can't have them?" Somewhere deep inside her memory, she remembers eating a hot dog smothered in ketchup and loving it.

"We all eat the same meal. Mother says it's a lot more work to make something different for everybody."

"Seems to me it's pretty easy to cook a hot dog."

"How would you know?"

Nicki doesn't answer, annoyed with this reminder that she doesn't get to know how to do anything they don't want her to learn. After a minute, she asks, "Do you ever get tired of doing what Mother says all the time?"

"She's good to me. She mostly lets me do what I want." He doesn't get how strange this sounds coming from an adult.

"If you're nice to her, she'll be good to you too," he adds.

"I'll try harder," she says, not really meaning it. "Can I bring Sadie her food tonight?"

Uncle stiffens up and wipes his lips with the napkin. "I already did."

She's not sure she believes him. "Can I just visit with her then? She must be so lonely."

"Not tonight. Mother says you have to earn back your privileges."

"Oh Mother this, Mother that!" She flings down her fork. "Screw that."

"Watch your language. And finish your meal." His voice has turned cold and harsh.

She lowers her head and picks up her fork. "Yes, Uncle."

Later when she's doing the dishes, he interrupts her. "Going out to chop some wood."

She glances toward the window. It's still early in the evening and the summer sun hasn't yet set. She resists the temptation to reply with sarcasm. *Don't we have a ten-year supply already?* He is out there chopping year-round. When she questioned him once before, he'd said, "Someone has to do it. We live in a forest. Can't just let logs rot on the ground."

"I need you to go to your room," he says.

"But you'll be right outside."

"Mother said that's the rule for now. One of us has to be inside if you're to have the run of the place."

Without arguing further, she turns off the water, dries her hands, and goes up the stairs with Uncle right behind her. After she shuts her door, she hears him lock it.

A zip of excitement runs through her. This is the first chance she's gotten to try out the bobby pins. Checking the window, she waits to see him come out back carrying his axe to the woodpile. Then she takes out the bobby pins and gets to work on the door. *Thwack, thwack* forms the background noise as she uses a bent pin as a lever to keep tension on the lock while she picks it using a second pin.

She works slowly, trying to get a feel for it, listening for clicks as a sign of progress. Fifteen minutes later, she still hasn't opened it and her knees hurt, pressed against the bare wooden floor by the door. After grabbing her pillow to put under them, she restarts from the beginning.

Ten more minutes pass without success and she pauses to rest her fingers. Outside, the *thwacks* have also stopped. *Crap.* She's about to put away her tools when the sounds of chopping resume. She dives back into her work, starting to feel as if she's getting the hang of it. Before long, the last pin clicks inside the lock and she turns the lever to open it.

Though it's the skill of a thief, her accomplishment fills her with pride. While Uncle continues with the wood, she locks and unlocks the door three times, getting faster with each attempt. She has confidence she can do it quickly now, but she'll continue to practice whenever she has the opportunity.

A glance at the window tells her the sun is nearly gone, and he'll be coming back inside soon. She locks herself back into her room, replaces the precious bobby pins, and goes to peer out the window at Uncle.

He puts the last log on the newest stack, wipes his hands with a towel, and pats his face with his handkerchief before heading across the clearing toward the shed. Pausing outside its door, he turns back toward the house, his gaze shifting to Nicki's window.

She jerks back behind the wall, but she might've been too late to prevent him from seeing her. Moving away, she rubs her hands against her jeans. Feeling dirty. Witnessing him there makes her feel like a party to his crimes. *Why haven't I helped Sadie yet?* Nicki bears responsibility as long as she allows herself to be paralyzed by fear of Mother and Uncle. It's not just about her. She can tolerate her life here with them. But she can't tolerate what they're doing to that little girl.

Getting an idea, she brings her pencil and writing pad to the bed and begins a list of everything they need to take with them when she and Sadie make their escape. At the top, she writes *Uncle's backpack*. She's seen him use it from time to time when he said he was going for a long walk. It should be just the right size for their needs, without weighing her down too much. The second item on the list is *map of the area*. There's one inside the kitchen drawer. When she gets an opportunity, she'll study it closely.

She doesn't know when the chance will come to make her move. But when it happens, she'll be ready. For Sadie.

14

———

Rebecca wakes with a spasm, vividly recalling how much it hurt to bang her skull against the hard surface of the cabin floor. Touching her head where the impact occurred, she no longer feels any pain or swelling, because that was six-year-old Rebecca and the mindcast has ended. She gazes at her adult-sized hand with affection, filled with relief to be herself again.

Sunlight floods her bedroom. Thirteen hours have gone by since she flipped into the past. She can't remember when she's ever remained in bed so long. Maybe her body needed extra time to recover from the trauma of the mindcast, disturbing beyond anything she's experienced in her life.

There are things she must do, but she can't get herself to move just yet. She's suffused with conflicting emotions of the sort she hasn't allowed herself to feel for years. Love, remorse, and longing for the living presence of her lost sister and mother. Judgment, guilt, and self-hatred regarding her actions that day, the worst of her life. Revulsion and loathing toward the man who destroyed her family. A man who now has a face, if not an identity.

Exultation underlies all of it. She's seen the man, and the license plate of the car he drove, and the place where he brought Sadie. So many clues, surely they'll lead her to him. She punches the pillow. It's impossible for her to fail now. She'll find him and bring him to justice, no matter how long it takes. No matter what she has to do. Determination surges through her.

Though her stomach craves food, she rises and goes straight to her computer. Opening a new document, she enters every detail she can recall. First the license plate number. Then a complete description of the kidnapper from head to toe. She even makes a sketch of his face. Unfortunately, she's incapable of drawing anything. Even her stick figures lack symmetry. Once when she played Pictionary, her partner couldn't guess a single one of her clues. No matter. Bob the Kidnapper suffering from facial paralysis greatly limits the field of possible suspects.

She records the details of their trip. The time it took for each section of the drive. The appearance of the clearing where they stopped, along with their conversation and all else that took place there. The sensations of riding in the car, the zigzags and ups and downs. The frequency of stop signs and stop lights. The times where traffic seemed to slow. And the final right turn off the highway.

Coming to her arrival, she describes the house and grounds. The clearing in the back, the possible stagnant pond, and the trees surrounding everything. *The shed.* She tries drawing a picture again, and although it's better than the face she sketched, it doesn't match her memory well enough. She crumples the paper and tosses it.

By the time she runs out of things to write down, she's tingling with anticipation. This has to be enough to find him, arrest him, and keep him from hurting any other little girls as he has hurt Sadie. She saves the document to her USB stick and prints out several copies. She will not be taking the chance of losing these notes, full of details that are fresh in her mind but will probably fade shortly.

She decides to place a copy of the document inside her letter to her father, telling him he can rely on the information though she can't tell him how she came by it. Most likely he'll consider it the ravings of a lunatic. But she will have tried.

Anyway, she's not planning on dying yet.

She wishes she could go to Freddie—the detective on Sadie's case with whom she still keeps in touch—and show him her description of Bob. Ask him to get a police artist to produce a sketch. Then have the police search their database for a match. But how could she possibly explain this description of the kidnapper that came out of nowhere? Everyone knows she never saw him, not even a glimpse from behind, because she was in the garage with Mikayla. She can't change that fact now, nineteen years later. Nor can she reveal her time-travel ability. Freddie isn't the sort to believe anything that doesn't sound rational. And even if she managed to convince him, what then? He'd be laughed off the force if he shared her story with any of the other officers.

Having completed her most pressing work, she allows herself to go out for another large brunch. She's been eating like a whale lately, just opening her mouth and letting gobs of food flow in. But a quick check on the scale shows no real change. The mindcasts seem to rob her of a great deal of energy that needs replacement in calories. She orders a stack of banana pancakes, planning to bring the leftovers home, but before she knows it, she has scarfed up the last bite soaked in maple syrup.

After leaving the restaurant, she sets out for a long walk since this version of her hasn't exercised in a couple of days. She calls Freddie, who doesn't answer—he never does—and leaves an urgent message for him to call back as soon as he can.

The phone rings half an hour into her walk and shows *Detective Lazo* on her display. "Hey Freddie, thanks for getting back to me so quickly."

"What's up? It's been a while." His voice still has the ability to comfort her.

"I've got new information. Can we meet somewhere in the next few days?"

There's a brief silence, and then, "You're in luck. I have to be in Milpitas this afternoon. Meet me at Kristal's Coffee on Hawthorne? Three p.m.?"

"Perfect."

They hang up without any more chatting. Freddie isn't the chatting type. Straight to business. Direct. Honest.

Rebecca returns home to shower and change. She reviews her notes, not planning to bring them with her to the meeting. Except she does jot down the license plate number on a slip of paper. If it connects to someone who lives within two hours of Windlake, she will be well on her way to breaking this case.

At the appointed time, she walks into the coffee shop to find Freddie already seated. He's a man of Chinese heritage on one side, Hispanic on the other. Trim and fastidiously dressed as always, he wears a sports jacket over a turtleneck, even though it's summer. Polished leather shoes. He rises when he sees her and shakes her hand when she reaches him. He isn't the hugging type. As usual, he smells like soap and looks as if he shaved an hour ago. His short black hair is neatly gelled to his head.

He smiles, which for him involves only a slight broadening of the lips. "Good to see you, Rebecca."

"Thanks, you too." She sits across from him and they delay talking until they can both order coffee. Freddie gets a chocolate croissant to go with his. "Missed lunch today," he says. The man has a definite sweet tooth, though considering she just polished off enough pancakes to feed a youth soccer team, she's hardly one to talk.

"It's about Sadie's case. Of course." It isn't as though they meet for coffee any other time. She slides across the piece of paper where she's written the license plate number. "Can you find out who owned this car in the year 2000?"

Freddie's eyes widen in disbelief. "Are you saying this has something to do with the kidnapping?"

"Maybe. I can't be sure."

"Where did you get it?"

"An anonymous tip."

"Did this person call you?"

"Freddie, I'm sorry, but I can't say any more about it."

"If they called, I can trace the number for you," he says.

"They didn't call."

"Email then? It'll be harder to trace if they know what they're doing."

"No email."

"That leaves handwritten letter. Can I see it?"

"I didn't get a handwritten letter." So far, at least, she has stuck with the truth. "That's all I can say. Can you just trace the number? What harm is there in that?"

He taps his fingers on the paper before raising his gaze to her. "I have to say this. If you found this source on the Internet… you can't trust information you find on the Internet. Nothing short of an article from a reliable source like the Times or the Post. Even then, it might've been doctored. Thousands of websites spout conspiracy theories. In some cases, people are trying to get revenge. What if whoever posted this has it in for whoever owns this vehicle? An ex-wife or ex-business partner. You can't believe stuff like this."

"It isn't like that," she says. "I swear."

"It's easy enough to find out all about the case. They could've targeted you. You didn't pay them, did you?"

"No." She knew it was going to be hard convincing him, but this is even worse than she expected.

He takes a bite of his croissant and chews thoughtfully. After a minute, he says, "I'll run it through and get the name of the vehicle owner. I suppose it can't hurt to do a quick check on them. See if they've got a record. If there's anything the slightest bit related, like he beat up his girlfriend or any other kind of assault, even if it's minor, it might be enough to justify talking to him. That's the most I can promise. But if the car owner is clean, never been busted for anything, I can't investigate. The chief would never approve it. I can't contact the FBI over this either. They'll think I'm crazy."

That he's agreed to run the plate fills her with joy. "Thank you, Freddie. That's all I'm asking." She had never imagined he would do more than this. Her fear had been that he wouldn't do anything.

He drains his cup. "Don't thank me yet."

15

———

Freddie's call comes a few days later in the morning. "It's a silver Ford Taurus belonging to a Daniel Ortiz of Draywood. D-R-A-Y-wood. You know where it is?"

"I don't think so." She's opening Google Maps, typing the name of the town. When she sees the location, she pumps her fists, mouthing *yes*. "I see it. Part way up the mountains."

"That's right. A one-horse town. Population around two thousand."

She clicks on *Directions* and enters "Windlake." When the app displays a roughly two-hour drive between Draywood and her former hometown, she bites her lip to hold back a shout. *This is it.*

"Sorry to have to tell you this, but Daniel Ortiz has led an exemplary life. Sixty-eight years old. A retired carpenter. Well-respected member of his community. He donates to charities and never got worse than a speeding ticket. The man's a mensch."

Disappointment fills her, though she isn't too surprised. A criminal is a law-abiding person until they're caught.

"Does he still live there?"

"No, he moved to Lodi a few years back." His voice dips to a lower register as he takes on a sterner tone. "I want to caution you not to approach him. I don't know where you got this number, or what role you think the driver of that car played, but it's just wrong. You need to let this go. If you take matters into your own hands, I won't be able to protect you."

"I'm not going to do anything," she lies. He can truthfully attest to having no knowledge of her plans, if it comes to that. This will all be on her.

He hesitates like he's not sure if he believes her but can't decide if he should say so. "Okay then," he finally replies. "You take care."

"I will, Freddie. I appreciate your help, even if it didn't come to anything."

As soon as she hangs up, she goes to her computer and looks up Daniel Ortiz of Draywood. There isn't much about him, except confirmation he used to be a carpenter and active member of the Sierra Club. However, another Ortiz comes up. His son, Martin, who works as a real estate agent in the area.

She can't find a photo of Daniel online. In any case, he's too old to be the man who picked Rebecca off the sidewalk and brought her to the shed. Nineteen years ago, Daniel was forty-nine, but Bob the Kidnapper could not have been older than his mid-twenties.

His son Martin, though. Could he have been driving Dad's car? She looks him up next, and thanks to his being a real estate agent, there are plenty of photos online. Movie-star handsome, he's clearly not Bob with the facial paralysis, even if the condition had been cured somehow. Martin appears to be in his mid-thirties now, making him sixteen or seventeen when it happened. Maybe he was working with Bob. Or maybe the father had been working with him. For all she knows, they could all be part of a network of child traffickers located in the Sierras.

She drums her fingers on the desk, considering whether she should pay a visit on Daniel Ortiz in Lodi. But what good would it do? He isn't about to admit anything to her, and she'll just be alerting him to the fact that she's coming for him.

Looking back at the map, she checks the route. It's easy to spot an extended section of the highway where the road follows frequent twists and turns. Figuring how long it would take to reach there from her old house, she matches this roughly with her description of when the constant swerving inside Bob's car began.

Certainty grips her. Draywood is where he brought her. The route matches her sensations of the trip, and the Taurus was registered to a man who lived there. Draywood is where she must go.

A bit more research reveals that Martin now owns the house that used to belong to his father. This could even be where she was taken. With growing excitement, she looks at the satellite view of his address, but she can't get an image of the back, and too many trees block the front to allow her a clear view of the place. She has to go see it in person. Her first step will be to visit the house. Her second will be to look for Bob. In a town that small, how many people could there be with a face like his?

She knows if she delays leaving it will cause her to hesitate. Being captured by that demon has left her frightened to face him again. Though she's back to being twenty-five years old, she is smaller and weaker than most men. And for all she knows, Bob might have a stockpile of automatic weapons as well. She has nothing aside from a can of mace she's been keeping in a drawer. The thought reminds her to move it into her purse, and then to add a roll of duct tape to her pile of things to be packed. If she can disable him with the mace, she might have a chance to bind him to a chair or something.

Returning to her computer, she looks up information about the area. The town is tiny, with a highway running through it and businesses lined up on both sides of it. A few small restaurants and cafés, a grocery market, a burger joint and pizza place, several gas stations—probably to accommodate all the skiers headed up and down the mountain—some retail shops, two real estate offices, and one motel. The Draywood Motel has a website displaying photos of the lobby and the front of the building, a phone number, and an email address. With no online reservation system, it seems like a holdover from the 1990s. On closer observation, the place looks more *rundown* than *rustic*—their word—but still several levels above the Bates Motel. She briefly considers staying in a different town, but decides she would be better off close to the heart of things, as she tries to sniff out Bob from wherever he might be hiding.

When she calls to book a room, they sound surprised she bothered to make a reservation instead of just popping in while passing in the area. And when she asks if she can keep the number of days open, they have no objection whatsoever. She hopes she isn't the only guest in the whole place.

Her next call takes a little more preparation. She usually doesn't drink wine this early in the day, but she needs a few slow sips to calm herself. The man she's about to speak with might be a villain who was involved in her sister's kidnapping.

She practices what she'll say to him a few times before finally making the call. After two rings, real estate agent Martin Ortiz answers, identifying himself in a clear, resonant tone. He probably spent years developing that voice, she thinks. It would go a long way toward convincing reluctant buyers to part with the obscene amount of money it takes to buy a home in California.

"Hi, this is Rebecca Jones," she says, having decided in advance to use a fake last name. If she were a real estate agent, she would Google every prospective client, and she expects no less of him. Particularly if in addition to selling real estate, he is somehow involved in child abduction. A search of *Rebecca Danser* shows her connection to missing child *Sadie Danser* on the first page.

Jones is a common enough name, he'll become overwhelmed trying to figure out which one might be her. She keeps her first name intact, knowing she'd be sure to forget to respond if she dubbed herself something else. "What do you think of that, *Susie*?" he might say, causing her to look over her shoulder for another woman in the room.

"I'm going to be in Draywood tomorrow and was wondering if I could meet with you to talk about local real estate," she says.

"Of course, I'd be happy to help you. What time is good for you?"

"Eleven?"

There's a pause as he checks his calendar. "That works. Are you looking for a vacation home, or a year-round residence for you and your family?"

"Year-round. I'll give you the specifics tomorrow." She ends the call, not wanting to spend any more time than necessary on phony details.

She packs a full-size suitcase, not knowing how long she may need to remain in the area. To make sure she won't have to find a laundromat, she includes a week's worth of clothing along with some warm winter outerwear. The altitude is considered below the snowline at 3000 to 3500 feet, but it could still turn frigid at night, and flurries are always possible.

At the last minute, she digs into the photo album for a portrait of Sadie taken not long before she disappeared. If Rebecca were to encounter a trustworthy resident who's been there for more than nineteen years, she could show them the photo and ask if they remember seeing a girl like her around town, or at anyone's house. This is a very long shot, but still worthy of an attempt.

It's late afternoon by the time she sets out. She listens to more podcasts about animal wildlife during the drive, though it makes her miss her friends at the refuge. When she stops for gas, she gets coffee to keep her awake since the monotonous drive through Central Valley tends to make her drowsy. She also buys a bag of chips to hold her till dinner.

It's about seven by the time she pulls into the motel parking lot. The place looks roughly equivalent to a Motel-Six, with design flourishes straight out of the 1950s, a big neon sign, and outside entrances for the two levels worth of rooms. She doubts they ever get close to filling the place, especially not now, too late for summer and too soon for ski season. Nor is there any major tourist destination nearby. All of this explains the near empty lot. She figures the two parked cars either belong to employees, or to people visiting relatives in the area.

Since the office is empty when she enters, she rings the bell. After a few minutes, a door to a back room opens and a boy emerges. He has freckles and long eyelashes and looks no more than sixteen. She assumes he must be older since he works in this place and doesn't appear to have parental control over his appearance, as evidenced by purple hair and full lower-arm tattoos.

He moves with nervous energy. "Good evening, ma'am."

Rebecca tries not to laugh. At twenty-five, she's not sure anyone has ever called her that before. "I have a reservation. Rebecca Danser."

"Is it just you, ma'am?"

"Yes, I'm alone."

"May I see your license and credit card?"

She slides them across and looks over the counter, where he inserts the card into a device connected to an iPad. His hands look too big for his arms, like they reached full size ahead of the rest of him.

He places the iPad in front of her. "Sign here, please."

She basically makes a line with her finger.

"Will you be staying past tomorrow?" he says.

"I'm not sure yet. Is that all right?"

"I don't know. We're expecting a busload of tourists from Hawaii."

She looks at him blankly, and he laughs. "JK, who would ever come here from there?" He returns her items and hands her an actual key, not a key card. "Room fifteen on the second floor. It's in the back. You can drive around and park there. Need help with your luggage, ma'am?"

She wonders just how old he thinks she is, and reminds herself to check the mirror as soon as possible. What if all this mindcasting is making her age prematurely, like a time-traveling *Picture of Dorian Gray*? Though actually, Dorian still looked young, it was only the picture that was a fright.

Declining the boy's help, she goes outside to her car, but when she turns and looks back through the glass, she sees him still standing there, watching her with a curious look in his eyes. It gives her a little chill, which she quickly shakes off, reminding herself she's grateful that although the motel looks ancient, thanks to this tech-savvy kid, she just had the fastest check-in ever.

Rebecca parks in back, gets her suitcase from the trunk, and carries it up the stairs. She has to jiggle the knob to get the key to open it. Inside it smells musty and the decorating is dated, with puke green carpet and tile in the bathroom that's the color of dried blood. At least from her quick inspection, the toilet and bed sheets look clean. It's good enough.

After freshening up and changing into a different blouse, she goes out. From her research she knows the few places to get dinner in town. She could order it to-go and eat in her room, but she figures it will be best to present herself in a public location as soon as possible, to reduce the amount of interest she might attract as she wanders through the area over the next few days. Most likely everyone else already knows each other. A stranger is bound to attract attention.

Since JJs Bar & Grill is only a quarter mile from the motel, she decides to walk. The so-called highway is more like a wide road with light traffic and sidewalks on both sides. She passes a gas station-slash-repair shop, a convenience store, and a building supply company. Eventually she spots the restaurant up ahead, its lights blazing like a beacon in the growing darkness. It reassures her to see vehicles in the lot, a sign that she's not the only creature remaining— along with the boy—in this post-apocalyptic town.

She steels herself before opening the door. There are so few choices of where to eat... what if the kidnapper is inside here right now? She prepares her face not to show any reaction before entering and pausing at the *Please wait to be seated* sign. Glancing around, she counts two families, four couples, three single diners. No Bob. She lets out her breath.

A waiter wearing a black bow tie over his flannel shirt approaches her. "One?" he asks.

Rebecca nods and follows the man to a table that's awkwardly too large, where he hands her the menu without comment. As she scans the list of entrees, she keeps an eye on activity around her. A gray-haired man seated alone is looking her way, but when she catches him at it, he shifts his gaze quickly. A little later, she notices an older waitress staring at her. But when their eyes connect, the woman smiles at her, holding her gaze until she's the one to look away.

After figuring out her order, Rebecca lays down the menu and checks her phone, not that there's really anyone in her life who would get in touch with her right now. A few minutes later, the waitress who was looking at her earlier approaches instead of the waiter who first seated her. The woman is past middle-age, but wears her hair in a ponytail and curled-in bangs that look childish on her. She's dressed in a pink blouse that ties with a bow at the neck, a straight, black skirt, and fat-heeled shoes.

"Hello, sweetie-pie. Can I get your order?" she says.

Rebecca masks her annoyance. She dislikes when someone she doesn't know calls her *sweetie*, or *honey*, or *darling*. "I'd like the grilled chicken with potatoes and red peppers," she says.

"Good choice. Anything to drink?"

"You have a local wine you can recommend?"

"Sure do. Laughing Duck pinot grigio will knock your socks off."

"I'll take a glass of that."

The waitress writes it down. "Your first visit here?"

"That's right."

"What brings you to our little town?"

"I just came for some fresh air," Rebecca says.

"You'll find plenty of that. Where do you hail from?"

"Bay Area."

"Well, I'm Patricia. I work here most nights. You have any questions about what to do around town, just come to me."

"Sure, thanks." Rebecca doesn't share her name.

"I'll get that food for you right away."

She wasn't lying about the food coming quickly. Though after taking a few bites, Rebecca thinks it might've benefited from more careful preparation. The wine is good, however. She works on a sudoku while she eats.

Later when the waitress takes her credit card, she scrutinizes it on her way to the register. Maybe she's supposed to do that when it's a stranger passing through town. But Rebecca has already decided she won't be coming back to this grill. Something about Patricia has left a sour tang in the back of her throat.

16

Rebecca gets up early and goes for a run along the tangled roads in the area behind the motel. Homes are few and far between. Streets are narrow, winding, and full of potholes. There are no sidewalks but it hardly matters given the lack of traffic. It's darker than she expected, with light from the rising sun shimmering through the towering pines.

This day will be a challenging one, emotionally and perhaps in other ways as well. When she returns from her exercise, she takes a shower, and dresses in comfortable leggings, with a thin cotton V-neck top and her softest fleece jacket. She walks down the street for coffee and a donut from a tiny building where you order at the window because there's no room for seating inside. She takes it back to her room at the motel, happy to avoid the chance of running into Martin Ortiz before their appointment.

To ensure she arrives on time, she drives to his office though that too is within walking distance. She's a few minutes early when she pulls into one of the three spaces provided for parking. Inside, there's a small reception area with no receptionist, leading to three equally small offices. Two are empty and Martin emerges from the third with hand outstretched. "Thanks for coming. Come on in." When he smiles widely, revealing dimples and beautifully aligned teeth, she has to remind herself he could be involved in terrible crimes. Otherwise she would find it hard to resist the green eyes, the wavy black hair with an errant curl on his forehead, the two- or three-day shadow on his lips and chin, and the way his polo shirt emphasizes the swell of his arm muscles.

He leads her into his office to a comfortable chair by the window. "Can I get you coffee?"

"I'm caffeine'ed out, thanks." She glances around while he settles behind his desk. She's not sure she's ever seen such a neatly organized office. Brochures are stacked at matching heights. His business cards, pen holder, and stapler are lined up in a perfect column on the other side. There's a vase with matching orchids, all poised in a state of early bloom. She thinks they must be artificial.

"If you don't mind my asking," he says, "what brings you here? A new job for you or your husband?"

"I'm not married." She's probably only imagining that his eyes show a dash of increased interest. "I'm a writer. I can work anywhere, and I love looking out at trees. It's affordable here, compared to most parts of California. I don't know. I think I could grow to like it. What do you think?"

"Obviously I love it, since I live here myself. People are friendly, but it's remote. Quiet. You have to be comfortable with that."

"I could be. Why don't you show me what's available? Not too large. It's just me."

He stares at her, thinking. "There's a place that just came on the market last week. Beautiful lot, but accessible."

"Accessible?"

"That means not too far from the highway. Do you have time to see it? Better than looking at brochures. And it's empty."

"All right." She almost feels guilty for wasting his time, but then, she has an excellent reason for doing so.

"My car's in the back," he says.

When she rises, her jacket brushes the brochures, knocking the top ones off center. He carefully straightens them before leading her out to a sporty-looking Subaru parked at the curb. To her relief, he doesn't try to open the passenger door for her. She can't stand when guys insist on doing things she can easily do herself.

"I think you might love this place," he says, getting into the driver's seat. "It has a great deck and lots of privacy." He elaborates on the amenities during the ten-minute drive, but since it's all a ruse to learn more about him, she doesn't pay close attention.

When they draw up to the house, she realizes he wasn't exaggerating. The place is beautiful. Rustic but modern. Surrounded by mature trees that look as if they've received regular care and pruning. Just the right distance from the neighbors: too far for prying eyes, too close to feel scarily isolated.

She follows him inside, where it's sparkling clean, with stunning wood floors and bright painted walls. They go into the kitchen.

"Oven and stove are electric but you can convert to gas."

"Why would I do that?"

"Oh, a lot of people think food cooks better with gas."

"I don't cook."

"Really? You might want to rethink that if you're going to be living around here. There aren't a lot of takeout options."

"I'll keep it in mind. I suppose you think it's odd, wanting a house for just one person."

"Not at all. I live alone too. Well, me and my dog, anyway."

"I love dogs. What kind is it? What's your dog's name?"

"Her name's Galleta."

"That's pretty. What does it mean?" She moves through a hallway into the first bedroom.

"Cookie. Or, more like a biscuit. Doesn't matter. I like the word, but now I just call her 'Guy' all the time."

"Guy. That's cute." She could see herself picking a name like that. "But are cookies her favorite food?"

"She doesn't get to eat them, so I don't know."

"What is her favorite food?"

"Anything that smells like bacon."

She can hardly believe her good luck in getting this information out of him. He doesn't appear suspicious either.

"There's three bedrooms and two full baths," he says.

"Good. I can have visitors." She pauses. "Be honest. Tell me what it's like to live around here. I've heard you can get oddballs in these foothill communities."

"I guess you don't have any oddballs in Silicon Valley?"

She laughs. "No, we're all one hundred percent normal. Whatever normal is."

"To answer your question, yeah, we've got oddballs. But overall, it's a nice community. Friendly. But not intrusive."

"Have you lived here long?"

"All my life. Well, except when I was at college."

"Did you come home in the summers?" She hopes not, because that would be around the time Sadie was taken.

But he gives a little laugh. "Yeah. Yeah, I did. I guess I'm pretty provincial. I even live in the house I grew up in now. My father sold it to me when he moved to Central Valley."

"And you haven't filled the place with children yet?"

"I'm not even married. My girlfriend was living with me, till we broke up last year." He gives her a curious look. "You know, for someone who wants to live alone in the woods, you're pretty talkative."

She decides it would be wise to give it a rest. They go out back to view the deck, which truly does look like a wonderful place to sit out in the evening, listening to the breeze rustling the branches of the trees. If she ever did live in a place like this, she probably would want a dog, though. Or maybe two.

"Let me show you another place you might like," he says.

"Um, thank you, but I have a meeting this afternoon. Need to go back to my motel room to connect."

"Okay, sure." He leads the way through the house, pausing to restore doors, window coverings, and light switches to the state they were in when they arrived. "Does tomorrow work for you? I assume you'll be heading back to the Bay Area soon."

"Let me think about this one. I'll let you know if I decide to look at any others."

The drive back to his office is fairly quiet. She feels guilty in a way, taking up his time. He doesn't seem like he could be involved in Sadie's kidnapping. But she has to be sure.

She actually does go back to her room, afraid if Martin sees her around town she's going to look like a liar. Luckily she brought several novels with her. She picks the most promising and stretches out with it on the comfortable chair by the window. She reads all afternoon, quitting by eight o'clock or so, in time to get dinner.

Anxious to get to the business of this evening, she buys a pizza and brings it back to her room. When she's finished eating, she rises to close the shade on her window. Noticing a car parked across the street from the motel lot, she draws back and turns out the light in her room. It's an odd place for someone to leave their vehicle, with nothing around except an empty field.

She's about to shrug it off when the light of a cell phone flashes inside the car, illuminating a person sitting in the driver's seat. But before she can make out any details, like what gender they might be, the light goes off.

Rebecca lowers the shade and sits down. Could someone be watching her? She's not sure what kind of car this is, but it isn't a red Kia. If Reamer is still following her, he must be driving something else. But she doesn't believe he would come all this way. It wouldn't have been easy for him to track her on the highway for so long without her noticing. Besides, he isn't the kidnapper. She has begun to believe his purpose in approaching her before was as simple as what he claimed—he wanted her to know he had nothing to do with Sadie's disappearance.

But if not Reamer, then who? Has Bob noticed her around town, without her noticing him? How would he even know who she was? After struggling with this thought for several minutes, she decides it's possible he's looked her up and seen a recent photo on the Internet. Maybe he keeps tabs on her family, wanting to be sure there are never any leads in the case.

She gets up again and folds back the shade to peer out. The car is gone. On the one hand, she feels relief; on the other, she wishes she could be sure it had nothing to do with her.

Before getting into bed, she chains the door and pulls the heavy chair in front of it. But even with these extra precautions, it takes far longer than she had hoped to settle down and grow more relaxed. The real work doesn't begin until she's almost asleep.

17

———

Rebecca travels back in time to the morning of the same day, landing inside her less-than-twenty-four-hour-younger self just as she prepares to leave the motel.

This time she doesn't drive to Martin's office but instead goes to the market, where she purchases bacon-flavored dog treats. From there she heads directly to Martin's family home, which she expects to find empty, save for Galleta—Guy—the Great Dane.

It's just past eleven when she turns onto his street. He's now in his office waiting for her to arrive, and she hopes he'll give her at least an hour. She turns off her phone to ignore the inevitable polite call or text he'll make in fifteen minutes or so, asking if she is still planning to meet with him.

She knows the instant she pulls up in front of Martin's house that it isn't the one where Bob took her. The property is similar but much better maintained, surrounded by trees and somewhat remote from its neighbors. This home is also a sprawling one-story, as opposed to an overshadowing two.

It brings her some relief to discover another piece of information that could clear Martin and his father of any involvement in Sadie's disappearance. But she can't yet discount the idea that her sister might've been taken here eventually. The involvement of the Ortiz family car in her kidnapping continues to be a damning detail.

Since Rebecca has come here via a mindcast she can afford to take more risks. She has already decided it will be necessary to get inside the house and search for any evidence of children being trafficked or kept as prisoners, or of a connection with the mysterious *Bob*.

Since there's no car in the driveway, she's hopeful no one else is at home. He said he and his girlfriend broke up last year, but a new one might have just moved in, or a relative, or a housekeeper. She should've asked more questions while she was with him, but she had been wary of raising his suspicions. Especially if he might truly have something to hide.

The best way is the direct approach, she decides. She rings the front doorbell, which causes a frenzy of barking to erupt from the backyard. Guy's register is low and deep, the kind that would scare intruders away if they didn't bother to go look at her. Great Danes are known for their gentle dispositions. Helen at the wildlife shelter, who used to breed them, told Rebecca the greatest threat they posed was the potential for whacking you with their whiplike wagging tails.

If anyone comes to the door, she has a story ready about confusing the address of his home and office. But no one does, even after a second ring. She waits a minute longer before trying the knob in case he accidentally left it open. No such luck, though.

She checks behind to make sure no one is watching before walking to the back of the house, rattling the treat box on her way to give Guy a preview of coming attractions. The dog is leashed to a long rope, allowing her full range of the yard from the back door to the edge of the forest. As soon as Rebecca rounds the corner, Guy bounds toward her, forcing a backward leap that keeps her barely out of reach. Her presence inspires another round of energetic barking.

"It's okay, girl. Look, I have treats." She opens the box and waves the smoky scent of bacon at the dog's nose. She grows quiet immediately and strains her head forward.

Rebecca tosses a treat that's caught in mid-air. "Good girl." She holds out the next one toward her mouth. "Gentle, Guy." The dog licks it off her palm and she keeps her hand extended to be sniffed. "See? I'm friendly." Guy allows herself to be petted now. "Good girl. What a beauty you are." The dog turns and presents her rump for scratching, a favorite spot for Danes. "You like that? Oh you're just a great big softie, aren't you?"

Rebecca is now free to cross the yard to the deck, pausing to pick up a tennis ball and toss it, not too far so it stays in Guy's range. The dog fetches it but instead of bringing it back for more throws, she settles on the grass chewing it.

Peering in through the back door, Rebecca scans the inside of the house. Sparsely furnished in a good way. Beautiful cedar floors. A stone fireplace like her family used to have. Is there a basement? She doesn't see any ground level windows, but there might still be something down there that they had specially built for potential appalling deeds. What if her sister is alive and a prisoner inside this house? Or what if another girl is being held captive now? The need to get inside and find out overwhelms her. Though it appears to be a normal house belonging to a normal man in a normal neighborhood, horrors might be hidden within.

This door is also locked, but unlike the front entrance, it has window panes above the knob. Breaking the glass might be beyond Guy's level of tolerance, but she sees no other way. She spots a toolshed on the far side of the house and manages to find a pickaxe inside it. *Martin, you shouldn't make it so easy for burglars.* Before using it on the glass, she puts out the treat box for Guy. As soon as the dog is distracted, she takes a great swing with the axe and shatters one of the lower panes. She pokes at the glass, pushing it into the house, and reaches in to open the lock from inside. When she pulls back her hand, she discovers she's bleeding from one of the shards cutting into her. It's messy but not deep. She wipes the blood on her pants.

Guy jumps up to accompany her inside, but Rebecca slips through quickly and pushes the door shut before the dog can get in. No way is she going to take the chance of the shattered glass on the floor cutting into the poor girl's paws.

She washes her hand with soap and water in the nearest bath-room, and wraps a small towel around it. No time to go looking for Band-Aids. Martin might soon get tired of waiting for her and decide to pop home for lunch.

Her first goal is to search for a basement, and it doesn't take long to locate the door in the laundry room. She opens it, her nerves prick-ling, expecting to see a burned-out bulb hanging from a string like in every horror film she's ever watched. Instead, she's pleasantly relieved to find a normal light switch at the top of the stairs, and a modern light fixture at the bottom. Still, she can't help feeling a shiver as she calls down the steps. "Hello? Anyone down there?" It would've amazed her if a reply came, yet when it doesn't, she feels disap-pointed.

She starts down the narrow, steep steps that creak underneath her feet. Maybe fewer pancakes and syrup would be in order. At the bottom, she finds the basement consists of two sections. On the right there's a tidy workroom, with a table saw and tools hung on the walls. In fact, this could be the reason for the basement, which isn't a common thing to find in California homes. Martin's father was a carpenter and needed a workshop. It's possible Martin learned wood-working from his dad and continues to use this space.

On the left, there's a door. Again, that nervous feeling runs through her. As she grasps the knob, she calls out again. "Hello? I'm a friend. Don't be afraid."

She pushes the door inward to darkness, but the light from the hallway allows her to find the switch inside the room. The overhead fixture comes on and reveals a carpeted area with two armchairs. Several boxes rest along the wall on one side. On the other side, there's an upright piano with a bench. Sheet music rests open in front of the keys.

Rebecca isn't sure what to make of this room. It certainly is not being used as a prison for little girls now. But it could've been. It has its own door. There are no windows. The walls and floor are finished. Remove the piano and chairs and replace them with a bed and a table, and it's the same as the shed, only more spacious.

The boxes might tell her something. She opens the first one and finds it filled with novels, mysteries by authors like Agatha Christie, along with books for a younger age, like Nancy Drew. She pushes this to the side and opens the next. Her breath catches in her throat when she sees the collection of toys inside. Things that a small girl would like. Dolls. Coloring books. Crayons. Building blocks. She turns with some trepidation to the last box. Her hands tremble as she lifts out a girl's flowered dress, small enough to fit a four-year old. Frantic, she dumps out the contents of the box, and with growing panic, picks through the rest of the contents. There are t-shirts, leggings, socks, underwear, bathing suits, sweaters, and jackets, all clothing that a girl might wear, in sizes that would cover ages four up to ten or twelve.

Though she doesn't find the unicorn t-shirt and red shorts Sadie wore on the day she disappeared, it brings her to tears to imagine these are the clothes she wore, toys she played with, and books she read. This was her prison.

A sudden noise interrupts her thoughts. Footsteps on the stairs, rapidly descending. Her limbs turn to jelly while her breath sticks in her throat. Before she can think what to do, Martin fills the frame, his face a dark cloud. "What are you doing here?" The calming, resonant tone has sunk to a growl.

Nothing that comes to mind is believable, the truth least of all. She remains crouched by the box, silent, her thoughts racing for a means of escape. *I will not let him take me.* Even being a prisoner in the shed for such a short time was horrific to her. She'd like to mace herself for leaving the can in her purse in the car.

He enters the room. His hands are empty; he hasn't brought a weapon, thank god. When he's a few feet from the door, she makes her move. Springing up, she dashes to the exit, banging the side of him, knocking him against the wall. She makes it through to the stairs, takes them two at a time, races to the front door. She hears him bounding after her. As her hand touches the knob, he reaches her, wraps a strong arm around her waist, and the other around her shoulders. He literally picks her up, drags her back to the couch, and sits on her. "You're not leaving till you explain yourself," he says.

She's weeping, she can't help it, she's so afraid of what he's going to do to her. "Let me go, let me go," she cries.

"I could've called the police. I've got a camera out back, you know. But a professional thief would look for that. Are you new to this? The camera and Guy are supposed to be deterrents. Admittedly, Guy sucks at her job."

It takes a few seconds for his words to sink in. Is it possible he really thinks she's a thief? She looks at his face. He almost appears as if he feels sorry for her.

"Why didn't you call the police?" *Because you don't want to attract their attention,* she thinks.

"I have no idea. Maybe because I couldn't believe what I was seeing? Also, Guy liked you, and she's a good judge of character. At least she used to be."

She decides to try a lie. "You're right. I'm a lousy thief. I lost my job and I'm out of money. I didn't think you'd have such good security out here in the sticks."

He stares at her like he's trying to read her mind. "Nope. I don't believe it. You're too smart. And this was too stupid. Why would you go in the basement? Hello? I keep cash in a drawer in the kitchen. I've got an iPad and a laptop in the study. Who keeps valuable stuff in the basement?"

Her mind races trying to make her lie sound real, but she's at a loss.

"You were going through the boxes my ex-girlfriend left here. Her daughter's old clothes that she hasn't bothered to pick up. What could possibly be of any value in there?"

His ex-girlfriend's daughter? Could this be true?

"Are you a friend of hers? Did she ask you to come get her stuff so she wouldn't have to come here?" He's basically talking to himself at this point. "But you only had to come to the door and I would've brought it out to your car for you."

He looks down at Rebecca, who's still refusing to talk, and takes out his phone. "Don't try to get away because if you do, I'll have to leap and tackle you to the floor, and that's really going to hurt." He enters 9-1-1 on the screen. "I'm going to report you unless you tell me what you were doing here." He raises his finger above the call button.

She can't be sure if he's bluffing. But she reminds herself she isn't in real-time. Mindcasts are for taking risks she wouldn't dare take otherwise. Mindcasts are for sharing information she wouldn't dare share otherwise.

"A silver Ford Taurus registered to your father was used to kidnap my little sister Sadie nineteen years ago," she says.

His face transforms. She has to admit, it would be extremely difficult to fake the level of astonishment he shows, unless he were one of the finest actors in the world. "What?" he says.

"Your father's car was used to kidnap my sister. That's why I'm here. I came to look for evidence of her having been held here. Finding a box of girl's clothing, toys, and books has definitely raised the probability."

He stares at her like he's trying to read whether she's lying or not. "If that's true about the car, why haven't the police ever been here?"

"I found out recently. I can't explain how. But it's true. Absolutely true."

He releases his grip on her. "Don't move or I'll tackle you, like I said." He gets out his phone. "What's your sister's name?"

"Sadie Danser. I'm Rebecca Danser."

His fingers move on the phone and he reads what's on the screen, his expression becoming grim. He does another search before pocketing his phone again. "What a fucking horrible thing to happen." He moves to the side of the couch, freeing her up. "You read about this stuff... you always wonder how the family manages to cope..."

"Not very well, obviously."

"If you want to leave now, go ahead. Just know that neither me nor my dad had anything to do with what happened to your sister. It turns my stomach just to think of it. And my dad... if you knew him, you'd know it's impossible he could ever hurt a helpless child."

She sits up but makes no move to leave. His offering to let her go weighs heavily in his favor. She can't believe he'd do that if he were guilty. "Why do you have a basement room like that, separated off with its own door?"

Martin lets out a small laugh. "You saw the piano, right? It was my mother's room. She was self-conscious about her piano-playing. Thought she wasn't any good and didn't want to drive anyone else crazy having to listen to her. After she died, my father didn't have the heart to change anything about that room. I didn't either. It's like a memorial to her."

His explanation, which came quickly to his lips, makes sense. Who would put a piano in a room meant to hold captives? They could be banging away on that thing any time someone came to the house, attracting attention.

"Could someone have borrowed the car?" she says.

His brows fold together in concentration. "No, I don't think so."

"It was a silver Ford Taurus, right?"

"Yeah. He had it for years."

"Could someone have stolen the plates... and put them on another silver Taurus?" Even as she says it, it sounds ridiculous.

"Weird to steal plates and put them on an identical car."

Something else occurs to her. If Martin is involved, this next question might seal her fate. But if he isn't... it's worth trying. "I have other information. The man who drove the car was young at the time. And the left side of his face was partly paralyzed."

Martin stares hard at her. It's clear this information triggered something inside him. "You sure about that?"

"Yes."

He gets up, walks across the room, pauses and runs his hand through his thick hair. "Tell me when this happened."

She gives him the date that's seared into her memory: July 28, 2000.

He nods his head. "It was that summer, I'm sure of it. I was back from freshman year at college. The carburetor was acting up and I took the car to the service station. This was early in the morning. He said he could do it right away and I walked home, planning to pick it up later. Then a little while afterward, he called my dad and said he wouldn't be able to get to it until Monday. Something about an emergency he had to deal with at home. Dad said, fine, we had the truck, so it wasn't a big deal to go without the car for a few days."

"Okay."

"But then on the Monday, when we got it back, we noticed a couple of things. First, the mileage. Dad had checked it a few days before we brought the Taurus in, because he was starting to think about selling it and wanted to see what it might be worth. So when we got the car back, he noticed it was hundreds of miles more than it had been. The second thing was the fuel level. It had more gas in the tank than when we dropped it off. Why would the mechanic fill up the tank?"

"Did you say anything to him?"

"You bet. My father went right over there and yelled his ear off. But he steadfastly denied using the car, and implied my dad made a mistake and didn't have the right mileage number or gas level. There wasn't any way to prove either one. So there was nothing we could do except take our business elsewhere. We never used his service station again, not even to buy gas."

A warm feeling of relief fills her, making her realize how badly she wanted Martin to be innocent. His story rings true.

"Please tell me the name of this service station owner," she whispers.

"Jeremy Toth."

PART IV

18

———————

Every evening for the last four days, Nicki has brought a bowl of chicken noodle soup and crackers to Mother in her room. This time when she carries in the tray, she finds Mother looking the worst she has since the flu began. She lies flat in bed with her face pale and lined, her nose red, and her eyes half-closed. Used tissues overflow from the wastebasket beside her, and the top of her bedside table is crowded with cold medications, throat lozenges, a Kleenex box, a water glass, and a thermometer.

"I can't eat," she rasps. It sounds like laryngitis. "Call Uncle up here."

Nicki sets the tray on the dresser and hurries back out into the hall. "Uncle! Mother wants to talk to you." She remains leaning against the wall while his steps approach from the family room. He climbs the stairs faster than usual because Mother never likes to be kept waiting. When he goes into the bedroom, Nicki listens at the doorway.

"My temperature's a hundred and four." Mother erupts into a coughing fit. When it ends, she says, "I might have pneumonia. You need to take me to Urgent Care."

"Okay. Right now?"

"Of course right now." This almost starts another coughing fit. "Nicki, bring my clothes."

Uncle waits in the hall while Nicki helps Mother change out of her pajamas into a long-sleeved shirt, sweatpants, and a zippered sweater. "Get my brother again," she says when they're done.

When he returns, Nicki retreats to a shadowy corner of the hall, hoping they'll forget about her.

The two emerge from Mother's room, with Uncle holding her purse and her leaning heavily against him. When they reach the top of the stairs, Mother pauses and looks back at her. "Go to your room, Nicki."

She swallows her disappointment and does as she's commanded. Uncle approaches behind her and shuts her door, locking her in.

Nicki listens carefully through the crack as they clamber down the stairs and out of the house. The car engine starts, and as soon as its sound grows distant, she erupts into action. *Now is the time.*

She empties the contents of Cinderella's butt onto her bed and gets to work on the door with the bobby pins. Having had other occasions to practice, she's gotten rather good at this. It takes no more than two minutes to open the lock, bringing with it a feeling of elation. But she can't delay, there's much to be done.

First, she changes into her *escape outfit*, as she's already designated it in her mind. Nights can dip to near freezing in November. A flannel shirt, her thickest jeans, her heaviest sweater, warmest socks, and sturdiest shoes. She takes out the only winter jacket that still fits her from the closet, along with a second jacket, the pink one she wore when she was younger, and one more sweater. These she lays on the bed for now.

From the pile of stuff, she pockets all the cash. She wishes there was far more, but it's been risky stealing as little as she has. Nothing could ever be swiped from Mother's purse, as the penny-pincher would be certain to notice. Only Uncle was forgetful enough not to miss a dollar here and a dollar there, which she snatched out of his wallet whenever he left it out of his sight.

She brings her list with her into Uncle's room, which she has never entered before in her life. She's glimpsed it from the hall many times when he's opened the door to go in or out of it. But no one, not even Mother, is allowed to enter, and surprisingly, she's always respected that.

It stinks of ripe garbage, and Nicki can see why. Used dishes are scattered across the room, on the bedside table, the dresser, a small table next to a chair by the window, and even on the floor. She has seen him carrying large piles down to the kitchen after they've accumulated for some time.

There's a wicker hamper in the corner, and this is piled high with dirty clothes, adding to the stench, no doubt. Likewise, his bed is unmade and it looks like the sheets haven't been washed in months. She wonders why he wants to live in such squalor, and why Mother tolerates it.

She dreads what she might find in the closet. The clothes hanging in there are cleaned and ironed, though. Mother does that for him. She supposes he must wait until he's almost out before delivering more items to be washed.

However, the other half of the closet is taken up by a bookcase filled with stacks of magazines. It turns her stomach to see the naked women pictured on the front covers. She looks away.

Forcing herself to check his dresser for anything useful, she's thrilled to discover the key to the shed in the top drawer. She had been expecting to have to use the bobby pins, but it was going to be hard outside in the darkness with no one to hold the flashlight for her. Also, it's a different kind of lock and she didn't know if she could work her magic on it. Finding the key makes everything faster and easier.

One other item that isn't even on her list strikes her—a baseball cap. It looks clean enough, probably because he rarely wears it. She tries it on, then adjusts the back to fit her smaller head. The cap will help disguise her appearance while they travel.

In the bottom drawer, she finds his gun and ammunition. She's heard him talk about it with Mother before. One time when they saw wild turkeys in the back, he wanted to shoot them. But she wouldn't let him, saying the neighbors might call the police, wondering what the crap was going on over here. *Crap* was Nicki's word; Mother considered that cussing and probably had said *heck*. They all had to put their hands over their ears whenever someone swore in a movie. Anyway, Mother told Uncle the gun was only to be used for their defense, like if a burglar broke into the house. Nicki couldn't imagine that ever happening. There was nothing here anyone would ever want to steal.

It flashes through her mind that she should take the gun to protect herself and Sadie, but just as quickly, she nixes the idea. She has no idea how to load it, never mind shoot anything. If she tried, the most likely outcome is her accidentally killing one of them.

At the same time, she doesn't want *him* to have it. He and Mother might be so enraged upon returning and finding the girls gone, she might just order him to hunt them down and shoot them like they were rabbits. She pictures Mother dressed like a witch, putting them in a giant oven to be roasted for dinner.

Holding the weapon gingerly, like it's a bomb waiting to explode, she carries it to her room. *Where should I hide it?* Glancing around, she decides *under the mattress* will do. It will be easy to find if Uncle searches here, but she believes he'll be convinced she took it with her. Because that's what he would do. Then she realizes she must hide some of the ammunition as well, to complete the impression that she's traveling with a loaded weapon and might even use it against them if they come after her. It may make them hesitate.

The search for useful items continues in Mother's room, where the powerful odor of Vicks VapoRub lingers. At least it clears her nasal passages. She has snuck into this room several times in the past, not just when she stole the bobby pins, and knows Mother keeps a jewelry box in her dresser. Nicki has no idea whether any of it is genuine or just cheap imitations purchased from garage sales, but that will be for the pawn shop to decide. Emptying the box onto Mother's favorite scarf—which is supposed to be silk and probably really is—she ties it up to make a pouch.

Stealing from Mother goes against all her instincts. It feels like a violation and a betrayal, because Mother has spent many years applying layer upon layer of guilt. *I went through hell giving birth to you. We work our fingers to the bone. Why? To pay for the house and everything in it so that you can live comfortably. To provide you with all the food your tummy desires. To buy books for your useless education.*

She claps her hands over her ears to shut out Mother's voice in her head. Nicki is only doing what is necessary to save Sadie. They'll need cash and her dollars and coins won't last long. She has an idea how much things cost from seeing receipts for groceries and other purchases, and from listening to Mother and Uncle talk. They have never once given her money of her own, since she's not allowed to go anywhere. The children she watches in movies or reads about in books often get an allowance. They're able to go out and make friends and live full lives. How is it fair that she's been denied these freedoms?

Her thoughts steel Nicki for taking the jewelry. At the same time, she prays she's not found and brought back here, because Mother will punish her for it till the end of time.

Once she's added the new things to her pile on the bed, she returns to Mother's bedroom for one more item of significance. During a previous snooping expedition, she discovered her own birth certificate inside a file cabinet hidden behind Mother's dresses in the closet. She has since learned from her reading that a birth certificate is an important document that's required for identification when a person applies for a driver's license or a passport. She actually can't imagine ever going to other countries where she'd need a passport, but she would like to drive a car someday.

She brings the document back to her pile and continues downstairs to the front closet, where Uncle keeps his backpack. After dumping out its contents on the floor, she recovers a utility knife with its own sheath from the mess and restores it to the pack. Then it's on to the kitchen, where she fetches the map from the junk drawer. She's studied this hard in the past whenever she found a few minutes alone in the kitchen, so she knows the general direction they plan to take, but the farther they get from the house, the more she'll need to rely on the map for reference.

A pair of Mother's sunglasses catches her notice. She tries them on and they fit pretty well. Between these and the baseball cap she'll have a decent disguise that will hopefully keep strangers from guessing how young she is. She puts them with the map in an outer pocket of the backpack.

Nicki takes all five water bottles remaining in the kitchen, hoping they'll last till they can reach a convenience store in another town. As for food, most of what they eat at home is frozen. But she takes the rest of the sliced bologna and American cheese, a bag of carrots, half a loaf of bread, an unopened box of Cheetos, and a package of Oreos.

Coming to the end of the list, she returns upstairs to pack everything she left on the bed. She places the birth certificate inside a plastic bag so it will have extra protection in case the pack gets wet. She adds her thinnest, lightest blanket to the top, along with the extra sweater and jacket, ready to be handed over to Sadie. Putting on her own coat, she pauses to think hard regarding anything else they might need. At the last minute she remembers her watch. It's a cheap thing they gave her for her birthday once, and she never wears it around the house because who wants to be reminded of time when they have nowhere to go? She finds it stuffed in the back of her drawer and makes sure it's working before putting it on.

No more time to waste. They might return any second. Mother might suddenly feel better and call off the visit. Or Urgent Care could be closed. Or Uncle might drop Mother off at the hospital and come home without her. One could not count on them following through on any plan.

She grabs the flashlight and spare batteries on her way out the back door, switching on the light as her feet crunch on pine needles. A drip of water lands on her forehead and she looks up at the solid bank of clouds overhead. It might be the first rain of the season, just her luck. She increases her pace to the shed and lets herself in with the key.

Sadie is crouched in the corner with her arms wrapped protectively around herself as Nicki enters and sprays the light on her. Seeing it's Nicki and not Uncle, she lunges forward and hugs her tightly. It stabs Nicki in the heart to think of her alone all this time. "I'm sorry. They wouldn't let me come before," she says.

"I missed you," Sadie whispers. "Becca and Mr. Fluffernutter missed you too."

Nicki kneels down beside her, slips off her backpack, and takes out the sweater and jacket. "I have good news. We're leaving here. Tonight. We won't have to be separated ever again."

She picks up Becca the rabbit and presses her into the pack. Sadie looks past her through the door. "Are we going in the car?"

"No. We have to go through the woods. I have a map. There's a back road, not too far."

Her eyes grow damp with fear. "The woods? Are Uncle and Mother coming?"

"They're not here now. Mother is sick. Uncle is taking her to the doctor." Nicki picks up Mr. Fluffernutter the dog. "We're running away."

"No!" Sadie screams. "No, we can't run away!" Tears start to roll.

Nicki pauses and grasps her twiglike arms. "It's okay. I've planned it all out. We'll be okay."

Sadie is hysterical. "They'll catch us and bring us back and hurt us!"

"We won't let them catch us." Nicki is not at all sure about this, but she tries to exude confidence.

"They'll hurt my mommy and daddy and my sister Becca if we're bad!"

"I know they told you that. But that's not going to happen. Your family is safe in their own house. They aren't here. Mother and Uncle can't get to them."

"How do you know?"

It's a good question. It's true she can't be sure. Uncle might find his gun or buy another. He might be crazy enough to go to Sadie's parents' house and try to shoot them.

But she can't allow Sadie to talk her out of this. She's a little girl and doesn't understand. Nicki is older and it's up to her to save them both. Dying is better than living as prisoners.

"Listen to me." Nicki makes her voice as calm as she can. "You know I love you. You know I won't ever allow you to come to harm. We have to get away from them. They're bad and we can't trust them. We'll run away and find your mommy and daddy and you'll have a real life again."

Sadie sniffs unhappily.

"Can you do this for me? Can you be strong for my sake? Because I can't live here with them anymore. But I can't leave you behind either."

"I don't want you to go without me," Sadie says.

"Okay, Good. We go together." She stuffs Mr. Fluffernutter into the pack. "It's cold out there." She helps Sadie put on the sweater and jacket, zipping it for her and pulling up the hood. Then Sadie gets on her sneakers with the Velcro fastenings.

Nicki swings the backpack over her shoulders and takes Sadie's hand. "We can do this. You're like my sister and sisters are strongest together." They walk out side-by-side and Nicki shuts the door behind them, hoping to delay the moment when Uncle or Mother notices they're gone.

Nicki switches the flashlight back on. "This way." Sadie clutches her free hand as they hurry toward the trees in the back. Lightning flashes directly in front of them, followed by a deafening blast of thunder. Rain cascades over them.

<h1 style="text-align:center">19</h1>

———————

As usual, Rebecca does not wake till morning. She must've returned right after learning Bob's real identity—*Jeremy Toth*—and slept soundly through the rest of the night. Having an actual name for him at last must've given her the feeling of resolution that brought her back to her own time.

Moreover, she feels a powerful sense of satisfaction in being nearly certain Martin had nothing to do with it. She quite likes him; she can admit that to herself now. She wishes she could make him a full ally by confiding in him, but years of false leads have made her cautious. Present day Martin knows nothing of what just happened in the alternate past, and she needs to keep it that way.

The first thing she does upon rising is Google Jeremy Toth of Draywood. This is sufficient to reveal his home address and the location of the business he owns. She realizes with a shock that it's the service station just down the road from the motel, the one she walked past on her way to JJs the first night.

Anxious to confirm that Toth really is Bob, Rebecca skips the morning shower, gets dressed, eats a granola bar she finds in her purse, and drives to the service station, hoping to find him on duty. It's one of those little independent stations one hardly sees anymore, a combination of two gas pumps and a small repair shop. She eases in next to a pump, shuts off the car, and peers through the front window. No one is visible at the register or in the garage. He could be using the bathroom, or doing paperwork in a back office.

Since the station doesn't even have a credit card scan at the pump, it gives her the perfect excuse to tromp right inside and see him up close when he comes out from hiding. Thinking about it makes her uncomfortable as hell, but it needs to be done.

The door dings as she enters and shoots her gaze across the two aisles with her stomach doing somersaults. It takes a minute, but finally she hears steps approaching and sure enough, *Bob* wanders in from a side door that connects to the repair shop.

It's definitely him, though the signs of paralysis on the left side of his face are slightly less pronounced than before. Having lost hair and gained weight, he looks twenty years older than when he tossed her in the back of Martin's Taurus, but it's still unmistakably him.

Seeing her staring, his expression stiffens and it's like a veil drops over his eyes. She figures people have been staring at him all his life, and at times, brutally mocking him for a condition he might've had since birth. Under normal circumstances this would evoke her sympathy, but her heart holds nothing aside from hatred and disgust for this beast.

"It's just me working here," he says, choosing to interpret her look as one of impatience. "Can't get to the register as quick as I'd like."

His name badge identifies him as Jeremy, in case she had any doubts. Not trusting herself to say anything, she takes out her credit card and looks for the card reader where she's supposed to insert it.

He holds out his hand. "Leave it here. I'll charge it after you fill up," he says.

Her throat goes dry as she stares down at her name on the card. Surely after stealing Sadie, he followed the news about it and therefore knows her last name and probably the full name of everyone in their family. *Stupid, stupid, stupid.*

"Wait, I might have cash." But like a lot of people her age, she rarely carries any with her. He watches as she opens her wallet exposing the empty billfold, recalling how she'd meant to stop at an ATM but then forgot.

Somehow she finds herself handing over the card, thinking who looks at it anyway? And he doesn't look at it, just sets it beside the cash register and shifts his gaze to the front window like there's something interesting to see outside, which there isn't.

But if he wants, he'll have all the time in the world to check out her name while she pumps gas into the car. Heading back outside, she berates herself for handing the card over and for forgetting to bring cash. She needs to be thinking further ahead. She's already made so many rooky mistakes. Her stomach churns the whole time while she fills her tank. Right now, he could be looking her up on the Internet, checking her photo for a match, confirming that she's sister to Sadie who was taken when she was four. By Bob the Kidnapper, otherwise known as Jeremy Toth.

Her hands are trembling when she pulls the nozzle from her tank, making her spill a bit of gas. Grabbing a paper towel, she wipes her hands over and over, dragging her feet back into the station to retrieve her card. He's already rung up the sale and wears a bored expression as he holds out the card and receipt for her. He says nothing and avoids eye contact, which just about confirms her fear that he now knows exactly who she is.

She can't get out of there fast enough, though she has to stop a few hundred yards down the highway to set her GPS to Toth's home address. Service is spotty, but it should get her there. She prays he doesn't anticipate her next move by closing up his shop and driving home to thwart her plans. She'll have to take that chance.

She heads up the mountain and within twenty minutes, the GPS tells her to turn right, just as she remembers from when Toth kidnapped her. There's a street sign identifying it as Pinyon Road, the right address. She hesitates whether to turn onto it, not wanting to attract attention from the neighbors or to accidentally drive too near Toth's house. On the other hand, an unfamiliar person walking down their street might draw more stares.

She makes the turn and passes several houses that are widely separated from each other, like a lot of places in this area. The one closest to the highway has been updated recently with light pine accents and is truly beautiful. But the others look unchanged since whenever they were built, maybe fifty years ago. Trees hug them close and cast dark shadows. She hopes the people who live in them are mentally well-balanced and not Unabomber wannabes.

Before long she comes to a mailbox with Toth's street number stuck onto it. Rebecca pulls over, peering down the long driveway, barely able to glimpse the roof of the house at the end of it. She'll have to park here, though if Toth does come home, he'll know instantly that she's at his house. She knows what she's doing is impulsive and dangerous and downright crazy, but a wild urgency has gripped her and she can't stop herself.

She's half-walking, half-running down the driveway, not even looking around, just focused on getting to the house as quickly as possible. Minutes later, the trees open up and the steep-roofed building she remembers appears before her, with the old wooden garage next to it. Without doubt, this is where Toth brought her. There's no pickup parked on the side this time; maybe Jeremy drives his truck to work. No other vehicles are in the driveway either.

Glancing up at the house, she searches the windows for movement, or the silhouette of a person looking out. She thinks there might be a light on in one of the upstairs rooms, but she can't be certain in the daylight, and anyway Toth could've left it on by accident.

Nothing can hold her back now from dashing between the garage and the house toward the clearing in the back. When she comes around the corner, she sees the dull gray shed exactly as it was nineteen years ago, perched on a rise, conveying a sense of forsaken solitude and isolation that fills her heart to breaking. Its high window— the one where she fell over trying to reach it—faces this side. *This is it, this is it.*

She sprints across the messy yard past piles of leaves and stacks of logs, mindless of the noise she's making, branches cracking, pinecones snapping beneath her feet. When she reaches the door, she rattles the knob and yanks at it with both hands, but it won't come open. She raises her arms and pounds her fists against the wood. "Sadie! Sadie, it's me, Rebecca, your sister. Speak to me. I've come to save you. Tell me you're there. Please, please, say something." She crumples to her knees and presses her head to the door, weeping.

All is quiet inside the shed. Most likely, no one is there. But it's also possible Toth has frightened and brainwashed Sadie—or some other girl now—so thoroughly, she doesn't dare call out for help.

Though Rebecca wishes she could take a sledgehammer to the place, now isn't the time. She forces herself to turn away, to retrace her steps to the car. As she passes the house, she looks up at the upper window again and wonders if there's a flash of movement, like someone drawing back so as not to be seen.

She's quite sure that if someone is there, they will not call the police to report her for trespassing. But they might well burst out of the house armed with a gun, prepared to shoot her down. It might even be within their rights to kill trespassers; she isn't certain of the law. These thoughts bring with them a spike of adrenalin, and she runs faster than she ever has toward her Honda, weaving as she goes to evade a speeding bullet if one comes behind her.

When she flings the car door open, she glances back without seeing anyone, but still she doesn't pause except to whisk up the keys after she drops them. Her breathing is ragged as she starts the car and drives away, trying hard to keep herself from flooring the gas. When she turns back on the highway, she lets out a cry, though she doesn't know whether it comes of despair for not finding Sadie alive, or triumph to finally have discovered the place where she was taken and who took her. To be so close at last to finding justice for her sister.

After reaching the downtown area, she parks near where she plans to grab coffee and brunch, and spends several minutes doing deep breathing exercises to calm herself. When she trusts herself to speak again, she calls Freddie.

His message says he'll be on vacation until two days from now. "Call the office if you need someone to help you before then," his message continues. "Otherwise leave a message and I'll get back to you as soon as I return."

Fuck. She leaves a short message asking him to call when he gets back, knowing he won't check it while he's away. He told her once he never gave out his personal phone number for exactly this reason. When he's on vacation, he wants to be on it one hundred percent.

She briefly considers contacting the local police department. But without any real proof, aside from, *I travelled back in time*, she won't be able to convince anyone to investigate Toth's background, let alone take out a warrant. Freddie should at least run a check on him like he did on Daniel Ortiz, Martin's father, and if something turns up in his past, the detective might be willing to go further than that, maybe even drive out here and help her. There might be DNA evidence inside the shed or the house. She just needs to convince Freddie, but now it's going to have to wait two days.

20

––––––––

After filling her stomach at the breakfast café, Rebecca takes a long walk through a heavily wooded neighborhood near downtown. It truly is a beautiful community, and under normal circumstances, she wouldn't mind living here, except her tendency to isolate herself would become even worse.

But mostly during the walk, she thinks about how she will nail Toth. She needs to time travel, of course, and she can do it tonight. She'll mindcast back to this morning when she drove out to his place and find a way to get into the shed. Its one window is too high up, and too small for her to fit through anyway. She'll have to break into the house, even if it means shattering more glass. Once inside, she might as well search the whole place for any evidence that Sadie has been there. Hopefully the key to the shed will turn up in the process. Toth being at work should give her plenty of time for a thorough going-over.

It's possible, though, that a friend or relation of Toth's might be living there too, and she needs to be prepared for that. This is why she brought the mace and duct tape. She's never used either one against a person before, but now isn't the time to shrink from unpleasant tasks. Of course, she'll do her best to avoid confrontation.

She didn't do well trying to fight off Martin. Not at all. But then, she wasn't prepared. Even the dumbest thieves—the candidates for Darwin awards—probably knew to check for cameras before breaking in anywhere, but this never occurred to her, even though her own apartment building uses them. Even if she hadn't noticed she was being filmed till she was already on his property, at least she would've known she only had a few minutes to search before police and/or Martin arrived.

Her phone rings while she's trying to decide if she should turn back from her walk. *Martin.* She's not sure if she should answer, until she remembers she's in real-time now, and everything that took place between her and him at his house happened during a mindcast. Sometimes she has trouble keeping track of which experiences occurred when.

Real-time Martin thinks Rebecca came here to purchase a house. He's probably calling to show her another place, or ask if she's still considering the first one. Feeling bad wasting his time, she decides to make an excuse.

"Hi Martin," she says.

"Hey. How are you?"

"Good. Enjoying a beautiful walk on a quiet street. I suppose you're wondering about my decision?"

"No. I mean, yeah, but that's not why I called... I don't generally do this sort of thing... shit, that sounds like such a line. Let me start again. Do you want to have dinner with me tonight? I'm not asking as your real estate agent."

She hesitates. Should she? She basically has nothing to do for the rest of the day, until she gets into bed and travels back in time to search Toth's house. It's not a matter of availability. But is this wise? She doesn't want to form any obligations. Nor does she want to hurt him by leaving him in the dust as soon as she gets Freddie to come help her.

"Yes," she says, surprising herself. "That sounds nice."

"Great. I can pick you up or..."

"I'll meet you there."

He gives her the location before hanging up. She hopes she doesn't regret this. She hasn't had a date since before she started mindcast-sex with Dev. Seeing someone in real-time creates expectations. The longest relationship she's ever had lasted three months, and it was eleven weeks too long. She can't stand having someone rely on her, like a boyfriend would. She can't bear to be in a position of letting anyone down. Not again. Not ever again.

When all this is over, she'll find another sex buddy. Not Dev. The last time they were together, she decided she didn't really like him. But maybe Martin. He's growing on her. Come to think of it, it's good she accepted the dinner date. That's more than she ever had with Dev. She can find out if she enjoys Martin's company. If so, it would add a new dimension to mindcast-sex. Maybe they'd even take time to have a meaningful conversation now and then. Not in real-time, however.

The more she thinks about it, the happier she is that she accepted his invitation. She's always led an isolated life, but here in *Sticksville*, she feels lonelier than ever. And more frightened. It's scary to think she could be the only person in town who knows the truth about Toth. Especially since he may be aware of her identity now. If anything happens to her before she speaks to Freddie, Toth could get away with everything.

After she's turned back and nearly reached her car, a familiar-looking older woman with bangs and a ponytail approaches Rebecca.

"Hello," the woman says. "I hope you're enjoying your visit." Seeing the blank look on Rebecca's face, she adds, "I'm Patricia. Your server at JJ's?"

"Right, I remember." She pictures her at the restaurant the first night, wearing an old-fashioned blouse with a large bow. "Yes, thanks, my visit has been very... productive."

"Oh I thought you were here to enjoy yourself. I suppose you're one of those people who hangs on her computer."

"I wouldn't say that." She steps past the woman.

"Are you coming to JJ's tonight?" Patricia says.

"Not tonight." To be nice, Rebecca adds, "Though the food's very good."

"If you're thinking of getting dinner somewhere else, you can't go wrong with Wild Mushrooms in Yellerton. It's just a twenty-minute drive down the highway. Everything on their menu is delicious."

"Thanks for the recommendation. I'm dining at another restaurant there, but I'll keep that in mind for tomorrow." She opens her car door.

"Have a lovely evening," Patricia says, turning back the other way.

After returning to her hotel room, Rebecca notices right away that the maid has been there. The bed is made and items have been straightened. The counter has been wiped and new towels supplied. But when she opens the drawer where she put away her clothes, it appears her things have been moved. She's quite sure she placed her black leggings on top, meaning to wear them tonight. But they're at the bottom of the pile.

Why get into the drawer? Maybe the maid is a thief, but she doubts it. They wouldn't last long here if they pilfered from the customers, and word that they were fired for stealing would whip through town faster than a California wildfire.

Rebecca checks to see if anything's missing, but she doesn't think so. Aside from clothing, she also left the duct tape, the photo of Sadie, and the printout of information on Martin in here. She should've taken those last two items with her, she realizes now. Any doubt Toth had regarding her identity would've been erased by Sadie's picture. Even worse, on the printout it says "Kidnapper's car" at the top, right above Martin's father's name and the address of their family home where Martin now lives. Below that she has notes about where Daniel moved, what Martin does for a living, and the location of his office. At the bottom she had added the name of his dog and her affinity for bacon.

A chill sensation grips her. Toth could've come here any time during the last few hours. He might have a helper at the station, and he also doesn't seem to mind closing up the place when he feels like it. Of course he would check this motel for her; where else would she be staying? Naturally he would know the young office worker along with everyone else in town. The kid would think nothing of revealing all he knows about the hotel's latest guest.

She checks the door for signs of anyone messing with the lock, but it looks normal. Not that she would be able to tell the difference if Toth picked it with a credit card, or if the kid let him borrow the key. She opens the door and glances out. The maid is nowhere to be seen. Cleaning wouldn't take long with no more than one or two other rooms occupied right now. The maid has probably left for the day.

Rebecca shuts the door and sinks onto the bed, thinking. She has to assume Toth has seen her page of notes and knows she's aware the Ortiz family car was used in the kidnapping. It occurs to her this knowledge might also put Martin in danger. More so because he has no reason to be wary of Toth. What happens in a mindcast stays in the mindcast, meaning present-day Martin doesn't know any of the things she told him during her visit to his home in the recent past. It may be best to fill him in during their date tonight.

Rebecca is the much more likely target, however—a thought that makes her shiver as she contemplates how the lock on her door is no deterrent to Toth. What can she do to dissuade him from coming after her? Maybe let it be known that she's "working" with the police. Actually, Freddie still doesn't even know where she is. When she left her message, she said nothing about her location. If he knew she'd come chasing after the owner of that car, he would be angry and unwilling to listen to anything she had to say. He might not even return her call.

21

Rebecca blocks her door with the armchair again before taking her shower. It's getting dark early these days, and she has no idea if Toth would take the risk of coming back to her room while she's here. She hopes if he's that crazy, this will block him long enough for her to call the police.

Turning her thoughts to Martin, she takes extra care with her preparations. No question he's her type and if this was the seventeenth century she'd probably swoon when he entered the room. Nothing will come of it tonight, but she can allow herself a little pleasure just looking at his handsome face and sexy male body. What she would really like to know is, just how hot does he think *she* is? Because that would really help her decide whether he's the right choice for her next round of mindcast-sex, whenever that might happen.

But she never in a million years thought she might meet a guy she liked on this trip, which is why she doesn't have anything stunning to wear tonight. She wishes she had her little red dress, though it might've been over-the-top for a first date. She has to settle for her black leggings and plunging off-white top made of light cashmere. And sneakers because that's all she brought for her feet, and her slate blue puffer jacket because the night is sure to get cold. At least she has one pair of dangling silver earrings and a diamond stud to add some sparkle.

After leaving the motel, it takes longer than she expected to reach the next town down the mountain and find street parking near Anthony's Organics. She's ten minutes late when she walks in and finds Martin waiting by the door. He gets up and touches her arm lightly by way of greeting. This was exactly the right move, because she hates being hugged or kissed before a first date even gets started.

"Do you want to sit outside? They have heaters."

She glances toward the patio, visible in the back. "Sure, that sounds nice."

They follow the hostess out the screen door to a table that overlooks a garden. The heater is on and Rebecca sits close to it. There's a lit candle and roses on the table, colored lights strung across the patio, and no one else seated near them. The ideal setting for romance.

The menu is mostly vegetarian, partly vegan, and has a wide range of food types from several different countries. She hones in on the Thai avocado curry, which sounds delicious if not quite authentic. "Do you only eat vegan?" she says.

He shakes his head. "I'm a vegetarian, but I don't have the will power to cut dairy and eggs from my life."

"I don't blame you. I'm mostly vegetarian, but I don't even have the will power to cut poultry or fish from my life."

He smiles as he adjusts the roses in the vase, and the positioning of the candle beside them.

"I can see why you became a real estate agent," she says.

He glances up. "This, you mean?" He nods at the items on the table.

"You obviously have an eye for detail."

"That's a nice way of putting it. I'm obsessive about things."

She shrugs. "It's better than not caring, if you ask me." That might be her flaw. Too much apathy, except for the single obsession that's driving her life at the moment. Something to work on eventually, if she can raise enough interest to do so.

They make small talk while waiting for the server to take their order. When he's left them alone, Rebecca says, "You're probably wondering what I've decided about the house."

"I don't want to rush you. That's not why I asked you out."

"Then let's not talk about it." She had been about to reveal the real reason she came to Draywood, but she stopped because it would put an end to any chance of having a pleasant dinner together. She knows from experience that *my sister was kidnapped nineteen years ago* is an absolute mood-killer.

"I have a game I sometimes play when I meet someone new," she says. "We tell each other something about ourselves, and the other one gets to guess if it's true or false."

"How do you know if they're telling the truth about whether it's true or false?"

"You have to trust each other. And I guess you could Google it later." She smiles.

"I'm game. You start."

"Hmm." She glances up at the dark sky, thinking. "I played the bagpipe from age ten to twelve."

He scrutinizes her. "Are you part Scottish?"

"No clues."

"Then I say you're lying."

"Yeah, I wanted to, though. I was fascinated by all things Scottish at that age." The waiter arrives with their wine.

After he's poured and gone away, they raise their glasses and clink them. "To... fulfilling our dreams," Martin says.

"For the record, playing the bagpipe is definitely not one of my dreams anymore."

"I won the county spelling bee in 7th grade." He takes a sip of wine.

She purses her lips. Could he be a former child geek? But there's something in his eyes that makes her think he's lying. "False," she says.

"I have dyslexia. I'm terrible at spelling. Though not that bad for someone with dyslexia."

Their appetizers arrive, distracting them. As the meal progresses, the conversation moves to what they like to do for exercise, for hobbies, and then for work. "You said you're a writer," he says. "Can I find a book of yours at Barnes & Noble?"

She laughs. "I'm not a published writer. Not even an agented writer." It's tempting to add, *not a writer of any kind, actually.*

He's silent for a moment.

"I know what you're wondering. How is she going to afford the house?" she says. "Man, you're looking at a trust fund baby."

The waiter returns to ask if anyone wants coffee or dessert.

"Not me," Rebecca says, thinking the caffeine will interfere with her upcoming mindcast.

"I'll take the check, please," Martin says. He turns back to Rebecca. "True or false. My mother died of cancer when I was twelve."

She's confused at first, thinking he's already told her his mother is dead, though he didn't mention how. But that must've been during her mindcast. It seems unfair that she already knows the answer, yet she feels certain she would've known this wasn't a lie.

"True," she says softly.

He nods. "I just wanted to tell you. It affected me more than anything else in my life. So, I wanted you to know."

"My little sister was kidnapped when I was six," she says.

His brow tightens as he looks at her, reading her, knowing she's sharing with him the same thing—the trauma that's affected her more than anything else in her life. "I'm so sorry," he says.

A silence follows as they leave the restaurant and he walks her to her Honda. On the way, his arm slips around her shoulders. When they reach the car, he wraps both arms around her and holds her tight. "I can't think of anything more heartbreaking than losing your sister like that," he says.

"It changed everything about my life. I think about her every day. It's worse, far worse, than if she'd died. At least then we'd know her fate. It's the ghastly stuff I imagine that... Do you know the story of Prometheus? How Zeus punished him for giving man the gift of fire? He was chained up and an eagle would come to eat his liver, which would immediately grow back so it could be eaten again the next day. This is how it feels to have someone you love taken from you, and each morning the first thing you remember is that."

He doesn't know what to say. How could he? She's never shared this part with anyone before. "I can't believe I just told you that. You probably think I'm demented." If he knew about the mindcasts, he would definitely think so.

"Then I must be too, because what you said made perfect sense to me."

He gets it, probably because he also had overwhelming grief to deal with as a child. This is when she makes up her mind to tell him everything. She draws back and says, "I'm not planning to buy a house here at all. That was just a ruse."

He almost seems to brighten. "A ruse to...? I wish I could believe it was a ruse to land a date with me."

"Sorry. I'm not handling this well. It was a ruse to find out more about you but not for the reasons you hope. It's because of... um, because of an anonymous tip I received. A phone call from someone disguising their voice. The person, I think it was a 'he,' named the kidnapper and the man whose car the kidnapper drove. This informant said he was dying and didn't want this hanging over him anymore. He gave no explanation of his own role, or anything else. Just the names. And then he hung up, before I could beg him to tell me more or to come forward and talk to the police." She takes a heavy breath. "The car belonged to your father."

He stares at her in disbelief. "That's impossible. This tip you got, it's bullshit. If you knew my dad, you'd know how insane that is."

"The caller provided a detail no one outside of the investigators could've known."

"I don't care. It's still bullshit. Who did he name as the kidnapper?"

She lowers her voice. "Jeremy Toth. He owns the—"

"Christ, I know who he is." He takes a moment to think about it and settle his thoughts. Slowly, he relays the exact story he told Rebecca in the past. How they had stopped bringing their car to Toth after he apparently drove it somewhere when he was supposed to be repairing it. "It's possible," he concludes. "I can't tell you how disgusted that makes me to think our car might've been used that way. What are your next steps?"

"I'm waiting for Freddie—a detective who was on the case—to get back from vacation. In two days. I may have enough to get him to act, especially with your information."

"Maybe you should go to the local police right now."

"It isn't enough. An anonymous tip. And only your word to go on that your car may have been used without your consent. No proof of anything. It'll be hard even for Freddie to get something going. Local police would just alert Toth of our interest. He'd probably get busy destroying any remaining evidence." She has to be ready with incriminating details before the police are brought in. She needs to find them tonight, when she uses her time travel super power to go back, get into the house, and search for clues.

"It's your call, of course. When you're ready, I'll be happy to tell them what I remember. I know my dad would be willing to come here and talk to them too."

"Thank you."

He rubs her shoulder. "You gonna be okay? Come to my place tonight if you want. I'm not putting the moves on you. I have a spare bed. You like dogs?"

"I do. Thanks for the offer, but I'm okay." His presence could make her time travel difficult or even impossible tonight. And she can't delay it.

"Call me tomorrow," he says. "If you don't mind. I want to know you're okay."

"Sure. Thanks again."

He waits while she gets into her car and drives away. She would've liked to go with him. But she has to finish this.

By the time she returns to the hotel she's feeling exhausted. It isn't that she expended much physical energy, but the emotional toll is heavy. She's relieved to see the lot empty and no cars parked across the street as she turns into a space below her room.

When she gets out of her Honda, and pauses to lock it, the sound of footsteps behind her comes out of nowhere. Before she can turn, something hard is smashed against her head. Her mind goes blank as she tumbles to the pavement.

PART V

22

If only Mother had fallen ill in the middle of summer, on a still, warm night with zero chance of the clouds opening up and drenching Nicki and Sadie. But no, she chose to get sick and go to the doctor at the worst possible time.

Without having gone far, they're as soaked and shivering as if they had jumped into a cold mountain lake. Sadie's teeth chatter noisily, though she continues trudging alongside Nicki with astonishing determination. Their pace is too slow, however. Nicki keeps glancing over her shoulder for the signs or sounds of pursuit. Not that she's likely to see anything in the rain-soaked darkness, or hear anything over the steady pelting of water.

The thunderous explosion that accompanies a series of lightning strikes causes Sadie to fling her arms around Nicki, her eyes wide with terror. Nicki holds her tight, fearing the next one might land even closer.

She should've thought of these dangers. She should've been much better prepared. She should've realized she hadn't the slightest clue how to survive beyond the four walls of her house. The house that had protected her all her life.

They are lost. She knows that now. When she looked at the map, it appeared all they had to do was walk in a straight line from the shed across the stretch of woods that would end when they came to a narrow road. It was no more than half a mile away and looked like hardly any distance at all on paper. But she should have known that in the dark, with trees closing in all around them, there would be no way of telling what was *straight* and what was *walking in circles for hours on end*.

The flashlight isn't helping. It produces only a narrow beam of light, and not enough for her to differentiate one tree from the next. Not enough to tell if they've passed this particular tree before or not.

The brush is thick. She had hoped they might find a deer path or something leading to the road, but no. In some sections she has told Sadie to hang onto her jacket behind her, while she batted at branches and kicked at bushes, trying not to let anything poke them in the eyes. Already she has a tear in her parka from one of the sharpest sticks. At least it didn't cut her.

"I want to go back," Sadie says in a faint voice.

With a sinking heart, Nicki realizes they can't go back, even if they wanted to. They're surrounded by darkness. She has no clue which way leads to the house.

But she knows when something is futile. They could kill themselves wandering around in the dark, hardly able to see anything even with the flashlight. Already she nearly walked off a steep incline, which could've broken her leg at the least. And if Sadie had followed her, tumbling to the bottom, Nicki never would've forgiven herself.

"We'll find shelter." She begins looking for anything that might serve. A cave would be nice, except she's not sure if bears might hibernate at this elevation. Usually they liked it higher up, but she had seen bears on the property on two occasions, the second time a mother with her cubs. She decides they will not be going into any caves.

But before long, she notices a large pine tree they may have passed earlier, with thick branches spread wide and low to the ground.

"Come here, Sadie." She leads her under the branches right up to the trunk.

"The rain isn't too bad here." It drips through the gaps instead of dumping on them. "Let's sit down."

"Do we have blankets?" Sadie says.

"Just the one." Nicki could kick herself for not packing more, but she'd run out of space in the pack. "Let's spread the pine needles first." She makes as neat a pile out of them as she can with her bare hands. But when she takes out the blanket, she finds it's nearly as soaked as the outside of the pack. "We can't use it. It'll just make us colder."

Sadie's face sinks as they settle on the pine needles.

"Let's eat something," Nicki says. The first thing she reaches, the Cheetos box, is soaked and soggy. She ignores that and takes out the bread, which was partly protected by the plastic. She assembles a sandwich with bologna and cheese, and hands it to Sadie.

"Not hungry."

"Are you sure? You should try to eat. You'll feel better."

"I don't feel good. I'm hot," she says.

Sadie's teeth were chattering only a short while ago. Swinging from cold to hot is not a good sign, Nicki knows. Putting down the sandwich in her lap, she reaches her arm around Sadie and draws her forehead to her lips. The girl is burning up. "Yeah, you're kind of hot," she says, not wanting to panic her. She gives her a water bottle from the pack. "Drink some of this."

While Sadie slowly sips, Nicki eats the sandwich, followed by three Oreos that managed to remain dry. She drinks from another bottle.

When they're done, she puts everything away, except for Becca and Mr. Fluffernutter. She gives them to Sadie, who wraps her arms tightly around them.

The cold is creeping up on Nicki inside. Like everything else, she woefully underestimated how low the temperature would dip in the foothills at night in the fall. She puts her arm around Sadie and draws her and the stuffed animals close. "We'll keep each other warm."

Sadie, with beads of sweat on her forehead, says nothing. After several moments of silence, they hear the crack of a twig breaking like someone stepped on it. "What's that?" Sadie whispers.

"It's probably just a squirrel or something." She prays it isn't Uncle coming after them. If so, they'll have no choice but to return with him.

"What if it's a bear?" Sadie says.

"They live up the top of the mountains. They don't ever come down here," Nicki lies. Still, she doesn't think it's a bear. A bear would make more noise.

"You sure?"

"Yup. I doubt it's any bigger than a raccoon. And they won't hurt us. We're safe here." She injects a confidence into her tone that she doesn't feel.

Hoping to distract Sadie, Nicki addresses the stuffed rabbit. "What do you want to be when you grow up, Becca?"

"A rabbit," Nicki says in Becca's voice.

"You already are a rabbit. I mean, what do you want to do?"

"Why didn't you say that the first time? I want to be a magician so I can pull a human out of my hat."

Though Sadie's face is pale and drawn, she smiles.

"What about you, Mr. Fluffernutter?" Nicki says.

"Hem, I would like to be a firefighter," Mr. Fluffernutter answers.

"That's very noble of you."

"A dog would never leave a burning building without leading his, hem, best friends to safety."

"You mean people?"

"Indubitably," the dog says. "We also like fire hydrants."

"I want to be a dog when I grow up," Sadie says in a voice so weak, Nicki can barely hear her.

"Why is that?"

"Because my owner would love me and take care of me and never let me be sad."

Nicki tears up at this and kisses her hair. "I want to be a doctor when I grow up. I'll love my patients and take care of them and never let them be sad, if I can help it."

Sadie closes her eyes and leans against Nicki. Before long, Nicki's eyes shut too and she falls asleep from exhaustion, despite the rain and cold, and her own fear and anxiety.

Dawn has broken by the time she wakes. Something feels off, and she realizes it's because Sadie no longer rests against her arm. Nicki looks around wildly, but doesn't see her anywhere. Sadie is gone.

23

———————

As consciousness returns to Rebecca, she becomes aware of a throbbing ache inside her head, an uncomfortable pressure over her mouth, and a burning pain running through her wrists, arms, and shoulders. When she tries to move her hands forward, she discovers they're securely bound behind her back.

Wherever she is, it's utterly dark save for a sliver of light coming from the gap beneath the door. She's lying on her stomach on a hard mattress, her face turned sideways and something—probably duct tape—stuck across her mouth just below her nose. Toth has taken her prisoner.

She can't be in the shed because this mattress isn't on the floor, it's on a bed frame. Plus if that's sunlight under the door, she ought to see it shining in from the upper window as well. This has to be a room somewhere inside Toth's house. Likely it's still nighttime, and a light has been left on in the hall. Still, his house is nearly as cold as the shed might be. Since he didn't bother to put a blanket over her, she only has her light puffer jacket to warm her, and it isn't nearly enough.

What are his plans for me? She can hope she's too old to be of interest to him. He likes little girls; he preys on the young, the weak, and the innocent. He's deranged.

He must want her alive, though, because otherwise he would've killed her in the parking lot with multiple blows to the head. After that he could've driven straight home, burned his clothes, and buried the murder weapon anywhere in the forest around their property. Barring an eyewitness, they wouldn't be able to pin anything on him, even if Martin came forward with the information she'd given him. Since there was no proof of any of her assertions, Toth would get away with his crime. Again.

But he has let her live, for now. He must have a purpose. Most likely he wants information from her. How did she figure out it was him? Who has she told? How much does she really know? Eventually he'll come to ask his questions.

In the meantime, she must try to escape. Shifting her body toward the edge of the narrow bed, she suppresses a groan at the pain shooting through her. She swings her legs down to the floor and stands on wobbly legs. At least her ankles aren't tied so she'll be able to walk.

She moves slowly, barely able to see anything. Maybe he didn't lock her in, counting on her being unconscious all night. When she reaches the door, she has to grasp the knob with both hands behind her back, but it refuses to turn. She tries pulling the door toward herself in case it's not fully closed or the latch is disengaged, but this also fails. The door is securely locked.

Looking around, she finds her eyes adjusting to the darkness. She edges her way to the left, her fingers gliding along the wall, before she comes to a wooden chair and small desk with nothing on top of it. She wonders if there might be something useful in the drawers, but with her hands bound behind her back, it's impossible to reach inside them. Above the desk there's a window with a heavy shade drawn over it. In attempting to raise the shade, she pulls down but then loses her grip, making it fly upward with a loud snapping noise that she prays wasn't heard outside the room.

She turns her gaze to the porch lit backyard—the pine-needle-strewn clearing with the shed as its centerpiece. Could Sadie be in there now? As crazy as it seems, Rebecca refuses to give up hope of finding her sister alive.

Pressing her forehead against the glass, she peers down, wondering if she could escape through this window. But she's on the second floor; it's too high up. If she had the use of her arms, she might find a way to climb down. As it is, she wouldn't be able to do anything but fall straight to the ground and probably break an ankle, knee, or most likely her neck.

She continues her survey of the room along the perimeter till she reaches a closet, its door partly ajar. This too is empty, except for a few hangers with nothing on them. Assuming Sadie is alive, this couldn't be her room. There would be clothes at the very least. She doubts Toth could've cleared out everything of hers so quickly.

Rebecca returns to the bed with her head pounding and her body exhausted by her efforts. She lowers herself onto her side—a painful position but better than lying on her stomach. Thankfully, she sinks into sleep before long.

The sound of a key rattling in the lock wakes her the next time. Opening her eyes, she blinks at the shaft of sunlight that cuts across the floor from the window.

Toth lets himself in, shutting the door behind him. His hair is mussed and his clothes wrinkled like he slept in them last night. *Good*, she hopes he was miserable.

He carries a water bottle and wears a large knife in a holster on his right side. His gaze shifts to the open shade but he makes no comment on it.

She tries to speak but it's all garbled due to the duct tape.

He says, "I'll take that off so you can drink. But if you give me any trouble, I'll put another one on. It won't come off again. Anyway, screaming won't help. The neighbors are a long way off. They can't hear a thing. Are you going to behave?"

Once she nods her head, he steps toward her, grasps the duct tape with two fingers, and yanks it off. She cries out, feeling like she just lost a layer of skin. When she licks her lips with her tongue, she's relieved not to taste blood.

"Open your mouth, I'm going to give you some water."

She does as he commands and lifts her chin, but he pours too fast, making her choke. "Slow down," she says, her voice coming out hoarse.

He does as she asks, while looking annoyed about it.

"I'm starving," she says after finishing the bottle.

"Are you? I might feed you later, if you behave yourself."

"I need to use the bathroom."

He nods toward a bucket in the corner that she hasn't seen till now.

"I don't think I can use that when I'm all tied up like this," she says. "Can you free my hands? I can't get out of here with the door locked anyhow."

"No." He forces her down on her back with her arms pressed behind her. "Why did you come nosing around my house?"

Her heart thumps wildly. "Because you kidnapped my sister." There doesn't seem any point in pretending she doesn't know.

"Who told you that?"

"No one. I found out on my own."

"How?"

"I travelled back in time and watched it all happen." *The beauty of time travel is you can tell the truth and no one will believe you.*

He pushes against her already pain-filled shoulder, bringing tears to her eyes.

"Who knows you're here?"

"The police."

"Why'd they let you come snooping around all by yourself?"

"They weren't sure if they believed me. But now that I'm missing, they'll be here soon enough."

"Why aren't they here already? I think you're lying. Nobody knows where you are or why you came."

"Where's Sadie?" she cries out, unable to hold herself back.

"Don't know who that is."

"If you hurt her, you'll never get away with it."

"I never hurt anybody."

"Then why am I here? You're hurting me. I beg you, tell me what happened to her." She might never get another chance to ask these questions.

Saliva drips from the paralyzed side of his mouth and lands on her neck. "I said I don't know who you're talking about."

"Yes you do, you sick bastard. How many other girls have you taken? Weak little children who had no chance of defending themselves. You're a coward and a monster."

He takes out the knife and points it at her chest. "Shut up! You don't know anything!"

"You need help. Your mind is sick. A normal person wouldn't do these things. Let me help you. Let me get you to a doctor."

"I said, shut up." He hesitates like he can't decide whether to kill her right now or not. Then he thrusts the knife back in its sheath. "Remember what I told you," he says. "You make a sound and I'll be back here with the duct tape."

"Please, please, tell me where Sadie is."

"She died years ago." He walks to the door. "You came here for nothing."

The way he says it, so unconcerned, so like he thinks her sister is nothing. The way he might talk about losing his pet chameleon. This causes a deep well of rage to rise up inside her. She makes a guttural sound in her throat as she lands on her feet and runs toward Toth. Moving quickly, he slips through to the other side and slams the door shut just as she reaches it. She pounds her head against it before collapsing on the floor, curled in a twisted heap, filled with impotent fury, listening to the sound of the key turning in the lock.

Eventually, she returns to the bed. But just as she's about to lie down, she notices several strands of her hair that must have come out when she was sleeping there. If she leaves them, they'll be easy for Toth to clean up once he's disposed of her, which is almost certainly his plan now that he's admitted killing Sadie.

But what if she hides the hair? What if Freddie comes looking for her, gets a warrant, and has the place searched? She needs to insure they find her DNA.

It's a painstaking job to work with her hands tied behind her, picking up a strand at a time, and depositing it somewhere hidden inside the room. She drops one in the corner of the closet that would be hard to reach with a vacuum. Another in a desk drawer, blowing it to the back where Toth will be unlikely to look. A third one she lets fall next to the bed and then presses it right up against one of the legs using her foot.

Pushing through her exhaustion, she stands back against the plain beige wall that looks uneven in spots, like it used to be wallpaper and they just painted over it. She rubs her head against it until more hair comes out. She has to kneel down and fall over on the floor to retrieve the strands and stick them into her back pocket. Maybe she'll find a use for them later. When she's done, she struggles onto her feet and flops down on the bed at last. Ready to fall asleep and send her mind back to yesterday morning, before she came here to see the shed. She thought she may have glimpsed someone in the house, and if so, she needs to find out who that person is and what role they might be playing in Toth's crimes.

24

———————

Rebecca spins through time and lands inside her day-old self just as she is stepping out the door of her hotel room. As sometimes happens, the abrupt transition makes her stumble and grasp the rail to steady herself. At the same time, a wave of relief washes over her at the realization that the agonizing discomfort she was feeling across most of her body has now disappeared.

She returns to the room to retrieve the duct tape and small pair of scissors she packed in her suitcase. These go into her purse underneath the mace, which needs to be the first thing her hand touches when she reaches inside.

Since she knows Toth is at the service station, she can skip that step and go directly to his house. This also gives her the advantage that if he does have a co-conspirator at home, this time he won't know to phone them and warn them about her possible arrival.

Same as before, she parks down the road from his driveway and takes it on foot. As she nears the house, she decides her best approach is to simply go to the door and ring the bell. If she were to try and break in, it would immediately tip off the person inside—if there is one—to the fact that she plans to make trouble for them. She hopes coming to the door will throw them off guard.

There's no doorbell, just a metal knocker that Rebecca raps three times. She waits with her hand at the top of her open purse. Several minutes pass while she wonders if she'll have to break in after all. If she could be sure no one was home, she wouldn't mind; it's the uncertainty that's frightening her. She knocks three more times, harder than before.

Finally steps approach from inside and the door opens a crack. A woman of around fifty or sixty with curled bangs peers out. *Patricia*, the waitress from JJs Bar & Grill, who somehow keeps crossing Rebecca's path. She's surprised and yet not surprised. The woman gives her a creepy feeling.

Patricia brightens like Rebecca is her best friend and opens the door wider. "Well, my goodness, you found me. Did you come to get those sightseeing tips I promised you?"

"Um, actually, I'm here to see Jeremy. I wanted to talk to him…" Remembering he's a car mechanic, she adds, "…about my Honda. Do you, um, work here?" Because it's hard to picture using the mace against this feeble-looking woman, Rebecca hopes she might just be the housecleaner or… she can't imagine what. Though Patricia seems like a phony, it's difficult to imagine her having anything to do with the murdering pedophile Toth.

But the woman laughs. "Work here? This is my house."

"Are you… are you Jeremy's wife?" She has heard of serial killers' wives having no idea of the crimes their husbands were committing. Patricia looks at least ten years older than Jeremy, but the age gap is the least of her problems if she's married to him.

"His wife? Oh no. I'm his sister. Why don't you come inside? As it happens, he'll be here soon. He forgot his cell phone this morning."

This isn't what Rebecca is expecting at all. Did he really forget his phone? He didn't look like he was going anywhere when she saw him at the station. But if he's on his way, she ought to get inside and prepare to mace him when he walks in. "Sure," she says. "Thank you."

Patricia gestures toward a chair. As Rebecca turns toward it, she feels something hard poke into her back. "This is a gun, and I'll use it if I have to, sweetie-pie. Walk down that hall. I'll be right behind you."

Fuck. She should've maced her. Now Patricia is probably planning to lock her in the prison room. She has to act now, or she'll be no better off than she is in the future. Whirling around, taking Patricia by surprise, she knocks the gun from her hand, whips out the mace and sprays it right into the woman's face. She screams, covers her eyes, and tumbles backward trying to escape another stinging blast.

Rebecca grabs her and pushes her into a kitchen chair. "Sit still or more mace," she says. Patricia lowers her face into her hands, moaning, while Rebecca tapes her to the chair. She doesn't cover her mouth in case she needs to ask her questions. But she does dampen a kitchen towel and presses it over the woman's eyes to help relieve them.

She doubts Toth is on the way, but to be safe, she takes the gun and the mace with her as she begins a rapid search of the house. Saving the kitchen for last, she moves out to a sitting room with a faded couch, old-fashioned TV, and stacks of movies on videotape. A dining room with a rickety table. A half-bath with a chipped mirror and rusty faucets.

Upstairs, the first door has a lock on its knob. Her skin tingles as she wonders again if maybe Sadie had been kept in this room at some point. He told her Sadie died long ago, but why should she believe him? He wouldn't want her to know if her sister was still alive and being held captive. *Sadie, sweet sister, are you here?* Her heart sinks once again as she slowly opens the door and finds the room empty. It looks just as it does when they imprison Rebecca inside, missing only the bucket they must've brought later.

She crosses to the window and opens it wide, leaning forward to fling the gun as far as possible into the woods at the edge of the property. Since this isn't real-time, she's not going to worry about anyone finding it. She just wants it out of the way because she isn't going to use it, not even during a mindcast.

Continuing down the hall, she comes to a bathroom and then another bedroom. It smells like shit, with dirty dishes scattered all over the place and clothes on the floor. She checks the closet, where issues of Playboy and Penthouse are piled up. Toth's room, obviously. It makes her want to puke.

She searches the room without regard to the mess she's adding to his own. In his bottom drawer, she finds more ammunition for the gun. But there's no law against owning one, especially if he has it properly registered, and she finds nothing else in his room that might indicate criminal behavior. She even forces herself to flip through the magazines looking for child porn, but it's all adult women.

The third bedroom upstairs obviously belongs to the sister. Rebecca goes through her things with as much disregard as she displayed for her brother. She's about to give up hope of finding anything interesting when she gets to a small file cabinet behind Patricia's dresses in the closet.

Scanning through the documents, she learns the sister's full name —Patricia *Gaunt*, not Toth like Jeremy. Maybe they're half-siblings or the woman was married. It doesn't appear there's any other man living in this house; at least, Rebecca hopes not.

The documents include the deed to the house, car titles, and old bank statements. Nothing interesting on first glance. But in a folder at the back of the second drawer, Rebecca finds a photo of a little girl.

Her heart constricts while for a fleeting moment, she thinks it's Sadie. She might've continued to believe this if she hadn't seen her quite recently. The girl has similar features, and appears to be roughly the same age as Sadie was when she disappeared, but her hair is darker, shorter, and wavier. It definitely isn't Sadie.

Toth must have a type, she thinks. This could be another child he kidnapped. If only she could take the photo back to real-time when the mindcast ends, but it isn't possible. She stares down at the girl's face a moment longer, trying to memorize it. *I won't forget you.* If, after returning to the future, she manages to escape from the prison room somehow, she won't leave the house without this picture.

Taking it with her to the kitchen, she holds it up for Patricia, who glares at her through watery, red-streaked eyes.

"Who is this?" Rebecca says.

Patricia turns her face away.

Rebecca aims the mace at her. "I said, who is it?"

"My daughter. Nicki."

"Where is she?"

"Not here."

"Tell me unless you want more mace."

"She's gone. She's never coming back."

"Is she really your daughter? Or another child kidnapped by you and your brother?"

"I don't know what you mean."

"Where is my sister Sadie? What did you do to her?"

"I don't know what you're talking about."

Driven by rage and frustration, Rebecca raises the mace to spray Patricia again. But before she can complete the action, the dizzying symptoms of her time travel coming to an end overwhelm her.

25

Rebecca's mindcast was interrupted by the cold metal pressure of Toth's knife pushing up against her Adam's apple. She opens her eyes to find him sitting on the bed next to her, with his lopsided face bent over her.

"You make a sound, this goes straight through your neck," he hisses.

Someone must be here. She holds her breath, straining to hear any sounds inside the house. A minute later, a rapping comes at the front door. Toth grips her arm with his other hand, hurting her. After a short pause, a man's voice can be distinguished. *Martin.* Patricia must've opened the door to him.

Rebecca's heart melts at his concern for her. They only met two days ago, and here he is, searching for her, trying to learn why she disappeared from the motel and hasn't answered his calls. He isn't like any man she's ever met before, and she wants so hard to cry out to him, but she believes Toth is desperate enough to carry out his threat. Worse, if Martin finds out they've taken her it could put his own life in jeopardy. Patricia has a gun that wasn't thrown out the window in real-time.

The conversation is too muffled for Rebecca to make out what they're saying. Patricia must be putting on her act of folksy friendliness and helpless innocence. She'll pretend not to have ever heard of Rebecca or Sadie Danser in her life. She'll pretend Jeremy isn't home. She'll be a convincing liar, and Martin will have no choice but to leave. Rebecca doesn't think he'll go so far as to force his way into the house. Not for someone he only just met, who might be mentally unbalanced given the crazy story she told. God knows, anyone else would have already decided Rebecca had a whole set of screws loose.

Sure enough, the conversation ends quickly. Shortly afterward, Rebecca hears Martin's car start in the driveway. He's leaving, taking with him the last bit of hope inside her. She didn't know it would hit her this hard. She's reached the end.

Toth withdraws the knife and stands up.

"He'll be back," Rebecca says with more confidence than she feels. "He'll bring the police."

He ignores her, going out and locking the door behind him.

She hears Patricia coming up the stairs, and then her words. "It has to be tonight."

They'll kill me tonight and there's nothing more I can do. She's weak from pain and gnawing hunger. There's no escape from her bindings. No escape from this room. For the umpteenth time, she fervently wishes she could go back and really change the past, not simply observe it.

She regrets none of her actions, though. She found the monsters who did this thing to her sister. She doesn't think they'll get away with her murder. Freddie will come, and Martin seems determined to help. She'll have to die, but her death will lead them to solve Sadie's disappearance. Toth and Patricia will be arrested and put in jail for the rest of their lives. This is her hope and solace.

She lies in miserable pain and sadness for hours, until the room begins to darken. She must've grown drowsy at last, because she suddenly feels her head heating up, and her vision blackening, like a new mindcast is beginning. The odd thing is, she usually has to be focused on it, concentrating on a particular time and place. But she suspects her subconscious is driving this. Her inner need.

When she arrives in the past, she and Martin are leaning against her Honda following their dinner together, and she has just told him about Toth and the role Martin's family car played in the kidnapping. Her first impulse is to throw her arms around him and tell him how grateful she is that he cared enough to come looking for her. But she holds herself back, afraid of confusing him. Afraid of scaring him off with her bizarre behavior.

The pain and hunger she was feeling in the bedroom prison are erased again. In fact, she's satiated from the delicious meal she just finished eating. They're almost at the point where she says goodnight and drives back to the motel, but she can't let that happen now. As soon as she leaves his side, there will no longer be anything to keep her in this reality, and she can't bear the thought of returning to that desolate room in which her life is surely going to end soon.

"Do you want to do something now?" A strange excitement pulses through her.

"Sure. You have something in mind?"

"Another game. I know, I'm full of weird games. I want you to imagine today is my last day alive. What would you show me in this town of yours? What would you recommend I do?"

He stares at her. "Should I be worried? Have you been threatened by Toth, or anyone else?"

"No, it's just a game."

"Because if you have, we should go to the police."

"I'm fine. This is just an exercise in making the most of each day."

He still hesitates.

"If you don't want to play, I get it," she says.

"No. It isn't that. I'm just worried for you."

"I'm not worried. If I've learned anything this year, it's that you can't stop the forward motion of time. Though you might pause it for a bit." She smiles to reassure him.

He thinks for a minute. "Okay, then. Carpe diem and all that. I've always tried to live that way. Experience every day as if it's your last... I've got an idea."

"Don't tell me," she says. "I want to be surprised."

"C'mon then. We have to drive there."

They go in Martin's Subaru. At the highway, he turns east toward Draywood, but when they reach the small town, he drives past it, climbing higher and higher into the mountains.

Already she feels better, enjoying the evening ride along the winding road. Magnificent trees on both sides of them. A man she respects seated beside her. A comfortable silence—an understanding —between them. And a surprise to come.

After forty-five minutes, they've left the lights of civilization behind them. Martin peers forward, searching for something. "I think this is it," he says a minute later. He turns the car down a dirt road, following it until it ends abruptly, blocked by forest. Martin shuts off the engine and pops open the trunk. "Here we are." They get out and walk around to the back.

Everything in the trunk is organized inside a basket stretched across the width of the car. Jumper cables, a collapsible snow shovel, a toolkit, spare water and snacks, maps, blankets, and more.

"Looks like we'll be fine here for days," she says.

"Weather's unpredictable in the mountains."

She gives him a crooked smile.

"What? You don't think this is normal?" he says.

"I wouldn't know."

He takes a blanket and uses his phone light to lead them to the start of a trail. Rebecca follows close behind using her cell, and before long they reach the top of a hill, where a vast meadow opens out in front of them. At the far side of the clearing, above the tips of the trees, the silhouettes of mountain peaks loom sharp, jagged, and infinitely fascinating.

"It's an incredible view," she says.

"C'mon, there's more."

They walk till they've reached the center of the meadow, where he spreads out the blanket. "Do you trust me?"

She can't remember the last time she trusted anyone. But when she searches for the answer inside herself, it emerges as a simple, "Yes."

"Lie down flat on your back, then." Once she's settled, he lays down beside her, with both of them gazing up at the night sky.

"The stars," she says. "My god, the stars."

"You have to go some distance from civilization to view them this well. And there has to be no moon."

"I've never done this before. I've never seen stars this bright. This distinct. There's so many of them."

"It's something everyone should get to see…" he trails off.

…before they die, she finishes inside her head. "Thank you for this." It could not have been a more fitting choice for her last night alive. "I suppose I should feel inconsequential compared to all these enormous and magnificent stars, planets, and asteroids. But actually I feel the opposite, like my life has been meaningful. Like I've made my imprint on the universe. Because here we are, living parts of this all-encompassing thing. We've had our roles to play, and who knows, if we'd never been born, the world might've been different in some small but significant way."

She wonders if when she's dust, her consciousness will merge with the universe. This seems all the more likely, given that she already has the power to separate mind from body and fly through space and time. All because of a spark from a mysterious rock. She wonders if it came from a planet of time-traveling wizards who probably have no idea what role they played in her life.

"We're interconnected in mysterious ways," she says. "I wouldn't be here with you now… I wouldn't ever have met you… if Toth hadn't used your father's car."

"Then it would've been better if we'd never met."

"I see it this way. A plant is fertilized with shit, but out of that excrement comes something beautiful and unique and living. I couldn't prevent him from kidnapping Sadie, but I can still welcome this precious feeling that grew out of a dark and sinister place." She shifts closer and slips her hand inside his.

They lie together under the brilliant stars until the cragged fingers of real-time pull her back.

26

The rain has ended and the sky is rosy with the light of dawn when Nicki rises in a panic.

"Sadie!" She hisses the name, aware of the danger that Uncle might be out searching for them at first light. "Sadie, where are you?"

Nicki stares down at Becca the rabbit and Mr. Fluffernutter the dog, abandoned on the ground. If Sadie had set out to find her way back to the shed, wouldn't she have taken them with her? Hopefully this means she only stepped away to relieve herself.

Nicki emerges from under the branches of the tree and scans the area. "Sadie!" she calls again. The leaves stirring in the breeze provide the only response. She widens her search, checking for footprints in the muddy sections. When she finds one, she grows excited until she realizes it's too large for Sadie and must've come from her own foot last night.

Nicki pauses to consider where Sadie might've gone. Her fear of being caught by Uncle after having run away may have driven her to try to find her way back to the shed. She might've chosen not to wake Nicki because she knew her friend was set on running away and would insist on Sadie remaining with her.

On the other hand, Nicki's first instinct that Sadie might simply have needed to pee could still be right. Only if that was the case, she must've wandered too far and now she can't find her way back. Or, after losing herself, and maybe calling out for Nicki, she might've been discovered by Uncle and taken back to the house.

As the sun's rays poke above the treetops, she gets her bearings. To reach the road, located to the east, she would need to face the sun and walk toward it. She could leave right now and set a much faster pace than would be possible with a four-year-old at her side. A sick four-year-old, no less.

But inside her heart, she knows she can't go without Sadie. She won't be able to live with herself if Sadie is back at the house, being kept prisoner inside that tiny room. If Sadie is the one who has to face the punishment for the escape attempt forced on her by Nicki. Mother and Uncle will make her suffer for it.

With a terrible feeling of resignation, she turns away from the sun and heads west. It doesn't take long before she glimpses their chimney above the highest branches in the distance.

But when she lowers her gaze, a patch of pink color next to an aspen tree catches her eye. Rushing forward, she finds Sadie's parka lying on the ground, abandoned. The air is crisp and cold; why would she take it off? None of this makes any sense.

Nicki resumes her search with new urgency, circling outward from the aspen, until suddenly she finds Sadie curled up behind a bush, her eyes closed. Nicki drops to her knees beside her. "Sadie," she whispers, "Sadie, get up, we need to go."

But the little girl doesn't move or open her eyes. Her face is unnaturally pale and feels like ice when Nicki touches it. With a deepening sense of dread, Nicki shakes her body gently. "Wake up, Sadie. Wake up." When she lifts Sadie by the arms, the girl's head falls limply backward and Nicki lowers her again. "Sadie, no..."

Tears roll down Nicki's cheeks as she looks down at the one person she loved unconditionally. How will she carry on without her? It must've been the fever, she thinks. Sadie must've caught whatever Mother had. Maybe she'd been sick for several days without receiving any treatment. Maybe she wandered away in a delirium last night. She might've grown hot from the fever and thrown off her jacket. Afterward, she would've become cold. The night had been freezing; there was frost on the moss when Nicki got up. Lying here without a coat... the cold must've killed her. That, and hopelessness.

She's not sure how long she cries, but eventually she gathers herself, determined not to let Sadie's passing be for nothing. It's their fault she's gone—Mother and Uncle, who left her alone in the shed, sick and dying, while Mother was rushed to the doctor. Nicki must leave now, before they can find her, and put as much distance between them as possible. She has to succeed in breaking free of them for Sadie's sake.

Filled with new energy, she stands and lifts Sadie. The child is light, even for Nicki, who isn't terribly strong. She carries her back to the tree where they slept during the night and lays her down. Wanting to give her a proper burial, she makes a clearing by pushing the pine needles aside, and attempts to claw into the soil with her hands and fingernails. But between the large roots of the tree and the cold, packed-in dirt, digging is impossible. Even with a shovel, she wouldn't be able to manage it.

She moves Sadie to the space she made and places the stuffed animals on either side of her. "Don't be frightened. Becca and Mr. Fluffernutter are with you." She kneels over her and kisses her forehead. "Sleep well, sweet sister."

Beginning with her feet and moving upward over her torso, she piles leaves and pine needles on top of her friend, covering the stuffed animals before pausing at her neck. The thought of sullying Sadie's beautiful face with the dirty mixture holds her back.

A voice carried by the wind distracts her. *Uncle?* She emerges from under the branches and listens. The sound comes again, and this time she's nearly certain it's Uncle calling out her name.

Nicki ducks back under the tree to finish the burial. But for some reason, Sadie's face is no longer visible. Did she fully cover her already? She could've sworn the task wasn't done. Nicki blinks hard, but when she opens her eyes again, she sees nothing but a mound of pine needles.

Her dislike for completing the job must've blocked her memory of it. Her grief and fear made everything seem confusing. But now she needs to leave. Sadie would be counting on her to succeed in their escape.

She blows a kiss at her dear friend's grave before turning away, putting on her backpack, and straightening her shoulders. A new feeling of lightness comes over her despite the weight she carries. Setting a brisk pace toward the east, she pictures Sadie dissolving into a puff of vapor and becoming the wind under her wings.

They come for Rebecca in the middle of the night. Toth's first act is to place a swatch of duct tape over her mouth. His second is to pull her up from the bed while Patricia holds the pistol on her.

"I think you met my sister," Toth says.

If not for her mindcasts, Rebecca would've been surprised by the revelation of Toth's connection to the woman who waited on her at the local bar and grill.

Patricia gives her a nasty smile. "I've kept track of you through the years. It was a shock when I thought I recognized you coming into the restaurant. I checked your credit card to be sure."

So they knew about her within hours of her arriving in town. That car outside her motel room the second night could've been Toth watching her. He must've known who she was before she even walked into his service station. Patricia was at home and certainly watching when she ran into their backyard and banged at the door of the shed. By then they must've decided they had to get rid of her.

She failed at sleuthing, but she never expected to make it her career anyway. If only she could get answers to her remaining questions, though. The tape over her mouth prevents her from asking them.

Her knees buckle when she takes her first steps, and Toth raises her back up. He forces her forward, through the hall, down the stairs, and past the kitchen to the front door. Outside, her Honda is parked close to the steps. Dread fills her at the sight of the open trunk.

As they draw nearer, Rebecca spots her luggage in the backseat. Toth must've taken her motel key after knocking her out. He could've dumped her back here before returning to her room to gather her things during the night. He probably left the key on the table to make it look like she checked out. Smart. It would be hard to convince the police she hadn't left of her own accord... unless they tried to track her movements from her cell phone. Toth must've destroyed it, and if so, wouldn't it be odd when it didn't show up anywhere? *But it's too late for me now.*

"Get in," he says, dragging her to the edge of the trunk.

She knows they'll just hurt her more if she resists. Without the use of her hands, she has to awkwardly sit inside it, tumbling backward, banging her shoulders, head, legs. The sleeve of her jacket catches on the latch, causing her arm to pull back painfully. When Toth pushes her further inside, the sleeve tears.

Once she is all in, he slams the trunk shut. She hears him get into the driver's seat, start the car, and back out. Eventually she feels a swerve to the right, which means he has turned onto the highway and is heading east up the mountain—just as Martin did with her earlier.

She keeps her eyes closed trying not to think how much like a coffin this is. The air smells musty and her stomach, though it's empty, feels queasy as they careen around each corner. She only hopes his driving is poor enough to attract the attention of the highway patrol.

Her eyes snap open again as she remembers something important —the hair in her back pocket. It *is* her own car, and anyone might lose some strands bending over their trunk, but if she scatters what she has, it might be enough for police to conclude she must've been riding in here. Anything that might lead to a conviction is worth a try.

She digs into her pocket for the hair and spreads it as best she can throughout the cramped space.

Given the length of time, it appears they're traveling at least as high up into the mountains as she and Martin did. There's a long stretch of emptiness before they would reach the ski area, currently closed, and she expects they'll pull off somewhere along that section. Sure enough, within ten more minutes the car slows before turning left onto a bumpy surface. With her banging over every ditch and stone, they wind along what must be a dirt road for some time.

Finally the car stops and the engine is shut off. Rebecca hears a second vehicle approaching behind them and for a fleeting instant, pictures the highway patrol. But then that car goes silent too. As she listens, Toth gets out and walks back to the second car, where he and Patricia share a muttered conversation. Of course, she's here to drive Toth back home after the deed is done. Rebecca figures they'll simply leave her dead body next to her car here in the wilderness. Her remains will be discovered eventually, but if they're lucky, not till after winter. If they're really lucky, police might assume she was stupidly wandering around and got caught by an angry pot grower. Though weed is legal now, she's heard some still work and live in the mountains and protect their property ferociously.

The trunk comes open. A glimpse past Jeremy shows Patricia still seated in her car, her gaze cast to the side like she wants nothing to do with this dirty work though she knows it has to be done.

When Toth grabs Rebecca and pulls her out, adrenaline shoots through her with the realization that now is the only chance she'll get, when he's off guard and not expecting any fight out of her. As soon as her feet touch the ground, she straightens, thrusting her head at Jeremy's chin. She hits it hard, even hears a crack. It hurts her like hell too, but what matters is he's crying out in pain and has fallen backward.

She turns the other way and runs into the forest, her only chance of hiding from them. Her eyes at least are used to the dark after all that time in the trunk. Her burning desire to live gives her a burst of speed, and though she's awkward and unbalanced with her hands bound behind her back, she puts distance between them.

But already she hears the sounds of him coming after her. The next thing she knows, a gunshot erupts behind her. The noise makes her body spasm but she doesn't think it hit her, at least she can't feel anything. She weaves and dodges to avoid the next shot and when a gap in the underbrush appears, she turns off the trail to make it harder for him to aim at her. But then the tear in her sleeve catches on a branch, stopping her, nearly knocking her backward. She yanks hard on it, ripping the material further, before she breaks free and sprints forward again.

Toth's footsteps crunch behind her, drawing closer by the second. The bushes and sweeping branches of trees slow her down, until abruptly the forest opens up and she finds herself on top of a rocky promontory. She runs to the edge of it, barely halting in time, teetering above a sheer drop.

Turning back, she glimpses Toth emerging into the clearing and pausing to raise his gun. The shot explodes from behind at the same second she leaps from the precipice.

PART VI

28

Martin wakes with the sensation of a long, wet, scratchy tongue licking his hand. When he opens his eyes, he's greeted by Guy standing next to the bed, resting her head on the blanket, staring at him with an aggrieved expression. *Do you mean to let me die of starvation?* those soulful eyes say.

It's 7:40, only ten minutes later than his normal rising time, but an eternity to his dog. He rubs her head and gets up. "It's coming, it's coming," he says. She follows him down the hall and sits like the good doggie she is while he pours her kibble. She waits for his signal before diving into the bowl and swallowing huge mouthfuls without chewing, like she's in a race to finish first, even though she's the only dog around.

When she's done, she goes out back to do her business. Martin makes a mental note to clean up out there later. For now, he needs to tend to himself. He's hosting an Open House at ten and has to drop by the office for some flyers first. Still plenty of time to shower and dress and make a decent breakfast.

First he returns to his bedroom to check his phone, though. It disappoints him to see there's no message from Rebecca, not even a quick text. He asked her to check in this morning, but it's still early and maybe she's asleep. He probably shouldn't worry, but he hasn't been able to get her, and the story of her kidnapped sister, out of his head since last night. After coming home, he spent several hours on the Internet reading articles about the search for Sadie. In the process, he learned that Rebecca's mother killed herself. He could only imagine how much that must have torn her apart, losing her sister and then her mother too.

But her actions in coming here by herself were rash, and he can't help fearing she might keep on acting rashly. Without knowing a thing about Martin except that his car was used to snatch her sister, she allowed herself to be alone with him when they went to view the house. She's just lucky he's not a serial killer. What if she's doing the same with Jeremy, who might actually be a serial killer?

While Martin showers, he considers the possibility that Jeremy is guilty. He never liked the guy, but he always tried hard not to show it. They went to school together, and it sickened Martin to see the way the other kids picked on him for his physical appearance and difficulty speaking. A few times Martin got involved and stuck up for him. One time he ended up in a fist fight, for which his father had to be called. But as soon as they got in the car, his dad said he was proud of him for standing up to bullies.

If Rebecca is right about Jeremy, she could be in danger. He easily could've seen her in town and might even recognize her. He might be keeping tabs on his victim's family. Or victims' families? Oh god, Martin hopes there's not more than one of them.

He makes himself scrambled eggs and a piece of whole wheat toast, and tries not to be too anal about cutting the bread exactly in half. Whenever he's anxious about something, his OCD tends to kick in harder.

As he gets up to do the dishes, the buzz of his phone stops him short, but it turns out to be an unimportant text from his coworker, Luanne. It still feels too early to call Rebecca, so he finishes the cleanup and then brings Guy outside to the line where she spends her mornings whenever the weather is nice.

He makes it to the office by 9:15 and heads to the Open House after grabbing the flyers. During the drive, he decides it's late enough to call Rebecca. He's willing to take the chance she'll be mad at him for waking her just to relieve his mind of worry.

It rings four times before going into her message. After the beep, he says, "Hi, hope I'm not calling too early but I just wanted to see how you're doing. Please give me a call when you get a minute." He hangs up, wondering if he's just ruined his odds of ever seeing her again.

When he gets to the Warrington's, setting everything up distracts his mind for a while. Turning on lights, spraying a bit of air freshener, checking each room to be sure there's nothing out of place. Luckily the owners have already moved out and they have the house staged with rented furnishings. That always works better than when sellers leave their personal items about. Still, there are always a few last things that need adjustment, like straightening a tilted lamp shade and closing the toilet cover.

The Warrington house has been on the market for a while so he's not expecting too many visitors. But the second couple to arrive shows a good deal of interest and plies him with questions for nearly two hours. At the end of this, they've decided not to make an offer, but they would like Martin to help them find something else. A lose-win, in other words.

When they finally leave, he checks his phone and is seriously disconcerted not to find a reply from Rebecca. *Fuck it.* He calls her again, and again she doesn't answer. His message this time says, "Hey, I don't mean to be a pest, but if you could please whip off a quick text, like even if it says, 'lay off, buddy,' I would feel better just hearing from you. Thanks."

After twenty minutes of still no response, he calls his coworker. "Luanne, I know this must be really inconvenient, but is there any way you can take over the Warrington Open House for me? It's only another hour. I have a family emergency."

He hears pages flipping like she's checking her day planner. She's old-fashioned in that she still prefers paper. "Sure, I've got nothing till three today. And then you'll owe me one, ha!"

"That's right, you can hit me up for something big."

"Oh I will, dude. I will."

There's a couple wandering through the rooms when Luanne arrives so she'll have some work to do after they finish looking. "I love you, Luanne," Martin says on his way out the door. Once he checks his phone, confirming there's still no response from Rebecca, he sets out in his Subaru for her motel.

Seeing that her car isn't there, front or back or across the street, he parks by the front lobby. Is it possible she just went back home? After doing his research on the Internet, he knows she wasn't lying about the kidnapping. But maybe she's a whack job who likes to make up stories about leads in the case. Milking her family history for sympathy.

Just to check, before getting out he does a Google search of "Rebecca Danser" on his phone, to find out if she might be in the habit of wandering the state, randomly accusing people of kidnapping her sister. If so, she must've gotten into trouble now and then. There ought to be an article or a police report, but nothing comes up. Did she escape from an asylum? Nothing like that either.

The thing is, what she said about his dad's car made sense. It really was gone that weekend. His gut tells him she meant every word she said to him. And therefore it's weird and somewhat scary that she's ignoring his calls.

He goes into the lobby. Richard, whose father is a friend of Martin's, comes out from the back. "Hey, how's it going?" Martin says.

"Fine." Richard looks puzzled to see him there. "You don't want a room, do you?"

"No, I do have a house nearby. I wanted to ask about someone who's been staying here. Her name's Rebecca Danser."

Richard gets a sly look on his face. "Oh the hot one?"

"Don't get any ideas, man."

His expression deflates. "Well anyway, she checked out."

"You saw her leave?"

"No. But when Sharon went up to clean the room, she found all her stuff gone and the key on the table."

"So... no one saw her leave? What time does Sharon start work?"

"Eight. Sometimes she's a little late, but no more than fifteen minutes."

"Is this office open all night?"

"With the number of guests we get this time of year? I go home at seven and leave out a number they can call."

Martin nods. "Thanks." Returning to his car, he just sits there. What now? She must've gone sometime between the time they left the restaurant and 8:00 a.m. Did she really just drive home without letting him know? Is it possible she has so little consideration for other people, she wouldn't bother replying to his messages? He thought they had a connection last night. Was it all in his head? He drums his fingers on the dash, until deciding to go to Jeremy's service station.

When Martin goes inside, he finds Greg, the assistant, at the register. "Hey, is Jeremy here?" he says.

"Took the day off," Greg says.

"Is he sick?"

"Didn't seem like it yesterday."

"Going on vacation?"

Greg shrugs. "He doesn't tell me anything. Should I say you were looking for him?"

"No, I'll call him. I have his number." Martin returns to his car, shaken. It doesn't feel like a coincidence, that on the day Rebecca seemingly disappears, Jeremy does too. He wonders if he has enough justification for going to the police, then he squelches that idea. He's got nothing at this point. They would laugh him out of the station.

He could go to Jeremy's house, though. What would he say? *I met this girl who thinks you kidnapped her sister. Did you take her too?* But with a little more thought, he comes up with a way to handle it.

Driving up to the house, he parks in the driveway behind a Chevy sedan that must belong to Jeremy or his sister. There's also a pickup truck on the side of the lot. If Rebecca was here, wouldn't her car be here too? There's a windowless garage. Not sure how he's going to get a look in there if anyone's home. Patricia is an odd duck too. Always doted on her brother when he was a kid. Fiercely protective of him, like she was his mother, not his sister. Might be that anything he does is fine with her. Their parents died young and she brought him up since he was nine or something. Like Jeremy, she keeps to herself, but she's always nice enough at JJs. He seems to remember she had a daughter, but it's been a long time since he heard anything about her.

Before getting out, he takes a minute to look around the place. He'd like to snoop around the back, but that might be taking it too far at this point. Glancing up, he glimpses a man, apparently Jeremy, at an upstairs window. The man immediately shifts out of view.

Martin gets out and knocks at the door. It doesn't take long before Patricia answers, blocking the opening with her body. Not that it wouldn't be easy to push past her if he wanted to.

"Hello." Her lips are smiling but her eyes are cold. "Nice to see you, Martin. How can I help you?"

"I was hoping to talk to your brother. Is he home?"

"No," she says. "Can I give him a message?"

Not too smart to lie about it. Jeremy must not have let her know he was going to show himself at the upstairs window. Martin tries to peer past her into the house, looking for any signs of Rebecca having come here. He also listens carefully for any sounds of her.

"Will he be back soon? I can wait." He stalls to give Rebecca a chance to cry out if she's inside. No way does he expect Patricia to invite him in.

"He won't be back for hours. I can have him call you then. What is it that's so important?"

"I have a client who expressed interest in buying the service station. I think he wants to build it up a bit. Add a café or something. The guy seems to have money to invest."

"Jeremy is certainly not going to sell it."

"Are you sure? It would be—"

"Good day." She shuts the door on him.

Returning to his car, he glances back up at the window, but

Jeremy is doing a better job concealing himself now. There's nothing Martin can do but leave. He's sure now that something suspicious is going on. Patricia lied about Jeremy not being there, and she clearly wanted Martin gone. And there's still the mystery of why Jeremy would take the day off just to stay home.

He can't let this go. From there, he drives directly to the county sheriff's substation. Unfortunately, Officer Fitzpatrick is at the front desk. Martin has never liked the guy. In school, Fitz was one of those bullies who loved picking on Jeremy.

Martin approaches and asks to speak with the sheriff.

"He's out on a call," Fitz says. "How can I help you, Martin?"

"When will the sheriff be back?"

"Not for a few hours. I can help you. What is it?"

Martin has no choice but to try to explain what's going on. That Rebecca Danser came to town telling him she believed Jeremy Toth was behind the Sadie Danser kidnapping. Meanwhile, Fitz is looking it up on his computer.

The explanation for how Rebecca became convinced of this comes out all wrong. The truth is, Martin can't really remember the details. Something about an informant, but the reason why they waited so long to say anything isn't clear to him, and he bungles trying to explain it.

"If this is true, why isn't the FBI here?" Fitz says.

"She didn't think she had enough proof to contact them yet."

"Uh huh." Fitz looks up at Martin. "You know, you may think you're another Pedro Pascal, but we all get rejected now and then. She went home. She didn't want to see you again."

"Pedro Pascal?"

"Aren't you Hispanic?" Fitz says.

"Half-Hispanic. So?"

"So, *Narcos*? He played Peña. And Oberyn in *Game of Thrones*. You watch TV?"

"Not much. Look, she might not have wanted to date me, but she was too nice to just ignore my messages."

Fitz rolls his eyes. "This the first time you dated someone who didn't answer your calls the next day? Lucky guy."

"This is fucking serious," Martin says.

Fitz stands up. "You don't fucking talk to an officer of the law like that. Come back when you've got something. This is nothing."

He's only wasting time with this idiot. Martin spins around and heads to the door.

29

———————

After striking out at the sheriff's office, Martin returns home, settles on the couch next to Guy, and considers his options. What else can he do, short of breaking into Jeremy's house? Maybe Fitz was right. Martin got rejected and he's having trouble dealing with that. It's true he hasn't been rejected too often. But in this case, there's an age difference. He might be ten or twelve years older than her. Maybe she thinks he looks like an old man.

He checks his phone again for messages. Still no word from her, but there's one from Luanne that he's needed at the office if he can make it. He grabs two energy bars since he hasn't had lunch, and heads off. It turns out to be a busy afternoon, with Luanne looking terribly relieved to see him after trying to juggle two different couples. He takes over with one of them, and it isn't till seven that the contract is filled out, signed, and delivered. Meanwhile he's been glancing at his phone every ten minutes.

When he gets home, he calls Rebecca and leaves one last message. "Look, it's fine if you didn't click with me. I'm a big boy and I can take it. But I'm seriously concerned about you. If you have a heart, you'll take one second to respond, 'I'm okay.' Please?"

Too demoralized to cook something real tonight, he just heats up a frozen pizza for dinner. His phone remains by his elbow while he eats.

It's too much. He has to do something or he'll never forgive himself if anything has happened to her. He remembers her saying something about a detective in Sadie's case who still keeps in touch with her. What was his name? Jeffrey? He's not sure. But maybe the guy still works for the same department, which ought to be in the town where they lived when the crime happened. He looks up one of the articles about Sadie to get the name of the place and puts in a call to their police.

After identifying himself, he says, "I'd like to speak with the detective in charge of the Sadie Danser disappearance."

The female officer on the other end says, "Sadie Danser? I'm not sure who that is."

"You must be new?" he says.

"Pretty new. Hold on, please."

He waits impatiently till her return a few minutes later.

"That was Detective Lazo," she says. "He's been on vacation, but he'll be back in the morning. Can I have him call you then? Or you can file a report with me."

He hesitates. Should he tell her what he knows? But after having tried to explain the situation to Fitz, he realizes how fruitless that will be. At least Lazo knows the case, and Rebecca may have already told him some of what she relayed to Martin.

"Please have him call me first thing tomorrow," he says.

He stays up late streaming action movies he's already seen before, unable to sleep. It must be two a.m. by the time Martin finally nods off. His phone ringing wakes him at six. He struggles out of a state of deep grogginess before lunging for it, filled with hope that it might be Rebecca. Instead, it's a male voice he doesn't recognize. "Hello, Mr. Ortiz?" the man says.

"Yes."

"Detective Lazo. Sorry for the early call. I just learned you were trying to reach me last night. Regarding Rebecca Danser?"

"That's right. I've been concerned about her."

"Do you know where she is? She left a message for me a few days ago. I called her a few times last night and she still hasn't returned my call."

"No, that's just it. I don't know where she is. And I'm worried about her. She was here in Draywood... to do with her sister's kidnapping. Do you know about that?"

There's a brief silence before Lazo says, "I know something about it. I told her to leave it alone."

"Well, she didn't follow your advice. And now she seems to be missing. I've been trying to reach her since yesterday morning, and nothing."

"I'm coming out there. Can I meet you at your house?"

"Yeah, I'll be here." He'll do whatever it takes to get Luanne to cover for him.

Martin fills the next few hours getting himself showered, dressed and fed, feeding and walking Guy, and doing repair work he's been avoiding at home. At a little before nine, the doorbell rings.

His initial impression of Detective Lazo is reassuring. Despite that he had to leave home at an early hour this morning, the detective is clean-shaven, neatly dressed, and ready to get to work. His handshake has a comforting firmness to it, and unlike Fitz yesterday, he's obviously ready to treat Rebecca's lack of responsiveness with the level of seriousness it deserves.

"Can I get you some coffee?" Martin says.

"Always. I like it with milk and sugar, please."

Once they're settled at the table, Martin pours out the whole story once again, brushing over the part about the informant, just focusing on the information Rebecca had. Recounting his visit to Jeremy's house, he expresses his suspicion of Toth and his sister in the strongest terms. "I'm sure they were hiding something."

"People hide a lot of things, but that doesn't mean they're kidnappers," Detective Lazo says. "Still, I'm very concerned about Rebecca. It isn't like her to get in touch and then ignore my replies. So, before I set out this morning, I requested a check on her apartment. Heard back an hour ago. When she didn't answer their knock, they got the super to open it up. She's not home, obviously, but the apartment looked fine, no sign that anything violent happened there. Her Honda wasn't in the garage, so I put out an APB on it."

"What about her phone? Can you find her from that?"

"Her phone is dead. Its last location was in the vicinity here, and that was nearly two days ago. So starting now, we're treating this as a kidnapping and we're going to do everything we can to find her. If you can assure me she told you she was going to Toth's house, the local police should be able to get a warrant to search there."

"Yeah, she was going there." Strictly speaking, she didn't tell him this. But if it helps get the police inside that house, he's willing to stretch the truth.

Lazo sets down his cup and gets up. "I'll keep you posted."

After Martin sees him out, he goes back to working on house projects he has put off for way too long. The waiting is hard, even with these distractions, and he jumps to answer his phone when a call comes in a little after noon.

"Okay, here's where it gets interesting," Detective Lazo begins. "The judge didn't want to issue a warrant since we don't have proof Rebecca went there, and we've got no evidence any crime was ever committed by Toth or his sister."

"That isn't good," Martin says.

"Sometimes you have to think outside the box to get inside someone's house. You look for code violations and things like that, small stuff, but enough to get you in. The sheriff had the idea to find out just who all is living at the house. They did a quick check of marriage and birth certificates. Patricia was married some years ago, but the guy died young of a rare illness, no question of foul play. However, before he died, they had a kid, Nicki Gaunt. This got the cops wondering, how come they never saw this kid around town?

"Next step was to call the local education department. They ought to know if she went to school, right? They told us she was home-schooled. Patricia filed an affidavit every year, until Nicki was sixteen. That year, after some prodding, Patricia told them she didn't file because Nicki ran away."

"How does this relate?"

"The people in the education department assumed she must have filed a report with the sheriff's office. But she didn't. They've checked; it was never reported. And that's not okay. You're responsible for your kid's well-being till they're eighteen. And it's really questionable when you don't report your kid missing. It makes us think there might be some parental foul play going on."

"Wow. Okay."

"They went back to the judge, and now she was interested. She granted a warrant for them to do a search and question Toth and his sister regarding what happened to Nicki. They're in there now. Rebecca's not there, I'm afraid. But they're taking forensics. We hope to have some clues soon."

The mention of *forensics* causes Martin's throat to dry up.

"Toth and Gaunt are starting to look suspicious enough, I got the sheriff to agree to send out a couple choppers to search around here for Rebecca's car. You probably know, there's a lot of old logging roads. Places where someone might dump a car. They might hope the snow will come soon and hide it till spring. It's worth checking."

"Thanks for letting me know." He felt better with the knowledge that things were being done, though it gave him a heavy feeling to think that if they found her car up there, it was almost certainly too late to save Rebecca.

"I'll call back when I've got more." Lazo hangs up.

Again, Martin waits. This time when he gets on the couch with Guy, they both nap. When the phone wakes him again, he's not sure how much time has passed.

"They found her Honda," Lazo says. "Pilot just called it in."

"No sign of Rebecca?"

"Not yet. I'm heading up there now."

"Can I come? I can help search. I've done search and rescue before, when hikers went missing."

"They've called for dogs. Not sure how soon they'll arrive," Lazo says. "Fine. I'll swing by and get you."

Martin watches at the window and rushes out to Lazo's car as soon as he pulls up. "Do you think she could be inside the car?" he says, belting into the passenger seat.

"If she is, she's not responding. The helicopter's making a lot of noise overhead and she hasn't come out."

"Right." He's too nervous to say much more as they drive up the mountain.

They reach the turnoff thirty minutes later, following some communication with the sheriff regarding the location. Martin thinks he's been to this spot before, sledding with his ex's daughter. But he's not certain. These side roads all look alike, with no signs and just a gravel surface.

A short while later they pull up behind a police vehicle parked next to Rebecca's white Honda. When they get out of the car, the sheriff approaches. Officer Fitzpatrick lags further back, avoiding Martin's glare.

"Hello Martin," the sheriff says before turning to Detective Lazo. "Keys in the car. Her luggage in the back seat. We noticed some hair in the trunk. Like, that's where she might've been travelling."

"Where have you searched?"

"Not far yet. We haven't been here long."

Two more squad cars arrive as they start to get organized. Before long, searchers are dispatched in groups of two, with Martin and Lazo paired. They're given a radio, a topographical map of the area, and a pack with water, snacks, and some emergency equipment.

As they head out, they look for tracks and other signs of anyone having passed through recently. They call out her name intermittently. But their progress is slow as they attempt to cover the area in methodical fashion, without leaving gaps in their search.

"Over here," Lazo says after twenty minutes have passed. He points out a footprint to Martin. "That's about a man's size eleven."

"Can you tell if it's recent?"

He bends down and peers at it. "I think so. Can't be sure, though."

They continue in the direction the footprint is facing. After several yards, Martin spots a bluish piece of fabric snagged on a branch. "Look at this." He touches it though he's not sure if he should. "It might be the jacket she wore the night we had dinner. It was this color."

Lazo comes up behind him and examines the material. "This is definitely new. It would be much dirtier otherwise." He scans the brush in the area. "Looks like she might've gone off-trail here. See... more broken branches."

They push forward through the undergrowth until coming to an open area with a rocky slope. Martin and Lazo creep to the edge and look down.

A body lies crumpled forty or fifty feet below, partly obscured by the branches around it.

Martin feels a stabbing sensation and has to turn away. *We're too late.*

30

Rebecca can't breathe. Dirt fills her nostrils and covers her eyes. It weighs down her body, forcing her deeper into the soil. She's aware that if she simply gives up and lets the earth swallow her, the grief and terror will disappear. *She* will disappear and never feel anything again. Death tempts her by being the easy choice. No effort required. If she wants life, she'll have to battle demons and endure excruciating pain, though she's weak and exhausted and has nearly lost all hope.

This is her state, poised at the brink of sinking backward or struggling forward, when she hears Sadie. "Becca," her sister whispers. "Becca, Becca, Becca," echoes inside Rebecca's head. *Is she calling me toward death or life?*

A beam of light shines over her. She's aware of voices and someone touching her. She no longer feels as if she's buried under the ground. That must've been a nightmare. They've come here to rescue her. She must not disappoint them.

Life is the word that floats through her mind, spoken in Sadie's childish voice, as Rebecca drifts back into unconsciousness.

~

SOMETIME LATER, possibly days later, she opens her eyes. All is blurry at first, but gradually her vision sharpens until she recognizes the face of the man seated beside her bed.

"Freddie." Her own voice sounds scratched and distant. She has an impulse to touch her mouth but her right arm won't move. She's in a hospital room connected to an IV bag, wearing a cast that wraps around her upper arm and shoulder right up to her neck.

Freddie pats her left hand and smiles at her.

"What happened?" she says.

"You broke your arm and collarbone. You got hypothermia and lots of cuts and bruises. But your spine is intact and you had no internal bleeding. You're incredibly lucky. It was forty-six feet to the bottom, but they think you bounced off the branches of the closest pine tree, which helped break your fall."

She remembers Toth chasing her, but doesn't recall anything after that. "I wasn't shot?"

"No. He had a gun?"

"I wonder why he didn't shoot down at me after I landed. To make sure the job was done."

"If you saw the drop again... you wouldn't think anyone could survive it. And even in daylight, it was a little hard to spot you at the bottom. At night he probably couldn't see you at all down there... Tell me who 'he' is."

"Jeremy Toth. And his sister came with him."

"Good. I needed to hear it from you. They've been arrested."

These words flood her with relief, though there's still much for her to learn. "How did you find me?"

He explains his failure to reach her on the phone, his growing concern, and Martin's involvement. He describes how they found the car, and then her.

"I want to know how you caught them."

"Your hair really gets around," Freddie says.

She brightens, pleased with herself for thinking of it.

"We found it in an upstairs bedroom of their house. More in your car trunk. Just got the DNA confirmation. They also left a clear tire tread behind your Honda in the mountains. Obviously one of them had to bring their own transportation for the getaway. We've matched the tread with one of their tires. And now, thank god, we have you to testify."

"Thanks to you and Martin."

"Should I remind you what I told you not to do?"

"I hope you can understand. I have no regrets. They took Sadie, I know they did. But have you found proof of it?"

His face grows somber. "And now we get to the best and worst of the news. Inside Toth's shed we found an armchair and a pile of dirty magazines. Adult magazines, though. No pedophilia, and nothing else in there. The team went through every inch of it like you wouldn't believe, and it paid off. They found a broken piece of finger-nail imbedded between the wooden floorboards. Small, about the right size for a four-year-old child."

She closes her eyes and takes several deep breaths to settle herself. "Has the DNA been confirmed?" she says.

He nods. "It's a match for Sadie."

It's what she's known since she went back in time and allowed Toth to kidnap her in her sister's place. Yet hearing these words in real-time—that there is actual, physical evidence of what she knew to be true—has the greatest impact of anything she's experienced since she began this journey. "Have you found her?" she says, her voice hoarse.

"No. But we've started looking."

He doesn't go into details because he knows she understands. They're digging up the property, just as they did to Reamer's backyard.

"We'll have closure now," she says.

"That's right." He stands up. "There's someone else who'd like to see you. We were told to come in one at a time, and everyone agreed you'd want the update first."

She reaches out and squeezes Freddie's hand. "Thank you. You don't know how much this means to me." But looking at his face, it occurs to her how hard he's worked on this case over the years. She recalls his excitement when they appeared to have breakthroughs, his deep disappointment when leads didn't pan out. Aside from Sadie's family, he wanted her found more than anyone else on earth. "Actually, I think you do know how much this means," she says. Moreover, she's grateful he hasn't brought up the subject of how she solved the crime. She hopes he never does.

Expecting to see Martin next, she's surprised when her father enters the room. In an uncharacteristic show of emotion, he bends over her and kisses her cheek, brushing her hair back from her forehead. His eyes brim with tears. "How do you feel?"

"I'm okay. They must've pumped me full of painkiller."

He sits beside her, lifts her left hand and kisses it. "You had me so worried."

"Did Freddie call you?"

"Martin. It's in the news now too. Sadie's kidnappers found at last. How did you do it?"

"I can't explain. I'm sorry. It just is."

"I should tell you that you never should've done this. You could've gotten yourself killed and then..." He breathes out heavily.

"But you know you would've done exactly the same as me, if you could've."

He nods. A tear slips from his eye and runs down his cheek. He kisses her hand again. "You saved us, Rebecca. We can find peace now. At least a semblance of it."

"I love you, Dad."

"I love you so much, baby. Forgive me for the way I've been."

They sit together a while longer, content to be together, understanding each other's feelings in a way that no one else would.

Eventually he gets up. "I don't want to tire you. There's one more person who wants to see you, unless you need to sleep."

"I can last a little longer," she says.

He kisses her cheek once more. "I'll be back tomorrow."

Martin appears shortly after her father leaves, and she takes his hand when he sits down. "I'm told I have you to thank for saving me."

"I was worried. You didn't seem like the type to just disappear like that. I guess I have a big enough ego to think our date went well."

"It went extremely well. You're right, I never would've run out on you like that." Her eyes grow moist. "But, man, one date with me and you get thrown into a ton of crap you don't need. I'm so sorry."

"I'm not. I mean, of course I'm sorry for what happened to you. But not sorry for my involvement. When we found you... okay, that was the hardest part. It looked like you were dead. It was a long drop and I couldn't imagine you surviving it. I feel like I went through some dark shit for the next hour or however long it took for the medics to reach you and shout out that you were still alive."

She squeezes his hand, so grateful for Martin's friendship.

"And look at you now. You're going to be fine. You are one tough lady."

"Never thought of myself that way."

"Most of all, I'm happy for you. At least, happy for the closure. I hope it'll bring you some peace."

"Thank you." She keeps her hand inside his. She barely knows this man and yet it feels right.

His phone buzzes, and after checking who's calling, he says, "I better get this." After a few seconds, he hands his phone to her. "Detective Lazo wants to talk to you."

"Guess I need a new phone." She takes his. "Hi Freddie. Didn't we just talk?"

The tears return as she listens to his report. There's concern in Martin's eyes when she hangs up. "He just heard from the team at the house," Rebecca tells him. "They found a burial site. The remains of a small child."

Martin leans his head gently against hers while she weeps.

31

———————

icki is working at Park's Organic Produce stand at the Ferry Building in San Francisco when she picks up a newspaper left by her last customer to put in the recycle bin. Her heart skips a beat as she glances down at the front page. A beautiful photograph depicts four-year-old Sadie, her eyes sparkling and face beaming in a way they never would again after she was taken from her home. The headline says, *Kidnappers Arrested in Draywood, CA*, and the first paragraph identifies Uncle and Mother as the kidnappers in question.

In between waiting on other customers, Nicki reads the rest of the article, which states that police have discovered a child's body buried in the backyard. Although this might refer to where she left Sadie in the woods behind the house, she isn't sure a covering of leaves and pine needles would be considered a *burial*. More likely this meant Uncle had found her under the tree and moved her closer to home. If so, she prays he laid Becca the rabbit and Mr. Fluffernutter to rest beside her. Sadie would not have wanted to be alone.

As soon as the body was discovered, the article says, Mother and Uncle were charged with murder in addition to kidnapping. Of course, Nicki knows they didn't strictly-speaking murder her, but in the years following her escape, she's come to believe that the responsibility for Sadie's death rests on their shoulders. Nicki has learned so much about how the world works since then, including how they were abusive parents and how they had no right to imprison Sadie—and her—as they did. But still she resisted going to the police, because there had been a time when she loved and relied on Mother and she had not wanted her to go to jail for her crimes. Besides, turning in Mother and Uncle would not bring Sadie back.

One part that interests Nicki more than the rest is the mention of Sadie's sister, Rebecca. Apparently she was the one who somehow figured out where Sadie had been taken, though the article doesn't explain how. The worst thing is they tried to kill her to keep her from telling anyone what she knew. But she survived and is going to be all right, thank god. Otherwise Nicki would blame herself for not turning in Mother and Uncle long ago.

Toward the end of the article, Nicki is surprised to find a mention of herself. It says Mother told the Department of Education that her daughter Nicki Gaunt ran away from home at age sixteen. However, since Mother never reported this to the police, and since no one knows anything about Nicki or where she might have gone, there's speculation that maybe she was also murdered and buried out back somewhere. The FBI are still searching.

She probably ought to contact the police and let them know she's alive. But what Mother and Uncle did to Rebecca has made her angry, and removed any motivation she might've felt to come forward and at least clear up the speculation regarding the possible killing of their daughter.

When it's time to close up the stand, she has to put off thinking about the matter for a while longer. But later when she returns to the homeless shelter, she thinks of Rebecca again. When she and Sadie ran away, Nicki had been planning to bring her back to her family. But after Sadie died, Nicki couldn't bear the thought of going to them and delivering such awful news. That was when she did not want to be responsible for Mother and Uncle going to prison as well.

But now, with them already arrested, and with Sadie's death being public knowledge, it seems the least she can do is go to Rebecca and tell her what really happened. It might comfort her to know her sister died quickly and without suffering. It's also possible Rebecca will blame Nicki, since she's the one who coerced Sadie into leaving, and maybe she would've recovered from her illness if they had stayed. But Nicki is older, stronger, and wiser now than she was then, and she thinks she can face Rebecca's anger if it comes to that. She owes it to Sadie to tell the rest of the story and let her sister know how she named her favorite stuffed rabbit after her, along with how brave she was right up to the end.

Nicki gets out her favorite possession, something she was finally able to afford after she started working—her smart phone. For someone who was isolated for the first sixteen years of her life, it's incredible to feel as if she's now connected to the entire world.

She needs to call Chelsey Heffron and ask to borrow her car. Chelsey is the saint-slash-social worker who plucked her out of Golden Gate Park, where she was living with other homeless people the first couple of years after she arrived in San Francisco. Chelsey arranged the bedroom at the shelter for Nicki, she found her the job at the produce stand, she helped her sign up for classes at the community college, and she told her how to get a driver's license using her birth certificate.

But before Nicki can make the call, a knock comes at her door.

"Nicki, it's me," Chelsey says.

She lets her in. "I was just about to call you."

Chelsey rushes forward and wraps Nicki in a tight embrace. "Oh sweetie, are you all right?"

"What do you mean?"

Chelsey draws back to scrutinize her face. "Did you see the news? I'm so, so sorry."

Oddly, Nicki hadn't even thought about her friends recognizing her name in the paper. She sits on the bed while Chelsey settles on the chair across from her.

"That's your mother, right? And your uncle?"

"Yeah, it's them."

"Did they really do that? I mean, obviously you're alive, so that part is wrong."

"They took Sadie," Nicki says. "But they didn't kill her. Not directly, anyway."

"Oh god. Do you still love them? Are you going to try to help them?"

Nicki lowers her gaze. "They've done terrible things. You read how they tried to kill Sadie's sister?"

"Fuck yeah. I can understand why you ran away now."

"It was crazy. You can't even imagine. I was a prisoner in their house."

Chelsey moves beside her on the bed and rubs her back. "Thank god you escaped. You did the right thing coming here. You've got a real life now."

"I have to go back."

"Go back? I mean, sure, you need to let the cops know you're alive. You don't want them wasting their time digging up the neighborhood looking for your body. And that's one crime your mother and her brother definitely didn't commit. But you can talk to the cops here. I'll go with you. You don't need to go back there. God no."

"Actually, I'm going to see Sadie's sister. She's in the hospital there. I need to tell her what happened, face to face. Before I talk to the police. I want her to hear it from me first."

Chelsey looks at her, thinking about it. "You're right, sweetie. Poor thing, losing her sister like that. And then, like, all these years go by, and she never gave up hope. She deserves to hear about her sister from you. Do you want me to come? I might be able to arrange it."

Nicki shakes her head. "I have to do this myself. I can handle it."

Chelsey removes her keys from her pocket. "Take my car. I'm not leaving the city for the next week. Take as long as you need. And call me if you change your mind and need help."

After Chelsey leaves, Nicki calls a classmate of hers, asking if she'll let her know about any new assignments that come up. She'll have to miss classes tomorrow, and maybe the day after that, so she spends the rest of the evening after dinner getting ahead in her homework. If there's one thing she learned to do well before she ran away, it's studying by herself. Her dream is to transfer to a real university next year, and get a scholarship if she can. She wants to fulfill her promise to Sadie and become a doctor someday.

She sleeps fitfully during the night and wakes early to set out. Her feelings of anxiety continue during the drive, growing more intense the closer she gets to her destination. Clearly she underestimated how it would make her feel to return to the place where she spent her miserable childhood. It's like journeying into a dark and terrifying cave, knowing that there's a monster at the end of it.

The only way she can force herself to keep going is to continually remind herself she isn't going to the house. She will never go there again, not ever. Not inside its dreary, suffocating rooms. Not outside with its clawing trees and stacks of hacked up wood. And never, never, never inside the shed. Now that Mother and Uncle are arrested, there is no one to make her.

Thankfully, the hospital is in Yellerton, lower down the mountain, so she doesn't even have to drive past Draywood. She doesn't associate Yellerton with past memories. Maybe Mother came here when she was so ill on the day Nicki and Sadie ran away, but if so, that was a long time ago and no one would remember.

After parking the car and getting out, she pauses for a moment staring at the building. A shiver runs through her and she hugs herself. It's going to be harder than she thought facing Sadie's sister. Her right hand shakes holding her purse, as it sometimes does when she's nervous.

She won't let herself turn back, though. One foot in front of the other, just as she made herself do after Sadie died and she kept walking and walking until, days later, she came to a bus station. That taught her she has a steely determination inside when she needs it.

At the front desk they try to send her away. They think she is a reporter pretending to be a friend. Apparently actual reporters have been doing this already. But finally she gets a nice nurse to agree to tell Rebecca that Nicki, a friend of Sadie's, is here to see her. A few minutes later the nurse returns and leads her to the room.

The sight of Rebecca fills her with a powerful rush of emotions. Probably because of her resemblance to Sadie, Nicki's heart goes out to her instantly.

Rebecca is drinking from a glass of water when she enters. But at the moment she sets down her glass and looks up at Nicki, her face transforms. Nicki has never seen anyone look so astonished before.

"Sadie?" Rebecca says.

Nicki is baffled. Why would she call her that? Sadie is obviously dead, and Nicki even told the nurse to give her name. "I'm Nicki Gaunt," she says. "My mother is Patricia Gaunt."

Inexplicably, Rebecca erupts into tears. Nicki approaches and pats her back gently on the side without the cast. "I'm sorry," she says. "I didn't mean to upset you."

A nurse overhears Rebecca's hysteria and looks in. "Are you okay?" He gives Nicki a dirty look like he thinks she's responsible. "Maybe you should leave, miss."

"No!" Rebecca cries out in the midst of her tears. She grabs some tissues and tries to get herself under control. "I want her to stay."

"All right then." The nurse moves on.

Nicki sits in the chair. "I guess it's a shock finding out I'm alive. I know the police are expecting to find me buried out there."

Rebecca blows her nose and nods. When she finds her voice again, she says, "You're right. Seeing you has been a huge shock. But I'm okay now. Please, tell me... tell me about yourself."

"I loved your sister very much. I was at the house when they kept her in the shed. I'm so sorry."

Rebecca keeps a tissue pressed to her face. "Please go on. I want to know everything."

"I snuck out to see her whenever I could. It wasn't easy. I was also a prisoner, only inside the house. I wanted to run away so bad, but I couldn't bear to leave Sadie alone with them. So I waited till one night when Mother was sick and Uncle took her to the doctor." Now Nicki tears up. "It was my fault, really. Sadie didn't want to go. She was too afraid of them and what they'd do to her if they caught us. But I insisted, and later I found out she was sick too. She died that night and I buried her under the tree, along with her favorite stuffed animals. She named the rabbit Becca for you. It all happened quickly. She didn't suffer."

"And you... you kept going after that? You got away then?"

Nicki nods. "It wasn't easy, but eventually I got to San Francisco. I live there now. I've had help from wonderful people."

Rebecca reaches forward and takes her hand. "I'm so happy for you. So proud of you. You got away."

Nicki hadn't expected it to be this easy. She thought there would be more blame. More questions about Sadie.

"Tell me Nicki," Rebecca says. "How... how old was my sister then? When you ran away?"

"She was four."

"And... and how old are you?"

"I'm twenty-three. I was sixteen then."

"Seven years ago. You ran away seven years ago. And you say Sadie was four then?"

Now Nicki is feeling confused. Why is she asking these questions? They aren't important. "Yeah, that's what I said."

"But seven years ago," Rebecca says in a gentle tone, "Sadie would've been sixteen."

Nicki blinks. She never really thought about their ages. "I'm not lying to you."

Rebecca holds her hand tight. "No... no, I don't believe you are."

"I wanted to save her. She was the sister I never had."

Rebecca draws her close and tries to hug her, though Nicki has to be careful not to put pressure on her cast.

"That makes you my sister too," Rebecca says.

32

———————

Rebecca didn't want Nicki to leave, not even for a second, but Nicki insisted she had to drive back home today because she was borrowing a friend's car. Rebecca had to be satisfied with a promise that she could come visit Nicki in San Francisco as soon as she was sufficiently recovered. She spent the rest of the day thanking and complimenting all the staff, chatting cheerfully on the phone with her father and Martin, and occasionally humming her favorite songs to herself.

In the morning the hospital releases her into Martin's care. Two days earlier, he refused to listen when she said she didn't want to be a burden to him. She gave up protesting before long, wanting to believe he was falling for her as quickly as she had already fallen for him.

She says nothing during the car ride to his house and waits till they're both inside. At this point he's starting to look nervous, obviously wondering if something's wrong between them and she's about to break some terrible news.

He's fussing over her when she orders him to sit down. "I have something to tell you and it's for your ears only for the time being."

"All right." He straightens two pillows while waiting for her to start.

"I had a visitor yesterday who told me she was Nicki Gaunt. Patricia Gaunt's daughter."

"Nicki Gaunt? Are you sure? The police think she might be dead."

"There isn't any doubt in her mind that she's Nicki Gaunt."

"She should come forward then," Martin says. "Why did she visit you?"

"She wanted to tell me how Sadie died. She said it happened when they ran away, seven years ago. She told me Sadie was four years old then."

Martin knits his brow. "Seven years ago? She must be confused."

The joy that Rebecca felt upon seeing Nicki the first time suffuses her again. "Her mind is confused, yes. And I understand why. Martin." She grasps him by the wrist. "*She is Sadie*. I knew it the minute I saw her. The thing is, *she* doesn't know it."

Martin is silent for a moment, taking this in. "Rebecca. I know how badly you want her to be alive. But—"

"I couldn't mistake my own sister. And when you see her, you'll know too. We look alike. We even sound alike."

"Then why does she call herself Nicki?"

"They must've called her that. They must've told her she was Patricia's daughter, over and over and over again. She was only four. I don't remember anything from that age.

"But a part of her consciousness was holding onto her own identity. And it caused her personality to split. It's the only explanation. It makes sense that she thinks Sadie *died* on the day she ran away. It was the day she broke free of their control. She didn't need the little girl she had been anymore."

He leans back, mind blown just like Rebecca's was the day before. "Have you told her?"

"No. I think it's going to take time. This has been her reality for many years. She was baffled when I pointed out the discrepancy in ages. It might shatter her to know she's Sadie, and Nicki is… no one?"

"She needs a psychologist."

"Yes. And I'm going to find a way to get her to agree to see one. Maybe a hypnotist would be best. We'll see."

"Have you told anyone else yet? Your father? Detective Lazo?"

She shakes her head. "I think the police and the press descending on her would be more than she could handle right now. And if there's a DNA test, and then they start calling her Sadie... it could be too much for her. For now, for just a little while, I'm going to keep her to myself and see if I can get her cured. Then we'll go to our father."

A brightness fills her. "But you see what this means... I have my sister back. I never thought I would. I only thought I would find out what happened to her. But she's alive, Martin. She's alive."

At the end of the day, Freddie stops by with the latest update. He comes outside, where Rebecca is tossing the ball for Guy. Martin hangs back, clearly wanting to give them privacy, but Rebecca waves him over to the picnic table. "No secrets from you after the hell you've gone through for my sake," she says.

As soon as they're settled, Freddie begins. "The DNA results are in on the child we found."

She struggles to keep her expression blank, and a glance at Martin shows he's doing the same. But inside, she's brimming with excitement, praying this is the confirmation she's been waiting for.

"It isn't Sadie." Freddie waits for a reaction from Rebecca, and looks puzzled by her silence.

"So they interviewed Patricia again," he continues. "She claims it's her daughter, Nicki, who died at the age of four. It happened when Jeremy was supposed to be watching her, and Patricia was at work. Nicki was eating some hot dog, and Jeremy left the room to use the bathroom, then got distracted doing something else. By the time he came back to the kitchen, she had choked to death."

"They never reported the death?" Rebecca asks.

Freddie shakes his head. "Patricia said she decided not to report it because she didn't want Jeremy to get in trouble. She wasn't sure if police might bring charges against him for criminal negligence. Also, he begged her not to tell anyone. Figured no one would use his business anymore. He already felt like a pariah in town and this would just make things worse. They ended up burying her in the backyard."

Rebecca looks down and hugs herself. Sad for Nicki—the real Nicki—who never got a chance at life.

"After the match with Sadie failed, and after speaking with Patricia, we checked her DNA against the child's. The preliminary results show a match. So, it's likely she's telling the truth about this being Nicki. But we can't be sure about the rest. Jeremy has refused to say anything, so we only have Patricia's word for it. Whatever happened, well, it may have been worse than a choking accident. But it's unlikely we'll ever know for sure."

"Poor child," Rebecca says.

"As for Sadie," he pauses, probably feeling puzzled Rebecca hasn't said, *well, where's my sister then*, but there's only so much play-acting she can do. "We haven't found any other remains. We'll keep looking, of course. But her body may not be at the house at all."

"I understand. I know you're doing your best. Thanks."

"Can we offer you some wine?" Martin says.

Freddie stands. "That sounds nice. But I'm driving back tonight. Not much more for me to do here."

Rebecca takes his hand and holds it for a moment. "Thank you. Everything you've done... you've been amazing."

"I'm happy the crime is finally solved. But I hope we find Sadie. The interrogations will continue. Maybe one of them will tell us where she is."

"You won't bargain for the information, will you? Do not, under any circumstances, allow them reduced sentences," Rebecca says.

"No, not a chance. Not for either of them. Don't worry. For all their crimes against you and your sister... they'll spend the rest of their lives behind bars."

Martin returns after seeing Freddie out.

Rebecca's face beams as she looks up at him. "You know what this means? The reason Toth took her? He killed his sister's daughter. He was bringing her a new one. Sadie must've looked like her. That's why they called her Nicki." Though their actions were abusive and unforgivable, neither one had been motivated by pedophilia or the desire to torture or kill a helpless human being. This was about redemption. Toth, who loved his sister, had been trying to atone. It's an emotion Rebecca understands well.

33

———————

Four-year-old Sadie lay on the lumpy bed clutching the blanket and sucking her thumb like she hadn't done for a year. The man who called himself Uncle had put her in this shed in the back of his yard and left her alone. It was pitch dark and there were scary noises outside, like animals scratching and bumping against the wood. She pictured monsters like the ones in *Where the Wild Things Are* surrounding the shed, peering in the upper window at her, waiting till she fell asleep before they would break through the door and eat her up. Never, ever was she this frightened before. Where were her Mommy and Daddy to protect her? Where was Becca?

Sadie blamed herself for ending up here. She had wanted to play with Becca and her horrible friend Mikayla, and after they disappeared, she thought they might've gone to the front believing Sadie would never look for them there. But even after Sadie saw they weren't there, she walked down toward the street, hoping to get her sister in trouble, knowing Mommy would be furious if she saw her out front by herself.

And now, because she had wanted to be mean to her sister, she was alone inside the shed belonging to this strange man with the scary face, and her parents were nowhere around and she was afraid and didn't know what to do. She could only close her eyes and suck her thumb and try to pretend she was home in her own bed, though this thing under her felt nothing like the soft, warm mattress she loved.

She had slept earlier for a while, but now she was wide awake, listening to every sound. She had cried a lot before falling asleep, until her throat was sore and her eyes red and her nose all snotty. She wiped it on the bed covers, which she now regretted because the sheet was damp and gross.

After a while she started to hum to herself. It was a song called *The Circle Game* that her mother used to sing to her while rocking her as a baby. She didn't remember all the words but she could hum it and it soothed her a bit and eventually she fell back asleep.

When she woke in the morning, she hoped when she opened her eyes, she would discover it was all a nightmare, and she would find herself at home in her own bed with her sister Becca sleeping in the bed beside her. But after she saw she was still all alone in the awful shed, the tears rushed out again and she cried so hard it gave her the hiccups. Worse, her throat was dry from lack of water and her stomach was like a gaping hole calling out for food. She wondered if the mean man would ever feed her.

Then a little while later there were sounds coming from the house, followed by footsteps and then voices.

A woman said in a grumpy tone, "What is this about? You know I don't like surprises."

"I did this for you, Patty. Just wait and see." This came from the bad man who took her from her family and called himself *Uncle*.

Sadie wasn't sure, but she thought maybe the woman would help her, so she called out, "Help! Help me!"

The adults were silent for a few seconds, like they were stunned. Then the woman spoke again in a voice of dread. "What have you done, Jeremy? What in god's name have you done?"

"Wait till you see her. She looks just like Nicki. Please. Give her a chance."

"I don't want to see her. Take her back where she came from," she said in a cold voice.

"Take her back? I can't do that. I'll be arrested. They'll put me in prison for a long, long time."

"You should've thought of that before you did this."

Sadie heard sounds like one of them was walking away. A minute later the door of the shed was opened and Uncle brought in a tray of food. She saw the back of a woman dressed all in black, going into the house.

"Eat this," he said.

"I want to go home. I want my parents."

He left the tray on the table and went out without answering her.

She wasn't sure how many days passed like that. The man brought her food but wouldn't talk to her or answer her questions. She cried and slept and cried again. Sometimes she played games with the stuffed animals, pretending they were real and they could talk to her. She would make up silly names and voices for them, like she was a ventriloquist. The rabbit, which she liked the best, she named for her sister Becca.

One evening after she had her dinner, she heard different footsteps approaching the shed, lighter than the man's. When the door came open, it was the woman who had been outside the shed before. Sadie had only seen her from behind but she could still tell it was her.

The woman bent down and peered into Sadie's face for what felt like a long time. Finally her expression softened and she even smiled, though Sadie wasn't sure if it was just a fake smile. "Hello, dear." She drew a lollipop from her pocket and held it out. "Would you like this?"

Tears were gathering in Sadie's eyes but she managed to nod. The woman tore off the wrapper and handed it to her. Sadie thrust it into her mouth.

"I don't want you to stay out here anymore, sweetie-pie." She took Sadie's hand, raised her into her arms, and carried her outside. The sun had set but it wasn't fully dark yet.

They went up the steps into the house, where the woman lowered her to the floor and shut the door behind them. "Your room is this way," she said. "Come with me." The woman held her hand as they walked up the stairs and through the first door into a girl's bedroom. It looked nicer and smelled nicer than the rest of the house, filled with toys and dolls and books and stuffed animals on the bed. Sadie would've liked it if she wasn't missing her family so much.

"This is your bed, dear." She helped her get into it, then sat beside her and pulled the covers up to her chin.

The woman had been so nice, Sadie finally dared take out the lollipop and speak. "Can you bring me home, please?"

"This is your home, Nicki. This is your bedroom and these are all your things. Aren't they nice?"

She tried to sit up but the woman held her down. "No!" she cried. "This isn't my house. I want my Mommy!" She started crying again and couldn't talk for a while as she coughed and choked and her nose ran. "I want my Mommy," she whimpered over and over.

When she wasn't able to cry anymore, the woman smoothed her hair and wiped her face with a tissue. "There, there," she said. "You've had a nightmare. You'll get over it."

"I haven't had a nightmare," Sadie said. "You're lying."

"You don't talk that way to your elders, Nicki."

"That's not my name!"

"Of course it is. Your name is Nicki Gaunt. That's always been your name. Anything else is just a terrible dream."

Sadie was confused. She believed adults always told children the truth. Was it possible that everything she remembered was part of a dream?

The woman stood up. "You need to sleep now. Do you like French toast?"

Sadie, in spite of herself, gave her a sullen nod.

"That's what we'll have for breakfast then." She walked to the door. "Will you promise me to try to sleep?"

She answered grumpily. "Yes, ma'am."

"Don't call me that. Call me Mother."

"But you're not my mother!"

"You'll remember soon enough. Goodnight, Nicki." She turned off the light and closed the door.

Sadie put the lollipop back in her mouth and sucked on it. She drew the blanket close around her. She knew this wasn't her home, and the woman wasn't her mother. But she didn't know what to do. She didn't dare get up and leave the room, because it frightened her to imagine running into the bad man in the hallway. She didn't dare do anything but stay right where she was until morning. Maybe when it was light, she wouldn't be so scared. Maybe when it was light, she would try to run away.

34

———————

In the time since Rebecca gained the ability to mindcast, her life has changed in every possible way. She's living in San Francisco now, sharing an apartment with the sister she thought she had lost forever.

Nicki earned a scholarship to UCSF and is on a pre-med track. Rebecca's little sister, going to be a doctor. She herself is doing what Nicki did before her—attending community college, hoping to earn the credits to eventually transfer somewhere else. Berkeley if she's lucky and works hard. She's not sure what she wants to do for a career, but it's looking like math or computer science. Just as her father always thought she should do.

Her collarbone and arm have fully healed, though she'll never be a wrestler. Now and then there's pain, but she's continuing physical therapy and hopes it will diminish over time. She feels incredibly lucky not to have paid a much greater price for getting Sadie back.

Martin visits weekends. She has given up sneaking around in the past, having furtive sex and then avoiding the man in real-time. With Martin, she shares much more than just a physical relationship. Since he has the kind of job he can do anywhere, he's planning to move to the Bay Area soon. For the first time in her life, she feels worthy of the happiness coming her way.

She doesn't think she can mindcast anymore. The last time she tried, just as a test a few months ago, it didn't work. It's always been a strange superpower, all tangled up with her emotions. It was as if her fairy godmother dinged her with a wand to fix all her broken parts, and once that was done, the spell ended.

Because she couldn't bear to watch her father wait anxiously while law enforcement searched for Sadie's remains, Rebecca told him about Nicki only a few days after her visit to the hospital.

Together they decided they also owed Freddie the truth, even though telling him meant the news would have to be released to the world. It didn't take long before a DNA test confirmed her identity and Sadie Danser's story filled the nation's headlines once again.

Nicki still insisted the police had made a mistake with their testing and she most definitely was not Sadie. But since Rebecca called her Nicki and made it clear they wanted her to be part of their family no matter what her identity, Nicki warmed to her newfound sister and father as much as if she were fully aware she was one of them.

She did agree to begin therapist sessions at Rebecca's urging, and now, months later, on a cloudless October day in San Francisco, she returns from her appointment and sits down to have dinner with her sister.

"I made real progress today," she says, barely able to hold in her excitement.

Rebecca gazes at her hopefully.

"I remembered the day I was taken," Sadie says.

The End.

BEFORE HE VANISHED

THE BEFORE SERIES BOOK THREE

For Tanner, Alan, and Derek

REBECCA

1

Rebecca had thought her sister's safe return would end her obsession with child abduction cases, yet somehow her walk has led her to the same *Missing Person* poster for the second day in a row.

The first time she had the excuse that sidewalk construction blocked her normal route. But today she actually chose this direction, although it brought her to a dark and dreary section of town. The buildings on either side of the street are stark and far-reaching, marked by splotches of mud and graffiti at their lower levels. Trash spills out from alleyways, suspicious-looking characters lurk in doorways, and the stench of urine overpowers every other smell.

As before, she has paused at the flyer tacked onto the utility pole near the X-rated bookstore. It looks like someone produced it using their crappy inkjet printer at home. The black ink is faded, and the white spaces are grimy. At the bottom, the paper has been cut into matching strips with the phone number printed on them. It's an old-fashioned thing to do in the age of the cell phone. But maybe it's only her place of privilege that makes it difficult for her to imagine someone tearing off a slip of paper instead of saving the number on their cell with a photo.

A thirteen-year-old child is pictured on the notice. Rebecca knows his age because it says so at the bottom. He has coffee-colored skin, rosebud lips, and charcoal hair cut close to his scalp. No smile. He looks impatient. Is it because he really doesn't want his picture to be taken? Or he's anxious to be somewhere? Or he's weary of a world that's become all too much for him?

The text underneath the photo says, "MISSING. Ethan Pitt. Last seen on…" a date that's roughly a year ago. The text includes the name of the city where he lives, and an exhortation to call the number "if you have any information regarding his whereabouts."

She doesn't call the number, but does Google his name and the date he vanished. One small news item turns up, reporting his disappearance several days after it happened. That's all. There is no further mention of him on the Internet. No way to know if he simply ran away and later returned home, or if he's still missing, or if his body has been found and whether his death was ruled an accident, suicide, or murder.

Simply no information at all.

Her thoughts fly to her sister Sadie. It was a huge story when she was kidnapped. She was an adorable little white girl. Though they failed, law enforcement put a great deal of effort into searching for her. Local police and the FBI vied for control of the investigation. News services swarmed their family and friends. Until they didn't.

Who cries for Ethan Pitt? she wonders.

ETHAN

2

Ethan slouches in front of the classroom, his hands trembling as he clutches the paper. "Amari is gathering wood for the fire when he hears the first scream coming from the village. Soon the air is filled with the cries of women and the shouts of men. Though the sound terrifies him, Amari runs fleet-footed back to the king tree and peeks out from behind it to find out what has happened.

"The invaders have pink skin, pinched features, and thick clothing that covers every part of them except their faces and hands. They have surrounded the villagers, including Amari's own parents and older sister. When Chikere—a young man who carves wood into animal shapes—tries to escape, one of the invaders snaps a rope at him. It cuts into his back and causes him to bleed. His anguished cry pierces Amari through the heart.

"The invaders bind the villagers one to another using a chain made of a hard, inflexible material like stone, not like the grasses his mother weaves into rope. They work quickly, before the villagers can figure out how to resist them. The invaders are, in fact, smaller and weaker than the men of Amari's village, but there are more of them, and they have used the advantage of surprise to good effect.

"Amari watches, frozen in fear and indecision. What can he, a thirteen-year-old boy, do to save his loved ones? He remains in hiding while everyone he knows in the world is shepherded away by the invaders.

"During the night, he curls up into a ball and weeps. But in the morning, the sunrise brings him new courage. He takes the spear that belongs to his father and a small supply of food and water before setting out to track the invaders and save his village."

Ethan lowers the paper and glances at Mr. Flannery, hoping to be allowed to sit down. But his teacher is slumped at his desk, looking oddly shrunken in his jacket that seems too large for him, and his neck extending forward like a turtle's. He peers at his students through his oversized black-rimmed glasses with the same expression he always wears—like he's resigned to bearing the burden of the world upon his shoulders.

"Pink skin?" Malcolm asks. No one ever waits to be called on in this class. It takes much worse infractions to trigger their teacher's temper. The cold venom that emerges during those rare moments is a terrible thing to witness, however.

"They have sunburns," Ethan says. "You know? White guys in Africa? They're gonna have sunburns."

Mr. Flannery, whose fungus green sweater contrasts with his own pasty hue, makes no comment.

"Why'd you say the women cry and the men shout?" Yolanda asks. "Seems really gender-biased."

Ethan was expecting this. He saw her scribbling a note to herself when he said that. Yolanda's comments are always about gender bias. "Yeah, I guess," he says. "I'll change it." It's easier not to argue with her, and anyway, he doesn't care about the kids in the back who snicker.

"What's a king tree?" This from the new student. Ethan doesn't remember his name.

"It's just what they call it. The biggest tree around, you know?"

"Ethan, you can sit." Though he enunciates every word, Mr. Flannery's sentences have a way of sounding flat. "Class, after hearing this first chapter, who wants to read more?"

Several hands shoot up while others give an unenthusiastic wave. The troublemakers in the back raise bored eyes to the clock.

Ethan drops into his front-row seat with relief. He wasn't happy when his teacher picked him to read his homework aloud, particularly since he didn't come up with the story idea himself. It begins like many told to him by his uncle over the years. Still, Ethan added his own details and came up with the wording. Uncle Ray never gave him written copies of his stories, though he had binders full of his handwritten scrawl. According to his uncle, Ethan has a way with language and he's miles ahead of other kids his age in writing skills. His problem is a lack of original ideas. When he started the assignment, he stared for hours at the blank page before deciding there wouldn't be any harm in borrowing from Uncle Ray.

Mr. Flannery zeroes in on Teshi, who's bent over her desk doodling on a piece of paper. "Why didn't you raise your hand when I asked who wanted to read more of Ethan's story?"

Ethan is thinking, *Why'd he have to ask her?*

"I do wanna read it." Teshi says.

"Okay then. Why?"

"Cuz Ethan wrote it. Gotta be good. Learned that shit from his uncle." Teshi flashes Ethan a knowing smile. The two of them hung together a lot in elementary school, and Teshi has listened to plenty of Uncle Ray's stories.

Mr. Flannery tolerates swearing unless someone goes on a rant. "You mean you trust Ethan to tell a good story?"

"Like I said. Got it from his uncle." Teshi seems one slip of the tongue away from accusing Ethan of plagiarism.

"How else does Ethan hook us into his story?" Mr. Flannery's gaze flicks across the room.

The bell rings, putting an instant end to any discussion. Chairs scrape as students leap up, forcing Mr. Flannery to raise his voice. "Work on your next chapters. I'll be picking someone else to read next time."

No one is listening anymore as they jostle to be first to the door. When Ethan reaches the hallway, Teshi catches up to him. "Weird," she says. "The pink faces, the king tree... feel like I heard that shit before."

He twists the dark brown and blue braided leather wristband his father gave him and tries to move past her. But there's a scent surrounding her, something delightful like peaches and honey, that makes him pause and look up. For the first time, it hits him how pretty she is. She used to be a scrawny little thing, and now she's taller than him. Though she's still thin, curves are forming in all the right places. Her smile radiates warmth and light and makes him helpless to do anything but smile back.

"Did you see these?" She nods down at her feet.

"Who'd you have to rob to pay for those fire Air Jordans?" he says. Teshi's family is dirt poor and probably ten bucks away from homeless. Maybe that wasn't nice of him to say, but he hasn't gotten over being annoyed with her.

His jab doesn't faze her, though. "What you gonna pay me to find out?" She parades her feet down the corridor, in no hurry to get to her next class.

3

———————

After school, Ethan plans to visit Uncle Ray to get ideas for the rest of his story. But when he reaches into his pocket, he discovers he left his money at home.

He considers heading back, but One Fine Burger, the fast-food joint where his mother works, is closer. And if he goes there, she'll get him something to eat too.

When he arrives, Ma is preparing food in the back, but as usual, she senses his arrival and looks over just as he's approaching. Her face brightens like it always does when she sees him.

He waits off to the side until she has a second to join him. "You want a burger?" she says. Off his nod, she teases, "Course you do."

"Ma, I need three bucks. I owe it to Lamar." He's a sixteen-year-old kid who lives in their building. Ma likes him because he's a geek who works hard in school.

"You shouldn't borrow money."

"Sorry." He feels guilty for lying. When he visits Uncle Ray, he always slips him a few bucks. If Ma knew it was for him, she wouldn't give Ethan a penny.

Cecelia, who always has a sour face, finishes with a customer before Ma squeezes past her to the register and pays for Ethan's order.

"Catch more flies with honey," Ma says to her. "Time to time, you might try smiling."

Cecilia scowls worse. "They gonna buy their burgers no matter what."

Ma returns to her work in the back and a few minutes later she hands over a medium Coke along with a bag that Ethan knows will contain a cheeseburger even though she ordered him a plain, a large-sized portion of fries though she ordered small, and four packets of ketchup. When he opens it, he finds the three dollars in there too.

Ethan polishes off the food in no time at all at a table outside. He sets off on his board and reaches the tent city under the freeway within twenty minutes. The place looks like an even worse shithole than the last time he came, and he has to cover his nose because it reeks like a garbage dump. He picks his way carefully, anxious to avoid stepping on syringes or piles of shit. A rat skitters from underneath one discarded food wrapper to another. It breaks Ethan's heart that his uncle has nowhere better to live.

He spots Uncle Ray looking worked up about something as he speaks to a man wearing a hat from the last century and a ragged, threadbare suit. Noticing Ethan's approach, Ray turns away from the man and hurries toward his nephew. He looks distraught, as close to tears as Ethan has ever seen him.

"What's happening?" Ethan says.

"It's gone." He shakes his head miserably. "It's all gone."

"What do you mean?"

He lowers his voice. "All my cash. Everything I saved up."

Ethan glances around and moves in closer so as not to be overheard. "You told me you always carry it on you."

Uncle Ray nods. "They picked my pockets while I was sleeping."

"You didn't wake up?"

Uncle Ray throws up his hands. "Sometimes I take a little something to help me sleep. Else how am I going to get any rest in this place?"

"Yeah, I get it." Ethan glances toward his uncle's tent. "Did you look everywhere? Maybe it fell out of your pocket."

"First thing I thought was I lost it. Tore through all my shit looking for it. It's gone, Ethan. I got nothing." His shoulders sag. "What am I going to do?"

If Uncle Ray was a person of means, who lived in a real home, who had connections in his community, maybe he could go to the police. Maybe they would actually make some effort to find the thief. But as it was, the police would laugh him out of the station if he went there to report the theft. There was no recourse for people like Uncle Ray.

Ethan takes out the dollar bills Ma gave him and presses it into his uncle's hands. "At least you can eat something." *Just barely.*

"Boy, I can't take your money." Uncle Ray always says this before taking the money.

"I'll try to bring more tomorrow." It won't be easy. Ma won't help Uncle Ray even if Ethan tells her what happened. She blames him for the drug deal that went bad and landed him and Ethan's dad behind bars. She blames him worse for his father having gotten sick and died in there, while Uncle Ray eventually made it out of prison alive.

"What about that job interview you had?" Ethan says.

He blows out air. "Train I was on just sat on the track for an hour. Nobody ever did explain that. So I didn't get there till late, and then the man just told me to leave, didn't want to hire anyone who couldn't get there on time. I was saving for a car, you know? It's all I need. I can live in it. I can get places, if I have a car. I was thinking of driving to San Diego. People tell me it's nicer there. I should've gone already, on the bus. Then I'd still have my money. Now I got to start from square one. Don't know how I'm going to do it. Nobody gives you the time of day when you got a record."

Ethan only wishes he could help. He's sorry he came here for the selfish reason of wanting Uncle Ray to give him more story ideas. Of all the stupid things, compared to the hell his uncle goes through every day of his life. It isn't fair. It wasn't his fault his money was stolen, dashing all his hopes to better himself and escape this pit of despair.

4

When Ethan opens the door to their apartment, he's surprised not to smell anything cooking. Usually by this time his mother has made soup, or beans, or mac and cheese, or any of the other frugal meals they typically eat. Before he turned thirteen, the burger after school might've held him till morning, but these days he's got a gnawing hunger that needs satisfying every few hours.

A glance into the kitchen confirms nothing is on the stove and the breakfast dishes are still soaking in the sink. Not a good sign. Ma doesn't start on the meal until the dishes are washed and put away.

He's thinking she must be out, maybe doing some shopping, but then he sees her in the family room, seated in the corner chair. She's not looking at him, doesn't even seem aware that he's there. Her eyes are glazed over, staring into space at nothing. This isn't like her. Normally she has the TV on, or if not that, she's reading an ebook on her phone. She downloads free romance novels wherever she can find them online.

"Hey Ma," he says. "Did you eat?"

She blinks and looks at him blankly, like she has to think about it. "I guess not." She doesn't move to get up, though.

"Everything okay?"

"Of course it's okay." Her tone is sharp. "Why wouldn't it be?"

He opens the fridge and the cupboards to see what their options are. "I can make us hot dogs," he says.

"I'm not hungry. Just make it for yourself."

"You sure?"

When she doesn't answer, he cooks two. If she won't eat the extra one, he will.

"Where were you?" she says, suddenly sounding more alert.

"Hanging with my bros." He doesn't want to tell her about his visit to Uncle Ray when she's already in a bad mood. "Don't worry, I did my homework, except English." He'll have to come up with something to move the story forward since he didn't get the help he was hoping for from his uncle.

"I saw Lamar in the hall. He told me you never owed him any money," Ma says.

"Thought I did."

"Well, you didn't. So let me have that cash back. We could use it."

His brain scrambles to think of a way out of this. He pats his pants like he thinks the money's still there. "Must've fallen out of my pocket."

She gives him the stink eye. "Don't you lie to me. You gave it to that no-good uncle of yours, didn't you?" It's not a question.

He's silent, knowing there's no point in lying because she can always tell just by looking at him.

"I told you not to go there," she says.

"He's my uncle."

"He broke the law. And he lives in that tent city full of addicts and rapists and who knows what all else."

"He's got nowhere else to live. You know how hard it is for him to get a job with his record? What's up with that? You serve your time, you should get another chance."

"He's a bad influence. You stay away from him." She is particularly ornery this evening, and he wishes he knew why.

"He needs help, Ma. Somebody found his money stash and stole it."

"That's what happens when you live with all the lowlifes."

He's never seen her this unsympathetic before.

"We can't help him. We're just barely getting by. You'll have to start working, Ethan."

He looks up in surprise. "You told me not to. School comes first, you always said."

"You were younger then. At thirteen, there's stuff you can do."

"Stuff like what?"

"I don't know. Deliver papers? Mow lawns?"

"I can't drive! And who's got a lawn big enough to mow around here?"

"Well, you figure it out. Ask your friends. Time you pulled your own weight." She jabs the TV remote and turns the volume high, making it clear she doesn't want to hear another word from him.

He sits at the table with his meal, but the lump in his throat makes swallowing hard.

5

———————

As soon as he wakes, Ethan looks over the chapter he wrote the night before. The visit to his uncle proved useful after all. The theft that happened while Uncle Ray slept, and Ma's talk of rapists at the camp gave Ethan the ideas he needed.

He's surprised to find the kitchen empty. His mother doesn't normally sleep this long. Although her shift doesn't start till later, she likes to help him with breakfast and see him off on the bus.

He toasts two pieces of bread and spreads peanut butter on them. There's precious little else in the cupboards. When he's done eating, he'll have to wake Ma up and let her know. Hopefully she'll do the shopping before heading to work.

He didn't get much rest last night. First, he stayed up too late writing his story. Then he slept fitfully through a series of dreams he can't remember now. It's probably because he's worried about Uncle Ray, and Ma too. Something was bothering her and it was strange she didn't tell him about it, because normally she talks his ear off when the slightest thing goes wrong.

Something must have happened at the job. Her supervisor yelled at her, or a customer talked smack to her. She tries to take things in stride, but she's sensitive and sometimes the shit people say gets under her skin. Ethan understands. He's the same way whenever one of his teachers raises his voice at him, or accuses him of something he didn't do. Like that time Mr. Howard thought he stole supplies from the classroom. It was so unfair and untrue. Luckily his last year homeroom teacher stuck up for him and put Mr. Howard in his place.

He pours himself the last bit of orange juice and puts his dishes in the sink. If he misses the bus, he'll have to use his board and then he'll get detention for being late to his first period class. After tossing his homework into his backpack, he checks on his mother. She's seated in bed, filling her glass from a bottle of vodka.

"Ma?"

She looks up, bleary-eyed.

"Why're you starting so early on that stuff?" It's happened before, like when his father was arrested and all the shit after that. But he hasn't seen her do it in a while.

"Don't you go judging your momma. Just for today, I need a little something to make me feel better."

"What're you feeling so bad about?"

"What are you doing here still? You're going to be late for school."

"We need groceries today."

"You pick them up after school."

"I need guap for that."

"Check my wallet."

He opens her purse on top of the dresser. "There's only eight bucks here."

She shrugs. "Get what you can."

During lunch break, Ethan slips away from school to check on his mother at work and see if she's gotten into a better mood. He prays she didn't drink too much, because that's how she got fired from her last job.

When he gets there, he doesn't see her behind the counter or in the back. He waits, thinking she's using the bathroom. But five minutes later, when she still hasn't come out, he approaches the heavy woman with spikey hair who's been nice to him before.

"Have you seen my Ma?" he says.

The woman scrunches up her face. "No, honey, not today."

"But she always works on Tuesdays." He wonders if she called in sick.

"Yeah, well, you better ask her about that."

Her tone conveys the worst. "Did she get fired?" he whispers.

The woman glances behind her nervously. "Like I said, you need to talk to her about that." She moves away to assist a customer.

That's it then, he thinks. She got fired. No wonder she wanted him to look for a job. Jesus. Thirteen years old, and now he's got to support Ma and Uncle Ray both.

REBECCA

6

2020 - PRESENT

Rebecca bangs the plate of Indian takeout leftovers on the kitchen table and drops into her seat. It grates that neither her sister nor anyone else will be warming the empty place across from her for she-doesn't-know-how-long.

Covid-19 did this. Beginning last month, the potentially deadly virus sent Americans scurrying back inside their homes, but only after they emptied supermarket shelves of hand sanitizer, toilet paper, and yeast. Why people seemed to require five-year supplies of the first two items is beyond her, but the run on yeast is even more baffling. Suddenly everyone is making their own bread, as if bakeries are the one mode of food production poised to disappear off the face of the earth. *C'mon, people. We're not homesteading here.*

She opens her laptop on the table to start the Zoom with Sadie. They used to have lunch dates in person, but now everyone has been ordered not to mingle indoors with anyone outside their own household. Those with a household of one can kiss human contact goodbye for the foreseeable future.

Sadie's face on the screen cheers her instantly, though. It's still surreal to have her little sister back in her life. "What're you eating?" she says.

"Chicken tikka masala. You?"

Sadie lifts a grilled cheese sandwich into the camera view.

"Again?" Rebecca says.

"Don't judge me."

"How's the fam?"

"Gone hiking at Tilden Park." Sadie takes a bite and keeps talking. "Becca, I wish you would join us here. You must be lonely."

She had moved out of Rebecca's apartment and into their father's home in Berkeley before the pandemic began. Martin had been visiting a lot then, and despite Rebecca's reassurances, Sadie had become convinced her presence got in the way of their romance.

"I'm fine," Rebecca says in a sharper tone than she meant.

"What about Martin? Is that really over?"

"He can't get himself to move away from Draywood. I mean, he's been there all his life. And I can't live there." She doesn't say she couldn't bear to occupy the same town where Sadie was kept prisoner for most of her life up till now. But her sister understands. "We might've been able to do a long-distance relationship if it wasn't for this damn virus. Anyway, it's over."

"Do you want me to move back in with you?"

"I'm fine. Really. You should stay with Dad."

Sadie sips her sparkling water before looking up again. "I do like being here."

"I know you do." It stings to see how close she and their father have become in such a short time. She even gets on well with his wife. Rebecca has always thought Marie couldn't stand her. How else to explain that they never asked *her* to live with them?

"It's not just him," Sadie goes on. "I can't get enough of our little brothers. It's just... amazing being part of a real family instead of one built on lies and intimidation."

What a gentle soul my sister is. Rebecca would've used a much harsher expression than "lies and intimidation." *Unfathomable cruelty,* more like.

"Little sis, you deserve to be as happy as you possibly can. I won't allow you to change anything. I'm absolutely fine."

"Tell me what you're doing these days," Sadie says.

With the pandemic going on, Rebecca's classes are in flux, neither in-person nor electronic at the moment. They're supposed to transition to online in a month. But she's already lost interest in them. She had started studying math and computer science at their father's urging. For years, he'd insisted she ought to develop the skills that would help her build a career. For years she'd resisted, until Sadie returned and it seemed as if she could finally have a normal life. But her life still does not feel normal. *She* does not feel normal.

"I'm keeping busy enough." She isn't, though. Her days consist of long walks with her face covered in a mask, getting takeout food for her meals, doing math puzzles, reading books, watching Netflix. *I hate my life*, is the thought that flashes weirdly across her brain. But she isn't about to tell Sadie. "What about you?"

"Still full steam ahead with pre-med. I'm lucky there's plenty I can do from home."

"Make us proud."

But Sadie is not done picking apart her sister. "I worry about you."

This makes Rebecca smile. Sadie, whose childhood was stolen… worried about *her*.

"Any time you need me, just let me know and I'll be there in a flash," Sadie says.

"It goes both ways."

"You've done your part. You nearly got yourself killed for me."

"I hadn't planned on that."

"I need to ask you something. I hope it won't upset you," Sadie says. "Dad doesn't like to talk about it, so I thought…"

Rebecca, chewing, nods for her to continue.

"It's about Mom." Her voice lowers. "That's been the hardest thing to accept since I got back. That she lost hope. That she gave up on finding me."

Imagine if you were the daughter who didn't go missing, Rebecca thinks. *Imagine if you were a needy eight-year-old living with said mother, but she didn't see you as sufficient reason to cling to life.* Rebecca says nothing, though. She doesn't want to burden Sadie with her pain.

"I wish I could've gotten to know her as an adult," Sadie says. "I remember nothing about her except a vague feeling of warmth and love. I know she was a writer. Do you have anything she wrote that I can read?"

Another sore point for Rebecca. "She finished a novel, then destroyed every copy before she died. Of all the things... I really can't forgive her for that."

"Did she leave a letter? Or a note?"

Rebecca's skin tingles. "A note?"

"You know... a suicide note. Something that could give some insight into her thoughts. I don't know. I was just wondering."

"There was no letter. No note. I'm sorry." But just as the words leave Rebecca's mouth, an image flashes inside her head. Her mother's body on the bed, and beside her on the table, a piece of paper.

7

2020 - PRESENT

In the evening, Rebecca fails to focus on the math problems she promised herself she would work on while her classes are in flux. All she can think about is how her mother might've left a suicide note she was never allowed to read. A debate rages inside her head over whether that piece of paper is a figment of her imagination, or whether it's a dormant memory that shot to the surface at Sadie's suggestion.

If there had been any such thing, her father ought to have told her by now. Maybe he didn't want her to see it when she was a child, but there was no excuse for not sharing it with her as soon as she reached adulthood. *Or was there?* If the note said something awful like *fuck you*, her father might be forgiven for simply destroying it. What good could come of sharing such bitterness with a child? She wouldn't want to show it to her kid either, if she had one.

Or maybe the note was just pointless. Something that revealed nothing about her mother. *Farewell*, or *I couldn't take it anymore*, or *yes, this really is a suicide.*

Eventually, she gives up on doing any work and tries to watch a streaming show. When it too fails to gain her attention, she shuts off her TV and prepares for bed.

Lying on her back in the darkness, she wonders if she still might have the power to travel through time. She thought she had lost it after Sadie was found, because the ability seemed to be driven by her needs and sense of purpose. But since then, she'd only tried once, and when the attempt failed, she thought that might be the end of it.

Now she wonders if it didn't work because she had nothing motivating her on that occasion. Since she became a time traveler, her mindcasts have always been driven by strong emotional need. Even the ones involving meaningless sex with Dev probably arose from wanting to fill the emptiness inside her.

It started the day she'd been hiking by herself and briefly wandered off trail. A tiny flash of light seemed to jump out of a black rock and prick her skin. It had caused a tingling sensation and nothing more. She paid so little attention to it, she continued on her walk and never thought there might be a reason to save that special rock. Now she would never find it again.

She still isn't one hundred percent certain her time traveling ability came from the rock, but since it was the only unusual thing that happened shortly before she discovered her new power, she has come to accept it as the explanation. Maybe aliens scattered them, thinking it would be funny to give humans a new power they had no clue how to use.

The first time she did a mindcast, as she later decided to call it, it was the strangest feeling. First her vision went black, then the inside of her head became hotter than her face the time she went to Florida and burned so bad she looked like a boiled lobster. As the heat lessened, dizziness overcame her, along with the sensation of doing reverse somersaults. *Like falling backward through time.* It was always backward, never forward.

Since her initial mindcasts brought her only to the recent past, it took several iterations before she was certain that only her thoughts had jumped back. In other words, when she traveled into the past there were not two Rebeccas wandering around. *Youth is wasted on the young,* they say. Here was a way for an older mind to experience youth again.

She eventually learned the other key aspect of her mindcasts—she could not change history. No matter what she did, when she returned to real-time, nothing in her life, or in the world, was changed. Maybe her mindcasts sent her into a parallel time thread, but she soon gave up thinking about it, since it only made her head hurt. Time travel allowed her to witness the past and to play with alternate scenarios that would never go anywhere in her own real-time. It had been all she needed to locate Sadie.

Tonight, for the first time since her sister came home, Rebecca has a powerful desire to revisit a moment in her past. She concentrates on that day, visualizing everything she can recall about it. And before long, a match is lit inside her head and she is spinning backward.

8

2002 - MINDCAST

Rebecca is eight years old and dreading what she and her father are going to discover inside her mother's house, although she knows what it is.

She's standing outside the front door next to Dad, staring up at his profile and wondering how she could have forgotten how handsome he'd been at this age. His clean-shaven face reveals the chiseled jaw that will later be covered by heavy bristle. He has smooth, dusty red hair that will, eighteen years from now, be reduced to thin gray strands across an otherwise bald head.

As he rings the doorbell for the second time, she looks down at herself and tries to wrap her brain around her much smaller, weaker self. She has mindcast into her little girl body twice before, but it's just as freaky the third time around. Because it's summer, she's wearing a tank top, shorts, and sandals. Her knobby little knees poke out below the shorts, but the real highlight is the pink glitter polish she must've spent hours applying to her miniature toenails.

"Did she say anything to you?" her father says, not really expecting an answer.

"No, Daddy." Her squeaky little-girl voice startles her.

He's annoyed because he has plans for tonight and wanted to get back quickly. But then he tries the knob, as Rebecca knows he will, and raises his eyebrows on finding it open. When she follows him in, she's overwhelmed by how surreal it feels, seeing her home the way it was all those years ago. She'll never grow accustomed to jumping this far into her past. It will always seem more like a dream than real life.

When he glances back to check on her, she notices the moisture beading on his forehead. It's like an oven in this place. They had central air conditioning added months before Sadie was taken, but it clearly isn't running now.

The rooms are far neater than she recalls. Everything in its place. The scent of lavender potpourri clings to the hot, suffocating atmosphere. Though it seems like someone contemplating suicide must have weightier matters to consider, her mother has shown a strange consideration in the details. *You won't have to clean up after me,* she hears her mother say. *You won't have to pay for air conditioning no one was using.*

"Take my hand, Rebecca," her dad says. Although his palms are sticky, she does so gladly. He knows something is wrong, but isn't sure if that wrong thing might involve a home invader. His instincts morph into protect-the-child mode.

They take a quick survey of the downstairs rooms, finding them empty. At the bottom of the stairs, they listen for movement. But the house is silent except for the ticking of the wall clock in the family room. Before, she would've taken that as a reminder of time's unstoppable forward motion, but lately she's been picturing it as more of a circular thing.

"Camille?" her dad calls out, not too loudly.

"Mommy," Rebecca says, she's not sure why, since she knows there will be no answer.

He calls her mother's name again. When no reply comes, he grips Rebecca's hand tighter and starts up the steps. He fears what they'll find upstairs, but the thought of leaving his child alone in this house frightens him more. He hasn't fully ruled out the possibility of an intruder yet.

She stumbles on a step, betrayed by her short, spindly legs. He lifts her up. This is a new detail. The genuine eight-year-old Rebecca would not have tripped over her own feet.

They reach her mother's bedroom door, which Rebecca remembers was left ajar. He lowers her, keeping her away from the opening, blocking her view of the room with his body. Only then does he turn and peer in. Rebecca knows he sees his former wife lying on the bed with her face turned away from them.

"Camille?" he says softly.

The same dread Rebecca feels inside her small torso is evident in her father's voice. This is so much harder than she thought it would be. To arrive here, at this moment, when it's too late to save her. If only they had come earlier... if only they had understood her state of mind... if only someone could've helped her and prevented her from taking this final act. It hurts even more knowing that if her mother had remained alive, she and Sadie would've been reunited. The rest of her life could've been filled with joy.

Her father moves around the bed and kneels beside her mother. Rebecca sees it now, a piece of paper on the bedside table. She runs toward it, but before she can reach it, he sweeps her up into his arms.

"Lemme go!" she cries in her childish voice.

Tears course down his cheeks as he holds her to him and carries her from the room. "You need to wait out here." He sets her down in the hall and returns to the bedroom, shutting and locking the door after him.

She bangs on the door with her round little fists. "Let me in! I want to see her!"

She hears him place a phone call to emergency services. Soon after, he opens the door again. "All right, Rebecca. Mommy is gone. You understand?"

She nods her head, sniffing.

"You can see her now. You can say goodbye to her."

At the time, she probably asked if Mommy was ever coming back, or how did it happen that her Mommy is now dead? But she says none of that now. When he lets her into the room, she dashes toward the other side of the bed, only to have her hopes crushed.

The piece of paper is gone.

"She left a note," Rebecca says. "Where is it?"

Her father gives her a curious look, surprised that she even noticed. "There wasn't any note," he says.

"You're lying! There was! Let me see it!" She grabs at his pocket.

He carries her kicking and screaming to the hallway and shuts the door on her again. As the lock clicks inside the room, her mindcast ends.

9

2020 - PRESENT

Three more times over the following week, Rebecca travels back to the day she and her father found her mother. She tries to outwit him by dashing up the stairs ahead of him, or slipping around his legs into the bedroom, but he blocks her every attempt to get her pudgy hands on the note. Eight-year-old Rebecca can't get past her father when he's determined to prevent it.

The situation infuriates her. How dare he keep her from reading her mother's last words? Why, after all these years, has he never mentioned it? Even if he thought she couldn't handle it as a child, he should have given it to her when she turned eighteen. But he's never said a single damn thing about it.

She considers telling him that a repressed memory regarding the note has emerged, and would he please show it to her? But if he's truly determined to keep her from reading it, he might deny its existence and then destroy it, if he hasn't already. She decides not to say anything unless the right moment somehow presents itself.

As for mindcasting back to that horrible day, she is done, at least for now. Each time they rediscover her dead mother's body is like another twist of the knife through her heart. She needs a rest from it.

· · ·

REBECCA WALKS the Filbert Street Steps as often as she can. This is one of the great benefits of San Francisco compared to where she used to live in the 'burbs, and the main reason she hesitates to leave the city, despite that rent would be cheaper almost anywhere else. The stairs are a challenging workout and on a clear day, she can view the broad expanse of the bay in exquisite detail. Other attractions include the quaint homes without parking spaces, the gardens with their flame-colored flowers, and best of all, the wild parrots.

Today, as sometimes happens, she questions her current life choices. She's known, almost since she started taking classes at community college, that she's really not interested in a career as a mathematician or a computer scientist or any other type of engineer. Only a reluctance to disappoint her father has kept her from quitting so far.

Why should she care? He didn't bother to consider how it might affect his daughter to hide her mother's last words from her forever.

Admittedly, she has no idea what she'll do if she drops the classes. No clue, really, regarding where to find contentment. She's been unhappy for years, but until recently, she thought it was because of Sadie being kidnapped. Now that they have her back, she wonders why her life hasn't been transformed.

Every second she spends in her sister's company brings her joy. It's the rest of the time that's the problem. There has to be more to living.

She slows her pace slightly to catch her breath on the uphill. Should she forget about a career and simply rely on her trust fund? That sounds boring, and besides, she doesn't expect it to last her whole life. She considers what skills she might have. Good at math, but uninterested in using that talent. Reliable, for the most part. Well-organized? Maybe not. Smart? Hard to judge.

Courage, though. She believes she has that. Not everyone could do what she did to save her sister. Courage and determination. When she decides to do something, she sticks with it.

She pauses to gaze at the Bay Bridge, its brilliant white lines etched into the deep blue sky. Her next thought makes her laugh. How could she have forgotten her one completely unique skill?

Visions of time travel lead her steps downward and onto a street she has visited twice before in recent days.

When she reaches the intersection where she believes the *Missing Person* flyer of Ethan Pitt was posted, she wonders if she made a mistake. The flyer is gone, though there are bits of paper hanging from tacks. Glancing around, she reassures herself that this was the spot. A thread of hope tickles her. Maybe Ethan's picture was removed because they found him.

Her hope is immediately dashed when she notices a crumpled wad of paper caught in the prickly branches of a dead shrub a few feet away. She snatches it and smooths open the page to find Ethan staring up at her with the N-word slashed in red ink across his face.

A wave of nausea hits her and she has to steady herself against the pole. The defilement of the flyer feels like a metaphor for Ethan's tragic life. Torn and sullied, abandoned and forgotten on this dismal, godforsaken street.

When she gets home, Rebecca opens her laptop and starts a new search for any mention of the boy. This time she finds him on a site called missingkids.org. The listing shows the same photo that was on the flyer, the date he went missing and from where, his race (black), his hair (black), his eye color (brown), his height (5'3"), and his weight (98 pounds).

The thought that he might not have lived long enough to push his weight into three digits makes her eyes well up.

Eventually she finds him on Facebook as well, sandwiched by a bra ad above and a cat meme below. Again, the identical photo, but different text. *Don't look away*, it says. *He could be your son, your grandchild, your brother. A thirteen-year-old child who disappeared. Don't you care? Doesn't anybody care? His name is Ethan Pitt. I'm his aunt. PM me if you know anything.*

That's all. Then beneath it, a name, *Yakeera McDade*, and the date of his disappearance.

Rebecca's cursor hovers over his picture for a long time before she clicks on his aunt's name. She writes, *Call me at...* and leaves her phone number. Let Yakeera make the first move, if *she* still cares.

10

2020 - PRESENT

Rebecca's phone rings a few hours after she reaches out to Ethan's aunt. She thought the woman might call sooner, but when this much time has gone by and you're not expecting anyone to care, you're probably not checking your Facebook messages every second.

"This is Ethan's aunt. Yakeera McDade. Is this Rebecca?" She sounds impatient.

"Yes, that's me."

"What's your interest in Ethan?"

"I'd like to ask you some questions about his disappearance."

"Lady, I thought you had information for *me*."

Rebecca hadn't actually said that, but there's no point in arguing. "I'm sorry. No. That's not the reason for my call."

"Look, I Googled you. You had a missing sister you found recently, right?"

"That's right. Sadie."

"So, are you just obsessed with missing kids now? Calling up victim's families to compare notes? I don't get it."

"It's not like that. I do care about missing people because I've experienced the anguish of it firsthand. That's what drew me to

Ethan's case. I'm a freelance writer. If I can gather enough information, I'd like to write an article about him."

"Freelance? You mean no one's paying you for this?"

"I hope to sell it to a newspaper or magazine."

"Why on earth do you think any paper would give good money for an article about Ethan?"

"Because people are finally talking about the fact that when something happens to a person of color, nobody in the white world is paying attention. The police don't put in much effort, the media barely mentions it. I want to change that."

"And we should trust you, a white woman, to tell our boy's story? Please."

"Is anyone else offering? You need publicity. People need to learn about him and be on the lookout for him. If the Chronicle publishes this, it'll put pressure on the police to do more. I'm going to do my best. Why not let me try?" Rebecca feels guilty lying to Yakeera, but she plans to make it up to her. If given the chance, she'll do her damnedest to find the boy.

"What do you want to know?" Yakeera finally says. "I've got nothing better to do right now."

A nervous shiver runs through Rebecca. Now that she's got the go-ahead, she almost wishes Ethan's aunt had called her bluff. If she had, Rebecca would've been saved from starting something that could be way beyond the scope of her meager abilities. Something that might be even more frightening and life-threatening than what she went through to save Sadie.

"Where was Ethan the last time anyone saw him?" Rebecca begins.

ETHAN

Just as Ethan is leaving the locker room, his teacher calls his name. He freezes, certain he's about to get in trouble for being a total fuck-up on the basketball court today. Ever since lunch, he hasn't been able to think about anything aside from Ma losing her job and drinking again.

When he turns back, Mr. Johnson takes in his scared face and says, "Ethan, it's okay. I wanted to talk to you about something. You're not in trouble."

Ethan relaxes a bit. Mr. Johnson has only been working at his school since winter break, and so far, Ethan likes him. The girls all have crushes on him because he has an English accent and they think he looks like a young Will Smith. Ethan doesn't see it, though no question his teacher's chiseled body is something to aspire to.

"I think you should try out for the soccer team. I've been watching you run and pass the ball. You'd make a good midfielder. What do you think?"

Ethan stares at him. Nobody ever asked him to join a team before.

"Do you want to play?" Mr. Johnson says.

Part of him really wants to say yes, but he knows he can't do it. Even before all this started, Ma was against after-school sports. *It's no good taking time away from your schoolwork*, she always said. A job is going to interfere with schoolwork too, but it seems he doesn't have a choice about that. "Sorry, I'm not interested." He doesn't say *I can't do it* because Mr. Johnson will ask why.

"Really? The team could sure use your help."

"My homework takes a lot of time."

"I talked to your teachers. They say you're doing well, especially in English class. They thought you could handle a sport, no problem."

"Look, I just don't want to, okay?" Frustration pours out of his shaking voice.

Mr. Johnson narrows his eyes like he's trying to read what's going on in Ethan's head. "Sure. Your choice. But maybe consider it a little longer? I think you'd have fun. I'll ask you again in a few days." He gives the boy a firm pat on his shoulders.

Ethan slips past him out the door, wiping the sweat off his forehead with his sleeve. Turning back toward the school's main building, he pushes past the tide of students leaving for the day. By the time he reaches Mr. Flannery's classroom, the halls are mostly empty.

The door is open. A younger boy who Ethan doesn't know is cleaning the whiteboard. Mr. Flannery is at his desk, hunched over papers that he flips through rapidly. He scribbles a mark at the end of the first set.

After hesitating for a minute, Ethan steps into the room and asks to speak with him.

Mr. Flannery raises his head and gazes at Ethan with cool gray eyes. "Have a seat." He glances back at the boy, who has just finished his job. "You may go now."

The kid grabs his backpack from a table and scurries away before the teacher can change his mind.

Ethan folds into the chair closest to Mr. Flannery. From here he catches a whiff of the cigar smoke that seems to have permanently settled into his teacher's clothing. It's very slight and maybe other kids wouldn't notice, but Ma has always claimed Ethan has a powerful sense of smell.

"How can I help you?" Mr. Flannery says.

Ethan holds his hands together under the desk. "I was wondering if, um, you might know where I can find a job?" He hopes his teacher might know folks with enough money to pay kids to do work for them around their houses.

"A job? Great idea. It's always best to be productive with your spare time."

Relief flows through Ethan. He'd been afraid his teacher would try to talk him out of it, and then he would be no help at all. "It might be hard to get one, though," Ethan says.

"That's why we have the Internet." He takes out his phone. "Jobs for eighth-graders... babysitting... what about that?"

Ethan shakes his head. "I don't have brothers or sisters. I don't think I could do it."

Mr. Flannery scrolls down the list. "Lawn mowing... stop me if any of these sound good to you... housecleaner... newspaper delivery... do kids still do that? House-sitting... dog-walking..."

"Dog-walking. I love dogs." He doesn't have one, but he's spent time with a few that belonged to friends. "How do I find someone to hire me?"

Mr. Flannery closes his eyes to think. "There's a woman in my neighborhood who dotes on her two dogs. I can ask her."

Ethan shoots to his feet. "Thanks, Mr. Flannery."

"You're a very special young man." He says this in his usual bland tone, but since he rarely praises any of his students, Ethan knows he means it. A warm sensation fills him.

"Not just because your writing is so polished," Mr. Flannery continues. "I think you have it in you to make something of yourself."

"I hope so."

"It won't be easy. Not around here. Others will try to pull you down to their level. Don't let that happen. Stay steady on your own path. Leave this place behind as soon as you're old enough. Don't let yourself get caught in the cycle of ignorance and poverty and crime."

Mr. Flannery hasn't spoken to him quite like this before. Ethan doesn't really understand what he's going on about, and he doesn't care much for the way his teacher has reduced his home city to its worst possible characteristics. He knows there's also plenty to celebrate about where he lives.

But the important thing is that Mr. Flannery has agreed to get him a job.

12

———

In the evening after Ethan returns from talking to his teacher, Ma makes them bean tacos for supper. After they sit down, she pauses and looks him in the eyes. "I lost my job."

"How come?" He decides there's no point in telling her he already knew.

"Oh, that Cecelia never did like me. She told the boss how I sometimes give you extra cheese or fries. He secretly watched me last time. You're my kid, for heaven's sake. I can't watch you go hungry and not do something about it. With the little they pay us, they ought to look the other way when we feed a little extra of their crappy-ass food to our children."

"It's not fair. You're a lot better worker than Cecelia. She always looks like she's going to bite my head off," Ethan says.

Ma sighs. "The boss likes her, and I can guess why. Nothing I can do. But we're going to be okay." Her voice is upbeat though her eyes tell a different story. "I went to the unemployment office today."

"They going to pay you?"

"It takes a few weeks before it starts. And it won't be the same as what I was earning. It's going to be less." She glances around the apartment. "We're going to have to move. We'll save money in a one-bedroom or a studio."

"A studio?" Having to share a room with his mother is not how Ethan was picturing his high school years. "Maybe we can move in with Aunt Yakeera." She lives nearby and has two bedrooms. The sisters ought to be able to share, and then he could still have his own space.

"What? You can't tell your aunt any of this. She'll just come in here like she always does and try to boss me around. Lecture me on all the shit I did wrong. No way can we live with her. Promise me you won't say anything about me losing my job."

He should've known better than to bring up Aunt Yakeera. His mother had a love/hate relationship with her sister. If Yakeera ever needed anything, Ma was there for her. But she hated when it was the other way around. *Too much pride.* All their lives they had vied to be the best looking and the most talented sister.

"I talked to Mr. Flannery, and he said he can get me a job walking dogs," Ethan says to change the subject.

Ma gives him a wistful smile. "That's good, baby. Every little bit helps."

"It won't be much to start. But once it gets going... once I get some more customers... it might really make a difference."

She tears up. "You're the best, baby. I love you. And I'll get a new job soon." Her gaze sweeps to the electronic keyboard in the corner, her prized possession. "I'm going to practice my singing. I've been away from it too long."

Three years ago, she was a backup singer for a talented rap artist who might've gone far if his drug problem hadn't caused his career to crash and burn. Maybe she can find something like that again, but it won't be easy, especially now that she's older.

She reads the doubt in his eyes. "Have faith in your momma, boy."

. . .

A FEW DAYS later he's on his way to the interview with Ms. Paladino, who's Mr. Flannery's neighbor. She lives in the next city over and Ethan will have to take the train to get there. Plus, he'll have to walk or ride his board to and from the train. He can see this will eat up a lot of his time unless he can find some other clients in the same area to make the trip worthwhile. If things go well, maybe she'll recommend him to her dog-owning friends.

Before leaving the apartment, he washed really well and put on his best clothes. He can still smell Ma's perfumy soap on him. When he reaches the lady's neighborhood, he's glad he put in the effort. It's pretty deluxe, no apartment buildings or retail stores, just all houses, and not the kind that look exactly like each other either. They all have lush green lawns and flowers blooming everywhere and sturdy old trees. Ms. Paladino's home is one of the nicest, bigger than most of the others and with the fanciest garden.

He checks himself and brushes off his pants before ringing the bell, which triggers two sets of high-pitched barking inside.

"Coming!" Seconds later, a woman flings open the door. "Shush, my pretties," she tells the mini-dogs at her feet. They stop barking, but one continues to emit a low growl.

"Hi, I'm Ethan," he says, taking the initiative.

"I'm Terry." The woman is plus-sized with clothes that look custom-fitted. Her blond shoulder-length hair is so smooth it could be a wig. "Come in." She and the dogs lead him to a chair.

"May I pet them?" he says.

"Oh yes, they're very friendly. That's Froo-froo, and this one's Diana."

He lets Froo-froo sniff his hand while Diana hangs back. "Good girl," he says.

"Froo-froo is a boy."

"Sorry. Good boy." At this point both dogs are crowding next to his legs, wanting to be pet. "They're really sweet."

"I think they like you. That's good. Have you been a dog-walker before? You're younger than I thought."

"Um, no. But I'm good with my friends' dogs."

"You don't have one of your own?" She frowns.

Ethan thought Mr. Flannery would've told her about him in advance. That was the whole point of getting a recommendation.

"Oh that's fine. I'll show you how to do it. We'll walk around the block together so you can see their favorite route. You must be careful not to let them eat anything on the sidewalk. Of course, you have to clean up their poo. And don't let anyone pet them." She has several more instructions before she finally finishes.

The walk around the block is awkward, with Ethan trying to hold the dogs' leashes while they pull in opposite directions, and Ms. Paladino issuing frequent commands from behind like a drill sergeant.

"I told your teacher he ought to get a dog," she says. "He said he prefers cats."

Ethan would've guessed that about him.

At the end of their walk, she offers Ethan the job. It doesn't pay much, though. He tries not to think about how many more customers he will need in order to come anywhere near replacing Ma's income with his own.

13

———

The velvety tones of Ma's voice seep out into the hallway as Ethan lets himself into the apartment after school. Though he would prefer if she were out applying for jobs, he can't help feeling comforted by Ma's flawless rendition of *Cry Me a River*.

She smiles at him and continues practicing her favorite songs, while he goes to his room and gets cleaned up for his first day on the new job. He puts on his plaid button shirt that doesn't need ironing, his newest jeans, and his hardly used gray rain jacket. When he comes out of his room, Ma steps away from the keyboard and raises her phone.

"Look at you. Let's take a picture," she says.

"No time. Gotta get to my job."

"I know, baby. Your first day is a big deal. C'mon now. Stand by the window."

He rolls his eyes before moving in place.

"It's too bright," she says. "Try the wall."

He hurries to the new position. "Ready."

She snaps his picture. "You look too worried. Big smile now."

He's too nervous to pose. She takes several more photos till she gives up on getting a proper smile out of him and sinks down into the armchair. "All that singing wore me out. Will you get me some cheese and crackers before you go?"

"You're making me late, Ma." But still, quick as possible, he prepares her plate and brings it to her with a glass of water.

"Thank you, my lovely son. Now go, make your mother proud."

He grabs his backpack and rushes out. It might be that she calls out for him as he heads down the corridor, but it's too late, he barely has time to get to the train, and she'll manage fine without him. He just hopes she doesn't hit the booze again.

Outside, the drizzle that started earlier has transformed into pelting rain. He jogs toward the station, splattering puddle water all over his good shoes and pant legs. Meanwhile his phone buzzes and he looks to see if it might be a text from Ms. Paladino telling him not to come because of the downpour. But he doesn't have a solid grip on it, and suddenly it's sliding out from between his wet fingers and flying into the street. He leaps out to get it but a car speeding toward him forces a retreat to the sidewalk.

By the time he's able to retrieve it, more than one car has run over it. The phone is smashed. He shoves it back into his pocket and runs the rest of the way to the station, arriving in time to watch the train leaving without him. It'll be fifteen minutes at least till the next one comes.

He looks at his phone but it's beyond repair. He can't get even the simplest function to work. This day has gone from shitty to complete disaster. He can't even call to let his new employer know he's going to be late. He leans against the wall, drenched and shivering, while he waits.

The train doesn't come for twenty-five more minutes. After it arrives at his stop, he sprints all the way to Ms. Paladino's house. At the front door, he stares down at his bedraggled self and prays she'll understand. Over here, the sun is shining and the streets are dry like it hasn't rained one bit. *Rich folk even get the best weather.*

His new employer takes a few minutes to answer his ring. The dogs must be in another room because he doesn't hear them bark.

"Yes?" Ms. Paladino says, looking like she doesn't even know him.

"I'm really sorry. The train was late and my phone broke so I couldn't call you." He shows her the pathetic instrument.

She squints at him. "Looks like you just got out of the bath too. I can't let you in here like that."

"Can you bring the dogs out? I can walk them."

"Sorry, but this isn't going to work. I'm in the middle of a meeting. You should have come earlier." She starts shutting the door.

"Ma'am, please, I really need the work."

"I understand, but I can't just have you popping in any time. I need someone who can be here at the same time every day. The train just isn't reliable when it comes to timing. I'll have to hire someone in the neighborhood." She closes the door before he can say another word.

When Ethan finally gets back home after his miserable day, he finds the apartment looking like a tornado just whipped through it. Drawers pulled out and upended on the floor. The carpet flipped over in the corner. Kitchen canisters tipped onto the counter.

Banging comes from his mother's bedroom. "Ma?" Not till after he calls her name does he think this might be the work of a burglar or worse. His gaze shoots around the room looking for a weapon to defend himself.

"In here!" she shouts back, relieving his worry over an intruder but introducing all new questions regarding her sanity.

He approaches her door and looks in. As he feared, her bedroom is like the rest of the apartment. While he watches, she empties the top drawer of her dresser onto the bed.

"What you doing, Ma?"

She bursts into tears. Throws herself down on the bed. "We have to find all our cash," she says between sobs. "You know how I hide it sometimes? We have to find it."

"Why now? What's going on?"

"They called from the unemployment office. Said I'm not getting shit."

"That can't be right."

"My boss told them I stole from him. I got fired for cause. That means I can't collect unemployment."

"Giving me a few extra fries? That's not fair."

"I don't know what we're going to do."

"You gotta settle down. We'll figure something out." But inside he's thinking, *why have I always got to be the adult?* On the surface, he's calm, but inside it's like all his nerves are tingling, getting ready to do something without having any idea what.

14

———————

The last few days have been a blur at school. All Ethan can think about is how he and Ma are going to get by without unemployment. At least he managed to convince her she needed to go out and apply for "regular" jobs while she waited for opportunities to reboot her singing career. She's been drinking again at dinner time and sometimes late into the nights, but at least there's been no vodka for breakfast lately.

It's been tough managing without his phone too. They don't have the money to replace it. He can't text his friends; he can't let Ma know when he's running late. He can't look stuff up on the Internet. It's like he doesn't have a life without his phone.

He's been avoiding any conversations with his English teacher since losing the dog-walking job. But when he spots Mr. Flannery in the parking lot after school, heading toward his old-fashioned Chrysler, Ethan forces himself to approach.

"Hello, Ethan." His teacher gazes at him with an unreadable expression, pausing with his hand on the door of his car. Ethan thinks he would make a good poker player.

"Can I talk to you?" Ethan says.

"Not now. I have an appointment."

"Oh, okay, sure, I just wanted to say I'm sorry things didn't work out with your neighbor. You know, the dog-walking. The train was late, my phone broke, I couldn't call her…"

"It isn't like you to make excuses, Ethan. You should've planned on taking an earlier train in case they were running late."

"Yes, sir. Sorry I disappointed you."

"I would think nothing of it if it were another student. But I have very high expectations of you."

"Thanks. I messed up this time, but it won't happen again. Do you know anyone else who needs a dog-walker?"

"I'm afraid not." He gets into his sedan but hesitates before closing the door. "Try Nextdoor dot com. Sometimes people post there when they're looking for services. You might find someone local, and not have to rely on the train."

"Thanks! Only my phone's broken and…"

"Use your computer. I have to run now." He shuts the door, starts the engine.

Ethan waves as his teacher drives off. He didn't get a chance to tell Mr. Flannery he doesn't have a computer. His phone was his computer. His phone was his everything.

He goes to the field and plays some pickup soccer with a few friends from school, trying to get his mind off things. It's getting dark by the time he heads home, so it's surprising not to see any lights in his apartment as he approaches the building.

"Ma?" he calls out as soon as he opens their door. He flips on switches and checks her bedroom. She's definitely not home, which is odd, because when she has errands to do, she usually completes them in full daylight. He hopes she's not out buying liquor with their dwindling funds.

Ethan assembles some quesadillas for their dinner and turns on the oven to preheat. Just when he's ready to put them in, he hears the key turn in the lock. *Good, she's back in time to eat.*

But when the door opens, it's Aunt Yakeera, not Ma. And from the look on her face, there's something terribly wrong.

"Ethan, I got bad news but your mother is going to be all right."

Right away his hands start to shake. "Where is she?"

"At the hospital."

Oh shit, oh shit, oh shit.

Aunt Yakeera sweeps toward him. "She got hit by a car. But man, my sister is strong. She doesn't have any broken bones! Just cuts and scrapes and bruises. And well, they say she got a concussion. But her head looks all right, she's just a little dizzy." Aunt Yakeera gives him a tight squeeze. "Your momma's going to be all right. They want to watch her tonight, but she should be coming home in the morning."

"How did it happen? Somebody run a red light?"

Aunt Yakeera blows out air. "Doesn't seem that way. Don't say this to anyone, but I think your mother might've had too much to drink before she went out. She tried to cross when the pedestrian light was red. The driver wasn't a bad guy. He stopped, called 9-1-1, stayed by her side till they came. The cops said he felt terrible."

"He should've stopped. There's a person in the street, you're supposed to stop."

"I know, I know. Sometimes people appear suddenly and you don't see them in time, though."

He reaches for his jacket. "I want to go to the hospital."

"No. You stay here with me. She's in good hands right now. We'll get her in the morning. I told her we weren't coming back tonight."

He decides not to insist. After all, he needs to get his homework done. And Auntie said she's doing fine. *No broken bones!* That was amazing. He wonders about the concussion, though. That sounds serious.

MA COMES home at noon on the Saturday after her accident. Ethan greets her at the door but doesn't hug her because she looks unsteady on her feet.

"Who's this handsome young man?" she says.

He's not sure if she's joking or not.

"She'll be loopy for a while." Aunt Yakeera leads her to her room with an arm around her waist. "Confusion is one of the symptoms of concussions. Also headaches and dizziness. She won't be leaving her bed for a few days. I'll get her into her pj's."

"I don't want to put on my pajamas," Ma says.

"C'mon, sister. You'll feel better when you're comfy under the covers." His aunt shuts the door to give Ma privacy while she changes.

Ma's phone rings as soon as Ethan sits in front of the TV. He tracks it to her purse, which Yakeera must've set on the table when they walked in. His first instinct is to bring the cell to his mother, but he pauses, thinking she's in no state to talk to anyone. Since the Caller ID only shows the phone number, he figures it's spam anyway.

On second thought, he answers in case it's someone from the hospital with instructions for her.

"This is Mike Wong from Dealmart. I'd like to speak to Laila Pitt." The man sounds annoyed.

"She's busy. Can I take a message?" Ethan says.

"She was supposed to be here half an hour ago for her interview. You tell her if she isn't here in fifteen minutes, we're removing her from consideration."

"She had an accident. She has to rest for a few days. Can she call you back after that?" Ethan's pulse races.

"Sorry. We need to hire someone now." The man hangs up.

Ethan lowers the phone. He doesn't actually know if she'll be better in a few days. What if she takes months to get over this? By then they'll be evicted. They could end up in the tent city with Uncle Ray.

Aunt Yakeera emerges from the bedroom. "She's sleeping now. I can stay here through the weekend, okay? Help her with the bathroom and stuff. And there's a visiting nurse going to come a few days a week till she's better. You don't have to do it all yourself, Ethan."

He looks down, nodding his head.

"Did you let her boss know she'll be out sick for a while like I told you?"

Since his mother doesn't have a job anymore, he hasn't done that. But he can't tell his aunt because Ma swore him to secrecy. "Yeah, I did," he mumbles, hoping not to be struck dead for lying.

Ethan goes to the library, taking advantage of Aunt Yakeera looking after Ma for the weekend. He has to wait awhile until one of the computers opens up. Following Mr. Flannery's recommendation, he navigates to the Nextdoor site and looks in the Services Wanted section. Eventually he finds three people looking for dog-walkers in the area.

Once he's got his list, he realizes how bad it will look that he doesn't have a phone where they can reach him. Nevertheless, he goes ahead and emails them to say he's interested, loves dogs, and is very responsible. He hopes they don't want a recommendation from a previous employer, because the only person who ever hired him immediately fired him.

After sending his emails, he hangs around the library for a while waiting for responses. He looks through the shelves and finds a book he wants to read. Then he gets back on the computer to find two out of three have replied.

The first says they already hired someone. The second says they require three positive references and they WILL call them.

Two rejections, and he's already beginning to understand how Uncle Ray must feel, time and again, when someone refuses to hire him. He settles into a bean bag chair and reads for a while before checking his email again.

The third one has replied. Their dog died.

Ethan checks out the book and goes home. There, things go from bad to worse when his aunt confronts him at the door.

"I was going over Laila's papers," she says. "I found a copy of her unemployment application." She glares at Ethan. "What've you got to say about this?"

Ethan's gaze shoots to the bedroom door, which is shut. He lowers his voice. "It's not my fault. She told me not to say anything."

"That's ridiculous. I suppose she's too proud to let her big sister know." She hmphs and haws for a minute. "Might be better this way, though. I doubt that job of hers paid sick leave. At least now she'll be getting unemployment soon."

He probably should tell her that's no longer an option either, but it doesn't seem fair that he's getting stuck with delivering all the bad news. While she rants to herself, he slips away into his own room and shuts the door. He's got enough to worry about without having to deal with the drama between his mother and his aunt.

Later Aunt Yakeera makes them the best dinner they've had for a while. Big juicy hamburgers with ketchup dripping down the sides. While Ma continues dozing in her room, they eat in front of the TV, watching a horror film. Midway through, just as the story is really heating up, he feels Aunt Yakeera's limp hand dropping on his shoulder. He turns and jerks away at the sight of her eyes rolled up in the back of her head, and her snarling mouth open like she's ready to bite.

"Stop!" he cries out.

She laughs. He should not have been surprised, because it isn't the first time she's play-acted during a scary movie. She used to work as an actress and managed to get bit parts in a few low-budget horror films. But when the acting jobs dried up, she turned to hairdressing to support herself. It was sad, he thought... both sisters having to give up on their dreams.

After he goes to bed, sometime in the middle of the night, he's woken by loud groans coming from Ma. She sounds like she's in awful pain. He gets up to help, but when he knocks on her bedroom door, Aunt Yakeera opens it just a crack.

"I got this, honey. Gave her some more Tylenol. Can't give her anything stronger with a concussion. You go back to sleep. I'll take you to church in the morning."

He returns to bed, but it's hard to sleep while Ma is making noises. Not just cries of pain, but it also sounds like she's in a delirium, talking to herself.

How he's going to handle this when Aunt Yakeera goes home, he has no clue.

15

———

Ethan's aunt went back to her own home on Monday. Ma is managing to take care of her personal needs, but Ethan is doing everything else, including grocery shopping, meal preparation, cleaning the apartment, and laundry. She's having more lucid moments again, but they're outweighed by all the time she can't move around because of headaches and stomach upset.

She's supposed to follow the BRAT diet for the nausea: bananas, rice, applesauce, and toast. Crackers and bouillon are good too. Mostly she's just not eating, though.

She makes a face when he brings her breakfast in bed.

"You should try to eat, Ma."

"I will, baby." She pats his hand. "I appreciate all you're doing for me."

He leaves for school feeling grateful that the nausea is keeping her from hitting the bottle. He hopes this experience will break her of the habit.

When he comes home to check on her, he finds her sound asleep in her bed, despite the TV being left on high volume. When he shuts it off, she opens her eyes.

"You want anything, Ma?"

She doesn't answer, just stares blankly at the empty screen. He brings her broth and a banana. "Here you go," he says.

Her gaze shifts to him. "I got to get ready."

"What for?"

"You know. I'm singing tonight with Gold Dog."

This was the rapper she used to work for. But his career sizzled after two years. "Gold Dog's not doing his music anymore," Ethan says.

"What? That can't be."

"It's the concussion. You're not thinking right. You just stay here and get better, okay?"

She makes a face and turns the TV on.

He nods at the food. "Don't forget to eat now."

"I will."

"You'll forget?"

"I'll eat it! Child, what is your problem?"

"It's hard doing everything." There. He said it, and now he feels like a terrible son, particularly since her face shows how much the remark stung.

"Come here." She opens her arms and pulls him into a hug. "I'm sorry, baby. I'll try to be better. I'm going to beat this, and then I'll spoil you like you never been spoiled before."

He draws back. "I have to go out now. I'll be back for dinner."

"Sure, baby." She leans her head back on the pillow.

He heads out of the apartment with his skateboard and rides it to the tent city. He's not sure, but it looks like it might've expanded since the last time he was there. His uncle's tent isn't where it was before and he has to search around until finally he almost trips over it. He shakes the tent flap and calls his uncle's name through the opening.

When there's no response, he repeats, "Uncle Ray? You in there?"

A man with a long gray beard peers out. "There's no Ray here."

"But that's his tent."

"It's my tent. Paid good money for it."

"My uncle must've sold it to you. Do you know where he is?" Ethan's eyes are searching the surroundings.

The man says nothing and retreats into the tent.

"I saw him waiting for a job at the corner of Main and Pine," a woman says behind Ethan.

Ethan turns around. "A job?"

"You know, where the illegals hang out, waitin' for trucks to pick 'em up and drive 'em to construction sites and shit."

"You know when he'll be back?" Ethan says.

"No idea." The woman moves on.

Discouraged, Ethan heads back the way he came.

"Ethan!" Uncle Ray's voice rings out behind him, bringing a smile to his face.

Ethan hurries toward him, though his happiness is short-lived. His uncle is bent over and covered in dirt. Though he tries to put on a cheerful face, he looks as beaten down as any man ever did.

"What happened to you?" Ethan says.

"I've been digging ditches all day. Hey, it's work. I was paid for it."

"You sold your tent."

"I needed the money for food. Things will be better now. The man who picked me up today says he has more work lined up."

The mention of work gets Ethan excited despite the way uncle looks after a day of it. "You think he'd hire me?"

"You don't want to do work like that."

"I need to do something. Ma's had an accident. She's not gonna be able to do anything for a while."

Uncle Ray stares at him for a moment. "I guess you could try. You'll have to wait for Saturday though. I don't want you missing school. They pick up once a day, eight am."

"I'll be there Saturday."

16

———

Ethan worked on the third chapter of Amari's story early in the morning, inspired by a dream that bees were chasing him. He couldn't sleep anymore after that, probably because he's worried about the upcoming work assignment, which previously left his uncle in such a worn and sorry state.

He puts on his oldest, least-cherished clothes, expecting to end up as filthy as his uncle was, and rides the bus to the intersection where they'll have to wait. Uncle Ray arrives a few minutes later, and they hover amidst other laborers who mostly speak Spanish. Surrounded by an aura of gloom, it feels like waiting to be picked for the least desirable sports team anyone could imagine. But at least they'll get paid.

"I bought back my tent with the money I earned," Uncle Ray says, trying to cheer Ethan with a bit of good news.

A half hour later, many of the men are gone. Uncle Ray begins to despair that the foreman who said he would hire him is not coming. But then he does, and true to his word, he picks Uncle Ray.

"How about my nephew here?" Uncle Ray says.

The man looks Ethan over and laughs. "We can't take children."

"I'm not a child." But Ethan's voice cracks, betraying him.

The man laughs again. "I'll take you but not the kid."

"It's okay, Uncle Ray," Ethan says. His uncle needs the money badly.

"Go on home," Uncle Ray tells him as he climbs into the truck.

"Sure, I will." But after the truck drives away, Ethan remains until the last worker is chosen an hour later. Nobody picks him. He drags his feet back to the bus stop, his pockets empty.

ANOTHER FEW DAYS GO BY, and Ethan's mother is not getting better. She lies in bed or on the couch watching TV when she's awake. More often than not, she's sleeping. The nurse who comes by to check on her every few days says that concussions can last months, if not years. Whenever Ma forgets to take her extra-strength Tylenol, the throbbing headaches return. Then she takes another two for good measure.

Today Ma is more alert when Ethan brings her food in the afternoon. "How is your job going?" Her words are slurred, but he can understand her.

He thought he told her he lost that job, but maybe he forgot. Or maybe it was not a good time to give her bad news then; he can't remember. "It's over. The lady lived too far away. I couldn't get there on time."

Ma blinks with concern. "Lord, I thought you were working. How are we going to manage? What day is it? Is the rent due yet?"

"We still have another ten days," he says.

They won't be able to cover it. The little money they have remaining needs to be saved for food.

"We better sell some things," Ma says.

He glances around the room at the furniture that came from thrift stores, wondering if they could even get five bucks for any of it.

"The TV has to go," she says.

Ethan eyes it, thinking it's so old and small, never mind selling it, they'd probably have to pay to have it dumped.

"Other one too." Meaning the one in the family room.

First his phone, now his TV. Next it'll be his bed and then he'll be sleeping on the ground in the tent city.

She holds out her hand and looks at the two rings she still wears—engagement and wedding. Both have small diamonds.

"No, Ma," Ethan says. "You can't. It's all you got left of him."

"You do what you gotta do."

"Not yet." He doesn't know what to do, though. His uncle can't help them, and Ma won't take anything from her sister. Mr. Flannery hasn't offered any more help. The only time Ethan had a chance to use a computer at school to apply for more jobs, only one person replied, and after they learned he didn't have a working phone, they told him they'd found someone else.

The next day after school, Ethan is headed to the bus when he spots Teshi. He almost doesn't recognize her at first, because she changed her hair and she's wearing a new jacket. The hair is braided and drawn into a ponytail. He knows from Aunt Yakeera that getting a style like that can cost a lot. And the jacket... it looks like suede in a creamy tan color. Paired with some skintight black pants, the girl has never looked so hot before.

That's his first thought; his second is, where's the money to pay for all this coming from? "Teshi!" He springs toward her. She pauses and turns his way, looking at him curiously.

He slows down as he nears her, suddenly feeling self-conscious about other kids watching him run after her like that.

"Hey, what's up?" she says. They step away from the crowd gathering for the bus.

"Um, nice jacket," he says, realizing he needs to work his way up to, *how the hell did you pay for it?*

She smiles and focuses her half-lidded gaze on him. Heat courses through him. *How did she turn sexy, like, overnight?* he wonders.

"You have something you want to say to me, or you just wanted to look at the jacket?"

He tears his thoughts from the unproductive place they were going. "I just, um, was curious. I mean, you've got these fine clothes, and your hair all braided up. What're you doing to pay for all this?"

"What's that supposed to mean?"

"I mean, did you get a job or something?"

"Here I thought you ran over here to ask me out."

A girl laughs behind him, but he ignores her and lowers his voice. "I need to find work. That's why I asked."

Teshi's expression grows more serious. "Hey, I heard about your mother's accident. Sorry. Is she okay?"

"Not really. She can't work right now."

"I get it. Yeah, I think I can help you. But I'm not supposed to talk about it till I clear it with the boss. He'll wanna meet you. I can set that up and text you later, 'kay?"

"I don't have a phone."

"What?" She looks the same as if he said he lost all his toes climbing Mount Everest.

"It broke. We can't afford a new one right now."

"When did this happen?"

"I don't know. Weeks ago."

"Dude, you need help."

"That's what I said." He lowers his voice. "Hey, this job... it's nothing to do with drugs, is it? I won't sell them. Especially not the hard shit." Weed might be okay, though. He's that desperate.

"It isn't drugs."

"So what is it then?"

"You gotta trust me. Let me set up the meeting." She glances back and sees her bus. "Gotta go."

"Okay, see ya." He knows he should be happy about the prospect of making money. But he's afraid about what he may be getting himself into. Teshi never had any common sense. She's been getting into trouble her whole life. He can only hope this is different.

17

———

Ethan sets out to meet Teshi the next day in the late afternoon, lying to Ma, telling her he's going to Chase's house to get help with homework. She'll be passed out in her bed in no time, and she won't know when he comes home or even *if* he comes home tonight.

Teshi is pacing outside. She's tense, nervous, which makes Ethan feel the same way. He's sure now that this must be some terrible shit, and he needs to get out of it. "I changed my mind," he says.

"Whoa, you haven't even heard what I got to tell you. I talked to Antoine—that's the boss. You know what he said? You do this job tonight, and he's gonna give you an iPhone."

"You serious?"

"Yeah, man. Just this once, cuz you need it. It'll be cash pay after that."

An iPhone. Once he's got that, he can get other jobs. That's the main thing that's been holding him back.

Teshi starts walking and Ethan falls in step beside her.

"Where are we going?" he says.

"You'll see."

"You still haven't told me what we're doing."

"You'll find out."

"How am I going to know what to do?"

Teshi turns on her heel and looks at him. "Stop asking questions. It's not that hard. Just do what I do. That's all you gotta do. Do what I do. It'll be over fast." She continues walking, upping the pace.

Ethan is still worried. "I'm not going to hurt anyone, if that's what this is."

Teshi coughs out a laugh. "Are you fucking kidding me?" She pats herself down. "I'm not packin'. You packin'?"

"No."

"So, you think someone would hire us to do a hit? Two fucking kids who don't have a gun between them?"

"Maybe they're going to give us some when we get there?"

"Listen to me. I swear on my dead grammy's body, there won't be guns. We're not killing anyone. We're not even punching anyone. It's not like that."

Ethan believes her. It's true, who would be crazy enough to hire two inexperienced kids to take somebody out? They'd be bound to screw it up. Still, inside he decides that if he gets a bad feeling about this, or sees any weapons, he will run as fast as he can away from the situation. They might kill him but he couldn't hold up his head ever again if he hurt someone.

After about twenty minutes they come to the corner of an alley and Teshi tells him they need to wait there. It doesn't take long before a car drives up and stops in front of them. Teshi gets in shotgun and Ethan slides in the back.

The man who's driving gives him a broad smile in the rear-view mirror. "Hey, Ethan. I'm Antoine." He has a subtle accent Ethan can't place. He's got stubbles that aren't quite a beard, and greasy, salt-and-pepper hair pulled back tight into a short ponytail. He looks old to Ethan, at least fifty or sixty.

"You nervous?" Antoine pulls out into the street.

"A little."

"That's okay. Everyone is the first time. You'll do great. Just do as Teshi does and you'll be fine."

"Okay, I'll try."

"I knew you would. You look like a nice kid."

"Thanks."

"Teshi tells me you need a new phone. You do this job right, you'll get one. Yeah? That'll be your first pay check. Good, huh?"

"Yeah, that's good." A lot better than the twenty bucks or so he had been expecting before Teshi told him. A new phone is worth a lot more than that. And Antoine is right, that's what he needs most of all. Can't do anything else without it. But at the same time, a little alarm is ringing inside him, telling him that if he's getting paid so generously, there's something wrong with this job.

"Try to relax," Antoine says. "We'll be driving a while first." He swivels his head to throw Ethan another smile. There's no warmth behind it, and it dissolves quickly. Then he starts some music—Drake —and nobody talks.

About thirty minutes later they turn off the freeway, some place Ethan's never been before. Antoine drives around for a while before they come to a downtown area. He parks near the front of a café that has outdoor tables.

For a while, he and Teshi just stare at the place. Nothing happens, as far as Ethan can tell. It's not crowded, and since the weather's nice, some customers are sitting outside. There's one couple, and two guys alone on their computers.

At a nod from Antoine, Teshi turns back to Ethan. "Hey. You and me are gonna go in here but we're not staying long. Just do what I do, okay? Antoine will be waiting for us. Afterward, get in the car fast as you can. Okay?" Teshi hands him a baseball cap. "Wear this and pull your hood up over it." She had told him in advance to come in a hoodie. She does the same with her cap and hoodie.

Ethan is pulling on his wristband real hard. "I need to know what we're doing."

"You're doing what Teshi is doing, yeah?" Antoine says. "That's all you got to know."

This is bad, he's sure of it now. "I don't want to," he says.

Antoine twists around to stare at him with cold eyes. "Can't change your mind now. That wouldn't be fair. We're counting on you."

"Please, can you just bring me back home?" He realizes how like a child he must sound. But he is a child. A stupid, foolish child.

"No can do. You're a part of this now. You've met me, seen our methods. You have to put your skin in the game. Otherwise, what's to stop you from squealing on us?"

"I won't! Teshi knows I won't."

"What do you say, Teshi?"

She shifts in her seat. Her eyes don't meet Antoine's. *She's fucking scared of him*, Ethan thinks. She shrugs her shoulders.

"Teshi!" They haven't been friends for a while but Ethan still hadn't expected betrayal.

"Just do it, man," she says.

"Listen to your friend. You're making a big deal out of nothing. Give it a try, yeah? Then if you don't want to do it again, no problem."

Ethan wants to say no. He wants to demand Antoine drive him back home right now. He wants to tell both of them to leave him alone after that and never contact him again.

But he knows he can't do that. At best, Antoine would kick him out of the car and leave him here. How would he get home? He doesn't even have a phone to call anyone. Even if he could reach his mother, she wouldn't be able to get him. They don't have a car. They don't have money for a taxi.

So he puts on the cap and draws his hood over it. Antoine gives him a big empty smile. "You can do this, kid. I trust you. Just follow Teshi."

And he does. Teshi gets out of the car and Ethan is right behind her. They walk up to the restaurant and she leads him to the front window where there's a menu posted. They both stare at it like they're trying to decide if they want to eat here.

Teshi shakes her head. "Let's try somewhere else." In a much lower tone, she says to Ethan, "You got Baldie."

Perplexed, he glances around and sees that "Baldie" must be one of the two guys working on their laptops. Meanwhile, Teshi weaves her way past the other guy. Acting fast, she snatches the guy's laptop, then races back to Antoine's car.

Cold fear grips Ethan. He knows what he's supposed to do. He isn't even really surprised. He hates himself for it, but he knows he'll do it. The alternative is worse. Antoine will drive away, leaving him here to be arrested for a crime he didn't even commit.

Though it seems like he's been frozen in place for some seconds, it really only takes an instant for him to make his decision, race to Baldie—who's distracted by the first theft—and rip the laptop out from under his hands. Afterward he hurls himself into the backseat of Antoine's car.

Teshi lets out a whoop of joy. "Dude, you did it!"

The car takes off.

18

No one talks during the drive back from the robbery. Ethan is too frightened to say anything, and too angry at himself for getting caught up in something like this. What if he gets arrested and thrown into juvey? They might even stick him in regular jail. He could die like his father. What will happen to Ma then?

He should've known it was something like this. Teshi always had bad judgment, which was why Ethan stopped hanging with her. In fact, this exact thing happened when they were ten years old and went into a Seven Eleven together. After they came out, Teshi pulled bags of candy out of her deep pockets. Candy she hadn't paid for. That was the last time they did anything together until now.

He wonders if she checked for cameras before going ahead with the steal. Every place has cameras nowadays. Since Ethan hadn't been sure what they were going to do, he hadn't looked for them. For all he knows, one was staring straight down into his face. He feels like he might throw up.

When they get back to their own hood, Antoine pulls into a parking space. He reaches past Teshi into the glove compartment and takes out an iPhone. "You did good, kid. Here's your reward." He hands Ethan the phone. "Call it a sign-on bonus, yeah?" He laughs at his own joke. "You need this for the job. Gotta be ready when I call. It's a burner, nobody gonna trace it."

Ethan stares down at the phone. Under any other circumstances, this would be the happiest day of his life. He never had an iPhone before. It truly is worth much more than he ever expected to earn.

But he can't rejoice. He sees this thing in his hand, not as a coveted object, but like a ball and chain that will bind him to Antoine forever.

"Aren't you going to thank me?" There's mockery in his tone. He knows exactly where Ethan's reticence comes from.

"Thanks," Ethan says. "Can we go now?"

"What's your rush?" Antoine laughs again. Then he takes out his own phone, opens up a photo, and shows it to Ethan. It's a crystal-clear shot of him running from the café with the laptop in his hands. His breath catches in his throat.

"Nice picture, yeah? People say I'm good at photography. Looks just like you."

"Why'd you take that picture?" Ethan knows he shouldn't ask, but can't help himself.

"Insurance," Antoine says. "Always gotta have a little insurance. I go down, we all go down. I got a lot of these in a safe place." He glances at Teshi to remind her too.

Antoine pockets his phone. "But we don't need to worry about that. You're a good kid, I can see it. Good at doing what you're told. And see, it wasn't that hard. In and out, you grab something and run. I drive us away. Nobody gets hurt. Rich assholes have to share the wealth, that's all. Why should they get everything and nothing for us? We're just taking what we deserve."

"Yes, sir," Ethan mumbles.

"Hey, we're not formal around here. You call me Antoine."

"Okay."

"Okay who?"

"Okay, Antoine."

"Okay. Get outta here now. Both of you."

Ethan has never opened a door so fast. Teshi grabs her backpack and follows him out. Antoine guns it down the street.

"I should've never gone with you," Ethan says.

She pats his arm. "Dude. I got you a phone. Where's the gratitude?"

"It won't stop, not ever. We'll have to steal for him our whole lives."

"It's not so bad. I kinda like it."

"You kidding me?"

"You didn't feel it? The rush? I'm tingling all over right before I snatch the thing. And then, like, my whole body goes electric. Running into the car and Antoine laying on the gas to get us out of there. It's like, I don't know, jumping out of a plane or something."

Ethan doesn't see it that way. Not at all. He's all fear, no excitement. But it's hard not to love Teshi at this moment. Her smile and the way her eyes lit up. She looks more alive.

She pinches his arm. "You wanna do something else?"

"No more stealing," he says.

"No, this is different. C'mon!" She grabs his hand and pulls him behind her.

He knows this is probably another bad idea. Yet he can't resist her. He's starting to feel exhilarated too. He stole something and got away with it. He must be invincible.

They hurry down the block and Teshi leads him across an empty lot to a dark section behind a warehouse building.

"This looks good." She takes off her backpack and opens the top. "What color you want?"

He looks at her curiously.

"I got red, black, and green." She lifts out the black spray can to show him.

"Shit." He looks around, but the place is empty. "Fine, give me the green."

She hands it to him. "Let's get started."

"What're we doing?"

"Making our mark. Lemme think. What's that dude, you know, the African boy in that story you wrote?"

"Amari?"

"Right." She sprays in a clear spot, making an "A."

"What should I do?"

"I'm doing the writing. Do a picture. Whatever you want."

He looks down at the green can and gets an idea. He sprays above where the writing is going. At the same time, he keeps an eye out for cars.

Teshi switches to red and makes the "m" in Amari look like a heart, then she continues with black again.

"Car," Ethan says. They watch as headlights pass the empty lot. When it continues on past the intersection, they go back to their painting.

"Oh look at that." Teshi stops again, staring at Ethan's picture. "Four-leaf clover. That's dope."

"Could use some of that good luck right now," Ethan says.

He finishes the clover at about the same time as she finishes her sentence: *Amari was here.* "This here's our mark now. 'Amari was here' with a four-leaf clover. We can put it everywhere."

Ethan's not sure he wants to make a career out of being a graffiti artist any more than he wants to steal shit. But he says nothing to dull her enthusiasm.

Another car turns down the street and seems to slow as it nears the empty lot.

"Let's get out of here," Teshi says.

They throw the cans in her backpack and slip away into the darkness past the side of the building. When they reach the sidewalk, they slow down again, not wanting to look like they were up to anything criminal. Ethan walks her to her apartment, which is just around the corner from his.

"You're cool." Teshi pops a kiss on his lips, taking him by surprise, before dashing into her building.

That kiss almost makes everything that happened tonight worthwhile.

When he reaches his own place, he wonders what the hell he's going to say if Ma is awake and in her right mind.

He needn't have worried. She's sleeping soundly in her bed. He shuts off the TV and gets under his own covers quickly. But sleep is a long time coming.

AMARI

19

Amari lopes across the open plain with the sun beating down on him. He wants to stop to drink from his gourd, but this water is all he has and it might be a long time before he can find more.

He must keep up this pace because he delayed too long before starting his pursuit. At least it is easy to track the invaders who captured all the people of his village except for him. They trampled the main road worse than a herd of rhinoceroses. Deep footprints everywhere, broken branches, and human waste mixed in with dirt and grass.

At midday, Amari finds the invaders' abandoned camp from the night before. It includes the remains of several fires, the bones of the animals they ate, and more human waste. He glances through the area without finding anything useful and is about to leave when he spots what looks like a person lying at the far end of the clearing.

His heart sinks when he sees it is Esi, the older sister of his best friend. From her state, it is clear the invaders violated her before killing her. Amari's blood boils with the desire for vengeance. He raises his spear, shakes it at the sky, and shouts out curses against the cruel demons.

He cannot leave her like this. It goes against all the teachings of his culture. Even if he went on to rescue all his people, they would still turn their backs on him for the crime of not performing the burial rites.

He searches for the softest ground before digging a shallow grave using a sturdy branch and his own hands. The sun is low by the time he finishes. He has to drag her body there since he does not have the strength to lift her. When he has gotten her in the grave, he takes his precious gourd and drips water onto her forehead and two hands, while reciting the words he remembers. The rite is not perfect but it will have to do. Then he pushes the dirt back over her, turning away in sadness as he covers her face.

After all this, he eats a strip of dried meat from his dwindling store and runs again. He follows the invaders' trail as long as light remains. Along the way he sees smoke from another village and considers going there to beg them to replenish his food and water. But some in these parts are known to be spiteful, and he does not dare chance that they may hurt him.

When he can no longer lift his feet to take any more steps, he settles in thick grass near the road and instantly falls asleep. He does not wake until the sun is high above him.

When he looks around, he discovers that his spear, his food, and his water are gone. There is no sign of the thief, who probably came from the nearby village.

His throat is parched, his belly empty, and his hope withered.

20

———————

A*mari has no hope but to go to the nearby village, since he will not get far without water and food. When he arrives, no one pays him much attention. All are busy with the daily tasks of village life.*

He asks to speak to the village elders and is directed to them. He tells them of the theft during the night and asks for their help in finding the culprit and restoring what was stolen from him. But they are old and lazy and do not want to be bothered. "What you describe is nothing unusual," they say. "Every man owns a spear, a water jug, and food."

"But my father's spear is inscribed with the marks of our ancestors," Amari says.

"Go, it is time for our meal," they say irritably.

Amari wanders through the village hoping to spot his father's spear, but hardly anyone carries a weapon. They must all be tucked away inside their huts.

By late afternoon his throat is parched. He approaches a mother for help. "May I drink a bit of your water?" he begs.

"We have had no rain for thirty days," she says. "I cannot allow my children to go thirsty. But I will spare you two sips."

She hands over her flask and he is careful not to take more than what was offered. "Do you know of work I might find in the village to earn food, water, and a spear?"

A man who has been listening speaks up. "Our honey gatherer is ill. Can you gather honey for us?"

Amari hesitates because he has never done it before. But he has seen the honey gatherer work and knows how it is done. "Yes, I will do that," he says.

This is how he finds himself climbing the tree to the hive hanging high above the plain. The action is difficult as he carries a lit branch for smoking out the bees, a curved blade for cutting into their hive, and a bucket for catching the honey as it drains out.

He manages to perch above the hive and begins waving the branch at the bees. But suddenly the entire stick lights up—it must have been too dry —and the flames spark his long hair, which is hanging down over his shoulders. He cries out and drops everything—the branch, the bucket, the blade—and bats his head with both hands to put out the flames. He loses his balance and his foot kicks the hive. The bees race out and begin a mad stinging frenzy against the intruder.

Amari slides and falls down from the tree, banging himself up, but still managing to get to his feet and run. He runs all the way to the mud hole with the bees following and stinging all the way. He throws himself under the dirty water, holding his breath for as long as he can. Finally, the bees go away.

But when he comes out from the mudhole, he sees an angry male rhino staring at him. The rhino must have thought the hole belonged to him. He gives chase.

Amari runs for his life to another tree and climbs up it just before the rhino raises his horn to spear him. The rhino misses him by inches and continues waiting at the base of the tree for Amari to come down.

The sun has set now. Amari is stuck hanging onto branches the whole night long while his body burns from the stings of the bees, and his stomach cries out for food, and his parched throat still has not had a proper drink for two days, unless one counts the mud-filled water he accidentally swallowed.

21

———————

By dawn, the rhino has left, and it is safe for Amari to climb down from the tree. He makes his way back to the mudhole to sip water as well as he can, because he does not know where else to find any. When he has drunk enough to satisfy his thirst, he returns to the village. He still has no food to sustain him for the rest of the trip to the coast, where he must stop the slavers from getting away with his family and the other villagers.

He has decided he has no choice but to beg for what he needs. In his village, this was considered shameful, and he hopes his family will never learn of it. But he is desperate.

He stands on a corner along the main passageway through the village, and asks for the currency of the village, or food, or anything he might barter. He offers to work for whatever they give him. But instead of earning anything, he is jeered by the village folk, who have heard the story of his setting himself on fire in the tree, being attacked by bees, and nearly killed by the rhino.

At the end of the day, when his throat is parched and his stomach crying out for food, a girl of about his own age approaches. She is very thin with large, angelic eyes, and dirty hands. She wears ragged clothing and *her feet are bare. Yet she offers him her gourd of water with only a few sips remaining, and a hunk of bread.*

Amari drinks a single sip and returns the gourd so that she may have what remains. He tears the hunk of bread and hands back half of it. They devour the bread hungrily.

"I am Panya," she says.

"Amari," he says.

"I am an orphan. The people in this village are not kind. If we want something from them, we must take it."

"You mean steal?"

"Shhh." She presses her warm fingers over his lips. "Will you help me?"

He never wanted to be a thief, but if he is to survive long enough to rescue his village, he must do what is required. He follows Panya through the village until she places a hand on his chest to stop him.

A necklace has been left hanging outside someone's hut. No one is around, and before Amari can say anything, Panya has run forward and taken it. Both of them race away from the hut without being seen. Amari thinks of the thief who stole his father's spear and blames himself for being no better.

Outside the village, they come upon a trader and offer the necklace for sale. In return, they ask for whatever food and water the trader can supply them with. The trader, sensing a bargain, gives them food and water to last several days.

They set out from the village before they can be caught for the theft, and walk on the main road through most of the night. Finally, when the sky is growing lighter with the approach of dawn, they find a place to lie down out of sight of passing travelers. They eat a bit of the food and drink a bit of the water before curling up together and falling asleep.

Amari's dream is full of nightmares of how he will be punished for his thievery by being cut up into many small pieces.

REBECCA

22

2019 - MINDCAST

A flash of blinding sunlight hits her and Rebecca feels rather than sees that she's behind the wheel of a moving vehicle. A few blinks and her sight returns, just as the car careens toward the edge of the road. *There's no fucking guardrail.* Only a few yards of scrub grass before the landscape plunges toward rocks and ocean below.

She shrieks, wrenches the wheel to the left, and veers dangerously into opposing traffic. A cement truck bears down on her, its horn thundering. She swerves back toward the cliff, her sweaty hands struggling to keep a grip. The truck hurtles past her, nearly swiping her side mirror. She pumps the brake, struggling to steady herself, until she's got the car under control. Her heartbeat races.

Rebecca pulls into the next turnout and cuts the engine. Lowers her head to the wheel, taking slow breaths to stop the trembling. She screams out a string of expletives.

When she's calm enough to think again, she pieces together how she ended up here. She has just begun a mindcast back to the day Ethan Pitt disappeared. Thinking she wasn't doing anything in particular then, she set her thoughts to land a few hours before he will be seen for the last time. But now she recalls she went to Half Moon Bay to visit her old friend Chi-Ling that day. Arriving early with time to spare, she drove along the coast to enjoy the rare fog-free view.

Mindcasts are disorienting enough without landing in a moving car at the edge of goddamn Highway One. But she doesn't have time to dwell on this. She's farther away than she expected to be. She'll need to drive fast to give herself time to stop at her old apartment and change her clothes before heading to Ethan's. She restarts the engine and merges cautiously back into traffic, planning to escape this death trap of a road as soon as possible.

After reaching home, she throws on her oldest jeans with the tear across the knee. Her gray hoody looks too new, so she switches to a faded black. She pokes a hole into one of her sneakers, with the goal of appearing homeless so no one pays her any attention. A worn outfit. No makeup or jewelry. No purse even. Her money and her phone in her pockets.

Since there's no time for a meal, she shoves down cookies and a chunk of cheese. Her cell rings while she's eating, but she doesn't answer. Afterward she finds a message from Chi-Ling, who's worried that she didn't show up for their lunch date, and thinking something may have happened to her, like, say, driving off the edge of a cliff. Rebecca texts her so she won't report her missing; cops searching for her might mess up her plans for the day. *I'm so sorry, but my dad had an emergency and I had to drive to Berkeley. Everything's okay now. I'll call you later to explain.*

That ought to hold her well enough. And if she doesn't believe the story and never wants to see Rebecca again... so what? To paraphrase a well-known saying, the beauty of mindcasting is that *what happens in a mindcast stays in a mindcast.*

Before leaving, Rebecca glances around for a mask to wear before it hits her that the pandemic hasn't happened yet. She's gotten so used to the mask routine, she practically feels naked leaving the house without one. It saddens her thinking how soon the world will change, and how many thousands of lives will be lost. If only she could warn everyone, but that isn't the way a mindcast works.

She reaches Ethan's apartment with time to spare, which is lucky because there's no place to park on his block. Circling the area, she eventually finds a spot on a parallel street some distance away. She speed-walks back, not wishing to miss anything else that might go on outside the boy's home.

Wondering how she's going to lurk without being noticed, she's happy to discover a bus stop from which she can see the apartment building entrance. She settles on the bench beside a little old lady with steel-gray hair and a large purple tote bag.

There's time for her to take in her surroundings while she catches her breath. Ethan lives in a three-story building shadowed by a tall warehouse across the street. Bars line its first-floor apartment windows, and a plot of weeds welcomes visitors to the front door.

From Ethan's apartment number, Rebecca figures he must live on the second floor, but she doesn't know which way his windows face. She can only hope there's no other way out, or else she might miss his departure. If the information Aunt Yakeera gave her is correct, the boy is inside the apartment right now, warming up soup for his dinner. His mother is passed out in her bedroom, and she won't notice the uneaten bowl he left on the counter till tomorrow morning.

Rebecca only has to observe from outside the building. Either someone came and forced the boy away—her job could be over instantly if that turns out to be the case—or Ethan left of his own accord and she will need to follow him. Hopefully not very far.

That he left without eating his dinner implies something crucial came up, because how long could it take for a thirteen-year-old boy to slurp down soup before going out? This makes Rebecca wonder if a phone call came in from someone demanding to see him instantly. Someone who frightened him.

But according to Yakeera, he didn't have a working cell phone. It had broken some days earlier, and they didn't have the money to get it fixed or replaced. He also didn't own a computer, so he couldn't even have received an email. They still checked his Gmail later, of course, but there were no messages that shed any light on where Ethan went this night.

A bus drives up, blocking Rebecca's line of sight. It remains there several minutes while the old woman uses her cane to creep to the door and up the steps.

Afraid she might miss something, Rebecca walks to the end of the bus to see what's happening across the street. Sure enough, Ethan has come out, and he's already halfway down the sidewalk. His pace is fast, almost a run. He definitely acts as if someone or something has spooked him.

Rebecca struggles to catch up to him without appearing to follow him. An impossible task.

ANY MINUTE NOW, Rebecca is going to lose Ethan. At a brisk walking pace, she's falling behind, but if she runs, he's going to notice her and that could change his behavior. She needs him to do exactly what he did on this night in real-time.

Luckily there's not a lot of pedestrian traffic or she would've lost sight of him already. When she glimpses him turning right at an intersection, she breaks into a jog, but by the time she reaches that street, Ethan has disappeared.

What now? She continues at a slower pace, glancing from side to side. The road is lined with small apartment buildings, interspaced here and there by tiny homes crammed between them. The kid could've gone into any of these places.

At the end of the street, she checks the sign. Oddly, she feels like she's heard the name before but can't recall the context. She hopes it comes to her soon.

In the meantime, she hesitates between continuing in a straight direction without knowing if he turned again, or returning the same way back to her car. It was ridiculous of her to have imagined she might solve the case with one mindcast. Obviously, it's going to take longer and she just needs to be patient. Next time she can simply wait on this street until Ethan shows up. She'll continue trailing him, and even if she loses him every few blocks, she'll mindcast for as many days as it takes to learn where he's going.

But then as she turns to retrace her steps, she spots Ethan rushing out of a narrow residence on the opposite side of the road.

"Don't go!" someone shouts. Her voice sounds familiar, and Rebecca finds out why as soon as the woman darts from the house. *Aunt Yakeera.* Of course, the street name Rebecca recognized. Yakeera had given her the address.

Even in bare feet and a bathrobe, the woman is beautiful, with long, wavy hair draping her shoulders. "Ethan!" she shouts.

He pauses without looking back at her, his face pinched in anger. She runs up behind him and says something at a lower volume than Rebecca can hear. When he tries to leave again, she grasps his arm and speaks urgently into his ear.

After she lets go, he grudgingly gets into the passenger seat of the car parked in the driveway. Yakeera disappears back into the house.

It looks as if they're going somewhere. If so, Rebecca will definitely lose his trail. She won't have time to get back to her own car to follow them.

Sure enough, Yakeera returns fully dressed and carrying her purse. She gets into the driver's seat, and one minute later they're passing Rebecca and she has no way of figuring out where they're going.

She should've known it wasn't going to be easy. *You can't trust anyone to tell the truth.* Not even his own aunt who claims to be desperately seeking him. Her Facebook post that seemed like the only positive movement in the hunt for Ethan, now bears the whiff of something sinister.

Rebecca feels the tingling sensation that often precedes her jump back to real-time just as one more person emerges from Yakeera's house, slamming the door shut behind him. A man with an arrogant expression, maybe in his thirties, tall, blond, and handsome.

She just has time to note the wary manner in which he glances around, and the speed of his departure, both indicators that this isn't his house and he isn't Yakeera's husband.

23

———————

2020 - PRESENT

Rebecca sleeps in the next morning. Time travel takes its toll on her, no question about it. When she does finally get up, her hollow stomach cries out for food. She throws on clothes and is about to head to her favorite brunch spot when she sees the mask hanging near her front door. *Damn Covid.* Her favorite brunch spot has been shut down until further notice.

Putting on the mask, she heads to the corner market for eggs and frozen waffles. Later, when she's seated with her coffee and home-made breakfast (if one can call frozen waffles *homemade*), she wonders if she could get used to cooking for herself more often. It certainly would save money.

During her walk afterward, she calls Yakeera. "I have some new information I need to talk to you about. Can we meet somewhere?"

Yakeera cups the receiver and speaks to someone in muffled tones. "Hold on a sec," she tells Rebecca. This is followed by the sound of footsteps and a door closing. "Just getting some privacy. You can say whatever you have to say over the phone."

"Are you worried about the virus? We can sit outside," Rebecca says.

"Of course I'm worried. Aren't you?"

"How about Zoom, then?" If Rebecca can see her face, she might be able to sense whether she's telling the truth.

"We're not Bill Gates over here," Yakeera says.

"Fine. The phone will do. So, I wanted to let you know I've been talking to some folks in the neighborhood."

"What folks?"

"Um, I can't tell you. Confidentiality and all that. But I learned something. Ethan's mom wasn't the last to see him before he went missing."

Rebecca pauses for a response but it's silent on the other end.

"A neighbor saw Ethan run out of his apartment building. So, like, no one snatched him or anything. After that, someone else witnessed him arriving at your house. According to them, he didn't stay long. But then you came out after him and convinced him to get into your car. The two of you drove off together."

Rebecca gives Yakeera a chance to respond, but she appears to have shocked the woman into silence. She continues. "And right after the two of you drove off, some guy my witness had never seen before left your house. Tall. Good-looking. Blond."

"You can't put that in that article of yours." Yakeera has lowered her voice like she doesn't want anyone else to hear. "It's got nothing to do with Ethan."

"You say you care about your nephew. But you had information about where he was that night, and you told no one."

"What difference does it make if he disappeared from his house, or from outside the restaurant? Anyway, it didn't matter to the officer we spoke to. Took him one minute to decide Ethan was part of a gang and it was a rival gang that killed him. That didn't even make sense. Since when do gangs bother to hide the victim? They just shoot each other down—bystanders too—and leave the bodies in the street."

"But it does matter where he was last seen. I need you to be honest with me if I'm going to get at the truth."

There's a deep breath on the other end. "If you promise me nothing about that man is going to be in your article."

Since Rebecca will never write an article, she can make that promise with a clear conscience. "If he's got nothing to do with any of this, you and he have nothing to worry about. I need his name, though."

"I can't tell you that."

Rebecca decides not to press her. "You mentioned a restaurant. Is that where you took Ethan?"

"His favorite place. Dos Amigas. He loves Mexican food."

"Me too. Was there a particular reason for going out to eat right then?"

"I'll level with you," Yakeera says. "Ethan walked in on me and my man. He's married. And his wife has some dough. I don't care about it; I just like having a little fun with this dude. But I didn't want to wreck things for him, so I ran after Ethan and told him we needed to talk. I had to ask him not to mention what he saw to anyone, especially his mom." She lowers her voice to a whisper. "She's a big gossip."

"Did Ethan agree not to say anything?"

"Sure. He's a good kid."

"After dinner, where did you and he go?"

"He didn't stay through dinner. Said he was using the bathroom and didn't come back. I don't know what happened. I assumed he saw someone he knew and went off with them. But that's the mystery."

Rebecca considers for a second. "What about your lover? You say he's got a wife. Maybe he was more upset than you thought about Ethan catching you two together."

"What're you saying? You think my man killed him? That's bullshit. No way."

Rebecca says nothing.

"Don't you go off in that direction. Just find out where Ethan went when he left the restaurant. That's the key. My man's got nothing to do with it."

"Okay," Rebecca says, just to keep the peace. "I'll see what I can find out. One other thing. It would help if you got me a list of anyone who was close to Ethan, with their physical addresses, phone numbers, email addresses. Pictures too, if you have any. I'm talking about relatives, friends, mentors. Anyone Ethan spent time with." She figures this may save her time while she's following the boy around in mindcasts. It would be good to recognize right away if he's meeting up with someone he knows, or if it's a stranger.

"You sure don't ask for much."

"Can't you find that stuff on his phone?" Kids' whole lives are on their phones these days. All their friends. All the websites they visit, the social media where they're active. All the texts and emails right there for anyone to read.

"His phone broke before he went missing. Remember? His mother couldn't afford to get him a new one. It was unusable, so we couldn't even check it to find out who's on his friend list, or who texted him recently."

Rebecca did remember, but she thought there must be other ways to get that information. "Couldn't the police find that out by checking with the phone company?"

"If they did that, they're not telling us," Yakeera says.

"Maybe you can use another phone to access his cloud storage?" Rebecca says.

"Like I said, we're not Bill Gates over here."

"Right." Rebecca isn't exactly Bill Gates either.

"I'm sorry I didn't tell you about the restaurant," Yakeera says. "Ethan's mother and I are grateful for your help. Please, find out what happened to our boy."

24

2019 - MINDCAST

Though a year has passed since Ethan's disappearance, Rebecca feels an urgency to find him. If he's alive, every day might be a fresh new torture. Now that she's begun this search, it would feel like a betrayal even just to pause for a bit. Concern for him has wrapped itself around her heart, squeezing and twisting to goad her into constant movement.

Which is why she dives directly into a new mindcast the night after her phone call with Yakeera. This time she avoids the near plummet off the ocean cliff, and still makes it to Dos Amigas Restaurant before Yakeera and Ethan.

She snags a table beside the window facing the parking lot so she'll be able to see when they arrive. It would've been nice to arrange a spot within listening distance, but even if she'd been able to time her arrival directly after theirs, and even if there was an empty table next to them, and even if she convinced the hostess to seat her there, she probably wouldn't hear their conversation. The restaurant is crowded with families talking (and screeching) at maximum volume, competing to be heard above all the other raised voices.

Rebecca orders an appetizer and a cup of coffee. "Can I pay for this now? I won't be getting anything else." She'll nurse her drink and guacamole for as long as it takes, and then she needs to be ready to leave in an instant.

"No problem." The server wanders off.

Before the food arrives, Yakeera's car veers into the lot and swerves into the first empty spot. She and Ethan spill out and head toward the entrance, the boy a few steps ahead of his aunt. His expression is troubled, his shoulders dipped. It hits Rebecca that this is the last time anyone in his family will see him. Something terrible is about to happen to this child, and she is now tasked with witnessing it. The thought makes her hands shake, causing a few drops of coffee to spill out.

The hostess seats them in the middle of the restaurant, giving Rebecca a view of Yakeera's face and the back of Ethan's head. She's way too far to eavesdrop, unfortunately.

Yakeera does most of the talking and she's quite animated, though that might be her normal state. After they place their order, she opens her purse, fishes inside for a wad of bills, then pushes them across the table to Ethan. He whisks them into his pocket.

Rebecca wonders if she's paying for Ethan's silence in the matter of the boyfriend. She didn't mention doing that. The whole thing strikes Rebecca as odd. Why was it so important to preserve this secret?

Maybe she should go outside and prepare to follow Ethan now. But their food hasn't arrived, and she doubts the boy could summon up the fortitude to give up a free meal at the restaurant his aunt said was his favorite, however much he might need to leave and possibly meet up with someone.

She waits, finishing her chips and dip. When her plate is taken away, she continues to sip her coffee as if she has all the time in the world, though several people in the waiting area are casting dirty looks her way.

When their food arrives, Ethan attacks it like it's going to bolt if he doesn't eat it all first. At this rate, he'll be done in a few minutes. She believes she's witnessed the one significant action here—the handing over of the cash. She gets up to leave.

Outside, she heads toward her Honda in the parking lot. Best to be out of sight when the boy comes out. But as she crosses in front of the restaurant, she notices a man seated in his car watching the dining area. At first, she figures he's just waiting for someone. But on further thought, it seems strange he's doing nothing but staring into the building. When she waits for someone, she does stuff on her phone. Checks email, listens to podcasts, plays games. He's not even holding his phone.

She turns like she's searching for someone in the lot, but actually she's throwing glimpses into his car. There's plenty of light spraying out from the restaurant, plus a nearby street lamp, so when he leans forward just a bit, she gets a better view of his features.

It's the man who was at Yakeera's place. The guy who's sleeping with her.

Her body tingles with excitement. *It must be him.* He has a motive to kill Ethan. He wants to silence the boy.

His gaze shifts to her. *Crap.* She hopes her face didn't reveal the surprise and even fear that she was feeling on seeing him. While the man watches, she pretends to wave at someone in the distance and moves on with determined steps. At the same time, she's getting out her cell, positioning it so that hopefully he can't see it. She clicks a photo of his license plate as she passes.

Continuing toward her car, she glances back and sees his eyes in the rearview mirror. His door opens; he must've glimpsed her taking the picture. Panic fills her as she throws herself into her car, wondering how she'll deal with him if he confronts her.

But then he pulls his car door shut again, starts his engine, and reverses out of his spot. Ethan has just come out of the restaurant by himself, having given Yakeera the slip. Rebecca gets out of her car, ready to follow him on foot.

Boyfriend drives up alongside Ethan, lowers the passenger window, and calls out his name. The boy stops and peers into the car. Looking both surprised and annoyed, he glances around as if seeking a means of escape. But Boyfriend must still be talking to him, and

Ethan keeps listening. After several more seconds, he opens the door and gets in. The car takes off.

Crap again. Rebecca dives back into her own car, starts the engine, flings it into reverse, and screams toward the exit, frightening an older couple on their way out of the restaurant.

But when she reaches the street, Boyfriend's car has disappeared. She drives to the nearest intersection and scans in each direction. No sign of them. They're gone.

There's still something she can do during this mindcast, however. She drives a bit further and pulls into a supermarket parking lot. It's 8:45, not too late. She gets out her phone and calls Freddie, the detective who was in charge of the investigation into her sister's disappearance.

He might not be pleased that she's still using his private number. That was for Sadie, but now that she's been found, there's no more excuse for her to have her own direct access to a cop. Still, she hopes he'll understand.

He picks up after three rings. His voice is gruff; maybe she interrupted something. "I hope everything's all right," he says right after greeting her.

"Yeah, yeah, it's all good. Except just this one thing." She wonders if she should have a little banter with him first to lighten the mood, but she feels the tension in his voice and there's no doubt he wants to end this call as soon as possible. "I'm wondering if you can trace a California license plate for me."

Dead silence on the other end. Then finally, "What's this about?"

"A car dinged mine in a parking lot tonight. The asshole left without a note or anything. Jerk."

"How do you know the license plate?"

"Oh, I... well, the car looked kind of sketch, so I glanced at the number on my way into the restaurant. You know, I'm good with numbers. I remember them."

More silence. "It might not even have been that same car."

"Pretty sure it was."

He sighs. "I wish I could help you. But the best way for you to deal with this is file a report with the local police. They should be able to help you. If they're not helpful, you can get back to me."

"Really? That sounds like it will take a whole lot of time."

"It shouldn't. Now, unless there's something else you want to tell me, I need to hang up."

It was her turn to sigh. "Well... if maybe there was some other reason I really need the number, what would you recommend?"

"What other reason?"

It hits her she's still in a mindcast. Whatever she says, Freddie won't remember in real-time. She can afford to take a chance. "It has to do with another kidnapping case."

"Oh boy. Do I have to remind you what happened the last time you investigated a case on your own?"

He is referring to her being left for dead at the bottom of a ravine and just barely surviving. "It isn't like that. This is about a boy who—"

"I'm sorry, I can't condone this. If you have some legitimate information, come talk to me about it and I'll see what I can do. Otherwise, we're done here."

They were definitely done.

25

2020 - PRESENT

The day after her time jump to the restaurant, Rebecca is planning her next move. Clearly Freddie is not going to be at her beck and call, and she can't really blame him. Sticking her nose into a missing person's case is probably not a safe thing to do, and Freddie, as a police officer, is all about preserving public safety. Plus, he knows her, and knows she'll take dangerous chances when she feels they're called for. He isn't about to make that lifestyle easier for her.

She needs to hire a private eye. Someone who can identify the owner of the car Ethan got into right after leaving the restaurant, on the night he disappeared. It's going to cost her, but she can afford it, for now.

Freddie must've encountered some private eyes in the course of his investigations. It can't hurt to ask. She believes there would be nothing illegal about his telling her the name of someone he respects.

She texts him so that it seems ultra-casual. *Do you know a private investigator in the Bay Area that you can recommend? Asking for a friend.* Hopefully, keeping it light will prevent him from getting concerned about it.

Only a few minutes pass before her phone buzzes with the reply. *Ian Slate*, followed by a phone number. Excited, Rebecca texts her thanks, calls Mr. Slate immediately. and leaves him a message.

He returns her call two hours later. "Ms. Danser?" His voice is a smooth baritone.

"It's Rebecca."

"This is Ian Slate."

"Thanks for getting back to me. I was wondering if you could help me trace—"

"If you don't mind, I prefer to meet with prospective clients in person first."

"During Covid?

"I mean, over Zoom."

"Sure, but it's just a small job at the moment. Might lead to more work, but I don't know."

"That's all right," he says. "No matter how small the job, my policy is to begin with a face-to-face meeting. Old-fashioned, I know, but it's the way I roll."

She hesitates. It seems like a lot of trouble just to trace a license plate. On the other hand, if she needs his services in future it's best to get the meeting part out of the way. "I'm pretty open." *Translation: absolutely nothing is on my schedule.*

"Tomorrow morning at nine?" he asks.

She agrees and after they hang up, Rebecca is left thinking it might be good for her to have a night off from mindcasting. Lately she has been getting headaches. Ibuprofen generally takes care of them, but she does fear they'll get worse if she pushes her body too hard. She doesn't have any way of knowing the long-term effects of traveling through time.

Yet the thought of delaying the search for Ethan even one more day causes a churning inside her.

A FEW MINUTES BEFORE NINE, Rebecca settles next to the small table she set up for Zoom conversations. Thinking that at some point she might need to interview for a job via Zoom, she actually Googled advice on recommended backgrounds and lighting before choosing this spot. Behind her is a blank cream-colored wall and a low shelf. The advice told her not to have anything too distracting in the background or whoever she's speaking to will focus on that instead of her. However, the advice then contradicted itself by suggesting one or two personal items would help to prove she's not a robot. For this reason, she placed a family portrait and a fake plant on the otherwise empty shelf.

However, because Rebecca is an extremely private type of person, the family portrait is not actually of her family. It shows two parents and two daughters, the older of whom looks a little like Rebecca. The daughters are roughly twelve and ten. Anyone who actually knows Rebecca would realize the photo could not be of her family, because at these ages, Sadie was kidnapped and her mother was dead.

The Zoom link arrives precisely on time, scoring one point for the prospective P.I. The connection goes right through, and she is immediately looking at a man of around forty, with his auburn hair and beard neatly groomed. He's quite slender, and it appears he is also tall, though it's hard to judge when the person is seated. Overall, he's like a cross between George Clooney and Andrew Garfield, with the face of the former and the lean physique of the latter. He's dressed with a European flair in a tan blazer over a plain black T-shirt. His neat presentation makes her wish she'd worked a little harder on hers.

After their greetings, he sips from a tiny glass filled with what looks like tea.

"Is that all you're having?" she says.

"The tea? I learned this in Istanbul. It stays hotter when you drink it in a small cup and keep refilling it. I like my tea very, very hot."

"I see. Do I need to tell you about myself, or have you already found out everything?"

"I'm sure you would expect no less of a P.I. Congratulations on the safe return of your sister. You were quite brave to stand up to those kidnappers."

"I wish I had done a few things differently."

"Don't we all. Tell me why it is you need a private investigator after having found your sister already."

She has thought about how she will answer this. "I'm sure you can imagine what it would feel like to have a family member missing for so many years. How you almost wish they were dead because at least then they wouldn't be suffering."

He gives a subtle nod.

"Having felt that for so many years," she continues, "I hate the thought of others going through it. I guess it wasn't enough for me to save my sister. I want to save others who've gone missing too."

"How do you propose to do that, aside from hiring me?"

"I have certain skills. I'd rather not go into that part. Let's just say, I'd like to use your services for the smaller jobs that require access to records and so on. In this case, I'm just looking for someone to trace a license plate number. There could be more jobs later, but I'm not sure. Maybe another case eventually. It kind of depends on how this one goes. Is this worth your while? Right now, I simply need that trace."

"I can do that for you. And I'm intrigued regarding your goals. I'd also like to make better use of my skills. Unfortunately, I mostly get infidelity cases. Although sometimes I help a person who really needs to be convinced to exit their marriage for their own well-being, it's more often an excuse for an overly controlling husband to keep his wife on a leash." He drains the tea from his glass before setting it down. "Can you tell me more about what you're working on now?"

She considers it, then shakes her head. "Sorry. I'm not ready to share. I barely have enough money to support myself and not much extra to pay for your services. At this point I expect to be doing most everything myself."

"All right. I can do this job for you, and if that's all there is, okay. I'll need you to sign paperwork and put down a retainer. If you send me the plate number, I can get on that later today. It won't take long."

"Sounds good." She's distracted trying to read the titles on the bookshelf behind him. It's clear now why the typical Zoom advice says to keep the background empty.

"You love mysteries, I see." She nods toward the books. One row features Sherlock, another, Hercule Poirot. Other classic sleuths are represented too.

"I always wanted to be a detective," he says.

"Do you play the violin?" A case rests at the center of one of the shelves.

"You might say so." Ian Slate seems rather on-the-nose, from his slick name to his European flair, his mystery collection, and his violin (that his hero Sherlock also played). But she rather likes him for it.

"Don't forget to water your plant," he says before ending their meeting.

She laughs to herself. Was he being sarcastic? She likes that too.

IAN SLATE IS true to his word. He calls a few hours after their meeting with the name of Yakeera's boyfriend—Craig Ballard—and his address and phone number.

"There's something else that may interest you." He sounds pleased regarding whatever he's about to reveal.

"Oh?"

"He's a lawyer turned politician. Running for the California Assembly in 2020."

"Really?" She can't keep the excitement out of her voice. It all makes sense now. Yakeera's story about being worried that Ballard's wife might find out the truth from Ethan did not add up. Even if the boy told his mother, and she blabbed to the whole neighborhood about Yakeera's hook-up with Ballard, how would that ever reach the man's wife? She definitely did not run in the same circles as Ethan's family.

If the man was aiming for a career in politics, though, that was a whole different thing. His opponent would be looking for dirt on him. Rebecca doesn't really know how it all works, but there's no question someone in public office has to be squeaky clean these days, or it's going to come out.

"Does that help?" Ian says.

"It could be related. Thank you."

"Let me know if I can do anything else."

After they hang up, Rebecca considers calling Ballard before rejecting the idea. Too easy for him to blow her off on the phone. She needs to go to his place, and the best way to do it is during a mind-cast. She relishes having the power to question him without his even knowing about it in real-time.

26

———————

2019 - MINDCAST

Rebecca decides on jumping back to a week after Ethan vanished. His disappearance will be public knowledge by then, at least for the tiny portion of the public that knows him. If Ballard is innocent, the details of where and when he picked up Ethan, and where and when he dropped him off, will still be fresh in his mind. And if he's guilty, he'll be more likely to be jumpy about it in these early days and possibly give himself away. He's probably not expecting anyone to connect him to the case, and it might really throw him off when she does.

After landing in the past, Rebecca sets out directly for Ballard's house. She turns up his winding driveway by 6:30 on the Monday evening following Ethan's disappearance. It seemed like a good choice for finding Ballard at home. *Who goes out on a Monday?* Rebecca never did, but then again, she rarely went out any other night either.

The house is a stunning contemporary, high in the hills with a view of the bay. If this place came from his wife's fortune, it gave him even stronger motivation—along with preserving his political career —to keep anyone from learning about his affair with Yakeera.

A Tesla and a Maserati are displayed in the driveway, more signs of their wealth. She hopes it's also a sign that he's home. She parks behind the Maserati and proceeds to the front entrance.

Rebecca rings twice before a woman's high-heeled footsteps approach. The woman speaks through the door. "If you're here to sell us anything, whether it's magazines or religion, you've come in vain."

"I'd like to speak to Mr. Ballard regarding a criminal investigation."

There's a brief silence. She definitely hadn't been expecting that. "Are you a police officer?"

"No, a private investigator."

Mrs. Ballard opens the door and looks her over. "What are you investigating?"

"I'm sorry, but I'm only authorized to speak to your husband about it."

The woman appears to hover between her desire to throw Rebecca out and her curiosity to learn what this is all about. Her curiosity wins. "Wait here."

She takes her time going up the stairs. A few minutes later, Ballard trots down with his wife following. Rebecca recognizes him as the man she saw leaving Yakeera's home.

"Mr. Ballard?" she says.

"Yes." He doesn't offer his hand.

"I'm Rebecca Danser. Could we speak in private?"

He throws a nervous glance at his wife, who directs a cold stare back at him. "Sure," he says. "This way."

He leads Rebecca to a study and closes the door. "Have a seat."

"I'm fine here." She leans against the desk, hoping to be at least a little intimidating in a way that wouldn't be possible if she sunk down into one of the plush chairs.

He also remains standing, probably for the same reason. Since he's taller than she is, it appears he's won the intimidation contest. "What's this all about?"

"A boy named Ethan Pitt. You probably heard he's gone missing?"

"Ethan…? I'm not sure who you mean."

"Yakeera McDade's nephew. I think you know him."

He gives her a puzzled look. "Yakeera, my haircutter? She might've mentioned him; she talks a lot while she's doing my hair. I don't know the kid. I barely even know her."

Unfortunately, he appears to be an excellent liar. Rebecca knows for a fact that Ballard picked Ethan up in his car, and yet he looks like he's telling the truth. Maybe they teach this skill in learning-how-to-be-a-politician school. Or maybe she needs to get better at reading people's expressions. She must find out if there's a class she can take. "Look. I'm not trying to embarrass you in front of your wife. But Yakeera told me she was having an affair with you."

He snorts. "That's a lie."

"Why would she lie about a thing like that?"

"How would I know what motivates her? Maybe someone paid her. Or maybe she's crazy and likes to make up stories about her clients. You know she's a wanna-be actress, right?"

His dismissive attitude only annoys Rebecca further. "You should know I have another witness. Someone who saw you leaving Yakeera's house."

Did that cause a little flinch? She's not sure.

He recovers immediately, however. "Again, this person is lying. I don't know their motivation. Maybe you should ask them. If you've got nothing better, this conversation is over."

"According to Yakeera, Ethan accidentally walked in on the two of you. And you were worried he might tell others."

"Is that what this is about? You think I did something to stop him from talking? That's truly ridiculous." He steps toward the door.

"Another witness saw you pick him up in your car outside the Dos Amigas Restaurant."

He hesitates. *Is that a line of moisture popping out on his forehead?* But he isn't ready to talk, that's for sure. He opens the door. "I think you know your way out."

Rebecca takes her time crossing the room.

"One thing I do remember," he says. "Yakeera was worried about that kid. She thought he was getting into some serious shit."

"Like what?"

"You know. Drugs. Gangs. Guns. He lives in a tough neighborhood. That's how it goes."

27

2019 - MINDCAST

The next time Rebecca mindcasts, she's back to the night Ethan disappeared, waiting in her car outside Dos Amigas Restaurant. This time around, she has not gone into the place at all. When she arrived, she eased backward into the parking spot so she would be ready to drive away at a second's notice.

She saw Ballard arrive twenty minutes ago. Since then, they have both watched and waited; him the mouse, and her, the cat ready to give chase.

She tenses as the restaurant door flies open and Ethan jogs out. The scene replays itself, with Ballard backing up, easing next to him, and the boy getting into his car. But this time Rebecca starts her car and follows them out of the lot.

Tailing Ballard isn't as hard as she thought it would be. Traffic is light, and even in the dark she can distinguish his Tesla up ahead. He doesn't appear to be worried about anyone tracking him. He signals before each turn, obeys the speed limits, and even drives courteously.

She's getting complacent by the time the light turns yellow at an upcoming intersection and Ballard makes it through. Though it's red when she gets there, she's planning to continue anyway, except a line of cars in the green light direction has already started across. She slams on her brakes, barely avoiding a collision. Fuming, she watches the back of Ballard's car as it signals a left turn up ahead.

When she finally gets the green, she floors it to the next intersection, where the red light blocks her again. Ballard is long gone by the time she turns onto the street where she last saw him.

She pulls into a gas station, parks on the side, and bangs on the steering wheel. Tailing a car is much harder than she imagined, especially in the dark. There has to be a better way to find out what happened to Ethan.

When Rebecca first became involved in the search for Ethan Pitt, she had imagined jumping back once, watching him get picked up by someone and figuring out who that someone was. *Voilà!* Mystery solved.

She knows now it's going to be much harder. Although Ballard still appears to be the number one suspect, she could spend forever just trying to tail him across town.

Naturally she had hoped for a quick solution. But this *following people about* no longer feels like the right approach. She needs to dig deeper, to get an understanding of Ethan and his friends and family. It will be a better use of her time to act like a cop or a private eye, by talking to people, hearing what they have to say, drawing out their stories. Then she should have a better understanding of where to focus her energy.

At first, she considered interviewing all the players in real-time. But a year has passed and their memories will be fuzzy. If instead she talks to everyone a week after Ethan has gone missing, their memories will be fresh, their emotions raw.

She should not have waited this long to seek out Ethan's mother. Laila must know her child better than anyone. It has to be possible to glean something from her.

Rebecca's next mindcast brings her to Ethan's apartment building, in the early evening a week after he's vanished. She has put some effort into her appearance for this visit. Unlike her previous time here, when she hoped no one would notice her, she thinks it might help to look like someone successful. Someone who has influence and might make a difference in the search for Ethan. Before coming, she styled her hair and applied more makeup than usual. She put on gold dangling earrings and three small hoops in the upper holes of her left ear. Also bangles on her right wrist. She dresses in the most fashionable outfit she has, basically *older student chic*. The goal is to appear hip, intelligent, and concerned. She has no idea if she's succeeded.

Ringing their apartment buzzer with one hand, and hanging onto a box of blueberry muffins with the other, she waits for an answer. Maybe Laila went out for an errand. It doesn't seem likely she'd be gone long, though. A woman whose child has recently disappeared isn't likely to stray far from her home.

Ten minutes later a man arrives and gets out his key to let himself into the building.

"Excuse me," Rebecca says. "Do you know Laila Pitt? She's not answering her buzzer."

"Laila moved out," he says. "Living with her sister, I think."

"Yakeera?" Rebecca doesn't know if there may be more than one.

"I think that's her name."

"Thank you."

He nods and lets himself in.

Rather than look around for parking again, Rebecca walks to Yakeera's house. The woman doesn't know her yet, which hopefully will be to her advantage.

Yakeera answers her door quickly, beautifully turned out, with flowing hair and large silver hoop earrings. The expert application of eyeliner adds a kind of soulful depth to her toffee-colored eyes. "Can I help you?"

"My name is Rebecca Danser. I'm a freelance journalist. I heard about your nephew, Ethan Pitt. I'd like to do a story on his disappearance and I was wondering if I could talk to you and Ethan's mother."

Her eyes sharpen with suspicion. "What paper are you with?"

"I'm freelance. I don't work for a paper. I write the story and then try to sell it."

"And why on earth would you think any paper would pay money for Ethan's story?"

This conversation feels like déjà vu. Rebecca repeats the same explanation she gave to Yakeera in real-time, how she wants to change things, how it's about time people of color got some respect and attention. Yakeera counters with the same objections as before, but eventually Rebecca's arguments prevail.

Ethan's aunt takes a deep breath before glancing back into the house. "Okay." She widens the door opening. "Come in. We'll see what you've got to say for yourself."

"Here, I brought these." Rebecca hands over her offering of muffins.

"How'd you know I love these?" Yakeera's face brightens.

Rebecca smiles and doesn't say she read it on her social media.

"Would you like some coffee?" Yakeera says.

"No thanks, just water." Rebecca glances around. Classic horror movie posters, beautifully framed, hang from the walls. *Psycho*, *The Creature from the Black Lagoon*, *The Bride of Frankenstein*, and *A Nightmare on Elm Street* are among those Rebecca is familiar with. There are several other films she doesn't know.

"I don't think I've seen this," Rebecca says, staring at the blood-splattered artwork for *The Beast of Hampstead Moor*.

The look in Yakeera's eyes deadens. She raises her arm and points with a limp hand. "May I show you the crypt?" Her voice quavers like a witch's cackle.

At Rebecca's incredulous expression, she laughs. "My one line in that film."

"Oh wow. You just sent chills down my spine. I didn't know you were an actress."

She shrugs. "You know how it is. Unless you break in big-time, you need another job to support yourself. Probably half the Uber drivers in LA are aspiring actors."

She gestures for Rebecca to sit down. The furniture is simple, modern, and there's not too much of it. Throw pillows and blankets add a sense of warmth to the main room. Dishes are put away, counters wiped.

A petite woman is seated in the corner. Her gaze is on Rebecca, yet her eyes seem unfocused.

"This is my sister Laila," Yakeera says. "Ethan's mother."

"Nice to meet you," Rebecca says.

Laila doesn't reply.

"How are you feeling, honey?" Yakeera says.

Laila nods.

"My sister got a concussion recently. It's been tough for her. Expressing herself is hard. She can listen all right. Have a seat, um..."

"Rebecca," she reminds her.

"Rebecca. Right," Yakeera says.

"Do you mind if I record our conversation?"

Yakeera looks at Laila, who nods.

"It's fine."

Rebecca can't bring a recording back with her to real-time, but she's doing her best to convince them she's an actual professional writer. It also could help her to review the conversation before leaving the mindcast. She sits near Laila and sets up her phone on the table between them.

"Before I start, I just wanted to express my deepest sympathy for what you're going through right now. I also want you both to know that I understand it because I've experienced something similar. My sister was abducted when she was four and has never been found." At this point in time, Sadie is still missing.

Yakeera's face fills with concern as she shifts her gaze to her own sister. Laila too appears saddened by Rebecca's disclosure. *Good.* She hopes this will make them more cooperative.

"I'm really sorry," Yakeera says.

"Can you tell me about Ethan? What's he like? What does he enjoy doing? Who are his friends? And so on."

Yakeera glances at Laila, but it's clear she isn't up to answering something so comprehensive. "I'll tell you what I can. Ethan is the sweetest, most good-hearted kid I know. Yeah, I'm his aunt, but still, if he was a mean little SOB, I would tell you."

"Okay."

"He's never had a lot of friends, has he?" Yakeera looks to Laila for confirmation. Laila shakes her head.

"But it isn't because he's not nice. He's just introverted. He daydreams a lot. He likes stories and writing. Laila, can I show her the story he was writing?"

She's getting up before Laila even finishes nodding. She goes into another room and returns with a folder, sits beside Rebecca on the couch, and opens it. "It's about this boy in Africa, trying to figure out what to do after his whole village is kidnapped by slavers."

Rebecca skims the first couple of paragraphs. "This is really well-written. Could I borrow it?" She hopes to get a chance to read all of it before the mindcast ends.

"Yes," Laila says, before Yakeera can ask her.

Yakeera hands Rebecca the folder. "You see, he's really smart and good at his schoolwork. I can't remember him ever getting into trouble. That's why none of this makes any sense."

"What about his friends? Has he made any new ones lately? Anyone who might be a bad influence?"

"We've been talking about that. We don't really know who his friends are now. You know, he's a teenager. Did you tell your parents who your friends were then?"

"Not if I could help it," Rebecca says.

"Right. So, sure, we know who he played with in elementary school, but we've got no idea who he's hanging with now."

"Is there anything else in his life that might be affecting him?"

Yakeera shoots a look at Laila, who finally speaks. "It's been hard for my boy, these last few weeks. I lost my job. Then I got hit by a car. I get these headaches... it's like someone driving a nail through your head. I have to take stuff for the pain. I haven't been there like I should for my boy. He's been taking it hard. Trying to get a job to make money for us. It's been so hard. Nothing to fall back on."

"I'm very sorry to hear about your setbacks. What kind of job was he trying to get?"

"Dog-walker and I'm not sure what else. But it's hard finding work when you're thirteen."

"So he didn't actually get a job?"

Laila shakes her head. "Least not that I know of."

Rebecca thinks for a moment. There's something here, for sure. A sensitive kid like Ethan might be frantic over his mother losing her job, becoming ill, and their having no income. He might've tried other ways of making money.

"Does he have any adults in his life, aside from the two of you? A favorite teacher, coach, or pastor?" Rebecca is thinking if there is such a person, they'll be the next one to interview.

"He likes Mr. Flannery. That's his English teacher. He helped him become a better writer. And he told me he liked the gym teacher. A new guy this year. I can't remember his name."

"Okay, good, that's helpful. Is there any adult in his life you think might be a bad influence?"

Laila gets an expression like she's fuming. "His no-good uncle."

"Oh? What's his name?"

"Ray Pitt," Yakeera says. "He lives at the tent city under the freeway." She describes how to find it after Rebecca asks for clarification.

"He talked his brother—Ethan's father—into some drug deal," Laila says, warming to her narrative. "They got caught, got prison time for it. My husband became ill and died in there. That's what they said. Wouldn't be surprised if someone stuck a knife in him and they lied about it."

"Ray served his time and got out," Yakeera says. "I don't think he's so bad. It's tough getting a job when you're an ex-con. I've seen him with Ethan. He loves the boy."

Clearly Laila doesn't agree. "Someone who broke the law is always going to be a bad influence on my boy."

"Do you think he might be responsible for taking Ethan somewhere?"

Laila shrugs. "Police said Ethan's not with him and he's just sleeping in that camp most the time."

Still, another avenue to be investigated, though Rebecca is not looking forward to visiting the homeless camp.

"Have you looked through Ethan's belongings? Did that turn up anything interesting?"

"We did," Yakeera says. "Didn't find anything that would explain his disappearance. Most interesting thing we found was that story." She nods at the folder in Rebecca's lap.

"Is there anything else you can think of that might be relevant to Ethan going missing?" Rebecca says.

After a moment's silence, the sisters look at each other, shake their heads.

Rebecca stops the recording and pockets her phone. She stands up. "Thank you. I'll be in touch if I learn anything new."

Laila's eyes fill with tears. "Let us know right away if you find out anything."

It's hard for Rebecca to restrain her own tears on leaving the house. But she straightens her spine. She knows from experience the only way to move forward is to force herself not to dwell on feelings of misery or hopelessness.

She tries to read Ethan's story inside her car but has barely begun the second chapter before the mindcast ends.

28

―――――――

2019 - MINDCAST

Rebecca did a little research to confirm the location of the homeless encampment where Ethan's Uncle Ray had been living. He isn't living there anymore because it was cleared out by local authorities.

But her focus is on the past. On the night following her mindcast to Yakeera and Laila, she jumps back to the same day again. It's helpful to know what she was doing that afternoon—hanging around her apartment until it was time to go to work. This way she doesn't accidentally land in a version of herself that's behind the wheel of a car.

She dresses down again for her visit to the tent city. Faded hoodie, jeans that have a tear in them, dirty sneakers. No makeup or purse. She almost looks homeless herself. To complete the façade, she arrives by bus. Seems safer than parking in or walking through a sketch part of town.

It isn't possible to miss her destination, a messy array of color and grime looming ahead of her. She has to admit, homeless people make her uncomfortable, maybe because some are aggressive panhandlers, and others just sound batshit crazy. They need help, obviously. Food, housing, and healthcare, *dammit*. America. The richest country in the world and you have to pay for healthcare.

Dozens of people are here. Many lie wrapped in sleeping bags, or even just garbage bags. A woman in a wheelchair who has a streak of purple in her white hair is petting a stuffed poodle in her lap. She glances up at Rebecca approaching and calls out to her. "Hey, you're new here."

Rebecca usually avoids talking to the homeless, a policy that suddenly strikes her as cruel and elitist. "That's right," she says to the woman, who has strips of cloth wrapped around her hands and wrists. Whether it's to bandage them or keep them warm, Rebecca can't tell.

"What's your name?"

"Rebecca."

"I'm Martha." She smiles, revealing a missing eyetooth on the left. She rocks in her wheelchair. "I think we're full up here. You should go to the other one."

"Thank you, but I need to be here."

"You should go, you should go." She gets agitated. "It's too crowded, too many people."

"I'm looking for someone. Ray Pitt. Do you know him?"

"He's a Ray of sunshine. Cray-cray, ray-ray." She repeats this a few more times and ends it with a hefty, uncovered sneeze.

Rebecca's hand goes instinctively to her face, and for a second, she's horrified at not having a mask on. She calms down when she remembers this is pre-Covid.

"Do you know where he is?" she says.

"That way." Martha points. "He lives that way. Watch your step."

"Thanks." Rebecca isn't sure if she's warning her to avoid soiling her feet with garbage or if she doesn't want her to tromp accidentally on some poor soul passed out on the ground. Either way, it's good advice.

As she continues through the camp, she wishes she had money or food to offer. But she didn't dare bring anything, afraid that if she gave something away, others would notice and overwhelm her trying to get a share for themselves.

Before long she spots a thin black man folded into a beach chair, scribbling into a notebook in his lap. It could be Ray; Yakeera said he enjoyed writing. Rebecca approaches and says his name.

When he doesn't look up, she wonders if this is some other writer in the group. But after she repeats his name louder, he squints up at her.

"Are you Ray? Ethan's uncle?" she says.

This gets his interest. "My boy. Has he turned up?"

She shakes her head. "I'm sorry. Do you mind if I ask you some questions about him?"

"Who are you?"

"My name is Rebecca Danser."

"Social worker?"

She nods. It seems easier than going into the whole writer ruse. "I'm trying to help find him. Like, trace his movements up to the day he went missing. When was the last time you saw him?"

"Police asked me this, and I said the same thing. He was here a couple weeks ago and I brought him to the pickup spot. You know, where contractors find guys to dig holes and stuff. The kid was worried about making money. I told him he could come, but they probably wouldn't take him. And they didn't."

"Did he go home after that?"

"I guess. I got picked, and I had to leave him there. I didn't think he was in any danger. The kid's been around these streets for a while. He knows how to handle himself."

That he's missing seems to contradict that, in Rebecca's mind. "Did he talk about what he might do if he didn't get picked? Like, other ways he might earn money?"

"He said something about walking dogs. I think his teacher recommended that."

Next stop, teacher.

"His teachers always like him. You know how smart he is?"

"I think so. I read some writing of his. It was amazing."

"Gets it from me." He raises the notebook and displays his tiny scrawl. "I've been writing since I was behind bars. I took classes there. I know all about it. Three-act structure, hero's journey, turning points... I taught Ethan how to write fiction."

"That's awesome. I hope you can get your work published."

He laughs. "Who's going to read stories by some ex-con homeless dude? Still, I can't help myself. They fill my head and I have to get them on paper."

"What are your thoughts on what happened to Ethan?" she says.

He taps his pencil. "I been thinking a lot about it. If anything happens to that boy, I don't know what I'll... I love him like my own son."

Rebecca waits to see if the answer is coming.

"I'll tell you what Martha thinks. I don't like my mind to go there, but... she said she's seen a guy lurking around the camp lately. Handsome black dude. I saw him once, a few days ago."

"What about him?"

"She says he looks at the boys... the young teenagers. We got a few of those around here, with their mothers mostly."

Rebecca feels a sickening sensation growing inside her at where the conversation is leading.

"She thinks he's a pedo... or maybe worse, maybe a child trafficker. Looking for kids to snatch and then maybe sell overseas. I heard about that before. Those are some sick fucks."

Wow. This feels like her first real lead. "Do you know the guy's name?"

"Nope. Don't know anything about him. I just seen him once. Hard to miss because he didn't look homeless. Nice clothes, and he smelled good. Not like anyone you normally see around here."

"Can you describe him for me? Other than he's good looking."

"Taller than him..." he nods at a young man with unfocused eyes and matted hair passing nearby. "Pumped like he works out. Not bald, but close-cut."

"Any tats or piercings?"

He considers this. "Not that I could see. But I think he had on long sleeves."

It's frustrating not to have something specific. "Anything else you want to tell me?"

He shakes his head. "Wish to god there was." He reaches out and grasps her hand. "If it's in your power, bring back that dear boy."

It's almost as if he senses she has a secret power that can help.

Leaving, she winds her way back to Martha. "Ray told me about the guy who might be a pedophile. Did you notice anything special about him, like tattoos or piercings?"

Martha shakes her head and shrinks into herself, peering around in case the guy might be watching. "No tats, hats," she whispers, "but he's a Brit Brit. Wore a Liverpoolian jacket. And he smells like crumpets."

29

2019 - MINDCAST

Rebecca's next mindcast brings her back to Ethan's school following his disappearance. Speaking to the principal first, she gives her story about being a journalist and asks who might know Ethan the best. Without hesitation, the principal refers her to Mr. Flannery, Ethan's English teacher.

She finds him alone in his classroom working on a crossword puzzle. When she asks to speak with him, he looks disconcerted to have been caught doing something for his own amusement during school hours. "Need to keep the brain sharp," he mumbles, sliding the paper to one side. "Remind me. Whose parent are you?"

At twenty-six, she doesn't expect to be mistaken for a parent of a thirteen-year-old. She guesses she could be a stepparent, though. The sudden thought of being someone's trophy wife amuses her. "No. I'm an investigative journalist." As soon as the lie emerges, she wishes she had come up with a different story. Mr. Flannery, being an English teacher, might be curious to find out more about her supposed career as a writer.

Fortunately, he displays a complete lack of interest. "I don't understand," he says.

"I'd like to speak to you about Ethan Pitt. The boy who went missing last week."

He straightens his black-rimmed glasses and scrutinizes her. "I'm sorry. Are you from the police?"

"No, I'm a journalist."

"I see. From the Chronicle?"

"I'm freelance. I took an interest in Ethan's story. I plan to write an article."

He still looks baffled. "Ethan's a gifted child. But an article? What would you put in it?"

"That's what I'm trying to figure out. I was wondering if you have any thoughts on where he might have gone, or what might have happened to him."

"I have no idea. He's an exceptional student. A fine writer. Smart. But there are negative influences in this community that sometimes affect our children."

"Is there anything specific you know about?"

"Of course not. He's not going to confide in his English teacher. But if I were to take a guess, I'd say, he may have gotten himself into trouble and doesn't know how to deal with it."

"So you think he ran away? Is that what you're saying?"

"It's certainly a possibility."

"Is there something he said that would make you come to this conclusion?"

"No. I told you. I try my best to get the kids to open up with me, but you know... middle school. An age where every child begins to reject authority. A time when kids are only focused on what other kids think of them. It's a tough time for them. Some can't deal with it."

"You don't think he might have taken his own life, do you?"

He spreads his hands wide on the desk, looking down at them. "I sincerely hope not. There's nothing more tragic than a child committing suicide. But I'm not a psychologist. Have you spoken to his family? Maybe he was seeing a therapist? I'm sure they would have much more insight on the issue than I would."

"Let me ask you this," Rebecca says. "Last week, when he was in class, did you notice anything different about him? Did he seem quieter than usual? Did he seem sad, or out of sorts? Any changes in his behavior that you noticed?"

"Miss, have you ever tried teaching a classroom full of unruly pre-teens? There isn't any time to observe nuances of behavior on a daily basis. From what I recall, he seemed normal. But I couldn't possibly say for certain."

"He went missing on the Saturday. Is there any chance he tried to contact you that day?"

"I was away for the weekend. I have a favorite camping and fishing spot up north, and I go there frequently. So, no, I didn't hear from him."

She stifles her frustration. After all, she could not have expected to learn much from Ethan's teachers. "Is there anything you can tell me that might shed light on what happened to him?"

He pauses, thinking. "Ethan is a very imaginative boy. I told you he's a talented writer. He's also an excellent storyteller. He might've wandered off on an adventure of his own imagining. If he does return... and I very much believe he will... he'll probably weave an excellent tale regarding what happened to him during the time he was gone."

If she hadn't come from the future... if she didn't know that he has now been missing more than a year with no sign of his ever returning... she might almost have been convinced by Mr. Flannery's optimism. No one wants to think the worst has happened to a child.

"Thank you." She rises and glances out the window at a striking black man passing by.

"Would you like to leave your card? In case I think of anything helpful?" Mr. Flannery says.

She has no cards and since she will be ending this mindcast soon, she also has no need of his ever calling her. She looks inside her purse like they must be in there. "Sorry. I guess I ran out. Can I drop it by the office for you later?"

"Sure."

She still has her eyes on the man outside when he turns toward the front of the school. The name "Liverpool" is printed on the right side of his jacket. The *Liverpoolian*, as Martha called the handsome creepy guy who had been hanging around the homeless camp.

"Who is that man?" Rebecca says.

Mr. Flannery follows her gaze. "Lou Johnson. The new P.E. teacher."

"New?"

"As of a few months ago."

"Nice guy?" she says.

"I don't know him very well." Mr. Flannery draws a stack of papers in front of him. "If you don't mind…"

She is already on her way, hoping to catch Mr. Johnson.

REBECCA CATCHES UP to the new P.E. teacher just as he enters the patchy school field where a handful of boys are currently running laps.

She calls out to him, but when he turns to her, he isn't smiling.

"Mr. Johnson, can I speak with you? I'd like to ask you some questions about Ethan Pitt."

"Who are you?" in clipped British tones.

"Rebecca Danser."

With reluctance, he shakes the hand she thrusts at him. His firm grasp along with the enticing vanilla scent surrounding him sets her insides aflutter, to her annoyance. For god's sake, shouldn't a gym teacher reek of sweat? But she remembers Martha saying he smelled like cake or something.

"I'm writing an article about missing children," she says. The scope of the article has expanded, now that she doesn't seem to be gathering much information about Ethan.

"I'm busy." He turns back to the kids.

"Please, Mr. Johnson. I'm trying to help Ethan and others like him."

"Are you? Or are you trying to capitalize on the trend toward diversity in publishing?"

"I'm not, but even if I were, my article could still potentially help him."

"What you write to sell an article might not be the same focus as if you're hoping to bring him home."

"You think he might have run away?"

"Actually, I don't think so. He struck me as a serious young man. I don't think he would do that. I'm very concerned that he's come to harm."

"Do you have any idea who would have a motive to hurt him?"

"No. I have to get back to my job."

"Mr. Flannery said you started working here a few months ago. Where were you before then?"

His expression hardens. "I thought you were writing about Ethan."

"Yes, but I need to get background regarding anyone who has touched his life. It would help to know if you're local to our area, or come from afar, like say..." Her eyes sweep over the word, *Liverpool*. "Like, say, the U.K."

"Do you have permission to be on the school grounds?"

"Yes, I checked in with the front office first."

"They should have told you not to disturb teachers at work." He steps away from her.

"Have you ever been to that homeless camp that's over by the freeway underpass?" she says.

His face turns explosive. "Not all black people live in poverty."

"What? No. I wasn't making an assumption. Someone there said they saw a man matching your description. I was just wondering why you would be there. Was it anything to do with Ethan?"

He tightens his lips and walks away. While she watches, he empties the ball bag and kicks the soccer balls out into the field. The kids retrieve them and start organizing for drills.

Rebecca knows she isn't going to get any more of a response out of him. But his silence speaks volumes.

The first thing she will do at the end of the mindcast is Google him and find out where he came from. If he was at another school, did something happen to any of the boys there? Why did he start a new job in the middle of the school year? And why is he so opposed to answering her questions?

30

____

2020 - PRESENT

Rebecca wakes bleary-eyed in the morning and decides she needs a day off from mindcasting. As much as she tries to stay in good health by walking a lot and eating oversized meals whenever she's in real-time, her nightly travels take a toll.

She steps on the scale and discovers she's down two pounds. It's part of a general trend; she's lost seven pounds since she began hunting for Ethan. She isn't too upset, however, since she's been meaning to shed five pounds since last year. *The Time Travel Diet*, she thinks. If everyone could mindcast, she would make a fortune on the book.

It would be funny if a lot of other people had gotten sparked by similar rocks that maybe landed in a meteor shower or were sprinkled over the earth by aliens. What if every other person who passed her in the street was also a time traveler? And all of them too frightened to talk about it, so they would never know that many others shared their skill. Maybe during a mindcast someday, someone would turn to her abruptly, give her a knowing look, and say, *so, um, what year are you from?*

She makes herself an English muffin with peach jam and peanut butter before showering. It's a weekday, meaning it's a good time to go visit Ethan's middle school.

She stops at the office first to get permission to talk to the teachers regarding her bullshit article about the boy.

"Where can I find the P.E. teacher?" she says, wondering if he would even have an office.

Apparently he does, and they give her directions. When she knocks on the door, a female voice replies from inside. "Come in."

Rebecca finds a buff woman of about her own age seated behind the desk, dressed like she's ready to work out. "Is Mr. Johnson here?"

At first the woman appears confused, then her expression clears. "Oh, you mean the last P.E. instructor. He left at the end of the school year."

Now it's Rebecca's turn to be baffled. "He left? After only half a year?"

"I'm his replacement."

"Was there a problem? Isn't that unusual for a teacher to leave a post so quickly?"

"Sorry. I'm just the new guy. No one told me why he left."

"Did he get fired?"

"I don't know."

It's clear she's not going to get any information here. Rebecca returns to the office and asks to speak to the principal. "I was hoping to talk to Mr. Johnson. I heard he was close to Ethan, the boy who went missing."

"Was he? I don't know. But I'm afraid he no longer works for us."

"Do you know why he left?"

"He told us it was because of a family emergency. His mother, I think. She became ill, and he wanted to move near her, to help care for her. In another state."

"Which state?"

"Hmm, I can't remember."

"Did he leave a forwarding address?"

"I don't know. You can check with my assistant."

"Overall, were you happy with his performance? There wasn't any problem?"

"Oh no. The boys liked him. Maybe the staff not so much, though."

"Oh?"

"Nothing specific. It's just, he wasn't very friendly. Didn't like to talk about himself. I don't believe he made any friends."

"I see. Well, thanks for your help."

She checks with the assistant on her way out, but there is no forwarding address to be found, nor does the assistant remember what state he claimed his ailing mother lived in.

When she gets home, she goes straight to her computer and launches a search on him. But the only thing that comes up is a brief mention of a soccer match won by the middle school team, coached by Johnson.

She checks social media too, and still can't find him. He has a frustratingly generic name, which makes it even more difficult to pinpoint this particular Lou Johnson. At the end of two hours, she leans back from the screen, her spine tingling.

A secretive man who has access to boys, and one of them goes missing. And then the man goes missing.

It has to be him. Despite her previous resolution to skip mind-casting tonight, she decides she can't put it off. She'll take a nap, eat a healthy dinner, and then nail this guy. Somehow.

ETHAN

31

———————

All week long, Ethan tries not to think about the stealing he did with Teshi and Antoine. But when he's outside, and a cop passes near him, he keeps his face turned away. What if they have a photo of him from a security camera and are looking for him right now? It makes him frightened to leave the house and be seen by anyone.

He only goes where he has to go, meaning school, and then right back home. Ma continues in a bad state and he has to take care of her. He shops and does the laundry and prepares their food and cleans up after. The money is running out, and he wants to try getting a real job, but he doesn't have any time to even look for one.

He hopes to never see Antoine again. Teshi is in his English class, but she runs off when the bell rings. He hasn't spoken to her since the night they were together and she kissed him. He's not sure what's up with her. After the kiss, he thought maybe she wanted to be his girlfriend, but now it seems like she's avoiding him.

It's Saturday afternoon when a call comes in from her. At first, his stomach flutters, but cold reality dampens his excitement. What if she's calling because Antoine wants them to steal again? Before he can decide whether to answer, the ringing stops.

Dude, where are you? Teshi texts.

Ethan rubs his wristband nervously. He can't just run away from this. Antoine has his picture committing a crime. The man threatened to turn him in if he didn't do his bidding. Would he really? Wouldn't he worry Ethan would then do the same to him? Maybe not. After all, chances are good Ethan doesn't know his real name, and he definitely doesn't know where to find him. Even if they did somehow pick up Antoine based on Ethan's description, there's nothing to prove the old man committed a crime, aside from Ethan saying so. Ethan is the actual person who committed the crime, and there's at least one photo that proves it.

With a sinking heart, he realizes he can't just blow Antoine off. But maybe this call from Teshi isn't about him. Maybe it's about her wanting to hang out with Ethan. He has to take a chance and respond. *Home,* he texts back.

She texts him to meet her at a specific street corner in ten minutes.

What are we gonna do? Ethan texts.

Antoines gonna take us for a drive.

Exactly what Ethan was afraid of.

Stop worrying. It's like she reads his mind. *Were not doing a job today.*

What are we doing?

You'll see. Nothing bad. She includes a kiss emoji at the end.

He hurries to get ready and checks in on Ma before leaving. Since reading now gives her a headache, she's watching TV again, and looking more alert than she has in a while. He makes up a lie about going to see a friend. He doesn't want to get *oh, is she your new girlfriend* comments if he mentions Teshi.

She's at the corner when he arrives, wearing her sexy new jacket, dope shoes, and slim pants. Her face brightens when she sees him. "Hey, it's cool. Don't look so worried, Ethan."

"Don't you think he's gonna want us to do something?"

"No, dude, I told you. This is what he calls a practice session.

Shows us how to get better. Last thing he wants is for us to get caught."

Ethan believes at least that much is true. Before they can talk more, Antoine's car pulls up and they hop in, with Teshi keeping her spot in the front. Antoine greets her then turns to look at Ethan. "Hey, nice to see you. Thanks for coming."

"You're welcome," Ethan mumbles.

Antoine turns on the rap music on his playlist, signaling he doesn't want conversation right now. They drive to a storage facility on the outskirts of town and follow Antoine into a large unit with boxes stacked on the sides, but empty through the middle. He rolls down the door with them inside. Though he leaves it open a few inches on the bottom, the place makes Ethan claustrophobic, wondering if they'll get enough air.

"Show him," Antoine says, turning his back on the kids.

Teshi approaches him quietly, slips her fingers into his back pocket, and pulls out his cell phone.

"Not bad," he says. "Quicker next time. Let's show Ethan his part."

"Come here," Teshi says to him. "You're going to be walking up to Antoine and bumping into him. Pretend it was an accident. Apologize but act annoyed too. Here, I'll show you."

She approaches Antoine, trips, and falls into him, banging his arm.

"Hey!" Antoine says. "Watch where you're going."

"Sorry! But dude, you were blocking the way."

"Okay." Antoine looks at Ethan. "I want you to do that now."

He nods and positions himself against the wall across from Antoine. When the old man takes a couple steps, he moves forward and bumps into him lightly.

"Try it again. Harder. I can take it." Antoine gives his frigid smile and they start over.

This time Ethan bumps him hard, enjoying it, taking out his aggressive feelings toward him.

At the same time, just when Antoine is thrown off by the bump,

Teshi is behind him, whisking the phone out of his pocket. He doesn't seem to notice.

"You see how it works, yeah?" Antoine says. "One to distract, one to take. Teshi's good at the picking part; we'll keep you as the bumper."

For about an hour, they practice the move over and over, concentrating on the best ways for Ethan to create a distraction, while Teshi works on refining her pickpocketing so that Antoine barely feels it.

"What happens if the dude realizes what we did?"

"You run," Antoine says. "But you'll be moving quickly anyway. As soon as she gets the phone or wallet, she's heading to the nearest corner, alley, or other hiding place. If it looks like the mark is onto you, don't talk to them after bumping. Just get the hell away from there as fast as you can. They can't really tie you to the theft. You accidentally collided with them; you didn't take anything."

Ethan looks at Teshi. "Have you done this before?"

She laughs. "Shit, yeah. A lot more than taking laptops from restaurants. That's riskier."

"Let's get out of here," Antoine says. After they pile out of the unit, he disappears around the corner to take a leak.

When Ethan and Teshi are alone, he says in a low voice, "You sure he's not a perv?"

"What do you mean?" she says.

"He likes having your hand in his pocket."

"Fuck you. This is business. He's a professional. He never tried to do anything pervy with me. We're all here to make money, that's it."

"A professional? He's an old dude getting kids to do his dirty work."

"I'm telling you, don't talk smack about him. I'm doing this because I like doing it. I can quit any time I want, but I won't, because there's nothing better than looking back at the mark and seeing that expression of panic on his face when he realizes you've swiped his fucking phone."

Sometimes he really doesn't know what to think about her. She says shit like this and sounds like an awful person. But at other times she's sweet, even vulnerable.

Antoine comes back around the corner and they all gather into the car. Ethan is feeling better about this so-called job. The pickpocketing seems easier than what they did before. More likely they can get away with it. They can choose their spots, making sure there aren't cameras around on the street. He had never planned on making money as a thief, but he's desperate. And Teshi makes it seem almost normal.

32

————————

Over the last week, Ethan has gone on pickpocketing expeditions three times. He's getting faster and more adept at his job of distracting the mark. The first time he screwed up, and they had to run away. The next two times they were well out of the area before the marks realized anything was missing. They got a cell phone once, and a wallet the next time. They turned it all over to Antoine and he paid them twenty dollars each for every successful hit.

He doesn't like what he's doing. He isn't proud of himself. But he's thinking he could live with it. If he's careful, he won't get caught. And Teshi's arguments, that life hasn't been fair to them... that rich whities get everything and black people don't get shit... are starting to make sense to him. It's not his fault his parents couldn't provide a good living for their family. Shit, it wasn't their fault either. When has a black person ever gotten a fair shake in America?

Antoine has another routine he likes. It's called driving around in his car looking for crimes of opportunity. Sometimes it's as easy as grabbing stuff from people's yards. More often, to get anything worth swiping, they have to find garage doors left open with no one watching. It has to be a house close to the curb, so Antoine can idle the car in front of the driveway, and Ethan or Teshi can dash out and snatch the first valuable thing before darting back.

Since Ethan joined them, they've nabbed a toolbox, a new pair of shoes, and the biggest prize—a snowboard. All without being spotted by anyone.

So that's what they're doing this Saturday afternoon, with Teshi riding shotgun, and Ethan in the back as usual.

"There's one." Ethan, leaning forward, is the first to spy an open garage up ahead. Antoine slows down as he nears it.

"There's a laptop on the workbench." Teshi's voice quivers with excitement.

Sure enough, the computer is open like someone's just been using it. Since no one is around, they must've popped inside for something.

"Teshi, you get it," Antoine says.

Ethan figures he picked her because she's faster and more experienced. A laptop is a prize you don't want to risk losing.

She's already wearing the big hoodie they keep in the car for jobs like this. She covers her head and face pretty well before getting out and glancing around. Seeing no one in the vicinity, she sprints to the garage and snatches the device.

"Hey!" A big man barrels through the door from the house.

Teshi doesn't pause or turn around, just keeps on moving. But this guy is fast, despite his size. "Gimme that!" He catches Teshi by the arm and spins her around. She swings the laptop and hits the man in the shoulder with it.

It's not too hard of a hit, but now he's furious. "You little shit!" He grips her on both sides and flings her back toward the garage. The computer flies out of her hands, and her head smashes hard against a concrete pillar, with the sound of a sickening thud.

Ethan watches this scene play out with dread growing inside him. *Fuck, fuck, fuck.*

Antoine pulls out into the street and they screech away from there. Resigning Teshi to her fate.

"You can't leave her!" Ethan cries out.

"Fuck I can't."

"She's hurt!"

"They'll take her to the hospital. She'll be fine."

"They'll arrest her!"

"And send her to juvey. She'll be out in no time."

Ethan shouldn't be surprised. He ought to know by now what a callous motherfucker Antoine is.

The old man says nothing during the drive back to the hood. He leaves Ethan two miles from his house, and the boy must drag his feet the rest of the way. To his surprise, Ma is in the kitchen, making homemade mac and cheese for them. "I'm feeling better today," she says. "Sit down and have some of this delicious pasta."

His stomach feels like he swallowed a brick already, but he forces down a few bites.

"What's wrong, baby?" Ma says.

"Not feeling so good."

She presses her wrist against his forehead. "I don't think you have a fever."

"It's my stomach."

"Maybe it's something you ate. What did you have for lunch?"

"I don't know. I just wanna lie down and watch some TV." He turns it on and stretches out on the couch. But he has no clue what he's watching, while the image of Teshi getting battered like a rag doll plays over and over in his head.

Ma manages to clean up and then goes to her own room. But later, after he's changed into his pajamas, gotten under the covers, and turned out his light, she comes in and sits in the chair by his bed. Her voice so soft and tender swirls over him:

Sing to me, sing to me, sing to me

Lullaby, lullaby, lullaby

Of the leaves.

He weeps with his face turned to the wall.

33

———————

The day after the assault, Teshi's mother calls Ma in hysterics and tells her that her daughter is in a coma and no one knows if she'll ever come out of it. Then on Monday, Mr. Flannery announces it to the class.

In the hallways, among the kids, everybody is talking about what happened. At least, what is known about what happened. How Teshi had been stealing from somebody's house, and then she got beat up, and that's how she ended in a coma. How she'll be in deep shit if she recovers, because the cops want to arrest her and maybe even charge her as an adult for attempted burglary of an expensive item. Ethan hadn't known until now that more valuable items count as felonies, and if the crime was a felony, they can choose to prosecute her as an adult.

At first everyone defends Teshi. Some kids assume she was beaten up by the cops because she's black and that's just what they do. Police over-reach. But then it comes out she was attacked by the home-owner. Somebody gets a picture of the man and everybody sees he's white. So again, all the kids are pissed that a white man was allowed to nearly kill a black girl just because she tried to take something of his. *Why isn't anybody arresting him*, they all ask. Teshi's crime was nothing compared to someone beating a kid so bad she ended up in a coma.

But apparently, it's allowed for people to defend themselves and their property when anyone trespasses. It's even allowed to shoot and kill a person who does that. But Ethan knows it doesn't work that way for black folk. If someone broke into Ethan's apartment, and his mother shot the man dead, you could be sure the police would show up right after and do the same to both Ethan and Ma. Especially if the intruder was white.

Ethan feels numb, almost like he's looking at himself from outside, making the motions of going through his day. He's in a daze, unable to concentrate on anything, let alone his schoolwork. When Mr. Flannery calls on him, he has no idea what the question was, or what his teacher had been talking about for the last ten minutes. But Mr. Flannery knows the kids are upset over the news about Teshi, and doesn't insist on an answer.

By the time Ethan reaches P.E. class, his last of the day, he's feeling at the end of his rope. Changing into his gym clothes, he overhears Jonas and Noah talking.

"Can you believe that about Teshi?" Noah says.

"Dude had no right to mess her up like that," Jonas says.

"What's she doing stealing his shit, though?"

"She's always been like that. One time I saw her swipe Vanessa's bracelet right off her desk when she turned away for two seconds."

"True dat. Nobody spent more time in the principal's office than her."

"That's what I'm sayin'. Girl had it coming to her," Jonas says.

The heat has been growing inside Ethan during this conversation, and finally, at these words of Jonas, he spins around to face him, grabs him by the arms, and slams him against the lockers.

"What the fuck, man?" Jonas shoves Ethan back.

"Hey, hands off each other!" Mr. Johnson comes around the corner.

"He started it," Jonas says.

"That true?" Mr. Johnson says.

Ethan stares at the floor.

"Go out to the field. I want everyone doing their laps." Mr. Johnson looks at Ethan. "Not you."

The other boys file out of the locker room. Mr. Johnson sits on the bench beside Ethan. "You and Teshi were friends, weren't you?"

He nods.

"Really sorry to hear what happened to her."

"Me too."

"You know what she's accused of doing, right?"

"Doesn't matter, nobody's got a right to hurt a kid like that." Ethan feels his head grow hot again.

"Calm down. I agree with you. But I need to ask... do you have anything to do with what Teshi has been up to?"

A chill sneaks down Ethan's spine. He hadn't expected anyone to make the connection. "No," he says. *Of course not.* What kind of idiot would admit to that?

Lou stares at him like he doesn't believe it. "I'm not asking to get you into any sort of trouble. I'm not the police. If you're in over your head, you can talk to me. Maybe I can help." He takes his phone out of his back pocket. "What's your cell?"

Ethan is about to tell him when he realizes he can't do that. It's supposed to be a burner. It's tied up in his criminal activities. Probably has texting evidence against Teshi, and himself. "I broke it." He prays Lou doesn't look in his locker, where it's in the pocket of his jeans.

"That sucks." Lou takes out the little notepad and pencil he keeps in his shirt pocket and scribbles down a phone number. "This is my personal number. If you need help, or just someone to talk to, borrow a phone from somebody and call me. Anytime. Anywhere. Got it?"

He nods, taking the paper handed to him. "Okay," he mutters.

"Get dressed and go home. You're excused from P.E. today."

"Thanks, Mr. Johnson."

His teacher leaves him alone in the locker room. Ethan gets out his clothes and starts changing back. He's never had a teacher like Mr. Johnson before. *Anytime? Anywhere?* Aren't there rules about not seeing kids outside of school? On the one hand, he desperately needs an honest adult he can confide in. On the other, he's learning not to trust anyone, especially those who pretend to want to help you.

34

Strangely, Ethan has never visited anyone in the hospital before. Even his mother after the car accident.

Apparently, you can just waltz right in and look around. But because he doesn't know where to go, he stops to ask at an information desk. They give him instructions to take the elevator to the third floor. Once there, he asks again at the nurse's station, and they direct him to Teshi's room.

Seeing her brings a sudden tightness to his chest. He forgets to breathe while he takes in all the machinery around her and attached to her, almost like she's part of it. A robo-girl.

She looks bad. Real bad. Her eyes are closed, her cheeks hollow, her skin wan. A bandage is wrapped around her head. She has stitches on her right arm and hand.

He can't turn his eyes away from the train wreck that is Teshi.

"Ethan," a woman says.

Only then does he realize Teshi's mother is in the room with them. Seated in the corner with yarn and knitting needles in her lap.

She pats her face with a tissue. "My little girl, Ethan. Look what's happened to my little girl."

"She'll get better, won't she?" he says.

Teshi's mother has no answer.

"I'm sorry." If ever an apology sounded inadequate to his ears, it is now. He should never have gone along with the stealing. He should've tried to convince her to give it up. She liked him. Maybe she would've listened to him.

"It's my fault," her mother says. "I been so busy. I should've known something was wrong. She told me she had a real job. It was a lie. I should've known. I should've checked on her."

Ethan doesn't know what to say. Her remorse is too much for him. He wishes he hadn't come. Some misplaced sense of loyalty. There's nothing he can do here. No way for him to help.

She sets aside her knitting, rises and grasps his arm. "Pray with me."

The room is suffocating him. He needs to get out of there as fast as possible. He can't stand looking at what happened to her a second longer.

But a nurse sticks her head in and smiles at him. "Are you her brother?" she says.

"Her friend."

"Nice of you to come visit."

"He's going to pray with me," Teshi's mother says.

He's trapped, with the nurse blocking the door.

"Come here beside me." She draws him to the corner of the room.

"I'll get another chair," the nice nurse says.

He leans against the wall, feeling dizzy. When the chair comes, he sits next to Teshi's mother, and she takes his hands in hers. "Lord Jesus Christ, by your patience in suffering...," she starts. Ethan doesn't know any prayers, except the one he would say with his mother at bedtime, but he closes his eyes and repeats, "my Lord and my God, amen," when prompted by Teshi's mother.

Afterward, she releases his hands, and he opens his eyes wishing for a miracle, but Teshi looks no different than before. What good are prayers if they never work? What good is a god who doesn't make your prayers come true? Ethan knows it's blasphemy to think this way, but he can't help himself. He prayed many times a day when his father became ill in prison. Then his father died.

Teshi looks like she's going to die too.

"You can talk to her," Teshi's mother says. "They say people in a coma can hear you. They say it soothes them."

Ethan approaches the bed. *What the hell am I going to say to her?* She wasn't his girlfriend. They were barely friends at all the last few years. "Um, I hope you get better soon, Teshi," he says.

"Hold her hand," her mother says. "Tell me if she moves her fingers."

He wishes he hadn't come. He hasn't ever held her hand before, and now is a weird time to start. "I have to go." He rushes out before her mother can protest.

"Come back tomorrow," he hears her say as he races to the elevator. He's not coming back tomorrow. He's not sure if he'll ever come back. He knows he's being a coward, but it doesn't change how he feels.

On the bus on his way home, his phone buzzes. A call from Antoine. It twists his stomach, thinking what that man did to Teshi. He doesn't answer.

The text comes after the phone stops ringing. *The pizza is here*, the message says. It's a code that means, *come to our meeting place asap.*

But he's already decided he isn't going. He's never going near Antoine again, if he can help it. He's going home, and he's going to lock the door, and maybe even pull the heaviest chair in front of it. He'll keep his phone next to him and call 9-1-1 if it comes to that. From now on, he'll be watching his back, and going nowhere except school and then directly home. Their money will run out soon, and if that means they'll be homeless, so be it. They'll live next to Uncle Ray and he'll watch out for them. He'll take care of Ma best he can.

It isn't till Ethan gets home and starts making dinner that one more text arrives from Antoine. *Last chance for pizza. Or else.*

Whether Antoine means he is planning to hurt Ethan, or that he's planning to turn him in to the police using the picture he took of him stealing the laptop, makes no difference. His life is over.

AMARI

35

———————

Amari tells Panya about his family and his village and his quest to save them.

"I will help you," she says.

"It is going to be hard."

"I am used to hardship. I lost my parents when I was seven and have survived on my own since then. Which way should we go?"

"The slavers will take them to their ships to carry them across the ocean. We must continue west to the water."

They walk for three days until their supplies are nearly gone.

"Maybe we can find work in the next village to pay for what we need."

"There is no time for that," Panya says. "We must steal. It is not fair that they have everything and we have nothing, especially since we are trying to save your village."

He does not argue because he knows stealing will be the quickest way, and they cannot afford to delay any longer. The ships could set sail any day now on the coast.

When they approach the next village, they decide to sleep hidden behind trees during the day, and enter at night to steal what they need.

They wake late after all the fires in the village have been extinguished.

Panya presses a finger to her lips before leading Amari. They are both bare-foot and step lightly. Only animals could hear their approach.

They have each brought a sack in which to store the things they take. They have gotten lucky in that the villagers appear to be very trusting here. Dried meats, fruits, and stores of water have been left out everywhere. Amari and Panya grab as much as they can carry.

But before they are out of the village, Panya spots an item of great value... a hatchet. She knows Amari's spear was stolen, and he needs a weapon to confront the slavers. Amari is walking ahead of her and does not know she has paused. She lets him keep going, not wanting to make noise in stopping him. She tiptoes to the hatchet and snatches it up. But in doing so, her pack tips open and everything she has already taken tumbles out, making a terrible noise.

Amari hears this sound and turns back. As he watches in horror, a large man emerges from the hut holding a spear. Seeing Panya holding his hatchet and surrounded by other stolen goods, he thrusts his spear right through her. Her body falls limp.

Amari is frozen in terror, not knowing if there is any point in trying to help her. It looks like she must be dead. And now the man has seen him and ducked back into his hut. Amari has no doubt he is seeking another spear to kill him.

Amari drops his pack full of all the food and water he so desperately needs, and sprints into the darkness, running like the wind and not looking back.

36

———————

Amari runs faster than he ever has in his life when escaping the village. He tries to wipe the image of Panya's body from his mind, but he cannot. The spear piercing her, the low cry she emitted, the slump of her slender form over the weapon... these pictures play out in his mind over and over as he flees.

He is only vaguely aware of things around him. The shouts of the villagers, and the noise of their pursuit. The sky being lit by their torches. The sharp rocks that cut into his bare feet; the branches that scrape his arms. Even the snarl of a lioness when he passes her, lying with her cubs. She is angry but fortunately cannot be bothered to chase him.

Soon enough, the raucous sounds of the villagers lessen. The sky darkens. They have given up and gone home. Amari is not even worth killing.

Despite his hunger and thirst, he runs all night and all the next day until he comes to the coast. He sees only the irony—that at last he made it to his destination, but without any means of saving anyone. Unable even to save himself, he collapses amidst a pile of rocks at the base of a cliff, and passes out.

When he wakes again, the moon has risen. He forces himself to get up and climb the promontory. He must crawl like an animal, dragging himself forward with slashed and aching hands, balancing on swollen, blistered *feet. The moon is in the other hemisphere by the time he reaches the top and stares out at the sea.*

He perceives the outline of a magnificent ship, twenty times the size of any boat he has seen before. Its glorious sails billow in the wind and spirit it away from the shore. This is the slavers' ship, bearing everyone he has known and loved across the sea, never to be seen again.

He drops to the ground and weeps, but even in that, he fails. He has no more moisture for tears.

When the ship is only a tiny speck in the distance, he looks down at the jagged rocks below him. He might as well jump and avoid the slower torture of thirst and starvation. Panya's death plays out in his head again, and he feels the spear as if it was thrust into his own torso. Life is too cruel and not worth living. He might as well jump.

REBECCA

37

—————

2019 - MINDCAST

Rebecca has been sitting in her car outside The Blazing Horse pub for the last ten minutes, pondering her next move. Upon arriving in this time, she went to Ethan's school and waited across the street for two hours until Lou Johnson the P.E. teacher drove out of the lot. She managed to follow him back to his apartment, which was lucky since she didn't know how else she would find out where he lived. Ian Slate's P.I. services would not help her here; he had no idea who she was in 2019, and the process of rehiring him and waiting for results would take much more time than she had during a mindcast. She's typically limited to only five or six hours, because once she falls asleep, when she wakes up again, she's always back in real-time. It's a rule she learned early on—no sleeping during mindcasts.

Instead, she has to do a lot of waiting around, trying hard not to doze off. Her phone entertains her. She reads articles (not too many, or they'll put her to sleep), listens to podcasts (same issue), and plays games. She's thinking about signing up for Duolingo if mindcast surveillance becomes an ongoing part of her life. Then she can learn a new language while waiting for her quarry to make a move. But she hasn't decided which one yet.

She's getting better at tailing cars through traffic too. Or maybe it's just that it's easier during daylight hours. Though she had to wait another hour and a half outside Lou's apartment, at least it was still light when he went out in his car again. The chase electrified her at first; she thought for sure he was on his way to find Ethan. But then, to her great disappointment, he turned into this English-style pub parking lot and went inside.

She's contemplating whether she should continue to linger outside, or go in and observe him. She might see something useful, like Lou talking to a suspicious character, or making or receiving a phone call that gets him excited. Anything that might have relevance as to what comes next.

On the other hand, if she enters the pub, she risks doing something that might change the timeline. If he notices her watching him, and thinks she might be a cop, he's not going to take the chance of kidnapping anyone tonight. And then this trip back in time will be wasted.

In the end, necessity drives her inside. During four hours of surveillance, she has finished two bottles of water and desperately needs to pee. With luck, she can use the bathroom without becoming a customer, and just take a brief glance in Lou's direction while she's coming and going.

The place has a large bar section and a smaller eating area next to the windows. It's crowded, though a few empty seats remain at the counter. Probably two thirds of the clientele is male. Most eyes are on the soccer game playing on two large screens, though there are signs of boredom setting in. Midway through the second half, the score is four - nil, and even Rebecca knows the game well enough to understand it's a blowout. The losing team has virtually no chance of turning things around.

Squeezing past other customers, she spots Lou at a table with two other men. He and his friends are focused on the game. *Good.* She pushes forward toward the restrooms.

It occurs to her Lou might leave while she's occupied in the bathroom. Looking back at his table, she glimpses half a drink remaining in front of him. Unless he downs it in one gulp, she should have time.

As soon as she finishes, she confirms with a look that he's still in the pub. Relaxing a bit, she notices a girl who appears no older than six waiting outside the door. Her arms hang slack at her sides.

"Hello," Rebecca says, glancing around for the girl's mother.

The girl sniffs and wipes her nose with her hand. She passes Rebecca into the restroom and shuts the door behind her.

Rebecca continues looking for any sign of a parent. The child is young to be sent alone to the bathroom in a mostly adult venue like this one.

That's when she sees Lou looking at her. *Uh oh.* Not only looking, but when he catches her eye, he gets up from his table and walks toward her. *Should I flee?* she wonders. But it's too late, she's affected the timeline, she might as well let this play out. Besides, she's over-flowing with curiosity.

He wasn't supposed to notice her, and now he looks like he's about to speak. Could he have remembered her from... when? Mind-casting can get so confusing, but she's pretty positive the only time she spoke to him was a week after today. In other words, a week after Ethan's disappearance. She hasn't ever even spoken to him in real-time, because she can't find him in real-time. At this point, he defi-nitely has no clue who she is.

"The girl's parents are over there," he says when he reaches her. He nods toward a couple seated in the middle of the room, engaged in a heated argument. "They didn't even notice when she walked away to use the toilet."

"You knew what I was thinking?" This image of Lou as someone concerned about children is so different than the impression she got when she first spoke to him.

"It was pretty clear from your expression.," he says.

"Poor kid."

"Yeah."

The girl emerges from the bathroom. Her eyes are red-rimmed and puffy.

"You okay, honey?" Rebecca asks.

Before the girl can answer, her mother rushes toward her, throwing dirty looks at Rebecca and Lou. "Come here, Jenna. You went to the bathroom? I was frantic when I saw you left the table." She grabs the girl's hand and pulls her back.

Rebecca and Lou exchange another look. "Should we have said something?" she says.

"Oh, I imagine she would just get defensive about her behavior. Possibly even blame Jenna for attracting the interest of two strangers. The only thing that might help is if there are friends or family members who can intervene."

"And then again, maybe it's a one-off. Can we give them the benefit of the doubt?"

He shrugs. "The way she spoke to her daughter left a lot to be desired."

The air grows thick between them as they both become aware that their conversation has grown strangely intimate.

"Liverpool or Man U?" His smile—which she realizes she hasn't witnessed until now—makes her heart rate skitter. She has entirely forgotten about the game.

"Sorry, too abrupt?" he says. "I'm a Liverpool fan myself, more's the pity."

Liverpool is the team that's nil.

"Condolences," she says. "I'm not a real fan, I just like watching the play." Better not to commit to a team because then he'll expect her to know something about it.

"Haven't seen you here before."

"No, I just… a friend told me about this place, and I was in the area, so I thought I'd pop in. First time." She decides, since she's already corrupted the timeline by drawing Lou's attention, she might as well take the opportunity to get to know him better. Does he seem like someone who could harm a child? Interestingly, he came across as far harsher the first time she met him than he does now. Maybe that change in manner came about because of guilt over whatever he might've done to Ethan.

"I was born in Liverpool," he says. "I never had a choice." He glances around.

"Where are you sitting?"

"Nowhere yet. I went straight to the bathroom. Would you like to join me at the bar?" She can't help enjoying his look of surprise at her forwardness. But he also looks pleased.

He follows her back and settles beside her.

"My treat," she says as the bartender approaches.

After they've given their orders, she jumps right into it. Mind-casting has taught her the value of time. "Do you have kids?" she says. "I'm wondering if that's what made you notice that little girl."

He gives her a sharp look, and she thinks she detects a second's hesitation before he says, "No."

If he's lying, then why?

"I teach them, though. Middle school P.E. So, yeah, I do like them. You could even say I'm trained to pay attention to them. You have any?"

She shakes her head. "Still time for that. In the meantime, I have a younger sister and little stepbrothers to contend with."

"I imagine you have lots of time." He glances at the feuding couple and their daughter, now rising from the table. The mother keeps a tight grip on her now.

"Ever wish you could save them all?" His voice is husky.

"Often," Rebecca says.

38

———————

2020 - PRESENT

The morning after her mindcast, Rebecca doesn't think Lou could be the culprit. His eyes were full of compassion when he looked at that sad little girl.

She wishes she could've eliminated him entirely as a suspect by not going into the pub, following him as planned after he left, and confirming he never kidnapped the boy.

But once she decided to use the bathroom inside, it was over. And then she made it worse by not ignoring him when he tried to speak to her. Instead, she got so chummy, he asked for her phone number after she said she had to leave. This wasn't good, her flirting with a suspect. She would have to make sure it never happened again. So unprofessional. Although no one is overseeing her actions, she aims to be as professional as possible.

There had been no point in following him after that. Her presence changed the trajectory of the evening and that was the end of it.

But now she's wondering what her next step should be. Another mindcast to the same place tonight, and this time she waits in her car? It's difficult for her to feel any enthusiasm for this plan, mainly because Lou has become an unlikely suspect in her mind. She would rather pursue a more promising lead. And if she were to be completely honest with herself, she would admit the other reason is, that the temptation to join him in the pub again might be too strong.

In the midst of her indecision, a call comes in from Yakeera. "Did you get that list I emailed you?" she says.

"I did, thanks." Rebecca has been avoiding the list of people Ethan knew, because it will require a whole new round of research.

"Well, there's one more Laila thought of. A girl, Teshi. They were friends when they were little. Her mother is a friend of my sister's. Troubled home, if you know what I mean. The dad. Laila thought she and Ethan weren't hanging out anymore, but then when Sharon called—that's Teshi's mom—when Sharon called and told her how Teshi had gone into a coma... the news upset Ethan. A lot. So, maybe they were better friends than Laila realized."

"A coma? What happened to her?"

"She got caught trying to steal something out of someone's house. The guy was brutal, smashed her head against the wall. And her just a kid."

"Poor thing. When did this happen?"

"Well, that's just it. Happened a few days before Ethan went missing. That's what got us wondering if it might be related."

It could be significant. "How's she doing?" Rebecca asks.

"She came out of the coma about a month ago. She was lucky; not many recover after so long. She's back home, still under medical care. Police want to book her, but the doctors got them to hold off a little longer. Laila spoke to her parents and they're okay with you talking to her. You want to do that?"

"Yes. Definitely." It might have no connection, but then again, it might. She gets the address from Yakeera before hanging up.

On her way over to see Teshi, she tries not to speculate too much. The girl and her stealing probably have nothing to do with Ethan. And she was in a coma for so long, she might not remember anything. Might not be coherent now at all. But it's worth investigating.

Teshi lives in a building that looks more rundown than Ethan's. A man answers the intercom and listens while Rebecca briefly explains who she is and that she got permission to come.

"I heard nothing about this," the man says. But after a pause, the door buzzes open and she lets herself in.

The apartment is on the third floor. The man, who must be Teshi's father, waits for her at the open door. He's short, with clothes that look baggy on him and a receding hairline. When he looks at Rebecca, he doesn't quite make eye contact, which, rightly or wrongly, lends him a shifty appearance.

He gives her the once over. "You're not from the police, are you? Got to tell me if so."

"I'm not, I swear it. I'm writing an article about Teshi's friend Ethan, who went missing. My questions are related to that. There won't be anything about your daughter in my article."

"I changed my mind about this. My daughter isn't well enough." He starts to shut the door.

She gets an idea. "There's payment, of course. Fifty dollars if you let me talk to her." Lucky she stopped at the ATM on her way here. She's been making that a habit lately, because cash comes in handy now and then. Helps to have it in advance, since there won't be time to get it in the middle of whatever she's doing.

He stares at the side of her face. "A hundred."

She hesitates before nodding. He holds out his hand for the money.

"When I'm done," she says.

He hesitates again, but seems to realize he has the power to keep her there until she forks over the cash. "Okay. First door on the left. She was awake a second ago." He moves to let Rebecca pass.

She goes to the open door and looks in. Teshi is sitting, or more like slouching, in a hospital bed watching TV with the volume turned way up. She's connected to an IV.

"Hi, Teshi," Rebecca says.

The girl turns toward her, a dull look in her eyes. Rebecca's heart sinks. "May I come in?"

Her eyes brighten just a bit. "Okay."

Rebecca settles into the chair beside the bed. "Do you mind if I turn off the TV for a minute?"

Teshi nods, which Rebecca takes as a *no-I-don't-mind*. She clicks the power button on the remote. "How are you feeling?"

Teshi shrugs. "They give me drugs." She looks at the IV. "I'm not normal yet."

"Can you remember stuff from before this happened?"

"Some."

"Do you remember your friend Ethan?"

She frowns. "Course I know Ethan."

"So you were good friends? Did you hang out with him last year?"

"Sometimes."

"Cool. Can you tell me what happened the day you got this injury that put you in a coma?"

"I don't remember that part."

"They say you were trying to steal something. Do you remember wanting to do that? And don't worry, I've got nothing to do with the police."

She pouts. "Don't remember nothin' about stealing."

"I'm asking for Ethan. What you tell me might help us find him."

"Find him?"

"Yes. I mean, maybe he's still alive. I'm not giving up hope."

"What the fuck you talking about? Where's he gone?"

No one told her. *Shit.* Now Rebecca has to. "A week after you went into a coma, Ethan went missing. No one has seen him since. It's been over a year."

Her eyes widen in astonishment. Suddenly she leans forward and grips Rebecca's arm. "Antoine did it," she hisses. "Antoine must've killed him."

An electric tingle runs down Rebecca's spine. "Who's Antoine?"

Teshi's gaze shifts to the door and back. She whispers, "the old guy who made me steal."

"Is he the one who ordered you into that garage?"

She nods. "I don't really remember, but it must've been him."

"What's his last name? Where does he live?"

"I don't know."

"Was Ethan stealing for him too?"

She nods her head.

"Why would Antoine kill him?"

She shrugs. "I don't know. But maybe if Ethan said he wouldn't steal for him anymore."

"Was Ethan with you when you got hurt?"

"I don't remember. Probably."

Rebecca learned where the attempted robbery took place from Teshi's father. No one, including the homeowner who assaulted her, had witnessed anyone else with Teshi, or waiting nearby. But just because no one had been seen, didn't mean they weren't there.

Having traveled back in time to witness what happened for herself, she waits in her car across the street, this time in a sleepy San Francisco neighborhood. An hour after she arrived, the man who nearly killed Teshi opened his garage door and began sawing a piece of wood, referring occasionally to instructions on his laptop. So far, he has left the computer on his workbench twice while he went into the house for several minutes at a time.

The third time he goes into the house, a gray Dodge stops abruptly in front of the driveway. Rebecca straightens in her seat, trying to get a glimpse into the vehicle, but the sun reflecting off the front windshield makes it difficult.

She gets out of her car at the same time Teshi springs from the passenger seat and runs into the garage. Rebecca's focus remains on the Dodge. She peers in at Ethan, hunched in the back seat. The man named Antoine must be the driver—a greasy, unpleasant-looking person in his sixties, she guesses. He makes her flesh crawl, the way he pimps children to carry out his crimes.

Antoine glances in her direction and is clearly unhappy to see a potential witness, but he waits for Teshi. If the homeowner hadn't returned, the girl would've been back in the car in two seconds. Tragically, the immense man with the shoulders of a linebacker charges her. Rebecca can't watch, though the sounds of the attack make her stomach roil. She tries not to listen as she notes the license plate number, repeating it inside her head. *I'm here for this*. She will use it to nail Antoine to the wall.

That cowardly motherfucker squeals his Dodge into the street and speeds off without Teshi, and with Ethan looking terrified in the back. She hauls back to her car, does a U-turn, and guns it after them. She means to track his next move and maybe find out where he lives right away, instead of waiting to see if Ian the P.I. can figure it out from his license plate number.

Rebecca manages to follow the gray Dodge all the way to Ethan's neighborhood, partly because of her initial assumption that they were headed there. Anywhere else and she likely would've lost them by now.

A mile or two from Ethan's building, Antoine jerks up to the curb and lets the boy out. Rebecca has to continue past them in order not to attract attention by stopping suddenly. In her rearview, she glimpses Ethan with hoodie pulled over his head, face lowered, and hands balled into fists. He can't get away from Antoine fast enough. She can only imagine the turmoil going on inside him.

A second later, Antoine pulls back into traffic. She waits until there's a reasonable distance between them before continuing her pursuit. It's going to be harder to tail him now that she has no idea where he might be going. Her tracking skills have improved compared to her early efforts, but even so, in her rush not to lose him, she swerves into two turns in a way that might be noticeable in his rearview. Still, he shows no signs of trying to shake her.

After five minutes of this, Antoine pulls ahead of a large truck on the right and veers onto the cross street ahead of him. Unfortunately, before Rebecca can follow, the light becomes red. The truck driver, who must be planning to continue straight, now blocks the right turn lane, forcing her to wait for the green light. Even then, there's further delay as the slow-moving truck rumbles forward.

Antoine is gone. She drives through the area for ten minutes without finding him again. At least she still has his license plate number in her head. With luck, that alone will give her the information she needs.

There's one more action she can take, though. Driving back the way they came, she parks as close as she can to Ethan's apartment. She hopes he hasn't gotten sidetracked and gone somewhere else.

Just when she's wondering if he might've reached home already, she sees him approaching along the sidewalk. His feet are dragging, and his shoulders hang low. She walks toward him, trying to make herself look as unthreatening as possible.

Deeply distracted, Ethan doesn't notice Rebecca until she moves in front of him.

"Can I talk to you?" she says.

He staggers back, nearly falling. "Who are you?"

"Rebecca Danser. I'm a social worker. I'm not with the police or anything like that." As soon as she says it, she realizes that was the wrong thing to say. Nothing says *I'm a cop* more than a statement like *I'm definitely not working with the police.*

"I gotta get home." He tries to get around her.

"I know you're working for Antoine."

His eyes widen. "What're you talking about?"

"You and Teshi."

"Leave me alone." His voice is thick. But when he attempts to pass her again, she grasps his sleeve.

"He's dangerous. You need to get away from him. Before he hurts you." She hopes this will reach him. He knows Teshi is already paying a terrible price for doing Antoine's bidding.

His face crumples. "What can I do?"

"Let me help you. Tell me his real name."

"I don't know it."

"Tell me where he lives, or where he meets you."

"He just drives up to street corners and picks us up. I don't know where he lives."

"Has he ever taken you somewhere?" Rebecca says.

He hesitates. "He brought us to a storage place once." He tells her the name, but it's a company that has facilities everywhere.

"What city?"

Ethan shrugs. "I wasn't paying attention."

"Why did he bring you there? He doesn't live there, does he?" She's not sure that would be possible, but it can't hurt to ask.

Ethan shakes his head and fidgets with a leather band he wears on his wrist. He describes how they practiced picking pockets while they were there.

"What else has he made you do?"

Ethan hesitates at first, but gradually opens up. The anger burning inside him over what happened to Teshi appears to be driving him. At the end, he asks, "What can you do to stop him?"

Gazing at the boy, she's reminded of Yakeera's words: *He could be your son, your grandchild, your brother. A thirteen-year-old child who disappeared. Don't you care? Doesn't anybody care?*

He deserves the truth, if only because his life may end three days from now.

"My little sister was kidnapped when I was six," Rebecca says. "I've never forgiven myself for leaving her alone. Then last year..." It was actually this year, but it's too complicated to sort out past and future at the moment. "Last year I got sparked by something and it gave me the ability to travel through time. I mean, my mind from the future comes back into my body during times in the past. So I know things that are going to happen."

Now he's staring at her like she's a crazy person.

"I actually found my sister using this ability. But it wasn't enough. When I saw your face on a poster, when I learned you were missing, I had to help you. I had to find out what happened to you."

He's no longer listening. He's written her off as a lunatic. "Hey, gotta go."

"I know you don't believe me. I wouldn't have believed me. But three days from now, remember what I said. Someone is going to try to hurt you. Protect yourself. Be safe. Don't let it happen."

"Lady, you sure you're okay?"

"You're very smart, Ethan. And kind. I read part of your story, you know. About Amari in Africa whose family is stolen by slave-traders. I hope I get to read the rest of it someday."

"Get out! Did my Ma show it to you?"

She shakes her head. "Your aunt will show it to me a year from now."

He glances around like maybe there's something to her claim of being a time traveler, and therefore the time travel machine must be nearby.

"Stay away from Antoine, and you should be safe." She knows whatever he does from now on will make no difference in real-time. But maybe it will change things for this version of Ethan. This particular thread in time, if that's what it is. "Go home. Be with your family. I'm sorry if I frightened you."

"You don't scare me," he says. "And don't worry about me. I'm not going near that son of a bitch again. It's Teshi who needs help, not me."

"She's going to be okay," Rebecca blurts. "She's going to recover."

He breaks into a smile that could light the sky. "Really?"

"Really." She can't help but smile back while he spins around and skips on his way to his apartment.

40

2020 - PRESENT

She's napping in the afternoon—something she does more and more frequently since she began mindcasting so often—when the buzz of her phone wakes her. It's a text from private eye Ian Slate, who she called in the morning to ask him to trace Antoine's license plate. *Are you available to zoom now?*

Yes, she texts back. When the link arrives a moment later, she's settled into her Zooming corner.

He looks as well put-together as the last time she saw him, with his miniature teacup poised at the tip of his fingers. "Some bad news," he starts off. "The license plate is fake. Not a valid registration. We can't use it to find the owner of the car."

"Aren't you required to have a valid registration?" she says.

"Sure. But it's a misdemeanor. It's better to be ticketed for that than to take the chance of being traced while you're committing a much bigger crime. If he's smart, he's a cautious driver who doesn't give traffic cops any reason to check on his plate. If he gets caught breaking other laws, the fact that he has a fake plate will be the least of his worries."

"I see. Thanks for checking." She wonders why he didn't just text this update.

"There's more." He gives a crooked smile, and she suspects he's enjoying playing with her like this.

"Please, do tell," she plays along.

"After calling a few of my contacts in law enforcement, I managed to find one who knew someone matching Antoine's description."

When Rebecca spoke with Ian earlier, she had opened up about the case to him. There seemed no reason to keep it secret that she was trying to learn what happened to Ethan. When she reached the part where she speculated the boy might've been thieving for a scumbag named Antoine, Ian had asked for a physical description of the man, along with information about his criminal activities and methods. He didn't explain at the time how that might help.

"Oh my god. Were you able to get his name and address?"

"His name is Alex Bosko, and he was arrested about seven months ago for possession of stolen property, fencing stolen property, corrupting minors, and related crimes."

Seven months. Meaning he was still a free man at the time Ethan went missing. Still her number one suspect. "Can I go talk to him in jail?" *And try to wrench the truth out of him.*

"I'm afraid he's not there. He made bail, and then he disappeared. They can't find him."

A shiver runs through her at the thought that he might've taken Ethan with him. "What's his address?"

"You won't find him there."

"I understand, but it would help to know how close he might've lived to Ethan. I mean, I don't really have proof this is the guy Ethan was working with." *But mostly I need the address so I can jump back in time and spy on him*, she doesn't say.

"Sorry, I didn't think you would need it at this point," Ian says. "I'll get back to you with that information."

"Thank you. You're awesome. You've been so helpful."

He shifts his gaze to something behind her. "Nice looking family. Any relation?"

Before she can answer, he has disconnected the Zoom. So much for her fake family.

41

———

2019 - MINDCAST

An hour after their meeting, Ian texted Rebecca with the home address of Alex Bosko, aka Antoine. Nothing could hold her back from mindcasting there the same night.

Since six p.m.—before Ethan has left his apartment—she has been parked down the street from Antoine's unremarkable gray house, without observing anyone coming or going. There's no way to tell if his Dodge is inside the one-car garage or not. She knows someone is in the house, though. Lights started flicking on after sunset.

She now wishes she had asked Ian to check who all was living here. A wife? A mother? *Abused children?* She needs to learn how to be more thorough, and less rushed.

Normally while surveilling a place, she keeps busy on her phone, but tonight she's too tense. She's convinced Antoine did it, he's the only one who really strikes her as a killer. Tonight she'll find out the truth, but the worst thing is, she doesn't see him as a kidnapper. A man who enlists kids to do his thieving... he's too lazy. It would be too much trouble for him to keep prisoners. He would shoot the boy and have done with it. This is the reality, and she needs to steel herself to face the atrocity she may witness.

By eleven o'clock, she can no longer stand not knowing whether it's Antoine or someone else inside the house. She checks to make certain no one is around before sneaking out of her car and silently approaching the front window. Creeping along the side, she peers through the glass and hears a late-night show on TV. However, she has to move to the next window before she's able to glimpse the small woman slouched in her chair, looking as if she has nodded off. *Must be the wife.*

Her heart leaps into her throat at the sound of an approaching vehicle. Headlights swerve around the corner. She looks around wildly for a hiding place. The car—which could be the gray Dodge— is coming this way.

She darts across the patchy lawn to the neighbor's driveway, where a mid-sized RV is parked. Just as the car is turning toward Antoine's house, she springs behind the vehicle and crouches down.

Next door, the car engine shuts off, the door opens and shuts. The car locks are beeped into place. Peering under the RV, she watches a man's feet walking toward the house. It has to be him.

Her heartbeat races. *What if Ethan's body is in the back?* It looks like a good-sized trunk, probably picked for that reason, to provide space for stashing stolen goods (and murdered children?) on the go. But more likely, Antoine would've already disposed of the poor boy some- where. In that case, there could be evidence he plans to remove tomorrow. She needs to pop that trunk and take a look.

After she hears his front door open and close, she waits a minute longer before slinking out from behind the RV. The front lights have been shut off; chances are he woke his wife, and they went to the bedroom. There's still a glow coming from the back.

She can't wait. This mindcast has lasted longer than any other, and it could end any second now. She sprays the light from her cell phone into the car. A few items of clothing are scattered around—a hoodie, a couple of baseball caps—but nothing to indicate he's recently been out killing or digging a grave. No shovel, or blood smears on the upholstery as far as she can tell. Of course, he's not likely to leave anything incriminating outside of the trunk.

She heard him use the remote, but in case he accidentally unlocked the car instead of locking it, she tries the driver's side door. Definitely locked.

There has to be a way to pry open the trunk. She kneels so she won't be seen from the house, and tries forcing each of her own keys into the keyhole. Her smallest key at least goes into the slot. She jiggles it around, making a mental note that she needs to look up lock-picking on YouTube when she gets back. Sadly, there's no time for that now.

Then, what feels like the muzzle of a gun is pressed against her back. "Say nothing," a man hisses. "Get up and walk to the house."

She struggles for breath. How did she not hear him approaching? With her legs weak and shaking, she manages to pull herself up and move toward the open door, with him following directly behind her.

The short woman is waiting for them in the kitchen, which is dark save for the beam of a street lamp through the window. She looks downtrodden, with thin strands of gray hair framing sunken features. She wears a bathrobe over her pajamas, and fluffy slippers on her feet.

But before Rebecca can make any further observations, Antoine smacks the gun hard into the back of her skull. Crippling pain overwhelms her, then dizziness and blackened vision. She clutches her head and drops to her knees in agony.

REBECCA PRAYS that she'll pass out, ending her misery and sending her back to her own time. But she doesn't.

She's helpless while Antoine presses her flat onto the floor and holds her down. "Get the whiskey," he tells his wife.

Rebecca is vaguely aware of her scampering to a cupboard and returning with the bottle.

"Open it," Antoine says. A second later he forces Rebecca's mouth wide open and pours whiskey into her throat. Choking and coughing, she's powerless to keep from swallowing. The excess runs down her face and neck. She remembers the movie *North by Northwest...* he's trying to get her drunk... then he'll run her off a cliff.

Go back, go back, go back, she keeps telling herself in the midst of her misery. But at the very second when she thinks her mindcast may be coming to an end, a crashing noise comes from somewhere in the house, and something in her subconscious with a need to know what that is keeps her here.

Heavy steps bang across the floor. Dark hands grasp Antoine's shoulders and yank him off her. He's thrown against a metal cupboard, the whiskey bottle splintering next to him. His head must've hit the edge of it; she sees blood as he crumples down and passes out.

The slipper-covered feet skitter out of the room. A door slams and a lock turns in another part of the house.

"Are you alright?" Rebecca's rescuer says.

She blinks up at Lou Johnson, Ethan's gym teacher, and her thoughts swirl in confusion. Has he been working with Antoine? Did one of them double-cross the other? But then, if he's one of the bad guys, why save her?

She wipes her hand across her mouth, her head pulsating like someone is flogging it with a hammer. "The gun... he had a gun."

Lou looks around, spots it on the table, and pockets it. "Can you move? We need to get out of here."

Trying to raise herself causes an acute stroke of pain inside her head.

"I'll get you." He easily lifts her and carries her across the room to the front door. She sees now that he must've kicked it open. He brings her outside and lays her on the grass, helping her to sit up.

"Please," she says. "Can you get his car keys? We have to open the trunk."

"Why?"

"I'm afraid of what he might've done."

He looks ready to ask more questions, then appears to change his mind. "Do you know where they are?"

"No."

A hesitation, and then he rises and hurries back into the house. She hopes it wasn't a mistake to send him back in there. What if Antoine woke up, grabbed another gun, and is waiting to kill Lou? Or what if the meek little wife is not really so meek, and she comes out of her room with an aim to shoot her husband's attacker?

But he returns quickly, the keys jangling from his hand. He goes straight to the car and opens the back. Not being in a position to see the trunk's contents, she waits, her heart thumping as hard as the inside of her head, while he stands hidden behind the raised lid far too long.

"What's in there?" she croaks.

Lou returns to her side. "It's full of stuff he must've stolen."

Relief floods her, though at the same time, she feels confounded. *Where is Ethan?*

"Are there any signs that he hurt someone?" she says. "Blood. A shovel. Anything like that."

He shakes his head, giving her a curious look. "Who are you?"

"I'm Rebecca. A social worker. Trying to find Ethan Pitt. Now your turn."

"Ethan? He's missing?"

"Yes."

His shoulders droop. "Fuck."

"Why are *you* here?" she says.

"I've been following Antoine, or whatever the hell his name is. Hoping to catch him with the goods."

"How did you find out about him?"

"I saw him with Teshi one time. You know her? You know she's in a coma because of that beast?" He waves his head toward the house, wearing a look of revulsion.

"I heard about what was going on from some of the kids," he continues. "I'm a teacher. I listen to them, sometimes when they don't know it."

There's the sound of a siren in the distance.

"I have to go," he says. "I'd appreciate it if you just say you don't know who called them. You thought it must be one of the neighbors who heard you cry out."

"Why don't you want to talk to them?"

"I'm black." He takes out the gun and wipes it with his shirt. "You want to hang onto this?"

"God no."

He tosses it into the shrubs and before she can ask any more questions, he has disappeared into the darkness.

"Thank you," she murmurs after him.

The siren grows closer. She doesn't want to talk to them either. Not here, not now. She needs to get back to real-time. She needs to find Antoine there.

As her vision dims, signaling the end of the mindcast, the throbbing inside her head mercifully comes to an end, while the question, *where is Ethan,* reverberates.

42

2020 - PRESENT

Rebecca hunches bleary-eyed over her breakfast. What now? Has she been looking at this the wrong way?

Antoine could still very well be guilty. He might've killed and buried Ethan and destroyed the evidence before returning home. But there are some problems with that thinking. First, Lou said he was following him, and clearly he didn't witness any foul play. On the other hand, Lou could not have trailed him the entire evening, because earlier he was at the pub watching the soccer match. She wishes she had asked for more details regarding where and when he began tailing Antoine.

Second, Lou told her the trunk was full of stolen shit. Which sounds like, no room for a body. It really feels as if she's back to where she started.

She opens a new document on her computer. It helps her thought process to see things in writing sometimes. She makes a list tracking Ethan's movements the night he disappeared.

1. *6-6:30 p.m., he's home making supper.*
2. *6:30, he leaves his building in a rush, goes to Aunt Yakeera's house (observed).*
3. *6:45ish, he runs out of her house, but she calls him back and he goes to dinner with her (observed).*
4. *7:40, he gives her the slip at the restaurant, then gets in Ballard's car (observed).*

After staring at the list for a moment, she starts a new one labeled, *The Suspects.*

1. **Antoine**, *aka Alex Bosko, is out in his car from 6:00 p.m. till 11 p.m.*
2. **Lou Johnson** *is at the sports bar from 7 p.m. till?? (can't be sure because I interrupted him). Sometime before 11 p.m., he tails Antoine back to his house.*
3. **Craig Ballard** *picks up Ethan from Dos Amigas at 7:40 p.m.. BALLARD'S CAR IS THE LAST PLACE I SAW ETHAN THAT NIGHT.*

Third list: *Conclusions.*

1. *Ballard kidnapped Ethan. He's the one who killed him or is keeping him prisoner.*
2. *Or, Ballard brought Ethan to his killer/kidnapper either knowingly or unknowingly. He knows who that person is, or saw the person and can give a description.*
3. *Or, Ballard dropped Ethan off somewhere but doesn't know who the killer/kidnapper is. Wherever he dropped him is likely to be a clue regarding the identity of the killer/kidnapper.*

Craig Ballard is the key. She needs to talk to him again, and this time she needs to be more intimidating and threatening. No more Ms. Nice Guy.

She doesn't need Ian's services this time. A quick Internet search turns up the name of the law firm Ballard works for, along with their address. Rebecca calls their office and asks to speak with him. As soon as they acknowledge he's at the office, she hangs up. It's all she needed to know.

She dresses quickly in a suit, nylons, high heels. Her hair loose and sexy. She wants to look impressive. The hotter you look, the more likely people pay attention to you. It's just the way things are. She wants the other lawyers in the office to notice her and wonder why she's there. She wants to make Ballard as uncomfortable as possible.

When she asks to see him at the reception desk, she is told he's in a meeting. She doesn't back off. "It's a family emergency," she says. "Related to a boy named Ethan Pitt, who went missing a year ago. Tell him that, please."

A few minutes later, he comes out to the lobby. He doesn't know who she is at this point; the last time she met with him was during a mindcast. He looks the opposite of pleased to see her.

"I'm Rebecca Danser," she says, rising and thrusting her hand into his. "I'm writing a story on Ethan Pitt. May we speak privately somewhere?"

"I don't know what you're talking about. Who is Ethan Pitt? If you don't leave right now, I'll have to call security."

"You know who he is. You gave him a lift outside Dos Amigas Restaurant a year ago. If you don't want to talk to me, that's fine." She lowers her voice. "I can go directly to the police, if you prefer. I have a witness stating you were the last person to be seen with Ethan before he went missing."

He lowers his volume too. "Why haven't I heard anything about this before?"

Rebecca glances toward the receptionist, who looks increasingly curious about their conversation. "Are you sure you want to talk out here?"

"Fine. Come with me." He leads her to a small conference room near the entrance and shuts the door once she's seated. "Who is this so-called witness?"

"Not saying. I'm a writer. I protect my sources." He will assume it's

Yakeera. Who else might've seen him arrive at the restaurant and take off with Ethan? Rebecca hopes this doesn't put Yakeera in any kind of danger. "Look, let me lay it out for you. I don't give a shit if you were having an affair with Ethan's aunt. I'm just trying to find the boy. If you tell me what I need to know, you're not going to feature in my article. You'll be a protected source and I'll make up a name when referencing you. No one will know about your tawdry affair. You don't have to worry about this ruining your political run.

"But if you stonewall me," she says, "I'm going straight to the police, and your actions will become public knowledge. Frankly, you're going to find yourself in legal trouble as well, for not coming forward with what you knew about the case. Is that what you want? I wonder how likely you are to win the election after that? Do you want the public to know you held back valuable information because you didn't give a fuck about what happened to a black boy who's the nephew of the woman you were fucking? Is that what you want?"

He's actually starting to sweat. "Why are you doing this? What do you get out of it?"

"It might be hard for you to understand, but saving Ethan is what I get out of it. That's my goal. If a decent article comes out of it too, great. But all that is secondary to finding the boy."

He's staring down at the table. Finally, he looks up. "I did give him a ride from the restaurant. I. uh, didn't want him telling anyone about my seeing Yakeera. The kid said he needed money, so we stopped at the ATM and I got out some cash for him. A few hundred bucks. I felt bad for the kid. I think I would've given him money in any case."

"Okay. Good. Where did you take him after that?"

"At first he said he wanted to get off at a bus stop. But after I gave him the money, he changed his mind. Said he wanted to see someone instead. He didn't say who. It took a while to get there. He told me not to wait for him."

"Was it a house? An apartment?"

"They were all houses around there. But I don't believe he had me drop him too near the house he was going to. I think he didn't want me to see that."

"How do you know?"

"When he got out of the car, he walked down the street and didn't turn into any of the driveways."

"Where was this?"

Her heart sinks when he gives her the name of the town. None of her suspects live there.

43

____

2020 - PRESENT

Rebecca goes for her afternoon walk, making it longer than usual. It isn't fun breathing through a mask, but the city streets are crowded and most other people are masked, so it's a matter of consideration if nothing else. To clear her head, she tries to think about anything but Ethan. She knows that when she avoids thinking about a problem for a while, a solution sometimes magically presents itself.

She returns a few minutes before five, in time for the Zoom she has planned with Sadie. They haven't spoken for two weeks, which is the longest separation they've had to endure since Sadie was restored to her family. Her sister is like a drug with no harmful side effects to Rebecca. Just seeing her face and hearing her voice makes Rebecca giddy, and prone to spontaneous bursts of laughter.

Uncharacteristically, Sadie joins the Zoom several minutes late, just as Rebecca is about to text her a reminder. It's obvious from her expression that something is wrong.

"Tyler's missing." She huddles with her arms crossed over her chest. Tyler is seven years old, the younger of their two stepbrothers.

Rebecca's stomach lurches. "What happened?"

"He and his brother were playing in the family room. They got into a fight over some toy, and Tyler ran off. The back door was open. Dad's looking outside. Kevin's here with me."

"Hi Rebecca." Nine-year-old Kevin greets her from somewhere offscreen. His voice is unusually subdued.

"Hold on, Marie just came home." Sadie moves away from her computer, but Rebecca can still hear her explaining what happened to their stepmother.

"Did you check everywhere?" Marie says.

"Yes, I think so." Sadie doesn't sound quite certain.

Rapid footsteps tapping against a wooden floor recede from the room, and Sadie returns to the screen. "She's checking upstairs again."

Rebecca's breathing quickens. An image flashes in her mind, her six-year-old self, trembling in the middle of a room, struggling but unable to understand the urgent questions of the police officers surrounding her.

"Have you called 9-1-1?" she manages to whisper.

Before Sadie can answer, their father speaks, his voice low and heavy. "He's nowhere outside."

"Found him!" Marie calls from upstairs. More pattering of steps.

A sensation of lightness fills Rebecca.

"Where was he?" Their dad's voice is still tight.

"He likes to read in the closet when he gets upset," Marie says.

"I thought we checked in there," Sadie says.

Tyler runs into the room and inserts his head in front of Sadie. "Hi Rebecca!" He gives her an enormous smile.

"Hey sweetie," she says. "I'm so glad you're all right. But next time you should tell someone if you're going to hide. Okay?"

"Sure." He runs off, and from the sound of it, he and his brother are soon playing happily again.

Their father appears behind Sadie and places a trembling hand on her shoulder. His face is pale. Rebecca knows exactly what he's feeling. They've been through this before, but in that case, it was the nightmare that didn't end for many years.

"Time for a glass of wine, Dad?" Rebecca asks.

He relaxes a little at the joke. "Not waiting till six, that's for sure. Hey, I wanted to ask, can you come for dinner on Saturday? Marie is making something special."

"What about Covid?"

"You've been wearing your mask, right?"

"Yeah."

"You're just one person. It's okay."

"Let me think about it. I don't want to accidentally get anyone sick." In truth, she's still not sure how she feels about spending time with them.

"Can we do our Zoom tomorrow?" Sadie says. "I think we all need time to breathe here right now."

"Of course. Everybody, relax. I'll be in touch soon."

They sign off, but Rebecca continues to stare at the screen. An idea is forming in her head. She's been concentrating so much on people who know Ethan. What if the kidnapper is someone who didn't know him? Like in Sadie's case. Or unlike Sadie's case, he might be a serial criminal. Maybe he's committed the same crime at least once before.

She texts Ian. *Can you check for any other missing boys that are similar in profile to Ethan? 11-14 years old, dark-skinned, low-income neighborhood, family not very well off. Good student? I'm not sure if that's relevant. Just in the Bay Area, for now. Last ten years?*

His response comes within minutes. *I'll get on that. Hope to have something for you tomorrow.*

44

2020 - PRESENT

After the first solid night's sleep she's had in weeks, Rebecca wakes to an email from Ian.

Five years ago in Penford, California, a twelve-year-old boy went missing. His parents are from India and they own a small Indian grocery store. Neighborhood similar to Ethan's.

Ian continues with the boy's name—*Kabir Ghosh*—followed by his parents' contact information. *Let me know if you want more names. There are several other possibilities to explore in the Bay Area, but this one was the closest match.*

Thanks and not yet, she emails back.

She quickly looks up Kabir Ghosh online. Like Ethan, he is barely mentioned in a brief local article several days after he went missing. She can find no further mention of him, aside from the listing on missingkids.org.

She decides to call the parents. It's the fastest way to find out the most she can about the case, assuming they're willing to speak with her. A woman with an Indian accent answers the phone.

"Hello, Mrs. Ghosh?" Rebecca says.

"I do not want whatever you are selling," she says.

"Please don't hang up. I'm calling about your son, Kabir."

There is a silence, during which Rebecca can imagine her jumbled feelings. Grief and fear reign on the surface, but underneath, the tiny light of hope always burns.

"Who are you?" The woman's voice is a whisper now.

"Rebecca Danser. I'm a journalist writing an article about a boy who went missing last year. I did a little research and found out about Kabir. There are some similarities between them. May I ask you some questions about your boy? It would be better to speak in person, but with Covid... I wonder if we could Zoom?" If they meet in person, they'll be wearing masks. Zoom is best because she'll be able to see their faces.

"We can Zoom." She sounds excited now. "Our oldest taught us."

They agree to Zoom in an hour, after Mr. Ghosh is back from the store.

At the agreed upon time, Rebecca finds herself staring into the faces of a middle-aged Indian couple who look like the type of husband and wife who resemble each other more and more with the passage of time. Mrs. Ghosh wears an orange and red translucent scarf over her gray hair. His hair is still black, combed neatly and gel'ed into place. They clasp each other's hands on the table.

"Thank you so much for agreeing to speak with me," Rebecca says. "Has there been any progress on locating Kabir?"

Mrs. Ghosh shakes her head sadly. "No. Nothing."

"Do the police have any theories? Any suspects?"

"There is one. An appliance repairman who came to our house to fix our oven shortly before our son disappeared. The police found pornography in the man's apartment. Nothing else, though. It doesn't seem like it could be him."

Rebecca makes a note to herself to get his name before they end their Zoom. "Can you tell me about Kabir? His personality. Things he enjoyed doing."

"He is our third and last child. Our baby. No one could be sweeter. I admit we spoiled him."

Mr. Ghosh nods his head in agreement. "He was a quiet child. Shy. And very smart. He received straight A's in school."

"Was he ever in any trouble?" She has to fish to see if there might be a connection to Antoine.

"Oh no," Mrs. Ghosh says. "He always did as we asked him. We almost never had occasion to scold him."

She sees it's going to be difficult to get them to admit their child could've been anything less than perfect. But she perseveres. "Is it possible, though, that he had any friends who might've been a bad influence?"

They exchange a look now. "There was one boy who Kabir knew," Mr. Ghosh says. "The police said the boy was a thief and asked if Kabir may have been involved in that. Of course, our boy would never do such a thing. He was brought up to be honest."

Second note—get name of this boy before hanging up.

"His teachers said so many good things about him. His English teacher thought he was gifted."

Gifted. Didn't Ethan's teacher say the same thing about him? Was this villain only interested in gifted boys? It might be worthwhile to talk with this teacher, who could be more forthcoming than Ethan's. "What was his English teacher's name?"

"His name?" Mr. Ghosh looks confused. "I don't remember."

"Mr. Flannery," Mrs. Ghosh says. "He isn't at our local school any longer. I believe he took another job."

It hits Rebecca like an ice-cold hand reaching into her chest and squeezing her heart. *Mr. Flannery.* Ethan's teacher. It can't be a coincidence. It can't be.

Mr. and Mrs. Ghosh are looking at her curiously. She struggles to pull herself together. "Do you remember his first name?" Her throat feels scratchy.

Again, an exchanged look, then Mrs. Ghosh shakes her head. "Is it important?"

"I don't know," she manages to say. "He might have noticed something in the classroom."

"Of course," Mrs. Ghosh says. "Would you like to come to our house? We are not worried about Covid. Maybe you would like to see Kabir's room?"

Rebecca feels like weeping for them. She knows so well how they feel. How desperate they are for someone to take an interest. Anyone who might give them hope their son has not been forgotten, abandoned, and presumed dead.

"This is all I need for the moment," she says. "I promise I'll let you know personally if I learn anything that might be useful. Thank you so much for speaking with me."

Mr. Ghosh bows his head, while his wife clutches his arm and presses her forehead against his shoulder. "We appreciate the call," he says.

It's only after the Zoom has ended that Rebecca shoots out of her chair. *Mr. Flannery.* She can't remember his first name either, so she checks the school website. *Todd Flannery.* She finds a short bio that lists Kabir's local school as the place he worked previously. *It must be him.*

When she thinks about it, she remembers feeling a little odd at the time that Mr. Flannery was the only person she'd spoken to who offered an alibi. An alibi she never bothered to check. She isn't much of a detective when it comes down to it. He said he was away camping or something the weekend Ethan disappeared. He easily could've been lying. But it would be hard to verify one way or the other if he said he went alone.

He's a school teacher. He isn't a despicable old Fagin-esque character who pimps out child thieves. He's not an asshole who cheats on his wife with his hairdresser and then hides that information instead of helping to find a missing child. He's either honest and reliable, or he's hiding something that's infinitely worse than marital infidelity. If Ethan went to see him that night... the fact that Todd Flannery never came forward to say so is damning.

She texts Ian once more, apologizing for the short notice. *Can you get me Todd Flannery's home address?* She explains he's an English teacher at Ethan's school.

Ian's reply comes a few minutes later. He's getting information for her faster and faster; she can tell he's getting caught up in the case as well. She checks his message, and cold certainty rushes over her. Flannery lives in the town where Ballard dropped Ethan off.

It's him. She feels it in her bones. She's aware she's told herself that before. But this time... this time, she has to be right. She checks the time—eleven fifteen. He should be at school for the next few hours at least. Is it all remote learning now? The kids for sure, but maybe not the teachers. They have all their resources in the classroom. She doesn't think they teach from home.

To be sure, she calls the school and confirms that Mr. Flannery is in his classroom. He lives about forty-five minutes away. It ought to be enough time for her to search the place before he leaves school for the day.

It would be safer to wait and do this in a mindcast. On the other hand, if Ethan is being held prisoner by his teacher, she can only save him by going there in real-time. If he's even alive to be saved.

She throws on sturdy boots and a jacket. At the last minute, she grabs a hammer from her toolbox and sticks it in her bag. It ought to break a window with no problem. What if she's wrong, though? Or what if there's no evidence? She could land in jail herself.

Past the point of caring, she rushes out to her car.

45

Her driving is erratic and Rebecca prays she doesn't get pulled over by a traffic cop. She breathes in deeply, trying to calm herself. For what she has to do next, she must be cool-headed.

Rows of trees on both sides add privacy to Flannery's house, which huddles at the end of a cul-de-sac. She parks along the curb across the street before crossing to his neat lawn and following a quick path to his front door. No one answers her ring after several tries. Unsurprisingly, a check of the knob finds it unyielding.

She steps back from the door to survey the place. No signs warn of a dog or an alarm system, nor do any cameras appear to be pointed at her. A front window that she could reach and break with her hammer can be viewed by neighbors across the street.

She hurries over the lawn to a wooden side gate. This too is locked. However, it isn't terribly tall, and it has no pokey things on the top. Making sure there are no witnesses behind her, she drops her bag on the other side. Her hope is to pull herself up and neatly vault over the gate. Needless to say, this takes way more effort than expected, but she finally manages to haul herself clumsily to the top, before falling on the other side. At least she lands on her rear.

In the back of the house, with no windows within easy reach, it appears she'll have to go all out for the sliding glass door. She checks it first in case he forgot to lock it. No such luck.

It occurs to her she ought to muffle the sound of the hammer, but she hasn't brought anything for that. Except she does have on a light hoodie over her shirt. She whips this off, wraps it around the hammer, and takes a wide, two-handed swing, imagining Flannery's smarmy face instead of the window. It cracks nicely, and she pounds it twice more until she has a clear reach inside to the latch.

Just as she steps gingerly over the broken glass, the ring of her phone makes her start. She should've shut that thing off. She silences the ringer inside her purse without checking who's calling. No time for distractions now; she needs to be quick.

She makes a rapid pass through three small bedrooms upstairs, two of them used for storage. Maybe later she'll have to search inside the boxes, but that will only happen if there's nothing larger and far more obvious to be found.

The place is neat and clean enough, though the scent of cigar smoke clings to its walls. Downstairs there's a kitchen and a separate small dining area, a living room and den, a bathroom, and laundry room. Except for the drab color scheme—fifty shades of brown—and the lack of decoration, the house could not be more normal. What if she's wrong and Flannery has nothing to do with these disappearances? Maybe it's only a coincidence that he taught both boys. She doesn't actually know if Ethan came here. Maybe he planned to visit his teacher but then changed his mind after getting dropped off. Some random sicko prowling the streets might've snatched him. She should've thought of that.

But she's here now and needs to make sure she's covered every inch of this place. The kitchen is the last room she enters, and that's where she finds the door to the basement.

Basements are not common in California homes. The presence of one makes her wonder if Flannery had this home built for himself. Or if he searched far and wide before finding it.

The light bulb at the top of the steps works, thank goodness. The stairs seem strong enough, certainly not like they'll break under her weight. She retrieves the hammer after removing the hoodie that's now embedded with slivers of glass and sticks it back in her bag. That and her phone might be needed in the cellar, though she doubts she can count on a signal down there.

Despite trying to reassure herself there's probably nothing but dusty old comic books and logs for the fireplace to be found, her throat goes dry as she begins her descent. At the bottom, she discovers the furnace, a set of faded wooden cabinets, and a mini-fridge that isn't plugged in. Before looking through them, she continues around the back of the stairs, where there's a door.

It's locked, of course. She prays this doesn't mean she'll have to search the entire house for the key. If it were her, she'd keep it out of sight in the basement. She switches on her phone flashlight to begin her search, determined to check for spiders before putting her hand into any dark crannies. She looks above the door frame, behind the furnace, and underneath the stairs. Nothing. She opens the mini-fridge to find a quart of milk on the shelf. *Ew.* She's about to move on to the cabinets—which she's dreading—when it strikes her that no smell arose from the fridge. It isn't plugged in; the milk ought to have curdled.

She grabs the carton and sniffs. Definitely no odor, and it's so light, it's probably empty. She sprays her light inside it. *Ha!* The key is here. She shakes it out onto her palm and unlocks the door with trembling hands. This is the moment of truth. If there's nothing here but garden tools, she'll have to start over. She won't give up, though. Not ever.

The door creaks as she pushes it inward. And there it is. She enters the room in a state of stunned disbelief.

Ethan is not here now, thank god. Not him nor any other child. But there can be no doubt regarding the purpose of this room. A flat table with shackles forms the centerpiece. He must've restrained the boys here. On the wall there's a selection of knives straight out of a medieval torture chamber. That's what this place is, she realizes. A torture chamber.

A shudder sweeps through her whole body. She thought she was prepared for the worst, but not this, she could never have imagined this. She clutches her arms around herself to still the shaking. *Ethan.* How he must have suffered. She turns to flee out of the room and back up the stairs, but Flannery forms a dark silhouette, standing in the doorway with a gun.

ETHAN

46

—————

Ethan loses his appetite after Antoine sends the threatening text. Thoughts race through his head. Maybe it's not as bad as he thought. He could leave home for a while and let things blow over. If enough time passes, the old man might forget about him.

He needs money to tide him over for a few months. That should be enough time. After that, he can come back home. If he doesn't go to the police—and he won't—Antoine will hopefully leave him alone.

Uncle Ray told him San Diego was nice. It's warmer there, summer is coming, and he can sleep on the street with other homeless people. Just for the summer, then he'll come home.

He'll write to Ma when he gets there, so she won't worry. Aunt Yakeera will help her. She'll take her in; she has enough room, since it won't be Ethan too. By the end of the summer, Ma should be recovered and can get a new job. When Ethan comes back, they can find a new apartment, a smaller one they can afford. It would be best if they move to another town, where Antoine can't find him. But none of this can happen till Ma gets better.

His mind races, putting together the plan. He goes to his room and gathers the small amount of cash he has. He glances around at the stuff he owns, wondering if any of it is worth selling. Sadly, he doesn't think so. Then he changes into his newest jeans and sneakers. Grabs his warmest jacket. He pockets the burner phone Antoine gave him, hesitating a minute, wondering if Antoine can track him from it, then scoffing at himself for such a stupid idea. Antoine isn't the police or the FBI. He's just a broken-down old son of a bitch.

While Ethan's getting ready, he's thinking about what to do first. Aunt Yakeera will give him some money if he asks, but he can't tell her what he's about to do. No way would she allow it. She'll tell Ma and they'll maybe call the police to find him and bring him back. She might even force the truth about Antoine out of him, which could be dangerous for all of them.

He needs a story, and he thinks he may have one that will work.

Before leaving, he checks on Ma. She's dozing, as she so often does these days. From the half-empty vodka bottle by her bed, it's clear she's been drinking again. Maybe that means the nausea caused by the concussion has gone away, but he can't rejoice over that if it just means she's going to return to the booze. He tiptoes over to her and brushes his lips against her forehead. *Love you, Ma*, he mouths.

He checks out the window for any sign of Antoine on foot or in his car. Since the coast looks clear, he heads out and sets a rapid pace for Aunt Yakeera's house. Her car is in the driveway so he figures she's home, but when she doesn't answer his knock right away, he lets himself in with his own key. He's about to call out when he notices movement on the couch. His aunt and a man he's never seen before. They're kissing and... *shit*. He immediately regrets coming here, wishes he could unsee what he just saw. Turning back, he stumbles out the front door.

"Ethan!" Aunt Yakeera calls out.

He actually pauses on her front lawn, not because she called him but because he doesn't know what to do now; he had been counting on her. While he's trying to figure things out, she hurries up to him.

"Ethan, you didn't see that. He's just a friend of mine, but... don't tell your Ma or anyone else, okay? Why'd you come over? Is everything all right?"

"Yeah… no. Wanted to talk to you, that's all."

"We'll talk, honey. My friend is leaving. Let me take you somewhere. Your favorite restaurant, okay? You wait in the car. I'll be right out."

Not knowing what else to do, he sits in her car and waits. A few minutes later she returns and gets into the driver's seat. The stranger is still in her house.

47

After a few minutes of sullen silence in Aunt Yakeera's car, Ethan abruptly opens up the subject he'd come to talk to her about. "Can I borrow some money?"

She glances sideways at him. "I've been helping out your mother. Does she need more?"

"Not her, me."

"You can ask her for it."

"I can't tell her about this. She can't handle it right now." He wonders if he looks as frightened and upset as he feels.

"Can't handle what?"

"I borrowed money for a new phone. I've paid back some of it, but there's a lot left. The guy who loaned it to me says if I can't pay it now, I have to sell drugs for him."

"Who is he?"

"Can't tell you that."

"Tell the police."

"Can't do that either. You know how it is."

"Boy, what kind of people have you got yourself mixed up with?" She almost doesn't brake in time to avoid hitting the car in front of her. "How much money do you need?"

"Two hundred bucks."

"If I give you this, you have to promise not to have anything to do with this guy again."

"Promise. I didn't know he was part of a gang."

"You also have to promise if he keeps bothering you, you come to me and tell me who he is then. Okay?"

"I promise. If he won't leave me alone, I'll tell you."

"You ought to have a phone, that's for sure. We'll stop at the ATM," she says. "There's one on our way."

Later when they're seated in the restaurant, she hands over the cash. "Remember what I said."

"I know. Thanks."

Their drinks arrive shortly after they place their orders. "Glad I got this," Aunt Yakeera says, sipping her margarita. "What a day. Honey, the man who was at my house… just pretend you never saw him, okay? He's married, and if his wife finds out, he'll be in a lot of trouble. You're old enough to know how that is."

Sometimes Aunt Yakeera forgets he's really not that old. How would he know how it is for a married man to cheat on his wife? "Why you wanna be with a married man?" Ethan says. His aunt is not that old, and she still looks nice. There ought to be plenty of unmarried men she could date.

"It's complicated. At first I didn't know about his wife. Anyway, after tonight… I don't think I'm going to see him anymore."

Ethan is anxious to get to a different subject. "I'm worried about Ma."

Yakeera focuses on him. "I know, honey. But she's going to get better, I'm sure of it."

"I guess so. But I worry cuz, you know, if something happened to me, who's gonna take care of her?"

"What are you talking about? *Nothing* is going to happen to you. And anyhow, as soon as she gets well, she'll be taking care of *you*, not the other way around."

"I know, but it might take a long time for her to get better. And you know, shit happens all the time around here. A two-year-old kid got shot three days ago. So I just wanna be sure, if something happens to me, you'll take care of Ma."

"Nothing's going to happen to you. But yeah, I'll always be there for my sister. You don't give up on family, not ever."

"You'll make sure she's okay?"

"Course I will. So will you. Because you'll be right here watching out for her alongside me."

He takes this as sufficient promise. The food clatters down in front of them, and he eats fast, hunger overwhelming him. At the same time, he makes a decision. He can't go back with Aunt Yakeera. Antoine might be hanging around the neighborhood looking for him. He can't take the chance of his aunt seeing him or learning anything about him.

When he's taken his last bite, and she's still barely midway into her meal, he excuses himself to go to the bathroom. He glances back to confirm she's not looking before ducking out the front door of the restaurant.

48

———

He's crossing the parking lot, about to check his phone for the nearest bus stop where he can catch a ride to the central terminal, when a car coming from the lot pulls up beside him. The window slides down, and the driver leans sideways to speak to him. "Hey, you're Ethan, right?"

Ethan recognizes him as Aunt Yakeera's boyfriend. *What the fuck is he doing here?* "Uh, yeah," he says, still walking.

"I'm John. I realize that must've been weird for you back at the house. Sorry. Can I give you a lift somewhere?"

John, huh? He could've been more creative with his fake name. But Ethan is poised between curiosity and thinking the wise thing would be to run like the devil out of here. Curiosity wins, mainly because he really does need a ride. Normally he would do anything rather than get into a car with some strange dude who might be a serial killer for all he knows. But with all that's happened in the last few weeks—Ma's accident, Antoine's threats, Teshi going into a coma—he's developing a real *what the fuck* attitude. Whatever he does, right or wrong, shit is happening, so he might as well pick what's convenient and worry about the rest later.

So he gets into the car with the white dude whose name probably isn't John, and they drive off.

"Where are you going?" John says.

Ethan doesn't want him to know his destination is the main bus terminal because he might tell Aunt Yakeera later on. Instead, he asks him to drop him at an intersection near there.

"Your aunt's real nice." The dude's smile looks like a leer to Ethan. This is a conversation he definitely doesn't want to be having. He turns to stare out the side window.

"But I'd appreciate if you don't tell anyone about me and her," John continues.

Ethan is about to tell him he doesn't give a single fuck about him or his sordid affair with Aunt Yakeera, but a sudden thought stops him.

"Sure," he says. "I won't say a thing." He pauses like the next subject isn't related. "Did you know my ma lost her job? And then she got hit by a car?"

"Oh wow. I hope she's all right."

"Not really. She's dizzy and confused all the time, so she can't work right now. We can't pay the rent. I think we're going to get evicted." Ethan gives the man his most tragic expression.

John gets it. "I can help this one time."

They drive a few blocks and stop at an ATM. When he comes back, he hands over a pile of bills.

"I got you a thousand," John says.

Ethan can't believe his eyes. He sure made the right choice to ditch his aunt at the restaurant. On the other hand, this dude is clearly bribing him to keep his mouth shut.

There's so much worst shit happening, he can't worry about that now. With this money, he and Ma can afford to pay next month's rent. He can't run away now. But he still has the problem of Antoine. He needs help, or at least advice. He glances sideways at his aunt's boyfriend, thinking white people hold more sway with the police. Maybe John could make a deal for him—turn in Antoine and they don't charge him with anything.

But then, this is a guy who cheats on his wife, bribes kids, and probably lied about his name. He can't be trusted to help Ethan. He doesn't want anyone to know he has anything to do with Ethan's family. All he wants is to keep his secret.

But Ethan knows another white dude who he actually trusts. Mr. Flannery. Maybe his teacher can help him. Maybe Mr. Flannery can find him a smart, free lawyer who can get him out of this mess. He should go talk to him. Maybe not tell him what he did. Say that he's asking for a friend. In fact, he can use Teshi. It's already known that Teshi was caught stealing. He can say, he wants to help Teshi once she gets out of the coma.

He turns to John. "I changed my mind about where I'm going." He gives John the address of the lady who fired him as a dog-walker. He can ask her which house belongs to Mr. Flannery.

His teacher will help him. He's sure of it.

49

It takes some time to get to Mr. Flannery's neighborhood, but John doesn't complain. Nor does he seem at all interested. He will do what Ethan wants this one night, as long as he never hears from him again and as long as Ethan does not talk about what he saw at Aunt Yakeera's house. That's how it seems, at any rate.

John does not appear at all concerned about letting Ethan out in this dark neighborhood with no one around. As soon as the boy shuts the door, he swerves into a tight U-turn and speeds away.

Unfortunately, the dog lady's house is completely dark. He checks the time—only a little after nine. Could she be in bed already? She might be furious if Ethan wakes her up.

He decides to walk down the street and check out the other houses. Maybe he'll glimpse his teacher through a window. If that doesn't work, he'll check Google to see if he can dig up Mr. Flannery's address somehow.

The suburbs, so unlike his own neighborhood, make him uneasy. Sure, where he lives, there are lots of sketch people hanging on the street, all day, all night. But there's some security in knowing people are around. Here, it's just like, dead. There are street lamps, but the houses are mostly dark. It's incredibly quiet; not even any dogs barking. Probably sleeping inside with their owners. It's so eerie, it makes him think of a sci-fi story where all the humans have been kidnapped by aliens.

He's beginning to wonder if he should've come here. He probably would give up on this idea right now, except it's a long walk from here to the train. Everyone he saw when he went on the practice dog-walk was white, and Ma has warned him about wandering in such places, especially after dark. Police get called when folks see you passing through, and then it's shoot first, ask questions later.

But he gets lucky when he reaches the house at the end—a plain gray home with narrow green trees on both sides that look like rows of soldiers. A barren hill looms behind the place. Most importantly, an old-fashioned dark blue Chrysler is parked in the driveway. Mr. Flannery's car.

He's relieved to see lights on in the house. He wonders if he should search for his teacher's phone number to give the man a heads up before Ethan arrives at his door. But Ethan knows he's just trying to delay the inevitable. Better to be bold, march right up, and press the doorbell with confidence. His teacher might be annoyed to see him at first, but he'll understand once Ethan tells him what's going on.

He does pause before ringing, though. Wondering for the first time if Mr. Flannery is married or has anyone else living with him, he listens for voices. But it's silent inside, without even the sound of a TV show. That seems incredibly strange to Ethan. At this time of night, the TV is always on in his apartment. Maybe it means his teacher is already asleep and just forgot to turn the lights out. He tries to peer in through the windows, but the blinds have been lowered on the first floor.

Fuck it. What's the worst his teacher can do? Ethan rings the bell, and listens for the sound of movement inside, but it's just as quiet as before. He waits, though. He's committed now.

Two minutes later, still no one has come. He rings a second time. All remains quiet inside. He waits a little longer before deciding to leave. But just as he starts to turn away, he hears something. Footsteps, definitely. Approaching the door. A pause while Mr. Flannery is probably checking the peephole. Ethan makes sure to stand in full view of it, to reassure his teacher it's only one of his students.

The door comes open. Ethan thought Mr. Flannery would look surprised or angry, but instead he stands there with the same inscrutable expression he displays every day in the classroom. He wears what must be a relaxing at home outfit—a light blue long-sleeved t-shirt, faded jeans, and slippers. Ethan doesn't think he's ever seen him wear jeans. The weirdest thing is seeing his teacher holding a cigar that looks like it was lit right before the door came open. Ethan had guessed already that Mr. Flannery liked them, but it's one thing to guess, and another to see proof.

"Come in, Ethan." His tone is relaxed, just as if he had been expecting him to show up.

"Sorry to bother you at home," Ethan says, even though Mr. Flannery doesn't seem bothered. He follows his teacher into the living room.

"I hope your mother knows you're here." He gestures at an armchair for Ethan.

The boy sits. "No one knows I'm here. I came to ask you for advice. For a friend."

"You walked from the train?"

"Yeah." Ethan's not sure why he lies about it. Maybe because he sensed Mr. Flannery wanted that answer.

"Did Ms. Paladino tell you where I live?" he asks.

Ethan shakes his head. "I saw your car."

His teacher settles into a hard-backed chair next to the table, sucks in a puff of cigar smoke, and blows it toward the door. He pulls a crystal ashtray closer to himself and pats the cigar over it.

"Which friend needs advice?" he says.

Now that he's with Mr. Flannery, Ethan is feeling more and more nervous about explaining the problem without implicating himself. He rubs his leather band, looking around the room. The wall paint is white, the carpets are light brown. The furniture is mostly brown too.

There are no pictures on the walls. It's as if Mr. Flannery doesn't want visitors to know anything about him.

"Teshi." There's no harm in naming her, since everyone already knows she's a thief.

Mr. Flannery looks puzzled. "I didn't realize the two of you were friends."

"We met when we were little kids."

"She isn't like you. She's made terrible choices with her life."

"I know that, but I want to help her. She's in a coma, you know." He forgets Mr. Flannery was the one to tell the class.

"I'm aware. Of course, we all hope the best for her. But it happened when she trespassed on someone's property and tried to steal from them. Such actions have consequences."

"Well, before that happened, she told me something about her situation. There's an older man who's like sixty that Teshi was working for. This guy's a real villain. Anyway, once she stole something for him, the man threatened her. Told her she had to keep doing it, or he'd turn her in. He had evidence, you know. Pictures. So Teshi was stuck. She had to keep stealing for this dude, like, forever. And I'm wondering, if she comes out of the coma, do you have any advice for her? How she can break away from his control?"

"Ethan, if she comes out of that coma she's going to be arrested. That's what she needs to be worried about. The criminal will disappear from her life. Teshi won't be any use to him anymore."

Unfortunately, Ethan's not ready with a counter-argument to this. "Well still, I mean, if something like this happens to someone else... what do you think they should do?"

Mr. Flannery's lips form a grim line. "Are we sure we're talking about Teshi here?"

Ethan moves his trembling hand out of sight under his thigh.

"Are you in trouble, Ethan?"

Mr. Flannery's tone frightens him. He lowers his eyes from his teacher's penetrating stare. This is when he notices the line of red on the edge of Mr. Flannery's sleeve. It looks like blood, though there's no wound that Ethan can see.

When he lifts his gaze to his teacher again, Mr. Flannery is staring at him with wide eyes magnified by his glasses. Ethan feels as if his teacher is seeing right into his mind and reading his thoughts. He shivers.

"You've disappointed me." Mr. Flannery's voice turns frigid. "I thought you were one of the special ones. Different. I believed you had it in you to break out of your toxic environment. Clearly, I was mistaken. You're stealing now, is that it?"

Ethan lowers his head. "I stole a few things. But I don't want to do it anymore. I made a mistake. But now it's like... this dude keeps threatening me."

"I wish you had thought of that before you started."

Emotion swells inside him and he's dangerously close to bursting into tears. "Can I use your bathroom?" he asks in a quiet voice.

Mr. Flannery glares down at him while he inhales from his cigar. He breathes out the smoke slowly, watching the shapes it forms as it drifts upward. "Down the hall," he finally says, with a nod in that direction.

Ethan follows the corridor to the bathroom. He has to go badly; the soda he drank at the restaurant has caught up with him. But while he stands there peeing into the toilet, his gaze wanders to the bathtub next to him. The rust-colored shower curtain is pulled shut. But near the wall, on the exposed edge of the beige tub, Ethan sees a thin streak of dark red.

At the same time, he becomes aware of an odor that's like what he has noticed before in the butcher department of their local supermarket. An odor he couldn't smell in the living room, with the cigar smoke overpowering all other scents.

The hair rises on the back of his neck as he finishes peeing and zips his pants. Like someone in a daze, he reaches to the curtain and draws it open. The shower rings screech against the metal bar, but he can't stop himself from looking now.

A motionless gray cat is splayed out on its back in the center of the tub. A horrible gash runs the length of its belly, covered in a sickening spray of darkened blood. At first Ethan thinks it's fake, someone's demented idea of a Halloween prank. But then he realizes it's real, and it's dead.

With all his nerves tingling in dread, he backs away from the disgusting sight. Mr. Flannery must've done this. Mr. Flannery, who Ethan believed was a moral, upstanding, responsible adult who he could count on for advice. Mr. Flannery, who tortures cats.

Ethan's instincts, heightened by recent events, kick-start his self-preservation mode. He turns and flings the door open. Runs out into the hall, ready to bolt from this house of horrors into the street, and take his chances running all the way to the train.

But Mr. Flannery is at the end of the corridor holding a gun. "It's a shame you had to see that, Ethan."

REBECCA

50

2020 - PRESENT

"Drop your purse and back away from the door." Flannery keeps the gun trained on her. "I don't know who you are, only that you'll regret breaking into my house."

Since she's not an expert in firearms—or anything else—she doesn't know what kind of gun it is, or whether it's even loaded. She can only assume it has the potential to kill her instantly, and therefore, she lowers the bag that holds the hammer along with her wallet, keys, and phone, and steps backward.

"Lie down on the table," he says.

Her gaze shifts to the torture table and her heart sinks.

"If you don't, I'll just shoot you right now. If you do, who knows, maybe you'll find a way to escape." He gives a dry laugh at the apparent absurdity of that notion.

Still, it's the exact reason she lies down on the table.

"Attach the leg cuffs around your ankles." He waits while she places both leather restraints around her ankles and buckles them.

"Now do your right hand with your left."

It's difficult since she's right-handed, but she manages it.

He approaches and sets the gun on the workbench. "Stay absolutely still. Otherwise, I'll take one of those knives and get to work on you. Also, just a heads up, the room is soundproofed so there's no point in screaming."

With only one hand still unrestrained, she knows there isn't any way she can disable him or free herself. She has no choice but to allow him to buckle the leather band around her right wrist. She's completely at his mercy now.

He opens her bag on the table, gets out her personal items, and shuts off her phone. "I assume that's your car across the street."

She says nothing. She's done making things easy for him.

He flips through the wallet, which doesn't have a whole lot in it. "Rebecca," he reads her name from her driver's license. "Why are you here?"

"I work for the police. Undercover. If you let me go immediately, things will go better for you."

"It's funny you don't have a badge. Or a partner, apparently. So I ask you again, why are you here?"

"I'm investigating the disappearance of Ethan Pitt."

He flinches at this. "Ethan. The boy who fell from grace."

"You kidnapped him and held him here."

Flannery gets a far-away look in his eyes. "He came here of his own free will. I tried to resist. At first I didn't answer the door, but he wouldn't go away. Even when I let him in, I wasn't planning to keep him here. But once he confessed his crimes, I knew what had to be done."

What little hope she had now drains from her. He would not be telling her this unless he planned to kill her.

"I cared for the boy," he continues. "He needed release from his earthly form, before the corruption grew so deep, there would be no chance of redemption. To keep my resolve from weakening, I allowed him to find the cat I had released earlier that evening."

"Cat?"

"Animals have a life force too. During release, their essence flows through me and brings me closer to divinity."

It's official, then. Flannery is completely insane. "I don't understand. Did you torture the poor thing?"

He screws up his eyes at her. "Torture? No. My methods are humane. I drug them. I don't want them to feel pain. That wouldn't do at all."

It gives her some relief to hear that Ethan didn't suffer.

"We start out life pure and uncorrupted," he says. "Some few manage to remain that way. Most fall prey to evil influences; by the time they reach adulthood, they're beyond help. But the children whose stars shine the brightest... if and when their light starts to dim, there's still time to save their souls."

"You seem to think you're doing them a favor by killing them."

"Even you might gain something from it." He takes a bottle out of a drawer. *That's it.* He's going to drug her, and then... her gaze shifts to the knives. "My team knows I'm here," she says. "They'll be coming any second." He gives her a look like he doesn't believe her. She's never been a convincing liar.

He brings a glass of water from the small sink and shakes out she's-not-sure-how-many-pills into his palm.

"Don't do this! I can help you. They're going to catch you anyway. If you haven't hurt me, they'll go easy on you."

He lowers the glass near her head and grasps her jaw, pushing her mouth open. Just like when Antoine forced the alcohol into her, Flannery drops the pills in the back of her throat. She tries to block them with her tongue and spit them out, but he prevents her. He pours water into her mouth, while she gags, unable to keep herself from swallowing. The pills go down.

"Bastard." Her eyes fill with tears. This isn't what she expected to happen. Why was she so foolish to have done this alone?

He returns the bottle and glass to their places. "It's going to take a little while to have an effect." From this, Rebecca figures he's given her sleeping pills, or something similar. Most likely he wants her alive when he cuts into her with those knives.

He puts her things back into her bag and takes it with him when he leaves the room. The snap of the lock from the other side saps the last tendril of hope from inside her heart.

51

2020 - PRESENT

ourage and determination. Not so long ago, she assured herself these were her special skills. *Use them, dammit. Don't give up. Never admit defeat.*

She looks down at her right wrist and wonders how she can possibly get free. Her hand faces up, and the back of the leather restraint is attached to a short metal chain, which is screwed to the table and probably bolted on the other side for all she knows.

The good news is she would not need a key to undo the restraint, which is buckled like a belt. The bad news is she can't do it without a free hand, or at least a way of rubbing her wrist against something. There isn't enough chain to allow her to turn her hand and move it against the table or even against her own body.

Without being able to reach over with her other hand, or swivel her wrist to press against the table, there appears to be no way to get the cuff off. Still, without expecting anything, she strains to pull her hand up. If the chain isn't securely attached, maybe she can break loose.

But it is secure, and pulling on it only makes her arm ache. Then she tries her left side, and both of her legs. She's not sure, but she thinks the left wrist might be slightly looser than the right. Turning her head sideways, she's able to glimpse the chain that's attached to the table. It looks old, even a bit rusty. This prompts a shudder at the thought of how many times it might've been used over a period of many years.

She yanks at the left chain again. Definitely looser than the other side. She thinks she sees a slight gap in one of the links. Maybe if she pulls hard enough, she can open it sufficiently to break the connection. One more time, and now she uses all the force of her left arm to resist the chain. Her muscles are screaming, and the edge of the cuff is digging into her flesh, but she won't let herself stop. *C'mon. C'mon.* She twists her body away to apply more force.

The link snaps free and a feeling of elation fills her. But it's short-lived; there's still much to be done. Flannery could return any second and he has the gun.

It's awkward and way too slow undoing her right hand, but she manages it. Sitting up to release her ankles, a wave of dizziness hits her. The drug is starting to do its damage. Her throat feels dry, but she can't let herself think about it. She frees her ankles before sliding off the table, nearly falling in the process. Her balance is off.

She's going to need a weapon, and there are plenty of them, though she recoils from the thought of stabbing anyone with a knife. Nevertheless, she's like Goldilocks, picking out the one that fits her hand the best. The one that has the right weight and size for her to use comfortably. She tiptoes to the door, trying to be as silent as possible, since she has no idea how close he might be.

The door is locked, of course. He would not be foolish enough to leave it unlocked, even with her restrained on the table. Her gaze sweeps the room, wondering if there might be a key in here. She seriously doubts it, though, and it might rob her off whatever wakefulness she has remaining if she were to search for it.

She'll have to wait for his return. She positions herself behind the door because there's no other hiding place. But while she crouches there, her symptoms grow worse. She feels nauseous and her head is starting to throb. It's a struggle to keep her eyes open.

She thinks she might've dozed off by the time she hears the key in the lock. Her eyelids refuse to raise more than halfway. She jabs her fingernails hard into her palms to keep herself awake a little longer.

The door comes open. She can't wait to see if he's holding the gun or not, she has to act. Driven by a rush of adrenaline, she whirls around the door and meets his shocked expression with a thrust of the knife into his side. He cries out and sprawls to the floor, blood gushing out.

It isn't in her to plunge the knife in again and again, as she probably should do to save herself. She draws it out and flings it across the room so she'll have her hands free, to somehow get around him and through the door. Her only thought now is to flee.

But just as she thinks she's gotten past him, he grabs her ankle, catching her in mid-stride. She crashes hard onto her knees. Turning back, she sees his hand reaching into his pocket where the gun must be. With her free leg, she kicks his wound with every bit of strength she has remaining. He screams, releasing her, and she scrabbles across the floor to the stairs on the other side, too dizzy to stand up.

Using the banister, she drags herself up each step. When she's almost to the top, a shot rings out. She feels nothing and hopes that means he missed her. Sheer terror gives her the jolt she needs to conquer the last onslaught of stairs, and stumble toward the table in the kitchen, away from the doorway.

There are noises behind her. A banging against the stairs. He's not dead, he's forcing himself up them. Probably pulling himself just as she did. Determined to kill her. Determined not to let her leave this house alive.

She's fading fast. Any second now, she'll be passed out and helpless. Grabbing the leg of the kitchen table, she struggles to pull herself up. But the table wobbles and a heavy crystal ashtray falls from it, landing on the other side. She falls back down and reverts to crawling. Halfway into the hall, her body collapses. This is it, she can't get up, can't move a single muscle any longer. She looks back to see him reaching the landing, blood smeared all over him. He raises himself to his knees to take aim at her. He's going to kill her.

But his hand trembles, his body sways. He's trying to steady himself before taking his shot. In the second this gives her, one final surge of energy allows her to lunge for the ashtray. In the same movement, she rolls up and hurls the heavy object at Flannery.

It hits his forehead. He staggers and falls backward down the steps.

She drops to the floor again, unable to keep her eyes open a second longer. As she lies there, strange visions flash inside her head. Her body shakes uncontrollably. She's not sure how much time has passed when she feels the touch of a hand on her back.

ETHAN

52

Under normal circumstances, Ethan would probably have frozen at the sight of a gun. But after everything he's been through—the stealing and the threats and Ma's accident and Teshi's coma—he almost doesn't care if Mr. Flannery shoots him. Almost. At least, he's reached the point where he'd rather be shot than captured.

These thoughts take a fraction of a second to ignite inside him, and then he's moving. He charges Mr. Flannery, taking him by surprise, knocking his right arm hard against the door frame. Mr. Flannery drops the gun, howling in pain. With no time to grab it, Ethan kicks the weapon away as he flies out of the room, sprinting faster than he ever has in his life, across the main living area and out the front door.

"Ethan, you fucking get back here!" Mr. Flannery bellows.

But he's on fire now. Bounding through the streets, he almost wishes someone would see him and call the police. He sprints all the way to the train station, though he fears Mr. Flannery may have driven here already and be lying in wait for him. He slows as he approaches, checking the parked cars, and the shadows for anyone lurking. So far, no sign of his teacher. Mr. Flannery may be too weak to do much now because of his injured arm. Or he might be afraid cameras would catch his movements.

Ethan has a bit of luck, finally. The last train of the night arrives within minutes of his reaching the platform. He gets in, keeping his eyes on the window, watching in case Mr. Flannery appears at the last minute and boards the train too. But soon enough the doors close and his teacher hasn't come.

Still, he remains nervous and walks through the train until reaching a section where several alert-looking riders are seated, as opposed to the two passed out homeless guys in the first car he entered. If Mr. Flannery appears out of nowhere and tries to kill him, at least there will be witnesses.

On the way, he makes his decision. When he reaches his stop, he no longer runs, but speed-walks to the homeless camp. He wanders for several minutes before spotting Uncle Ray's tent in a new location. Ethan kneels by the opening, listening to his uncle's light snoring.

"Uncle Ray," he hisses.

No response.

"Uncle Ray," he says louder.

There's a snort and then, "Who is it?"

"It's me. Ethan."

"What you...? Get in here, boy."

He climbs into the tent as his uncle pulls himself into a sitting position. "You alright?" he says.

At that moment it hits him how definitely, positively not all right he is. His eyes fill with tears and the story of his life these last few weeks pours out of him, except he leaves out the part about Mr. Flannery, afraid that his uncle might do something rash. When he finally finishes, Uncle Ray leans forward and wraps his arms around him.

"What am I going to do, Uncle Ray? What am I going to do?"

"'Run like hell my dear,'" his uncle says softly, "'from anyone likely to put a sharp knife into the sacred, tender vision of your beautiful heart.' A brilliant poet named Hafez said that."

He nods at his uncle. "Will you come with me?" he asks.

.   .   .

THEY LEAVE before dawn and take the train into San Francisco. Uncle Ray gives Ethan his tent and helps him settle into a camp. He tells the boy not to go anywhere aside from fetching food occasionally.

Uncle Ray returns to his camp on the other side of the bay for several weeks, as long as it takes to convince police he has nothing to do with Ethan's disappearance.

Then he returns to his nephew in San Francisco, and together they take the bus to San Diego. Ethan feels guilty for not reporting Mr. Flannery to the police, but he's certain they're not going to believe his word over that of his respected teacher. Especially if Antoine spreads it around that he's a thief, and then he'll be the one going to jail. It's a terrible thing if Mr. Flannery continues to cut up cats or other animals, but after all, Ethan is just a kid and can't be expected to solve the world's problems himself.

He pretends to be Uncle Ray's son as they build a life together. He takes a new name for himself. *Amari.*

From time to time, he thinks about calling his mother. But he's afraid she won't be able to keep it to herself that he's still alive. And if word gets around, Antoine might threaten her to force Ethan back under his control. For now, it's better if they all think he's dead.

REBECCA

53

2020 - PRESENT

Rebecca wakes up in a hospital bed with Sadie seated beside her. She squeezes her sister's hand.

"They pumped your stomach." Sadie says. "You could've died."

"I know," she says. "What about Flannery? Is he dead?"

She shakes her head. "They took him off to jail hospital or something. They found the stuff in the basement. Jesus, Becca, how many kids are you planning to save?"

"All of them. I need to work faster."

"Just as I thought. I didn't tell Dad, by the way."

"Thanks." When Rebecca asked her to be her emergency contact, she made her promise not to tell their father if anything happened, unless death was imminent. "How did I get here? Did the neighbors call the police?"

"Oh no. A man called Ian Slate. Nice name. Do you know him?"

Rebecca smiles. Over the next hour, she tells Sadie as much about the case as she can without mentioning time travel. Hopefully Sadie will assume any confusing parts are a result of her sister not being quite clear in the head yet. Rebecca isn't ready to reveal her mindcasting superpower to anyone, not even Sadie. Her sister might question her sanity, or leak it to their father, who would definitely question her sanity. Maybe she'll confide in them eventually. But not today.

By afternoon, Rebecca is able to check out and return home. The first thing she does when she's alone is arrange a Zoom with Ian.

"How are you feeling?" he says.

"Not bad. Thank you. I'd be dead if not for you. How did you know where I was?"

"I'd be a lousy private eye if I couldn't guess that. I've observed you; you're impulsive. The last thing you did was ask for Flannery's address, and after that you stopped answering my calls. I did some research of my own and learned he was also Kabir Ghosh's teacher. Then I drove to his house, and just as I was tracing the plate of a nearby car to see if it was yours, I heard a gunshot."

"Oh man, that was lucky," she says.

"Lucky it didn't give me a heart attack. I called the police, and then I went in through the back like you apparently did because I wasn't sure they'd arrive in time. But there wasn't much I could do till the ambulance arrived."

"He wasn't moving around, I hope."

"He looked dead. So did you. This was very traumatic for me. Do you think you could give me a heads-up next time?"

"Seems like a typical day for a hard-boiled detective like you," she says.

"I told you, my typical day is following women to hotels and hanging out in the lobby, trying to snag free lemonade while I'm waiting."

"Do you even play the violin?"

He gives her an enigmatic smile before signing off, leaving Rebecca feeling like she'd be happy to actually hang out with him instead of only ever seeing him on her computer, but... Covid. In-person meetings will have to wait.

. . .

A FEW DAYS after Rebecca returned home, she heard from the police that the bodies of three juveniles were found buried in Flannery's back yard. So far. The news hit her hard, and for the next day she found herself weeping on and off at unexpected moments. She had really believed she might find Ethan alive.

His family was notified that he might be one of the victims, due to Flannery having been his teacher. DNA results had not come in. Rebecca had not yet spoken to them, nor to Kabir Ghosh's parents.

She did not regret any of her actions. As the sister of a kidnap victim, she knows it's better to learn their fate than to spend your life wondering if they might still be alive and suffering in the den of a monster.

The police questioned her regarding her role in exposing Flannery. She managed to gloss over the information she learned through time travel by describing it as conjecture. Her choice of journalist as a cover turned out to be a good one, as they accepted her refusal to divulge the names of "witnesses" who spoke to her. That Ian was known and respected by some of the officers helped her credibility.

On the fourth day after Flannery was exposed, she's getting ready to call Yakeera. But Yakeera calls her first.

"Rebecca?" Her voice is filled with a joyous excitement Rebecca doesn't understand.

"He's alive," Yakeera says.

Rebecca's breath catches in her throat. "What?"

"Ethan. Ethan is alive. We just spoke to him on the phone." It all comes spilling out in one rapturous run-on statement. "The night he disappeared, that devil Flannery tried to kill him or take him prisoner, I don't know which, but our boy got away. His uncle Ray helped him. He loves Ethan, always did. Ray hid him, and then they went to San Diego together, and they've been doing well. They got a tiny apartment somewhere, and it's not bad. Ray got a steady job in construction and bought a used car. Ethan's doing remote school. And can you believe it, he's taking care of dogs for six different families.

"Ethan didn't actually know his teacher was murdering kids; he thought it was just cat torture, which is bad enough, but I don't blame the boy for running, there was so much going on back then, way more than a thirteen-year-old could handle.

"Anyhow, Ethan saw the news about Flannery getting arrested and bodies turning up in the backyard, and he knew what we would be thinking so he called us. Rebecca, he's grown so much, so mature, he wants to testify against Flannery and another lowlife called Antoine. He was so, so happy to hear Teshi came out of the coma. He's dying to see her too.

"I'm calling to let you know he and Ray are driving up here and will arrive around noon today. Laila and I thought you might want to be here. You made this happen, Rebecca. It's thanks to you our boy's coming home to us."

Tears of joy stream down Rebecca's cheeks. "Thank you, Yakeera. It means a lot to hear you say that."

As soon as they hang up, Rebecca leaps out of her chair, shrieks, and does a happy dance. She calls Ian next and probably sounds a lot like Yakeera just did in relaying the information.

Arriving early for the reunion, she parks across the street, trying to peer in through the windows to check if Ethan has come yet or not, but the glare makes it impossible. After waiting in her Honda for about fifteen minutes, she decides Ethan probably is inside and she should go to the door. But just as she grabs her purse, a car approaches, slows, and parks on the other side.

She recognizes Ray in the driver's seat. He remains there while Ethan pops out the other side. It gives her a shot of euphoria to see him, looking completely different than when she spoke with him during the mindcast. Then he was gaunt with bent shoulders and a vacant stare. He's alive again now, approaching the house with bouncing steps and a wide grin spread across his face.

Laila flings the door open and rushes out first, wrapping her arms tightly around her only child, who she hasn't hugged for over a year. Yakeera gives them no more than two seconds before she flies out and joins the embrace, hopping up and down for joy.

Arms still clasped around one another, they squeeze into the house, with one of them kicking the door shut behind them.

All the effort, all the fear, and all the pain were worth it for this. Rebecca starts her car and drives away. This is a moment when four would be a crowd. Ray gets it too.

54

2020 - PRESENT

At the end of the week, Rebecca decides to go to dinner at her father's house after all. They greet her warmly when she arrives, even Marie. Rebecca is beginning to believe she hasn't given her stepmother a fair shake. Or her father.

She and Sadie assemble Legos with the boys while her father and Marie prepare the meal. At dinner they talk about Covid, of course, but also about politics and philosophy and art and math and lots of silly subjects too. When Marie goes off with the boys to help get them ready for bed, the three remaining adults dispatch the kitchen cleanup quickly.

They play Pictionary after the boys have gone to sleep, and it's the most fun Rebecca has had in a long time. But scribbling on pieces of paper reminds her of the suicide note her mother wrote and makes her heart harden against her father again.

Maybe it's the wine they had with dinner, or maybe it comes from observing Ethan's courage in returning home and facing his demons... but after her father finishes using the bathroom, she meets him in the hall to have a private word.

"Can I talk to you, Dad? It's important."

"Sure, Rebecca." He leads her into the small room he calls his study.

"Something has been weighing on my mind," she starts right in. "Something that came out in therapy." She's not even in therapy right now, but he doesn't know this. "I remembered that when we found Mom, there was a piece of paper on the table next to her. You took it away and never showed it to me. Was it a note? Did she leave us a note?"

He looks at her blankly before getting up and leaving the room. She hears his footsteps on the stairs.

She's not sure what she's supposed to do. Did she upset him with her question? Does he want her to go now? Her father can be infuriatingly uncommunicative at times. But just as she is resigning herself to leaving without any resolution, she hears his steps returning.

He has a folded piece of paper in his hand. "It was in the safe in our bedroom," he explains. "I'm so sorry, Rebecca. I should've given it to you years ago. In all honesty, I forgot about it. Or more accurately, I pushed every memory of that day as far from my mind as possible."

"But why didn't you let me see it then?"

"You were so young. I guess I was thinking, we could pretend it was an accident. Not that I ever thought for a minute that it was. But... I wanted you to think that. It's such a terrible thing to believe someone you love could've killed themselves. You feel responsible. Though it isn't anyone's fault, you can feel a crushing guilt. I blamed myself. I still blame myself in some ways.

"But it was wrong of me to hold this back from you once you were an adult. In fact, it was written for you, not me." He holds it out to her.

She hesitates before taking it. For better or worse, she must read it.

THE NOTE SAYS: "Dearest Rebecca, I wish I could've been the mother you deserve. Forgive me." While her father waits, she reads it over and over again, its words washing over her. *Dearest. Forgive me.*

Nothing will ever cure Rebecca of the guilt and remorse she feels as a result of her mother's suicide. But the note brings relief. Her mother isn't blaming her for anything. Quite the opposite. She recognizes her own incapacity to mother after having lost one child. It isn't that she didn't love Rebecca. It's that she felt herself deeply inadequate.

She's not sure how much time passes before she rises and lets her father take her in his comforting embrace. She doesn't cry; those tears have been shed before. Instead, she feels like she can breathe again.

"I love you, my darling girl," he whispers. When they break apart, she discovers he's the one whose cheeks are damp. He wipes his face before they rejoin the others.

Before leaving, Rebecca hugs Sadie and Marie, and then holds Marie's hands while thanking her warmly for the dinner. She hasn't been fair to her and it's time to change all that.

Sadie and Marie clearly know something happened in the study, but they are wise enough not to ask about it now. She will share the note with Sadie the next time the two of them are alone together. Now is not the time. The note was for Rebecca. She needs to savor it for a while.

At home, she learns from the news that Kabir Ghosh has been confirmed as one of Flannery's victims. She calls his parents immediately to express her condolences, but no one answers. Their grief, like Laila and Yakeera's joy, is not to be shared, at least not yet.

She prepares herself for bed, hoping the closure will at least allow her to get a decent night's sleep at last. But when she settles under the covers, her thoughts go to the night she shared drinks with Lou inside The Blazing Horse pub. It's the one remaining mystery of this entire adventure. What happened to him? Where is he now? Why did he leave the school where he had just begun teaching?

It's clear he cares about the welfare of children. She wonders if that means he's wounded like her. She felt a connection to him that night.

The curiosity is killing her. She closes her eyes and pictures that night in the pub. Before long, her head heats up, her vision blanks out, and she spins backward through time on her way to solve the mystery of Lou.

AMARI

55

____

As Amari stares out at the ship that is now a tiny blip on the horizon, he remembers the words of the village Wise Man: "Do not confuse futile pursuits with those actions that are within your power to accomplish."

His gaze shifts to the waves crashing on the rocks below, but he no longer considers dashing himself against them. He climbs back down from the cliff and heads in the direction of the largest village along the coast.

At first, he is reviled as a beggar and a thief, because word has reached them from the other villages. But he humbles himself, and is satisfied to earn pennies from the washing of villagers' feet. He sleeps along the side of the road like a dog until a family takes pity on him and invites him to share their home. They do not regret it, because not only is he kind and honest, but he is also hardworking and helps every member of the family with their chores.

As he grows older, his skill as a storyteller begins to emerge and he earns his keep that way. Eventually he becomes so accomplished at weaving his stories that he is elevated to be the new village Wise Man, as the previous one unfortunately passed away. At eighteen years of age, he is the youngest Wise Man the village has ever seen.

He could, if he wishes, live out his life in this place that has welcomed *him and made him one of their own. He could find a bride and with her, make a family of children. He will be prosperous and respected and live a happy life.*

But one day word comes of a group of like-minded people in a faraway country called England, who have gathered to condemn the practice of slavery. They mean to fight those who think they have the right to rob the health, happiness, and freedom of others.

Amari knows much he could tell them about this practice. He can bear witness to the crimes against his family and the people of his village, wrenched from their homes, and forced into slavery in a foreign land.

Thus he finds himself, six years after the cruel act that tore his world apart, on a ship headed for England. He leans into the wind at the bow, leaving behind the home he worked so hard to construct. But someone must stand tall against the brutality of evildoers if they are to be stopped.

The End.

***

Thank you so much for reading *The Before Books 1-3*. If you enjoyed this collection, please help other readers to find it by rating it, writing a review, or simply telling your friends. You are awesome.

Read on for a preview of *Dreadmarrow*, Book One of *The Thieves of Magic Trilogy*.

DREADMARROW

PREVIEW

Today, my fifth time as a russet sparrow, I felt as if I'd been flying all my life. I left caution behind, soaring over the town square, catching a beakful of rancid smoke rising from the shops and ramshackle homes. My wings flapped according to instinct and carried me toward Sorrenwood's outer edge, over rows of broken shelters. I continued across a field dotted with bent farmhands, past a thicket of trees that gave way to the swimming hole.

I flew lower to watch the three bare-chested boys who approached the water. I'd seen them before but they were younger than me and I could not remember their names. The dark one swung out on the rope and when he reached the highest point, he released with a shout and a splash. His friends followed in rapid succession, nearly landing on him. Their joy was infectious. I sailed up higher and dove down, letting myself fall until—an inch above the water's surface—I pulled up. The pale boy saw me and looked puzzled. He had probably never seen a bird play before.

I rose higher for my second dive. But as I shifted downward, a huge silhouette appeared above me... *a hawk*, its wings spread wide, a monstrous beast to sparrow-me. Shaking, I dodged left and then right and then back again, hoping to confuse it with my odd movements. I followed an erratic course and didn't realize until it was too late, that I'd crossed over the outer wall and now flew above the Cursed Wood. Gray mist seeped upwards like steam from a giant cauldron. The tips of black tangled branches reached toward me, but I knew better than to land on any of its foul trees.

The air whooshed as the hawk dove for me, and I felt a stinging sensation as it clipped off a wad of my feathers. I beat my wings in a panic, angling toward Fellstone Castle. It was a dreary, forbidding fortress but the only place I might find refuge. A shadow formed over me as the hawk prepared to dive again. My confidence shaken, I swore at myself for having so little practice flying. Whether to flap my wings or coast on the wind—I had no idea which would get me to the castle quicker. And so I flapped and coasted and flapped again, aiming to reach the nearest tower. The hawk's breath grazed my back as I flew over the moat, ducked under the edge of the roof, and hurled myself into a tight corner, where I crouched, trembling and desperately wondering what defense I could use if my attacker crawled in after me.

The hawk didn't come. Yet I feared it might still be out there, perched on the roof, waiting with uncanny stillness for me to emerge. That didn't sound like normal hawk behavior, but I knew so little about them. By now I should've been an expert on any animal that wished to make me its supper. I'd grown careless, caught up in the novelty and excitement of flying. My first time out, I only hopped across the yard and took a short flight up into the nearest tree, growing accustomed to the odd sensation of seeing things behind me. With each day I flew, I grew bolder. I'd half-believed, half-hoped the magic lent me a kind of protective shield, keeping other animals from perceiving me. I knew better now. In future, I would watch for shadows, and feel for subtle shifts in the air that flowed around me.

Movement below caught my eye. Down on the castle lawn, six armed boarmen huddled together, speaking amongst themselves in snorts and grunts. Their pig heads with sharpened tusks were disturbing enough at the best of times, combined with the bodies of herculean men, broadened by thick padding covered in chain mail. Here, alone and unprotected at the castle, I shivered in dread, and shrank further into my corner. Their leader glanced upwards, revealing heavy scars across his eyes and snout. Even from this distance, or maybe because I knew the way they always looked at you, I felt the chill of his cold, black piggish eyes, devoid of feeling. Of course he wasn't looking at me, a little bird under the roof, but at an open window below me. Seconds later, a man extended his arm out the window and lowered it in signal.

The scarred boarman bellowed at another whose ear had been partly chewed off. The group opened up, revealing a frail man on his knees at their center, his hands tied behind his back. Pale and filthy with his clothing torn into strips, he looked as if they'd dragged him from the dungeon only moments earlier. Two of the boarmen lifted him to his feet and shoved him in the direction of the forest. His poor legs appeared weak and spindly from long disuse, but still he loped toward the trees, driven by a final, desperate hope that defied all logic. *If only I could help him.* But even if I flew down to lend him my wings, by the time I changed back, and before I could show the man what to do, the boarmen would surely have murdered us both.

Run, I silently urged. *Run as if the world were on fire beneath your feet.*

The boarmen salivated and raised their spears on their leader's command. The man stumbled just before reaching the trees, clawing his way up, fighting his way forward. *Faster! Don't give up!* The leader signaled for the boarmen to unleash their blood lust, and they pummeled each other to be first to their prey. They thundered across the field, hunched over and pig-like despite having the bodies of men. Their high-pitched squeals formed a grating war cry as they crashed through the bramble into the woods.

Please visit margiebenedict.com for purchase options.

ALSO BY MARGIE BENEDICT

DREADMARROW (The Thieves of Magic Book One)

GRAVENWOOD (The Thieves of Magic Book Two)

KINGSHACKLE (The Thieves of Magic Book Three)

THE THIEVES OF MAGIC TRILOGY

BEFORE THE KILLING (The BEFORE Series Book One)

BEFORE SHE WAS TAKEN (The BEFORE Series Book Two)

BEFORE HE VANISHED (The BEFORE Series Book Three)

BEFORE BOOKS 1-3

INVADER

BLOOD AND VEIL

LAST GIRL STANDING

THE TRIALS

ACKNOWLEDGMENTS

My deepest love and gratitude goes to these dear friends and voracious readers for their willingness to read and honestly critique all that I write:
Karla Sheridan
Katherine Liscomb
Sheri Davenport
Susan Rendina
Tanner Kaptanoglu

Thank you to the many readers who have lent their support to indie authors like me. By showing your appreciation of my work, you motivate me to continue this writing journey.

ABOUT THE AUTHOR

Margie Benedict writes emotionally charged, genre-spanning fiction centered on one powerful theme: second chances. Whether set in a magical kingdom, a dystopian society, or a time-twisted reality, her stories follow women and girls as they rediscover their strength, rewrite their stories, and reclaim their power.

Formerly publishing under the name Marjory Kaptanoglu, Margie is an award-winning author whose books have earned praise from Kirkus, the BookLife Prize, and Publishers Weekly. Her work blends emotional depth with genre thrills, resonating with fans of *Outlander*, *The Hunger Games*, and Tamora Pierce's *Song of the Lioness* series. Before turning to fiction full-time, she helped develop pioneering software at Apple and wrote screenplays that were recognized at Slamdance and produced for film.

Margie is now building a brand readers can trust for gripping, transformative storytelling—books that don't just entertain but empower. From middle grade fantasy to adult thrillers, sci-fi, and women's fiction, she invites readers of all ages to ask: *What would you do with a second chance?*